Praise for th

2022 Royal Dragonfly [...]
Fic[...]

"This is dark fantasy at its best... The more creative descriptions of the darkness that threatens humanity pull the narrative somewhere between horror and fantasy... a delightful read with a voice that works and prose that is bold and enticing. But it is the immersive world of this creation that will have most readers turning the pages."
—The Book Commentary

"...stunning page-turner ...original, captivating, and readers may be surprised to find this is the author's debut novel. The storyline is absolutely mesmerizing, and Thornbury has a knack for telling a dark story. And I do mean dark."
—Reader Views

"This was a really great introduction into the Sundered Web series. Alex is wonderfully skilled in world building and this book is a prime example of that. Her wonderful descriptions create beautiful and vivid imagery. It's almost like the reader becomes Elika."
—NetGalley Reviewer

"An intriguing YA fantasy featuring harsh magic, a brutal world, and a tenacious hero. In many fantasy stories, magic is assumed to be a force that reflects humanity itself: wielded by a few adepts for their own purposes, and therefore likely to be benevolent, cheerful, or amusing. The first book in Alex Thornbury's Sundered Web series does something different and surprising…"
—Independent Book Review

"A wonderful fantasy story for teens and adults... The author has a great imagination and whilst this book is a complete story in itself I look forward to the sequel."
—Booksprout Reviewer

"Expertly crafted and highly readable… Mesmerising. A horde of surprising plot twists and magical intrigue mark Thornbury's debut instalment in The Sundered Web series. "
—The Prairies Book Review

"... thought provoking ... enchanting novel."
—Sally Altass. Author of the *Witch Laws*

"The Bridge to Magic is well written and draws you in from the start. Well-paced and filled with good characters... a quality entry into the fantasy genre."
—Christian Warren Freed, Author of *The Lazarus Men*

"The Bridge to Magic" is a magnificent high fantasy debut by exciting new author, Alex Thornbury. Dark and foreboding, while equally alluring and addicting—as the first book in *The Sundered Web* trilogy, Thornbury lays the foundation for an unforgettable journey … The despair, the suffering, losing hope—it's a gloomy formula, and combined with the meticulously drawn settings, Thornbury's words have the authority to shroud the reader in the eerie gloom that threatens humanity."
—Reader Views

"A thought-provoking parable of ecological and civilizational collapse, that which we grapple with today. Thornbury delivers this tale with gravity and sensitivity. Within what might appear to be a simple framework of life and death, good and evil, our attention is drawn to how difficult it is to ever know for certain what is happening and what we can do about it."
—Independent Book Review

The BRIDGE TO MAGIC

THE SUNDERED WEB BOOK 1

ALEX THORNBURY

Shadow Lore
PUBLISHING

The Bridge to Magic is a work of fiction. Names, characters, places, and incidents either are the product of the author's imagination or are used fictitiously. Any resemblance to actual persons, living or dead, events, or locales is entirely coincidental.

Copyright © 2022 Alex Thornbury

All rights reserved.

Distributed by Shadow Lore Publishing

First Edition: February 2023

No part of this book may be reproduced or modified in any form, including photocopying, recording, or by any information storage and retrieval system, without permission in writing from the copyright owner, except for the use of quotations in a book review.

Cover artwork by Alejandro Colucci

Paperback ISBN 978-0-6454970-0-7

US Edition

www.alexthornbury.com

Shadow Lore
Publishing

To my friend and mentor Brian Keaney.
For your tireless insights and endless patience.
Thank you for helping me cross my own bridge to
magic.

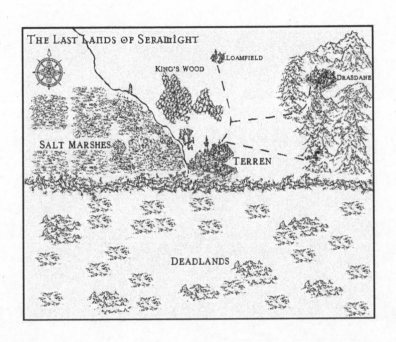

CHAPTER ONE

The Bridge to Magic

"To understand the history of our realm of Seramight, we must first understand the nature of the world we live in. Three realms of life circle each other in the dark Abyss, bound together by the Great Web. The celestial realm is ruled by the gods, the ethereal by the tsaren. Our own earthly sphere was ruled by the Kings of the Sacred Crowns for three thousand years, before Tsarin Reval destroyed their illustrious houses in the Sundering War."

History of Men, Gods and Magic,
By Priest Oderrin

All stories began and ended at the Bridge to Magic.
So it has been for six hundred years—the story of this age, the story of the battle against magic and its banishment after the Sundering War. And Elika's story, too, began with the bridge. Were you to ask any man, woman or child, they would say their earliest memory was the first time they beheld its dark path or heard whispered tales of it in their cots.

There was a time before the bridge was forged, but those stories had been mostly forgotten. The dark history of that bygone age was now buried in the archives of the priests.

Only the echoes of it remained on the tongues of minstrels and drunks. Elika had heard them all and each tale seemed more terrible and unimaginable than the other.

Those were dismal times of endless wars—men against magic, magic against men. The time when even the storms and rains were at the mercy of magic and its fickle moods. It might snow in the summer, or the hot winds might carry sand upon them, burying entire cities. Honest travelers feared to ride through the forest, lest the trees attacked them. A farmer might wake up to find his river flowing the wrong way or dried up altogether. Those days were gone and might have been forgotten, but for this stark reminder before Elika's eyes.

And who had not stood before the dark bridge in their last moments, facing that choice they all must one day make?

Like that hoary, old codger in the ale-stained uniform of the city's Blue Guard who had stood before the bridge for nigh on an hour; unsteady on his legs, his sour breath steaming in the crisp, winter night, drinking deeply of the cheap gin, which was as likely to kill him by morning as what he now faced. He took a long swig out of his bottle as he braced himself for the unknown fate ahead.

Elika sat huddled in the doorway of an abandoned house, watching him, needing to know whether he would reach the other side or die crossing. Her ears filled with the howling winds rising from the great chasm, and she did not need to imagine what he was thinking, staring as he did at the monstrous bridge and the lifeless bank beyond, for she was thinking the same—*surely it is better than what remains at our back. Better than what approaches.*

She clutched the cloak tighter around herself against the biting gust of wind trying to rip it from her. She had scavenged the woolen cloak some days ago from a dead beggar, and it still smelled of his mustiness. She pulled up her knees to her chest and clamped her icy hands under her arms. The stone wall was cold at her back. Her breath steamed. She waited and watched the old guard take another wobbly step toward the bridge, seeking courage in his gin-dulled mind.

He took another gulp, stared at the empty bottle in surprise, then threw it aside with a foul curse. The bottle hit the frozen ground and rolled off the edge of their world into the chasm, to fall for eternity in that endless darkness.

It had been a long and depressing day, and Elika was almost glad the old guard was finally here. Only that day everything had changed. Only that day they had learned that Terren, their city, now stood alone in the relentless advance of the Blight.

That day, as the sun was rising, Elika was there, high above the gathered crowds, watching from the rooftops as the Blue Guard rode through the city gates, whilst melancholy bells announced their return. This old guard was amongst the rag-tag force who had left not twenty days ago to scout the boundary of the remaining lands still untouched by the Blight. Sent out by the king, they had set out to discover the fate of the only other remaining city, to find out why the trade caravans from Drasdark had not arrived that summer whilst those that left Terren had not returned. Now, the Blue Guard had finally come home.

They rode silently, their faces haunted, the desolation in their eyes as stark as the lands beyond the bridge. The same desolate silence had engulfed the crowd, and the slow clip-clopping of hoofs on the street sounded loud and final.

Behind the returning guards walked a long line of stony-faced, bleak survivors of Drasdark, carrying the barest of their possessions in fur bundles. There would be no more trade caravans. Terren was now the last refuge of man. Magic had won after all. And soon, like everyone else, Elika too would have to face the impossible choice, the only one left to them now; fall to the Blight or face the Bridge to Magic.

With the shadow of that choice looming high overhead, it was easy to fall into despair, and it had taken great effort to push it aside and remember her daily task. That choice was still too far away, she had told herself, whilst her stomach was hungry now. Besides, there was still time. The king and his priests would find a way to stop the Blight. All they needed to do was purge every echo of magic left in their world that drove the punishing Blight. She had clung to that hope even as she watched the drawn faces of the guards who had lost theirs.

It was said those who had faced the Blight often returned to face the bridge. Often enough it was true, and an orphan like her did not reach the age of fifteen years without learning how to see the signs of men on the edge. And she was better than most at reading men, at seeing those who fought to hang on to the shreds of their decaying hope. It was barren hope, nothing more, which led them to believe that perhaps whatever lay on the other side of the bridge, death or some manner of uncertain existence, was better than the Blight. All you had to do then, when you saw those death-walkers, was stalk them and wait.

So when the Blue Guard had ridden through the city gate, her gaze had instantly settled on this old picket with a frost-nipped nose. She could read men and instantly knew he would face the bridge that day. It was not in his eyes, as Bad Penny had taught the young ones in their pack—his gaze was dull, uninterested like the rest of them—but in the set of his lips. They were pressed together in a determined way, stubborn almost. Elika could almost hear his thoughts—*thinking any more about it won't change me mind. I've seen enough. I know what it is that approaches, and I know what it is I must do. It's the bridge for me.*

She had been the first to mark him. It was why Bad Penny always sent her out as a spotter before anyone else. She did her part and signaled one of the younger kids milling about on Tollgate Corner to run and tell Penny that she had sighted the target to follow. Penny would send the scouts to learn what they could about the death-walker. And when they found his home, they would send for the looters. Until then, she had to keep him in her sights.

So she had followed him in the shadows all day, whilst he stumbled from tavern to tavern, chasing that evasive courage in the bottom of his tankard. It was his last day of life in this world, after all, and a man had a right to drink himself to oblivion if it pleased him. Except, there was not enough gin in the city to douse him in the courage needed to cross the bridge. That always came from within. She had seen many a staggering drunk turn away from the bridge, and many a sober man take that fateful step onto it. And she was certain this one had enough stubbornness to take it. His mind, as he was no doubt telling himself, was made up.

As he drank his last coin, he told any near enough to listen of all that befell the Blue Guard on their way to the new border of the Blight, and all they had seen since they came upon it. She'd heard enough such stories to pay them little mind. They were always the same. Aye, it was creeping toward them, and all it touched slowly died and turned to dust. And aye, only Terren was now left in its path. You did not dwell on it, else the temptation of the bridge or the eternal chasm it spanned might sink their tendrils into you. If she listened too closely, she might just start thinking of things other than getting enough food to live through the winter.

Still, as the day waned, her mood grew more and more dour. She had learned more about the guard than she wanted to know. Learned of his wife's death from the sweating fever, and his son who took the bridge after he had lost the use of his arm in a bar fight and could no longer earn his keep, of his daughter who was heavy with another child she did not want. He suffered pain in his knee from an old wound that plagued him more and more each passing winter. He hated the darker ales, for they turned his stomach at the end of the night ... Elika did not want to know any of it, did not want to become bound to him. But she had listened and came to like the old codger and now she would not rest until she knew his fate.

So here she was, sitting, waiting in the swirling snow flurry, long past when she should have returned to the safety and warmth of her den. He took another staggered step forward, past the black, grasping roots which anchored the bridge to this world. They sank into the cobbles of the old street like talons, glowing like slick skin in the flickering oil lamp across the street. It was the only light in the whole of Rift Street alongside the edge of their world.

The old guard stood there for another long, undecided moment, then cursed on a steaming breath and took another step toward his uncertain end. Again, he halted. Only the blood-salt barrier, a thick red line in the melting snow, lay between him and the magic of the bridge. Salt soaked in blood was the only defense against magic. It was how men long ago defeated it in the terrible war that sent the mighty tsaren fleeing.

Elika took a deep breath and hoped he would be spared the fate of reaching the other side. She had watched many a wretched soul face the bridge and thus knew the first step onto it was the most important. Once taken, another would follow, and then another, each one less labored, more determined, and then resolute. One step after another coming quicker, until they reached the point of no return ...

Once, she might have tried to stop him. Just as once she had tried to stop a noblewoman with a babe in her arms from doing the same.

"Lady, there is hope," Elika had told her urgently. "They say the king has found a way to halt the Blight. He sent the priests out toward it ..."

The woman had turned her empty gaze to Elika, handed her the babe and without a word strode out onto the bridge, and perished before reaching the end. Elika had been only six then, but as she was the one to bring the babe to their Hide, it was up to her to look after it. Those were the laws of their pack. She tried, but the babe cried and cried and refused to eat the stew, taking only bread soaked in water. There was no milk to be had unless you were gentry, and the babe died soon after in her arms.

No one tried to comfort Elika. She should have known better than to torment the poor babe for pity's sake. It would have been kinder for her to perish on the bridge in the embrace of her mother.

It was a hard, bitter lesson, and Elika had learned it well. After that, she never stopped mothers with babes, never picked one up from the frozen streets where they were left to face a quick, merciful death. She had learned to shield her heart from the endless river of misery and hunger that flowed through the streets of Terren. Aye, it had diminished her, made her less somehow, but it had kept her alive where she had watched others perish.

Since then, she only watched the desperate take the bridge from afar.

Bad Penny was right; there was nothing you could say to change their minds. Their hearts no longer lived in this forsaken world.

Elika caught a flash of movement in the shadows between the buildings. It was inevitable the others would sniff out the old death-walker before the day was done. One-eyed Rory of Peter Pockets' gang emerged to lean on the corner. He was, as ever, impeccably dressed in a silk shirt and silver vest, with black kid gloves and a long fur coat. You'd never mistake him for the gentry, however. He did not carry himself as one, did not talk like one either. He was as much a thief as any of them, and despite his plush, stolen clothes, just as desperate. She paid him no mind.

Rory nodded to her, a wicked glint in his remaining dark eye. "Still here, is he?"

Elika continued to ignore him.

Unlike the others of her pack, she did not bother to hide. Little Mite would be angry with her, but why bother hiding from the other watchers? They all knew each of them was there. Farther away, she had already spied the other looters, waiting for the signal to the race to claim the old man's remaining earthly possessions—waiting, like greedy vultures, for death. And she was one of them.

If she could, she would have found another way to be. But there was no other way. She had not only herself but the pack to look after. If it meant robbing the dead, then she'd do it. As one of the oldest in their pack, the weight of responsibility for the young ones rested with her as much as with Penny and Mite.

Today, luck was on her side. The old guard was one of those few who took nothing with them across the bridge, except the clothes on their back and their wits—not even the hope of reaching the other side. He left everything behind: food, grain and flour, coal lumps, blankets, clothes and shoes ... everything their pack desperately needed.

Unfortunately, he was also a city guard and thus one of Captain Daiger's men. Likely, they would have already gone through his home, laying claim to and hoarding the best pickings. They would not have taken anything, though. No, not yet. Not until the old man was dead or on the other side. Else claiming his possessions was thievery. And the king hated thieves more than murderers. Looting, however, was tolerated. After all, those who took the bridge never returned. Captain Daiger's men were likely guarding the doors until they received word the old picket was gone and not coming back.

"Bloody hell! Looks like he's about to change his mind," Rory said to no one in particular.

"He won't," she said.

"Confident, are ye? Why are you here, anyway, Spit? You won't be getting his loot. My men are already outside his home, and they'll cut any ragamuffin who tries to sneak past us."

She hated being called Spit. It was the name they gave the orphans. "Name's Eli," she mumbled, though why she bothered she did not know.

Rory knew her name, knew all their names, for it was his job to know. He was the one Peter Pockets sent out to catch and bring in those young 'uns who might be worth something to Pockets' gang. He was also the one who delivered the less savory messages to competing gangs when they strayed from their own hunting ground.

"Sure it is, Spit." He gave her a mean, toothy grin. His yellowing teeth were large in his long, gaunt face, and made her think of a fox's snout. "Why don't ye just go back to your mouse hole and save yourself being cut again?"

"Not here for his loot," she lied and instinctively scanned the buildings for Little Mite, in case Rory was of a mind to cut her now and be done with it.

Mite was also watching, though she'd never see him unless he wanted to be seen. Mite only needed to give the signal across the roofs for Tick to slide down the chimney into the old guard's home before Captain Daiger's men got their own signal. Tick was fast and wily. He'd be quick to grab what he could and be gone before anyone had the mind to chase him. She'd already seen his pleased face from afar when he had signaled to Mite that he was in position. There was good looting to be had with this one.

"So, here for the spectacle, then?" Rory smirked. "Always thought you were morbid like that, watching them with those large, icy eyes of yours, as if you were death itself urging them on." He shuddered. "Evil pup. Maybe you be thinking of taking the crossing yourself, hey Spit? Like your ma and pa."

Again, Elika ignored him. He thought everything was there for his amusement. Rory was cruel when the mood struck him. She had seen him cut a finger from Fast Flint's hand when he had mistakenly tried to pick the other thief's pocket. He laughed when he did it too, telling the skinny boy to mind whom he stole from the next time.

Rory pointed to a rheumy-eyed wretch in the distance, wrapped in a woolen shawl. "See him over there, the one with the walking stick. Watching. Making up his mind to do the same."

Elika had already seen him, studied him, and dismissed him as a target. He would never put a foot on the bridge. He watched it from afar, fearful of approaching the magic in it any closer lest he became infected with it. Yet, drawn to the bridge as a starving man to rotten bread, watching it with the same amount of disgust and want.

The bridge was a frightening sight. A grotesque creature that sometimes stirred and groaned in the dead of night; an ugly, ever-present reminder of the time when magic had existed in their world. Slick, spindly tendrils wove together to form a thin, narrow path, just wide enough for two men to walk side by side across the enormously wide chasm. The railing was little more than a thin, black web which could not possibly hold a man's weight were he to lean on it. No one touched it, not ever.

For a long time, like everyone else, Elika thought the bridge had been woven by magic. Then one day, she had stood at the chasm and stared into those endless depths that had swallowed many a man. And as she looked into the eternity of darkness, a thought came to her, a whisper on the rising wind from the Abyss; the bridge was woven *from* magic. It was more than a mere thought; it was a surfacing of some deep, innate knowledge. It made no sense, other than the stark resonation of the truth through her.

The bridge was magic itself, solid and menacing, and not some invisible force men imagined it to be. Like something out of old Bill Fisher's tales, which he spun over ale in the *Fat Fish* tavern. Bill sometimes spoke of magic taking on the shape of some object or walking amongst men as one of them and no one being any the wiser. She'd always thought them just tales, but what if they were true? The bridge had to be alive, for it had been forged by Tsarina Arala with her last breath, and she commanded the magic of life. The bridge ended the age-long war between men and magic, for it allowed magic to flee men's domain once and for all.

Since then, nothing had ever crossed into their world, and no one who had crossed to the other side ever returned.

At the chasm, their city of Terren ended as abruptly as if a giant knife had sliced through it. The city wall stopped at the bottomless precipice. The old streets ran to their crumbling edge and went no further. The other half of the city, with all its occupants, had vanished when Syn'Moreg, Lord of the Abyss, had sundered their world in two. At the chasm, their world began and ended. Only the bridge whispered cruel temptations to the forlorn and those as broken as their world. Like the old guard here, who still clung to hope that there was some manner of escape from the ever-relentless approach of the Blight. Except there was no refuge on the other side. Anyone with eyes could see that.

Deadlands, the land beyond was simply called.

There, the sky was gray, dull and cloudless in the day and starless at night. There were no splashes of sunlight on the ground—even when the sun was high—no snow, no rain, no breeze to stir the dust. Only the deadlands to where magic had been banished. The rocky land was flat, endless and desolate. Nothing stirred, no life, no creature. It was as gray and lifeless as a memory. A reminder of the destructive force of magic. If men could have destroyed the bridge that anchored it to our world, they would have done so long ago.

Finally, Elika saw the guard find his cagey courage. She knew the signs well—a deep breath, a stiffening of the shoulders, clutched fists, a final gaze back toward the city. A glance that was as desolate as the land beyond. He looked back and his deep, tired eyes locked with hers and held. There were others around, and yet it was her gaze he sought his strength in. For long moments, he simply looked at her and she at him. She was careful not to change her expression, not to urge him on or hold him back by anything as small as a careless blink.

His lips twitched into a sad smile.

A choking lump appeared in her throat. She wanted to look away but forbade herself to do so. She would give him the last piece of humanity he would likely ever see again. He did not need pity, just understanding. His passing would not be unobserved, his fate would be witnessed. She would watch and know his fate and would always remember why she hated magic.

He touched his hat to her, turned away and took a firm, bold step across the blood-salt line, quickly followed by that final, irrevocable step onto the bridge. As soon as he did, the roots of the bridge moved and clung harder to the ground. The bridge groaned and heaved, as if taking a soft breath.

The lump in her throat grew larger. There was no turning back for him now. Once there, they never turned back. Whether it was the pull of magic or some insurmountable resolve, she never knew, but the second step always followed the first. And then another, and another. The winds rising from the chasm tore at his coat, ripped the hat off his head and sent it flying into the dark abysm. He paid it no attention, neither halting nor slowing in his step. They never looked back, never wavered. And all too soon, it seemed to her, he reached the apex. He stopped there, at the point where some capricious power decided your fate.

Elika held her breath, her heart racing with dread and fear of that same distant choice before her. She had seen this part countless times and thought this the worst and cruelest test. The uncertainty, the simply not knowing what the next step would bring, what fate awaited you beyond the apex. Worse still, the not knowing which fate was kinder; that you should reach the other side or ...

The old guard spread his arms, as if offering himself to the mercy of magic, and took his last ever step from this world. In the blink of an eye, his form turned to dust and was swept away in a vortex of uprising winds.

Elika closed her eyes and held back tears with everything she had. She never cried, forbade herself that weakness.

Everything began and ended with the bridge. It was at the heart of all that was wrong in their world, at the heart of the Blight and the great chasm. It had stolen her very first memories, fed her very first fears.

Aye, her story, too, began at the bridge, her first memory, the memory of loss and grief and abandonment. She recalled the faceless shadows of a man and woman hugging her, kissing her ... and leaving her. She had watched them cross the bridge into the night, growing distant and fading from her memory. She had wanted to run after them, but the firm, bony hand of a stranger held her back. Elika must have seen what had happened to them. But since then, no matter how hard she tried, she had never been able to recall whether they perished at the apex or reached the Deadlands.

She remembered trying to wrench herself from the dry hand holding her back, and an old woman's crackly voice saying, "Not your time, precious. I told them so. Told them you must stay behind to hold the world together for just a little longer. And what if you alone made it across without them? What would have become of you then? What would have become of us all?" the voice added in a whisper.

For so long Elika had pondered that memory, seeking some sense from it, some understanding why her parents abandoned her here. What drove them to seek escape in that other lifeless world? Why not wait until she was older and they could have taken her with them?

She was older and wiser now and had seen the rotten heart of Terren where humanity was likened to weakness. She had seen the hunger without end, the sickness, the dead unclaimed on the streets, the wealthy looking aside. She knew better than most what drove the broken to the bridge, the despair that drove them to the unthinkable. Some took their children with them. Others left them behind in the world of man to fend for themselves as best they could. There were times when she, too, craved some escape from the filthy streets of Terren. Yet even in those moments, she found herself grateful to have been left behind.

She recalled those vague days of being alone, frightened and hungry, when she had sat there, watching the bridge, imagining her parents walking back across it and sweeping her up in their arms. It was Bad Penny who had found her and taken charge of her. She owed her life to Penny and Little Mite.

She owed only hatred to the cursed bridge for all it had taken from her. And despite her fear and hatred of it, one day, she too would be left with nothing but the dreadful choice—face the Blight or the Bridge to Magic. Death or endless existence as a phantom, haunting the plains of

Deadlands, were she to reach the other side. To become a shapeless shadow swallowed by the gray land. Neither alive nor dead, slowly drifting away into that fathomless distance, fading, then vanishing.

Magic was the enemy of man. Its echoes drew the Blight toward them. And the bridge kept their world linked to the place where magic and the terrible tsaren had been exiled. Elika lifted her head and filled her vision with the slick, black monster, ugly and menacing, like a misshapen tree.

The street was dark and empty. All the other watchers had run off to loot the old guard's home of all his scant possessions. The beggar with the walking stick also had gone, having lost his courage. She was alone, just her and this creature of magic that did not belong in their world. It was twisted and ugly, and she hated it—hated it above all else.

She wanted her parents back. She wanted to know whether they had turned to dust or crossed together to become shapeless phantoms; wanted to know why they had not taken her with them. She hated the magic that had irreparably broken their world. The bridge was meant to free men from their terrors. But even now, the Blight was nigh upon them, driving good folk across the chasm to nowhere, save that it was away from here. She sprang to her feet and advanced on the beast before her, wanting to hurt magic as it had hurt so many others.

The bridge was made from magic, man's foe forged into dark flesh. Everything alive could be hurt, killed, destroyed, even the gods themselves. Destroy the bridge and you will stop the Blight, said the priests. Many had tried. Nothing had worked, not fire nor sword or blood-salt. Since the day magic had been vanquished and purged from this world, no power men possessed could damage Arala's creation. It did not matter. Elika wanted to try. If only to stop it offering false hope to the desperate.

She pulled out her bone-handled knife from under her tunic. Fury surged through her, solidifying into a ball of power and strength inside her. It grew and grew, feeding on her anger until she could not hold it back from erupting out of her.

Her foot crunched on the blood-salt ... sudden stabbing pain struck her stomach. She cried out and bent over, her whole body afire. She stumbled forward, across the salt line, and just as suddenly the pain was gone.

She did not think more of it, for the ball of rage was still inside her, and she was there, beside the bridge, closer than she had ever dared approach before. She could feel the heat of it, smell the faint sweet odor, fresh and earthy. It smelled like spring and summer fruits, and rich, tilled earth. Somehow, she had imagined this monster would smell of death and decay. But magic was deceptive. She raised the knife and with a roar stabbed the vile beast.

The blade dug in deep to the bone hilt, and the bridge groaned and shuddered as if in pain. Except ... the knife was not meant to pierce it. Many had tried ...

Elika staggered back and stared at the steaming, black blood pulsing gently from the wound onto the snow.

She had seen city guards and priests use swords and stones and ropes and fire in trying to destroy this relic of days long past. She had watched the king's own personal Red Guard try to cut it down with axes made of blood-salt. Nothing had ever broken through its impenetrable magic. But her knife slid in as easily as if the bridge was truly spun from mere flesh.

She backed away. It was impossible. How could she have done this? The knife was still lodged in the black flesh, and the blood continued to trickle, staining the snow a deep, dark red.

Her chest tightened with fear. She glanced around. The houses across the street were long abandoned and crumbling. No one wanted to live so close to the bridge, lest they became infected with its magic. She could see no one, yet she felt watched. There were always watchers by the bridge, waiting for that next loot the death-walkers left behind.

Something brushed her foot. She yelped and jumped back. One of the inky roots was creeping toward her like a fungal tendril. It probed the ground, this way and that, searching for her, reaching for her. Horror gripped her chest. She had never seen it do that, like some foul, unnatural creature of old tales.

She turned and fled without looking back. She ducked behind a corner and stilled, listening.

Silence. No one followed.

She looked down at her hands. They were shaking. Only magic could hurt the bridge. And no one, not even the most powerful of Echoes, those poor souls who had somehow become infected with an *echo* of magic, could command it. Only the tsaren ... or their human mages. But the mages were also all gone, banished to roam the Deadlands as phantoms, or burned long ago in the blood-salt fires to destroy the magic inside them.

Magic inside her ... Her skin crawled with disgust. Everything inside her tightened. There could not be magic inside her. She could not be an Echo. Surely, she'd have known before now if she was. But if anyone had seen her ... the priestesses would hear of it. They would find her ... unless, of course, no one had seen her. Maybe she had not used magic. Maybe it was ... it was ... what? It did not matter. She had to leave. She would just go back to the Hide, where the orphans were likely dividing the old man's loot amongst themselves.

She pulled down her hood to better cover her face, blended with the shadows of the street, and began to walk as fast as she dared.

Behind her, she heard a soft footstep crunch on ice-laced snow.

"Well, well, lil' princess. What have you gone and done now?" said a dark, knowing voice.

Without looking back, she quickly turned another corner and ran.

CHAPTER TWO

The Echo of Magic

"Many a scholar has tried to determine when the ethereal and earthly realms collided and joined into one. Some date it to a thousand years ago, when the tsaren first appeared in our world and tried to wrest Seramight from men. But even before that, there have been countless intrusions of magic into our world whenever our realms brushed past each other. Before the arrival of the Tsaren Reval, Ilikan, Dragan and Arala, men contained and fought magic with blood-salt and fire. No other ward or prayer token had ever been an effective defense against it."

History of Men, Gods and Magic,
By Priest Oderrin

The dark voice she had heard at the bridge continued to haunt her steps as she fled through the streets. She knew who it had belonged to. How could she not, for she had listened to his strange and frightening tales since she was a wean? She'd recognize Bill Fisher as well as he'd recognize her from two streets away. And not a moment ago he had seen her stab the bridge; Old Bill, who could not hold back a good tale.

A toothless beggar grabbed at her cloak and muttered an incoherent plea. Even if she had a morsel to spare, she'd give it to her own pack of sallow-faced orphans before all others. So she strode past, trying to appear calm, though her hands were still shaking in her pockets. It would not do to appear agitated on the streets at night. That was certain to draw the attention of the predators.

As it was, women with babes pestered her for spare coin. The drunks harassed anyone in sight. The sick only moaned as they lay there dying. Each day she was forced to make her heart cold and hard, to be one of those countless others who looked dispassionately on the suffering that filled their streets. And when she looked at the desperate and desolate, she felt only dread at how many hungry mouths there were, vying for the same scraps of food as her pack of orphans.

She peered around the corner, down a street illuminated with a single, flickering oil lamp. Three guards were harassing a sleeping drunk slouched against a garden gate. When he did not stir, they searched through his pockets and found nothing of worth. She ducked behind the wall and walked in the opposite direction.

If the guards saw her, it was likely they'd simply ignore her. But you could never tell when the mood to pick on a street orphan might take them.

Captain Daiger himself paid the orphans as much attention as he might a scurrying rat in his path. Some days he ignored them. Other times he took it into his head to rid the streets of the pestilence. She held no genuine dislike for the captain. He was as greedy and mean as the rest of them, but he still had ideas about keeping order in the city. He went about it in his own way, trying to appease the deserving, respectable folk by not turning a blind eye to the crimes that offended them.

Tonight, he had a different purpose. Since the survivors of Drasdark had arrived earlier that day, Captain Daiger's guards were out in force on the streets, looking for homes to commandeer from the weak, the sick and the poor, to generously redistribute to the more worthy.

That was the way of things. The wealthier gentry of the Silver Circle had barricaded the streets against the encroachment of homeless migrants and thieving dog-gangs, the disorganized rabble of brutes. Likewise, the nobility hid in their stately homes inside the Golden Circle, where archers atop the inner city wall would gladly shoot a drunken beggar who strayed too close to the gilded gates. In the rest of the city, coin, savagery or cunning got you a roof over your head.

Many slept on the streets. Others formed dog-gangs to seize ill-defended or abandoned homes. They rarely kept them for long. Captain Daiger was constantly on the lookout for easy coin and would step in to chase off vagabonds and squatters. The title registrar was also on hand to swiftly reassign titles to men of respectability with heavy pockets and *generous* natures.

With so many city guards about, no street was safe tonight, especially those close to the chasm in Riftside, where the poorest and most desperate lived. Each street she turned into, seeking a safe way back to the Hide, she encountered a group of guards peering through the windows, knocking on doors, demanding to see titles and leases. She kept out of their sight. Only their uniforms told them apart from the dog-gangs they often hunted.

It was the same eight winters ago when the survivors of Foxway came in their thousands. The merchant town, which traded sugar and rice, lay in the last pocket of the Wetlands. Those who arrived with plenty of coin to spare and share turned to Captain Daiger to find them a vacant home.

She would never forget that haunting night. They all thought they were safe in their hideout. It was an abandoned, crumbling building a few streets away from the chasm, with a leaky roof, missing doors and boarded windows. The downstairs stank of rot and excrement. No one had bothered them there before—not so close to the bridge.

But in the dead of night, she startled awake to screams, torchlight and gleaming swords stained with blood. Blue coats were everywhere. Those who slept closest to the entrance lay in their beds with their throats cut. The older ones of their pack were fighting, the youngest scattering in all directions. Elika had just enough sense to scramble from her bedroll and dart for the nearest bolthole. Someone grabbed her foot and dragged her back. She screamed. But Little Mite was quickly there to cut the guard's throat. He turned and stabbed another guard, then shouted at her to run. She had escaped. Few of them did.

Later, she learned those who were not killed had been captured and forced to take the bridge. The guards jeered and laughed and wagered on whether they'd reach the other side. One of the older boys fought them. Him, they threw into the chasm alive. Only ten of their pack were left. Too few to defend any den, even against drunken dog-gangs. After that, there was no place for them to go, except the one place even the most desperate shunned—Rift Street.

Elika turned another corner and emerged into it. It was dark and empty. No one dared to live on Rift Street. It faced the bottomless chasm that sundered their entire world in two. The cobbles sloped sickeningly down to the frayed edge of the abyss where the last of the road had tumbled in. From the chasm rose the undying vortex, mercilessly buffeting any who dared to come near. She hugged the building wall as she went, the clawing air pulling at her cloak and trousers, forcing her to keep one hand on the brickwork. Now and then, like tonight, those winds carried on them the faint smell of death. And it was said that, in the quiet of the night, if you listened, on the keening updraft you could hear the screams of those who had fallen into the chasm.

She glanced about and peered into every shadow whilst straining to hear beyond the restless wind for sounds of pursuit or lurking threat. Nothing moved, save the dust sweeping the old, cobbled road. In the distance, the bridge was dark and menacing in the yellow glow of the street-lamp. The rest of Rift Street was shrouded in shadow.

She turned in the opposite direction to the bridge and walked briskly. Their pack did not shun superstition. Only fools did that. So they had been careful to choose a section of Rift Street as far away from the bridge as they could. They named their new den the Hide.

There were many ways into it. She chose the first one she came to, snatched another glance about, and slipped through the door hanging askew on its hinges. This one was the farthest from where they slept. But even here she could smell Penny's delicious stew on the air. She avoided the traps Mite had set up and tended daily, then jumped and skipped over the gaps in the floor where the timber planks had been ripped up for the fire.

Only the one forest remained between here and the Blight, and the king had forbidden all from cutting a single branch of it on the punishment of death. It was a stupid law, she thought. Once the Blight reached the forest, it would be no good to man or beast. Might as well take what they could now. But then, there was always that hope which got in the way of men thinking clearly.

She bounded up the stairs, two at a time, following the aroma of stewed mushrooms. The promise of food did not cheer her, however. She was an Echo. How could that be? She always did those rituals that Penny made them do to keep the echoes of magic away. She ate raw garlic in the morning when there was garlic to be had. She cut and burned her hair in summer and inhaled deeply of the smoke. She even carried a Sachi ward against magic, a small wooden carving of an eye, the symbol of the old gods men had long ago abandoned. None of it had kept her safe.

Her foot broke through a rotten step, and she fell.

She had ever been careful to avoid that step. She was being careless. Inside, she was still shaking from what had happened. It would not do. If she returned flustered, Penny would realize something was wrong and demand to know everything. And Mite would be there, making certain she missed nothing out whilst she told it. She took a deep breath and steadied her nerves. She could not reveal that she was an Echo. Not even to Penny or Mite. Not yet. She had to think. She must tell no one of what she had done.

But Old Bill Fisher has seen you, the niggling voice at the back of her mind whispered. *He'll tell everyone.*

Maybe Bill's mind might wander again, and by morning he'd forget what he had seen. Besides, everyone knew Bill was full of fanciful tales … No, they would believe him, for she had left her knife behind.

She sat down, lowered her head, and just breathed. No one except Bill knew it was her who had stabbed the bridge. She was wearing a cloak and hat, and from afar she looked like so many others. The next few days she would just have to be more cautious, maybe change her appearance. She had done so plenty of times to fool the city guards. And even if she had stabbed the bridge, they were more likely to thank her as not. After all, the priests believed that if you destroyed the Bridge to Magic, you would destroy the Blight.

She forced herself to push away all thoughts of magic, focusing instead on the delicious smell of cooked mushrooms drifting down the corridor. The Sewer Sisters, Ell and Mill, had found a secret patch of them growing where the brick sewer walls had crumbled and mingled with the dirt. Secrets, however, were as hard to keep to yourself as coin, and there was always a thief on the prowl for both. For now, it kept them fed each night. Her stomach rumbled loudly. No, there was no need to panic. Not yet. She took another calming breath and continued up the stairs more cautiously.

Over the years, the successive leaders of their pack had reorganized the Hide to suit their extended family. Walls between adjoining buildings had been broken through to create the large room they all lived in. Over the windows, they hung old moth-eaten rugs to block the sight of the chasm and the desolate, gray deadlands beyond. For Elika, it was no longer habit but instinct to check all the boltholes. Some led down, some up. And over time they had carved out many small, secret ways between the abandoned buildings. They would not get ambushed again. This time, there were enough fleeing holes for them all. Little Mite had also set up traps and alarms around every entrance to the Hide. So far, only the rats and the stumbling drunks had set them off.

Elika looked over the Hide.

They had grown in number since the day the ten of them had claimed this den. They were thirty strong now, a formidable number for other orphan gangs to reckon with. And soon the youngest of them would be out there, bringing their share home to the pack. They sat around the small fire, watching the stewing pot with wide, hungry eyes. The older kids sat by themselves at a distance, throwing dice and wagering pebbles, whilst passing around a bottle of Lazy Eye's sour wine. Lazy Eye was already snoring in his blankets. He'd gotten himself work in a tavern, and on those nights when there was a big brawl, he would steal a bottle of their cheapest wine with no one the wiser.

Having satisfied herself that nothing was amiss and no one was paying her any more attention than usual, she made her way to the fire. She put out her stiff hands to warm them, trying to appear calm and composed. She yawned for good measure and flexed her numb fingers to get the heat into her bones a little faster.

"The priestesses say we're next," Pit the Picker was saying miserably to Bad Penny as he warmed his own hands. "I heard 'em talking about it when I was waiting for their charity."

With everything happening that day, she had forgotten about the charity. Every seventh day, the Priestesses of Mercy brought out bowls of torn bread to give to the hungry. Pit the Picker was small for his age. He had large eyes on a round, freckled face, with a head which seemed too big for his body. He was the best at earning pity. With his sweet, cheeky smile, the priestesses could not resist giving him a few extra pieces and an occasional half penny. These he was meant to bring back to the Hide, to be shared amongst the pack.

Penny did not give her trust to those who had not yet earned it and had sent Elika to spy on him the last time.

She had watched from above and seen him pocket the coin and eat some of the bread. But which of them had not strayed before? She could not bring herself to rat him out to Penny and Mite. Might be they'd just cuff him. But then, they might just decide to make an example of him. Whenever she thought that, she remembered Lucky Lick and what they had done to him.

So Elika had taken it upon herself to cuff Pit, warning him to bring back everything he foraged. Those were the laws of their pack. He had sworn he'd do so in the future. Today, she had been planning to keep an eye on him again, to be certain he heeded her warning. Instead, she had followed the old guard. She looked at Pit and saw how he studiously avoided her gaze. Aye, he had strayed again. She'd have to have another talk with him later. Might be she didn't cuff him hard enough.

Bad Penny stirred the stew in the pot over the fire, whilst hungry eyes watched her from around the room. "'Twas always going to happen. I said so years ago when traders from Drasdark said they could see the Blight from their city walls, from up high atop the mountain."

"But that's not the worst of it," Pit said. "I heard them saying that the Blight sped up at Drasdark when it had gotten close. Like it charged into battle. Then it slowed again when it was done killing them."

"What nonsense have you brought up here?" Penny threw him a stern look. "Charging to battle, indeed. It's a slow-moving beast, Pit. Old women can out-walk it, even babes can out-crawl it."

"But I heard 'em talking about it. They said it moved faster than men could run. 'Tis why Drasdark was taken by surprise. They thought they had many years left before it reached them."

Elika could see what Pit could not; Penny was just as troubled as the rest of them. She was pale, her eyes darting to the young ones as Pit spoke. It was them she hoped to spare the nightmares. "Why don't you do something useful, Pit and …"

"Doesn't it scare you that we are next?" Pit asked, heedlessly. "They say it won't be long now. Maybe a year or two. Maybe even less than that. And then … then there'll be no way out … just the bridge." He grew more and more agitated as he spoke.

Penny flicked her deep copper hair, the color of an old coin, behind her shoulder. "Then you've got two years to work out how not to die of hunger. So quit your fretting. We can't even see the Blight yet." She tasted the stew and seemed pleased with it. Penny could make boiled leather taste delicious.

"Besides, the king has sent out the priests again. They think they've found a way to stop it," Elika said with an indifferent shrug, despite feeling sick with dread herself. She had heard tales on the street of how Drasdark had perished, saw it all in her mind—the harrowing fear, the slow death, the helplessness. But Penny was right, what use was there worrying over it now?

"They said that before, remember?" Pit whined.

"He's not a king but an imposter. And a useless one at that," Little Mite said in his deep voice from his bedroll. He was lying back with his hands behind his head, looking up at the jingle-jangle alarm he had crafted in the rafters of the ceiling.

"Don't you start with that one, again," Penny replied.

"Everyone calls him a king," said Pit.

"It's because no one knows any better," Mite countered. "Except the priests and the imposter-king himself, and those wastrels passing as nobles around him. Only those with the blood of the Sacred Crowns, ordained by the gods, can be kings."

There was nothing little about Mite. Penny said he'd once been the smallest kid in the gang, small even for his age. That was before Elika joined their pack. Now he was taller than any of the older boys, all wiry muscle, lean as a whip. All the boys looked up to him, and some whispered that Mite should take over the Hide from Bad Penny. They'd never whisper it where Mite might hear them, for he was unwaveringly loyal to her.

"And where's your professed heir of King Northwind now, that rebel Lord Silvering?" Penny asked, waving the spoon at him. "Dead, he is, like the other rebels who joined him in stirring unrest. And good riddance too. War's the last thing we need. The old kings have been dead six hundred years. Leave them be in the past where they belong."

Mite's jaw tightened. "Maybe if the old kings were still here, they'd stop the Blight in truth."

For her part, Elika gave the king no more thought than she did to anyone else in the Golden Circle, for she was certain they gave no thought to the folk beyond their gilded gates.

"Might be they could. No one knows that for sure, now do they?" Penny said. "And they're not here to tell us. There's only our king to stop the Blight now."

The two of them often argued about things that seemed unimportant to Elika. Her stomach rumbled again. She scooped up an empty bowl, which seemed too small in her hands for the size of her hunger. As one of the older kids, she had *first picking* rights. Tonight, she would not squander them.

Little Mite picked up his bowl and lined up beside her. She eyed his larger bowl with a pang of envy. Penny decided who got how much food, and Mite was bigger than her and Penny combined. Still, she was hungry enough tonight to eat three of Mite's portions of stew. It was as if there was another hungrier creature inside her demanding its share too. She tripped on that thought, caught her breath, and her stomach shrank back.

Don't think of magic, she told herself harshly, *else they will see something's wrong.*

"Don't care about the dead kings," grumbled Pit the Picker. "It's them Echoes. They say Drasdark fell to the Blight 'cause they couldn't get rid of all the Echoes. It's them Echoes that are feeding the Blight with their magic. The sooner they find them all and shove them across the bridge, the better."

Her heart skipped a beat. She stared at her bowl as Penny ladled a small amount of stew into it, then retreated to her bedroll.

As she ate, she thought of what Pit had said about the echoes hiding inside unsuspecting folk, like her. It made her feel like a traitor, hiding the enemy within. She had to tell Penny ... she'd be thrown out of the Hide until she was purged of it. And rightly so. She should leave. But then Mite would look for her, and he'd force the truth out of her.

She looked down again. All her stew was gone. She had not tasted any of it. And her hunger was still there, fiercer than before. She had not eaten all day, but that was not so unusual. She should have been sated. Instead, she was even more ravenous.

The weans were lined up for their share of the stew, and she could already see that the last few would go without. She remembered those times when she had to be faster than the other kids if she wanted to be fed. There was never enough food for them all. Some had to wait until the next day to sate their hunger. She put the empty bowl aside, resigned to another hungry night.

"Here, take it." Mite thrust half a bowl of stew before her.

She blinked at it. Mite was *big*, so big that she knew he was secretly always hungry. And now he was giving her half his portion. She shook her head. "Give it to them." She nodded to the ones at the back of the line.

He chuckled. "They already ate today. Fast Flint brought back a mud eel earlier that he filched from Sticky Tom's eel barrel. And I saw you eyeing up my bowl. Just take it. You look half-starved and I stole half a loaf from Pretty Bessy earlier."

She scoffed at his lie. There was no stealing involved. Bessy took a special liking to Mite, and everyone knew she liked to feed him. Elika was not so naive not to know why. Mite's beard had thickened this last year, and he looked almost like a man. He had developed men's appetites long before that, however.

She snatched his bowl. She was too hungry to refuse and it annoyed her that instead of keeping an eye on the pickers and looters, he was rolling around in Bessy's bed again. She ate quickly, just to give him back his bowl and get rid of him. Mite had a way of seeing things others didn't want him to see.

He chuckled at her. "I won't steal it back from you, kid, so slow down."

"Not a kid," she said through a mouthful of stew.

He suddenly grew serious. He crouched beside her and gave her an odd, thunderous look. "Wanted to talk to you, besides."

Her heart skipped and began to race. "About what?"

"The bridge."

Her insides jolted. He knew. Had seen her. He always seemed to be just there.

She stuffed her mouth with another spoonful and said nothing.

"Look, I saw what you did. I was there, and so was one of the captain's men. He took off as soon as he saw you stab it. I tried to catch up to him and silence him, but ..." He gritted his teeth. Mite would have cut his throat had he caught him. She had seen him do it when Seena was snatched and dragged into an alley by two guards. "Do you understand what I'm saying? They'll be looking for you."

She shrugged, trying to appear unafraid. "Then they'll be looking for a boy. Might be I'll change back into a girl."

His face turned red with anger. "And how many *boys* will they snatch from the streets before they find you?"

She had not thought of that. "I didn't mean to ... it was an accident," she blurted out.

He glanced around furtively. "You did something no one has been able to do before. No one. Not any Echo. Do you even know how you did it?"

Elika could tell he was bewildered, just as much as she was.

She shrugged. "Maybe I'll just surrender and get myself purged, like Mad Maddy."

His jaw tightened. "And if they can't purge you, like with Nails?"

She did not want to appear afraid, especially in front of Mite.

"What's the worst they'll do? Shove me across the bridge?" She said it flippantly, though her heart raced with the fear of it.

"The worst they'll do? Burn you alive in blood-salt fire," he snapped back. "Didn't you hear? It's what the Prince of Drasdark ordered when they saw the Blight approach. Only they didn't manage to burn all the Echoes. The migrants are saying there are too many of them still left in the world, and that Terren would do better to start the burnings sooner than later."

She thrust the empty bowl into his hands. "The king would never do that. His father banned the bonfires eighty years ago."

"There is nothing men wouldn't do to survive," he said with a savage glint in his eyes.

He rose to his feet, taking his bowl with him, then barked some instruction and pointed at four older kids. Pit the Picker led them out. Two had to watch the bridge day and night in case another death-walker chose to leave it all behind. The other two patrolled the roofs above their Hide.

Elika curled up on her bedroll. Clever Kit was already asleep, and she shuffled closer to him for warmth. She lay on her side, listening to the distant howl of the wind, unable to sleep. And when the winds grew shrill and piercing, she was certain she heard the chilling screams of countless souls damned to fall in darkness for eternity.

For long hours, she twisted and turned, her mind churning. It was said that those who slept under the eye of magic were likely to be claimed by it. So they avoided sleeping in those rooms that faced the abyss and sprinkled blood-salt by the windows to keep it out. And in the summer, they cut and burned their hair to cleanse the Hide of any lingering echoes of it. Despite all that, she had somehow become infected.

Her gaze found Mite in his bedroll, sleeping in that wild abandon of his, with arms and legs flung wide, his woolen blanket half cast aside. His dagger peered from under the roll of rags he used as a pillow. He was right. Mite was always right. By morning, they would be looking for her. Echoes had to be purged or exiled. She knew the law, and with the Blight so close, there was only one thing to do. All those infected had to go to the Temple of Mercy to be cleansed. And they did. Except not everyone came out.

She remembered Nails, who was quick to mischief where mischief was to be had. He walked around with a big smile on his face and quick wit on his tongue. One day, he was caught by the guards for thieving. They beat him, took his loot, but would've let him go except that they checked him with a blood-salt crystal. They had done it to him before, but this time Nails screamed in pain. He'd been infected. They gave him to the priestesses for the purging. But the magic clung to him, like an invisible leech, so they took him to the bridge. With magic, it had always been destruction by blood-salt or banishment.

She had watched from afar. They all had. He had wept and pleaded for another chance to be purged. The priestesses shook their heads. The guards shoved him onto the bridge. Cross, or face the fire. Nails trembled and walked and wept all the way. He reached the other side. Few ever did. And like them, he stood there unmoving, still as a picture, a dark phantom alone in the vast, empty landscape surrounded by magic. Neither alive nor dead. The next day he was farther again, growing fainter. Each day his form grew more distant, yet frozen as before in the bleak landscape. Until one day he vanished, and the desolate wasteland beyond was once again empty.

A whimpering came from the dark, followed by stifled sniffles. All thoughts of magic forgotten, Elika propped herself on her arm. The Hide was quiet. The faint glow of the remaining embers cast menacing shadows onto the walls. Her gaze settled on a small bundle wrapped in a filthy blanket beside the fire. Rosy Rose, the new addition to their pack, was crying again.

Penny had found her hiding behind a water barrel in Market Square, alone and frightened. She was filthy, lice-infested, her cheek bruised. Penny was quick to claim her before some foul pander had. The pack, however, resented new arrivals who brought nothing but another mouth to feed. And now she was weeping where everyone could hear her.

Elika shook her head in exasperation, and leaving her warm bed, tiptoed over to the bundle.

She crouched down beside it, glancing around to see whether anyone was awake. "Shh," she whispered to Rose. "Don't let them see you cry, else they'll think you weak and will steal your food when Penny's back is turned."

Rose recoiled with fright, sat up and clutched her blanket to her chest. She was one of the Winged Folk, and feathers adorned her hair, though it was a dreadful tangle now.

"Nana … mai arra …" she sniffled. "Nana …"

That was another thing about the Winged Folk. They had come to Terren three hundred years ago when they lost their forests to the Blight. They had settled in Treeside, as it was now called, for they planted miniature trees in pots and every spare space they claimed. And since then, they had clung to their exotic language and strange customs.

The strangest of which was their propensity to breed fanciful birds for their bright feathers. They used those feathers to adorn their hair, clothing, jewelry, and every manner of item they traded in the city.

Elika sighed and sat down next to the girl. "Penny said your Nan is dead."

The girl's lip shook.

"Can you speak our tongue?"

No answer.

Winged Folk taught their own language to their children before allowing them to learn the common tongue.

"You'd better learn, else how will you know what you must do?"

Rose wiped her nose with the back of her hand. "Do?"

"To survive, you know ... to eat." Elika motioned to indicate food going to the mouth.

"Cama inna," the girl said in distress and patted her stomach. "Eat."

Elika's shoulders slumped. "There's none now till tomorrow. You have to be fast, see? Faster than the other kids. And remember to hit them if they try to take what's yours. Hard as you can. They might hit back, but they'll like you more for it."

Rose looked down at the bright-blue feather she clutched in her hand and her eyes welled with tears again.

"Is it your ward of protection?" Elika asked, speaking quietly so as not to wake the others. She pointed at the feather.

"Mikka," the girl said miserably. "Mikka," she repeated and brushed the white and blue feathers in her hair. "Ma faira."

"Your bird? Mikka was your bird?"

Rosy Rose nodded. "Ma bird. Dead. Boy kill to eat."

Elika stuck her hand in her pocket and pulled out the wooden carving of an eye. She showed it to Rose. "This is my ward. See? It's the eye of the gods. The Sachi believe that if you carry it, the gods' gazes will be drawn to you and they will watch over you. It keeps me ..." *Safe*, she was going to say. Except it had not kept her safe from magic, had it?

"Eye ..." Rose repeated.

Elika gave her a small smile. "If you ask nicely, Fast Flint might show you his ward of protection. It's his little finger. It's all shriveled and black. He carries it in the small pouch around his neck." She stuffed the wooden carving back into her pocket. "And stay close to Penny until you learn what's what around here. It's likely she'll cut your hair soon. She hates lice."

Rose scratched her head, yawned, and lay down again.

Elika left her there and returned to her own bed. She glanced at Mite, as she did so. His eyes were open, watching them. She quickly looked aside, feeling as if she had been caught in some misdeed. She lay down and pulled her blanket over her head.

When sleep finally came, she dreamt of the dark bridge, of standing at its apex, feeling her body fall apart and rise on the winds into eternity ...

She awoke to the distant sound of temple bells and a hive of activity around her.

"There's an announcement from the king," Pit the Picker said to her on his way past. "And that's never good."

Elika sat up and rubbed her raw eyes. The others were already scattering through every bolthole up to the roofs. She sighed. It had to be about the bridge. By now the whole city must know what had happened. She rubbed her eyes again.

When she opened them, Mite was looming over her. "You look like you've been touched by Moreg himself."

She felt as if she *had* been touched by the God of Death. She ached all over and felt as if she had not slept at all.

"Last night …" she began awkwardly. "Mite, it's not just the guard who saw me. Bill Fisher was there, too. He followed me."

Mite was silent for a moment, his eyes flickering sightlessly the way they did when he was thinking intently about something that needed fixing. "Let's hear what the king has to say and then we'll see what Bill wants for his silence." And that was that.

There was an intent look in his pale eyes and an odd intellect that did not belong in the face of a street urchin. He never spoke of his past, none of them did. He moved with a certain grace and steady pride. But the thing she liked best about Mite was that he would set this right. He set all their troubles right.

His steadiness gave her courage. It gave them all courage. She threw aside her covers, put on her hat, grabbed the cloak and followed him to the roof.

The sun was as high overhead as it was going to get. It was a crisp morning, but there was a little heat from the low winter sun to warm her face. Spring was near at last. The ice had melted on the sunward side of the roofs, and the footing was certain and no longer slippery. Even the enormous palace, raised from the ground by the tsaren, looked neither foreboding nor menacing, but magnificent and brilliant. The slender black towers shone in the sun as they stretched into the sky. On those gray, rainy days of autumn she had seen them touch the clouds.

She followed Mite above the barricades in the Silver district, racing toward the outskirts of it, toward the

Temple Square. Mite ran ahead with those long legs of his, pausing often to wait for her to catch up. The thieves' highway was busy today. In the distance, other gangs also made their way to hear what the king had to say.

There was no better place in Terren than the rooftops. Here, above the streets, she could never become lost. The expansive webbing of roofs could take you anywhere in the city without needing to touch the ground. Many different races had carved their own small patch out of Terren, building homes into every corner and nook they could find. Sky-homes spanned the streets overhead between buildings, forming roof-bridges across every street and alley. And with so many shacks on tall stilts, there was barely a place in the streets where one could look up and see the sky. But up here, the world was bright and vast. The air was fresh and the land beyond was boundless. Or so she imagined.

There were as many pockets to Terren as you might find on a pedlar, with just as many little treasures. Every roof had its own story to tell of them who lived below it.

For centuries, the refugees brought their customs and their own ways of building homes. The painted Dash loved their inks, and their tiles were brightly colored and adorned with fanciful lattice. The Sachi built tall spires above their homes, as if they were trying to poke the celestial gods they still worshipped. The dark-skinned Islanders she knew by the delicious scents of spices on the smoke from their chimneys. The Barbs, or the Barbarians as they were once called, built low-lying, narrow homes, squeezed between buildings. Often these huts formed dead ends along alleys. Elika liked them the best. Their low roofs formed stepping stones and an easy path down to the streets.

Only the Golden Circle, where the nobility lived, was beyond her reach. As she ran high along the ridgeline, she could see over the wall into another city of stately homes and vast green spaces surrounding the palace. There, ladies clad in bright silks rode their horses or strolled arm-in-arm with their lords through wintry parklands. They picnicked beside sparkling fishponds, serene and joyful, as if the Blight would never touch their pristine streets, nor dare to march over their walls and taint the elegance and beauty of their noble world. But no one was beyond the touch of the Blight. Nor were the shining nobility beyond the reach of despair and fear. They might remember that one day, she thought.

By the time she and Mite reached Temple Square, dense crowds had gathered in the streets below. Mite settled down with a warm chimney at his back, and Elika sat next to him. The Temple of Mercy loomed large before them and dwarfed the surrounding buildings.

In the distance, another gleaming temple spire broke through the gray sea of slate. The red-stoned Temple of Nerabyss was the home of the priests. Once, long ago, the temples had been places of worship and prayer to the old gods. No one worshipped the gods anymore. They had abandoned men long ago. Only the few remaining Sachi still clung to the old faith. The temples were now places of wisdom. The priests were scholars who spent their days reading ancient scrolls and crumbling books, and thought themselves wise enough to advise the king on all matters relating to magic.

The priestesses began to emerge from the temple onto the balcony above the gathered folk. They were followed by the High Priestess Herra. She wore a green robe adorned with silver leaves, a wreath of flowers and a serene expression. The crowd grew silent as she surveyed them in a slow wide sweep of her gaze.

"Hear me, people of Terren," she called out, and her voice carried strongly across the square. "I am here to bring you a message from our benevolent, glorious King Tesman, whom we faithfully serve."

"Tell the king to give us the grain he's been hoarding and might be we'll listen," someone shouted from the crowds and laughter rang out.

"And the coal," another shouted.

"And the goat meat. I'm sick to death of eating rats and the cats that chase 'em."

More laughter swept over the crowd, disguising the general rumble of anger.

High Priestess Herra continued as if she did not hear them. "Long ago, Arala, beloved daughter of Goddess Neka, sacrificed herself to save men from the wickedness of magic when she banished it to the Deadlands and rid our world of its malice. Yet its echoes remain, for it is a cunning beast. And those echoes have conspired to bring forth the Blight."

Murmurs of discontent went through the crowd. "So what's the king going to do about it?" a shrill voice shouted.

Again, the high priestess ignored them. "Yesterday, we learned that Drasdark has fallen. We are now the last in its path. But it is not fear you should fall prey to, but hope. For our wise king has neither given up hope nor the fight. Days ago, he sent the priests with more wagons of blood-salt toward the boundary lands ..."

"They tried that before," Mite scoffed. "It didn't work."

"They're burning it this time to create a wall of blood-salt smoke," Elika whispered back.

"They've tried that before as well," he said.

"How do you know?" She stared at him. He seemed to know a lot of things no one else but the priests knew. "I heard the priests discovered another ingredient that can kill magic. And it's certain to halt the Blight."

"… a darker threat than ever before," the priestess was droning below. "Though our glorious King Tesman has found a way to defeat it once and for all, he cannot undo it himself alone, for the magic is a formidable foe. The battle also falls on to each one of you, man, woman and child …"

"This is how it always starts," Mite mumbled with a shake of his head. "The hunt for Echoes."

"… an Echo, more powerful than any we have seen before," the priestess continued. "One who holds such power as has not been seen in six hundred years. Power to strike and wound the bridge …"

"A mage!" someone shouted from the crowd.

Elika held her breath, afraid to move lest she drew the attention of the high priestess' shrewd dark eyes. Beside her, she felt Mite tense but his gaze remained forward.

High Priestess Herra ignored the outcry. "Though we are grateful for his service in hurting the bridge, which still links us to the banished magic, that *Echo* must be found, and his magic purged. Through no fault of his own, he poses the greatest threat to us all in this war. And unwittingly, he might yet bring the Blight upon our city. But with his help, we may yet defeat it …"

"They're going to kill me," Elika breathed. "If they think I'm a mage …"

"We won't let them," Mite said grimly.

"… and if you are out there, come to us willingly, so we might free you from the curse of this infectious magic. Free you from its evil hold over you."

The hum of the crowd rose again to discontent and higher still, to anger.

"Burn the mage!" someone shouted in the hard accent of the mountain folk, and a rolling wave of consent came from the crowd.

There was something about the high priestess' keen eyes that Elika did not trust. Her gaze roamed over the high priestess, trying to see inside her mind. There was a tension in her shoulders caused by fear rather than anger. She looked pale compared to the priestesses beside her. Her head shifted this way and that as if she desperately searched the crowd for the rogue mage. The priestess had deliberately not used the word *mage*, likely to stop the masses from turning into a frantic mob. But Elika saw she was thinking the same as the crowd were shouting. Only a mage could have hurt the bridge fashioned by the tsaren. But she could not be a mage. They simply did not exist anymore. How could they, without the tsaren to form them, to merge magic and man into one body?

The priestess raised her hands. "As per the king's law, we call upon all Echoes to come to us in this most desperate time of our need. Come to us before it is too late to save our city. Never has there been greater urgency to be vigilant for those echoes of magic hiding inside those you love. Now is the time to do everything you can to cleanse our world from it, once and for all."

"Burn them all!" someone shouted to a sweeping roar of approval.

Elika felt sick. They had done that in Drasdark in the end—men, women, children, no one was spared.

"Burn them!" the shouts went through the crowd, in a wave of fear and hate.

"The king calls for calm," the high priestess called out. "No fires will be lit. Bring out the salt stones."

Priestesses emerged from the temple, carrying boxes of small, red crystals on twine.

"Our wise king has passed a new decree. From this day forth, all men must wear a blood-salt crystal around their necks, displayed for all to see. Those who do not wear one must touch a blood-salt wardstone as they pass it in the street. Willing or not, the infected must come to us freely or be brought by force to be purged."

Elika remembered the moment she had stepped on the blood-salt by the bridge and the terrible pain that had gripped her. She raked her memory, trying to remember the last time she had touched blood-salt, but could not recall a time when she was ever tested. Was it possible she had never touched a piece of blood-salt in her life? Was she infected as a child? And what if magic was left untreated for so long? What if it had seeded itself deeply in her, and like Nails, she could never be rid of it? She could not go to the priestesses. They would send her to the Dead-lands or worse …

"Burn them!" the crowd shouted.

Mite's large, solid hand covered hers, steadying her. "We'll think of something."

"I'm not a mage," she said desperately. "You know I'm not."

"It wouldn't matter if you were."

"All the mages followed the tsaren across the bridge," she insisted as if it proved her innocence.

Mite looked away abruptly, as if afraid to meet her eyes. "Would it be such a terrible fate compared to what approaches? What is there for us in this city?"

She could not believe what he was saying. "You always said it was better to face the Blight, to fight, to die fighting."

He did not reply, and his silence frightened her. He was watching the crowds below push their way toward the priestesses to grab their blood-salt pendants from the boxes, before hanging them around their necks as if they were wards of protection. But everyone knew the blood-salt pendant did not stop the echoes of magic from infecting you.

There was a sudden cry of pain. A brawny man stared at his large hands in horror, where a moment ago he had held the blood-salt crystal. It now lay on the ground at his feet. The priestesses were quickly there, surrounding him, comforting him, leading him away into the temple.

Elika could not bear to watch anymore. She had to get away from here. The blood-salt pendant would cripple her. But if she didn't wear it, everyone would know. She had to throw herself on the priestess' mercy … no, she could not. She had seen the high priestess' pale face when she spoke of the powerful Echo, had seen her stark fear of whoever had stabbed the bridge. None of the Echoes had ever shown any ability to command magic. Elika did not know what it meant, only that she was not like the other Echoes. And if they could not purge her …? Worse still, what if they thought she was a mage? There was no cure then, only banishment or death. And blood-salt fire was the one sure way to kill magic.

She scrambled to her feet, ducked behind a rise in the roof, and fled from the square.

Mite was there beside her. "Stop," he panted. "You can't outrun this. We must think."

She stopped and turned on him. "Why aren't you telling me to go to the temple for the purging?"

He looked toward the distant Stoneward Mountains, where Drasdark city was now a silent tomb. The broiling, steaming black mountains, home once to Draygan, the Tsarin of Stone and Earth, had also been cleaved by the chasm. Half the mountain was a sheer face as if a giant sword had sliced clean through it. On the other side of the chasm, where the other half of the mountain should be, there was nothing but those endless, desolate, rocky plains of Deadlands.

"We have to slow down and think," he said at length.

She did not want to think. She needed to act, to run away, to do something ... but what? There was nowhere to run but the bridge. Nothing to do but try to be purged.

"You don't think I can be cured of magic?" she choked out her own fear.

"It's not that ... of course, you can ... It's just that ..."

She laughed, if only to stifle the rising tears. "You are a terrible liar."

"Don't cry," he said gruffly.

"I never cry," she bit back, though it came out choked.

"Sure you do," he teased with a weak, pacifying smile. Then his gaze snagged on something behind her.

She turned as the gilded gates of the Golden Circle slowly opened, and the king rode out on a magnificent horse. A line of courtiers followed in his wake. There were beautiful ladies there too beside their lords, sparking like snow in sunshine. A wave of royal Red Guards cleared the streets for the procession.

"The king never rides into the city," she whispered and watched, transfixed, as the procession turned toward the Bridge to Magic.

When the spheres of life had collided,
And the gods turned their gazes aside.
When the world stained with death had been sundered,
And the bridge twined across the great chasm.
When the fires of hope have subsided,
And your courage is fading away,
Cast your gaze at the endless, vast wasteland,
There awaits your uncertain, dark fate.

CHAPTER THREE

The Uncontained Magic

"Many a scholar has tried to understand the creature we call Magic that lives in the ethereal realm. For a long time, we believed it was a single governing sentience that wrought mischief whenever it could. This creature, it was argued was either malign or simply ignorant of the natural order, for it certainly wrought much destruction when some juvenile whim took it. Its nature was likened to a rabble of mindless rats, driven by instinct and the immediate whims of life. With the arrival of the four tsaren, men came to realize that Magic was a hive of many different sentient beings and there was a greater mind behind the formless creatures, one which might subdue or incite it."

History of Men, Gods and Magic,
By Priest Oderrin

The bridge was dying.

The priests had examined it and confirmed it. Neither the sullen Priests of Nerabyss, nor the worried-looking Priestesses of Mercy, knew what it meant. No one appeared to be pleased with it. Then the king rode in.

The crowds gathered in the streets shouted and cursed and demanded that he stop the Blight.

"Burn the Echoes!" they shouted.

"Burn the mage!"

The king's Red Guard whipped those who threw stones at the glorious cavalcade and rode through those who tried to block their path.

It was rare for the king to ride through the city. Rare for him to bestow his eminent gaze on his filthy subjects who demanded more food when there was barely enough to feed the nobles.

Elika watched from the roofs, following them as they rode toward the bridge. Mite had gone ahead to get close enough to the priests to hear what they were saying.

She slipped into one of the abandoned houses which overlooked the bridge. She was not alone. Something was afoot, and all the gangs were eager to learn what, and whether there was any coin to be made from it. She spied One-eyed Rory sneaking up to the upper windows. He acknowledged her with a nod. She ducked into another room, crammed herself through a narrow hole in the wall, and crawled into the back of a secret cupboard. There was a crack in the outer wall, large enough to look through at the bridge whilst remaining unobserved.

The king dismounted his great black horse and strode to the bridge, where the grim-faced high priest clad in plush red robes was waiting for him. The king was old, but he did not move like an old man. And despite his grief at the death of his only son, the Prince of Drasdark, no emotion showed on his face.

He knelt before the bridge as if paying homage to it, with one knee planted on the blood-salt line for all to see.

The bridge continued to bleed, a slow trickle so dark it seemed as black as the bridge itself. The wound was not healing, even though someone had removed her knife from it. She did not know who.

With his gloved hand, the king touched the pooling blood on the snow, rubbed it between his fingers, smelled it, turned and said something to the priest. The priest nodded sagely in reply.

The bridge appeared sicklier, less menacing, as if some vigor had gone from it. She had hurt it, where many others had tried and failed to do the same. But instead of joy, Elika felt a pang of doubt. She shook herself inside, refusing to feel pity for the dark creature. But it was much easier to tell herself that than to believe it. Kill the bridge and you will stop the Blight, said the priests. Then why did the high priest and the king look so grim and worried? And why was her stomach filled with those wriggling knots of dread?

As if in reply to her thoughts, the king looked up and toward her. Instinctively, she shrank back against the cupboard door and it popped open. But he must have seen her, or else he had seen some of the other watchers in the windows. He called out a command and pointed in their direction. A moment later, heavy footfalls bounded through the building.

There was a scurry of movement all around. She bolted into a crawl hole. There, she pushed open a hidden panel in the wall, crawled through and replaced the panel quietly and firmly. Somewhere behind her, she heard a child's abrupt scream and shouts from the guards. "Stop in the name of the king!"

Elika darted between the walls of the adjoining rooms into another hollowed-out crawlspace, climbed the rope ladder, and squeezed through a narrow hole onto the roof. Others were already there, scattering in all directions. The Red Guards were climbing out like clumsy bears to chase after the slowest runners.

Never lead anyone to the Hide, she chanted in her head and forced her feet to move in the opposite direction to the Hide and safety. A burly Red Guard gave chase.

She sprinted as fast as she could across the capstones. In the distance, she spied Rory expertly slide down the roof, and then brace and crab down the wall between the narrow buildings. She had just enough sense to follow him to the streets. Rory had never been caught and knew how to evade the guards better than anyone. And they didn't call her Eli Spider for no reason. She slid down the gutter pipes and leapt between balconies above an alleyway, losing sight of Rory as she did so. She dropped to the street, stuffed her hands in her pockets and merged with the faceless crowd.

A moment later, she was strolling; one of the faceless masses seeking to catch a glimpse of their king. Her heart was racing, her chest was heavy with exertion, and it took great effort to appear calm and not look behind her.

Ahead, she caught sight of a Red Guard grab Tiny Timmy, one of her pack. He kicked and wriggled to no avail. The guard produced a blood-salt crystal and put it against Timmy's cheek. He did not react.

The guard shook him and demanded answers to questions. Timmy shrugged his shoulders and said something. With a curse, the guard let him go, shoving him away, and Timmy darted into the crowd. Elika breathed a sigh of relief. But more royal Red Guards appeared in the streets, joined by the city's Blue Guard. One by one, they seized who they could to test them with blood-salt crystals. She turned the first corner she came to, and after quickly picking a familiar lock, ducked into the washerwoman's shop.

Milly the washerwoman had once been in the pack—long ago, before she found honest work. But she never forgot her life on the streets and allowed Penny's pack to use her shop as a hideout, as long as they did not steal anything. Elika closed the door softly behind her and replaced the latch.

Milly was not home. She lived alone in two tiny rooms on ground level. One where she slept and ate, and one at the back where she did the laundry, which she hung out to dry in the narrow stone courtyard. Elika touched nothing. She sat in a chair and ran her hands over her short-cropped hair.

A door opened silently, but instead of Milly, Mite came in, looking flushed and harried.

Without saying anything, he slid down the door to the floor. They sat there for a long time, waiting for the disturbance outside to pass. Gradually, the shouts grew distant, before fading altogether along with the afternoon sun.

"Milly's doing well for herself," Elika said, if only to break the intolerable silence.

Mite was distant in that thoughtful way of his. He tried to hide it, but she saw the hues of despondency in his face. She looked closer and realized what she had not realized before. Mite was not a boy anymore. She had mocked him for pretending to be a man, but he was not pretending. It made her suddenly uneasy and awkward. He was older than her, though not as old as Penny. He must be approaching twenty … or more. She searched his face, thinking back, trying to remember him as he was when she first arrived. And it occurred to her now that soon, he too would leave the pack.

As if he read her mind, he glanced around and said, "Been thinking of joining the guard myself."

"Red or blue?" she asked, though it was a foolish question. It was no secret that Mite hated the king and the squabbling, simpering nobles around him.

Oddly, he seemed daunted by the question. "Not sure if I could be one of Daiger's thugs. Might be the red would suit me better." He did not seem too pleased by that prospect either. "Should have gone years ago, though, but Penny and the pack needed me."

They still needed him. Mite had always kept them safe. But everyone left eventually. They all grew up, and it was easier to look after yourself than a litter of unwanted children.

She grinned to hide her fear of him leaving. "If you had it your way, you'd be serving the gods, hey Mite?"

He looked intently at her, and her smile faded. "If I had it my way, I'd be the king and serving men." He said it so seriously, laughter died on her tongue.

"Like Lord Silvering wanted to be?" she asked at length.

Mite's jaw clenched and he glanced aside. "Aye, like him."

Fifteen years ago, as more towns and villages fell to the Blight and their city was drowning in refugees, Lord Silvering led a rebellion against the king. He accused the king of being an imposter and failing his people by doing nothing to stop the Blight. The rebellion failed, and Silvering was banished from court and never heard of again.

"I think the guards are gone," Mite said abruptly and rose to his feet. He peered through the gap in the curtains without moving them. "No one's about ... damn. They're dragging the blood-salt wardstone to the corner."

Elika was on her feet heading toward the window to see for herself. She crammed herself beside Mite to look through the same gap, and the heat of him hit her, unexpectedly, dizzyingly. Her mind scrambled. She could smell him. Strange how Mite did not stink. Boys stank. It was not their fault; it was just how they were. But Mite's smell was pleasant and ... oddly heady. Her breath quickened. The house shrank around them and she became acutely aware that they were alone. Why would it matter now? They were often alone.

He shifted, the tiniest motion, and his shoulders filled her view, solid and strong. And she realized she was just standing there, staring at the buttons of his shirt.

"Eli ..." he whispered and his breath stirred her hair.

Her name was a gentle question on his lips.

Why are you standing so close? Why are you staring at my chest like a fool? Why don't you say something?

She was being ridiculous. From the corner of her eyes, she saw his hand move, then halt, then slowly rise again ...

She spun on her heel and walked to the door, her cheeks burning. "I think they are gone." Her voice sounded oddly hoarse. She cleared her throat.

For a moment he did not move and she felt his eyes bore into her.

She fumbled with a lock and flung open the door, unthinking. She needed air. The house was small and stifling.

He uttered a foul curse and was beside her, scanning the alley. "Do you want to be caught?" he growled.

Again, she felt his unsettling heat. She moved quickly, walking away. Behind her, she heard him softly close and lock the door with a pick.

The streets had grown quieter. There were no guards about, and the crowds who had followed the king had dispersed, leaving behind the usual throng of locals. Those who did not wear the pendants, walked by the blood-salt wardstone, touching it as they passed. She fell behind a wide, buxom woman, and put out her hand as if to do the same. Her fingers flitted close to the stone but never touched it. Even so, a pulse of tingling pain shot through her fingers and up her arm, as if a bolt of lightning had struck her. She flinched, stuck her hand in her pocket and kept walking.

Mite fell in step with her. "Where are you going?" he demanded.

"I have work to do and you have yours."

Mite's hand was on her arm. "Don't. You need to stay hidden for a little while."

She snatched it back. "And how am I to earn my keep?"

Bad Penny did not give charity. Those who did not bring their share to the pack were placed at the back of the food line or cast out altogether.

His expression softened. "I'll look after you."

"I'm not a child needing looking after."

"Damn it, Eli. The king is searching for you."

"He doesn't know who he's looking for. Now go away and let me find a death-walker to track."

"Stubborn woman," Mite muttered and fell back, letting her go.

She hated that she could still feel him watching her. So she turned the next corner and walked right into the path of a brawl between a group of Drasdanes and Terrenians.

You could tell them apart easily enough. The people from Drasdark were paler in complexion and clad from head to foot in hide and leather. All their cloth came from the animals they hunted in the mountain forests. Their women were larger, too, for they worked beside their men as builders and tanners, miners and even blacksmiths. Now they fought beside their men. She had seen many such fights between migrants and locals.

Elika deftly swerved aside to avoid the brawlers, but as she did a Drasdane collided with her. Elika stumbled back, tripped over a small pig and fell on top of it. Instantly, a large woman yanked her up by the scruff of her neck.

"Keep your filthy hands off mey pig, ye thief," she yelled in the thick accent of the mountain folk as she pushed Elika against the wall, then threw a punch.

Elika had just enough sense to duck and slip past under the woman's giant arm whilst pulling out her knife. "Not here to steal your pig," Elika said and backed away. "Come close and I'll cut you."

The Drasdane woman looked her up and down, then withdrew her small axe from her belt. "Will ye now?"

Elika's heart began to thunder. This woman was a head taller, her shoulders the size of most men's. But the mountain folk were not thugs or thieves. They fought when they thought there was a reason to fight, no matter how slight.

Elika stuffed her knife back in her belt and raised her hands in supplication. "Not here to fight you, lady, just walking past."

That stopped the fair-haired Drasdane in her tracks. She thought about it, then jerked her head. "Then shoo, little mouse." With that she put away her axe and dragged a Terrenian man by his hair from another hide-clad woman.

Elika walked away hurriedly, without meeting the eye of any mountain folk, who leaned on the walls watching the brawl. They were a hardy, practical people. Some had already set up mending stalls and smithies in this alley. They knew better than anyone how to work and shape metal, and how to treat animals for sickness. She swerved around another pig and a goat. A chicken ran underfoot, chased by a small boy in furs.

It was always the same. The migrants brought their animals. Which was allowed. Trouble was, those without gardens to keep them had to rent animal pens and stockades around the city. They were expensive, filthy, and the animals were often stolen. So the migrants kept them in the streets or inside their homes to the dismay of their neighbors and anyone who had to walk the grimy streets.

And each day, more and more folk kept arriving from the remaining lands, fleeing the ever-encroaching Blight. They often arrived in their hundreds, sometimes in thousands, when another town or village succumbed. When they did, Elika's dread and trepidation grew a little more.

They filled the streets, slept where they could, defecated in narrow alleys, and washed using precious rainwater collected in barrels on street corners. And it was hard not to feel resentful at their hapless invasion, to remember that there was no other place for them to go.

As it was, the Terrenians had long ago exhausted their charity to migrants fleeing the Blight. Some merchants refused to sell their goods to them, and street brawls were common. Elika suspected there was some migrant blood in her too, and she had been chased out of a shop a time or two for looking too much like a Sachi.

In the distance she heard a city crier shout, "A chest of gold from the king for finding the mage. Hear, hear! A chest of gold for the mage."

"Keep your chest of gold," someone shouted back. "If I find the mage, I'll burn him meself."

"Burning's too good for them magic lovers. Traitors, they are," a woman nearby scoffed.

They were wrong, thought Elika. She hated magic. That alone must mean she was not a mage.

A shape detached itself from the wall and blocked her path.

She stopped in her tracks.

One-eyed Rory smiled menacingly. "Hey, Spit."

He was idly spinning a blood-salt crystal on a string. She glanced around. He appeared to be alone, but she was certain his men lurked within his whistle's reach. She could bolt, but it would do little good. Rory was fast—too fast for any of them.

His smile broadened. "No need to run. Not here to hurt you. Just have a nice, friendly question for you."

Her eyes fixed on the blood-salt crystal he spun around and around. "What do you want, Rory?"

"Last night, at the bridge, you were the last one there, as I recall. Might be you saw something ... or someone ..." He trailed off, his dark eye watching her closely. He wore a patch today over his empty socket.

"I didn't see anyone. I left soon after you." She tried to stay as close to the truth as she could. Lies did not trip as easily off her tongue as they did off Pit the Picker's.

"You know, Peter Pockets is mighty generous to his friends."

"So I hear," she replied. Peter Pockets would also gladly cut your tongue out if you crossed him. "Anyway, you asked your question ..."

"Did I? I don't recall asking anything. My question is, would you tell me if you did see something?"

His mildly spoken question chilled her. Peter Pockets had manners and a certain sense of honor. He never invaded another thief's abode, unless they stole from him. He was also the one to settle disputes between warring gangs. Above all, he abhorred those who did not follow the Code, like the unruly, disorganized dog-gangs who attacked where whim or greed took them. It made them unpredictable and more frightening than even Rimley's gang. Though Rimley's men only went hard against you if they wanted something you had. Still, when Peter Pockets asked a question, you did not refuse to give him an answer. And there was this thing in the Code about lying to him, which gave Pockets the right to cut out your tongue or blind you in one eye.

She thought quickly and remembered something she'd heard earlier. "If I was to tell anyone, it'd be them Red Guards, for a chest of gold. So, as I have nothing to tell them, I've nothing to tell you. See?" She smiled, trying to appear cocky.

His smile fell away. His one eye roamed over her face. "Might be Pockets will give you more than the king for the information."

"Look, Rory, if you want to speak to one of ours, you've got to talk to Mite first as he's the one who speaks for Bad Penny. It's the rules. Or is Pockets thinking the Code no longer matters?" Peter Pockets was nothing if not an adamant enforcer of the Code. It was the only thing keeping the gangs civil to each other. "Even if I knew something, Mite and Penny would cull me if I betrayed them. So if Pockets wants our help in finding the rogue mage, then he'd better be prepared to share the reward with us. So how is it to be?"

Elika already knew the answer. Peter Pockets never shared.

His eye dropped to her bare neck. "You know, Spit, it's dangerous to be seen on the streets without one of these, nowadays." He lifted the blood-salt pendant to show her.

"With the guards grabbing everyone in sight who doesn't have one, and the ruffians beating up every Echo they see. Heard a mob of Drasdanes threw two of them into the chasm."

Never show them fear, she reminded herself. "Why don't you wear it then?"

There was a sly, amused glint in his eye. He touched his hat to her. "If ever you wish to rise up in the world, come to us and Peter will have a place for you." He hung the blood-salt pendant around his neck and strode past.

Elika fled in the opposite direction, glancing around to see whether anyone followed. She resisted the urge to flee to the rooftops. She had work to do. There was always someone thinking of taking the bridge.

For a while, she strolled the streets, without paying attention to where her feet took her, only being careful to avoid the guards. There were many dead ends, and narrow alleys beneath bridge-homes, and rickety stairs to the upper-level walkways. The ramshackle upper streets were built of wood planks and iron. She climbed the stairs to Upper Brewer's Street, populated largely by the gin distillers. Despite the king's orders to abolish them and save the grain for bread, Captain Daiger lived too well from the distillers' *shiny handshakes*. As long as they brewed ale at the front of the shop, he never checked what they brewed in the back.

From the upper street, it was easy to keep everyone below in her sights. Beneath the distilleries, drunks slept away the day and bruised whores plied their trade. Few begged anymore, mostly they lay there in their own piss, waiting their turn to die. She spied many watchers, like her, looking for an easy target. They recognized each other and anyone who did not belong in this hunting ground.

Mite had traded hard and fought even harder with the other gangs to expand their pack's hunting ground. It now ran between Rift Street and Temple Square. Without his efforts, Elika was certain they would have starved long ago. She was careful never to stray. In her collar, she wore a copper button to mark her as one of Bad Penny's pack.

She did not mean to meander back toward Temple Square, but her treacherous feet took her there, anyway.

From the streets, the Temple of Mercy looked far more formidable and immense than from the skyline. The houses beside it appeared shrunken, like beggars' huts. The square was busy. Most here were simply homeless and had found a corner to sleep in or sought charity from the priestesses. Instantly, her eyes were drawn to a man who did not belong.

He stood beside the drinking well in the square, staring at the temple, agitated and anxious. He was not wearing a blood-salt pendant. His hands were smooth and he wiped them often on his trouser legs. His clothes were as plain as any around, except they were made of a fine cloth which marked him as a man from the Silver Circle. Gentry disguised as a commoner, thinking it would keep him safe. He'd never fool anyone. Already, many small eyes were on him.

He stood there for a long while watching the temple, then he turned and walked away brusquely. Elika followed.

There was a skill to following men without them suspecting they were being tracked. Mite was a master at that and had taught her all the tricks. Unfortunately, other watchers followed him too, and not so subtly.

The man headed in the direction of the bridge, glancing about him often like a blind man lost in the dark. When he saw guards ahead, he took a quick right turn. Elika shook her head at him, for it was clear he did not know where that street led. And true enough, he walked straight into a checkpoint.

The king had ordered many such checkpoints to be set up around the city, and they were often moved. It took good knowledge of the streets to know where they were on any one day, and how to spot where they were likely to be by closely watching the movement of people before you stumbled into one.

She hid around the corner and listened.

"Where's your blood-salt, then?" the guard asked.

She heard the man patting his pockets. "Must have left it at home. I am Master Penilworth's secretary. He will vouch for me."

"Don't matter if you are the king himself, only blood-salt can vouch for a man nowadays. But never mind your forgetting. Just touch this crystal here and you can be on your way."

There was silence. Then the man burst past her. The guards gave chase, blowing their whistles as they ran. For one of the indolent gentry he was surprisingly fast and might have made it but for the two brawny men from Drasdark who brought him down.

"Bloody Echoes. Burn them!" they shouted as they hit and kicked the poor fool curled into a ball on the ground. Someone doused him in lamp oil and to Elika's horror, another man was running toward them with a lit lantern in his hand.

The guards were there, breaking up the fight. "Get off him, you filthy dogs. Beating an honest man like that. Not his fault magic got him. Might be it was you who brought it here."

The Drasdane with a lantern spat at the guard's feet, shed a foul curse and retreated.

"Take him to the temple for the purging," the other guard commanded, and they dragged the oil-soaked Master Penilworth's secretary to his feet.

"Wishful tripe, is what it is. All this dribble about purging them clean," the man from Drasdark said. "Fools, ye all are. Them Echoes are conspiring with the magic. It's why so few are coming forward for the purging. Nothing but the blood-salt fire will rid the world of magic and the Blight ..."

She did not see the rest, for she walked away before they noticed her lingering about and tested her. She raced up the steps to the upper street, and from there up a gutter pipe onto the roof, breathing heavily after the horror of what she had seen. They were going to burn the poor fool alive for nothing more than being an Echo. Fear was spreading through the streets and fear always brought out savagery. How long before she could not walk the streets without one of those pendants around her neck?

She forced herself to calm. She'd find a way. Besides, there on the horizon she could see the red smoke. The sunsets had been redder than normal these last few days. In the boundary lands, the priests were setting the grass-lands on fire, adding powdered blood-salt and their secret ingredient to the flame.

As she watched the smoke, another, more pressing problem intruded into her mind. The days were short, and it was already near dusk, and she had nothing to bring back to the pack. Some days were like that. Still, she found she did not want to go back, did not want to face Penny and the expectant faces of the young ones ... of Rosy Rose with those pleading, hungry eyes. So, she walked north instead toward the city gate.

Only guards milled at the open gates. More patrolled the walls and the watchtowers, waiting for that ever-encroaching enemy. The land beyond was quiet. There were no travelers anymore, and only a few trading wagons still left the city for the outlying farms and villages. Once, long ago, countless wars had been fought at those city walls. Some against neighboring kingdoms, most against mages and magic. Marks of those fierce wars were etched into the stone. Since that time, they had known six hundred years of peace, tainted only by the Blight destroying all in its path.

As she stood there, she watched a figure appear on the winding road, racing toward the city on horseback. She watched as it grew closer. His red robes marked him as a priest. He did not stop at the city gates and the guards did not halt him. Instead, he rode straight up to the palace. Even from afar, Elika could tell whatever news the priest had brought would not please the king. The thought disturbed her.

Mite was suddenly there, as if he had never left her. "I thought I told you to stay hidden."

"I lost my target," she blurted out. "Penny won't be happy if I return empty-handed."

Tomorrow she needed to do better at finding food or coin. Perhaps she'd ask if Milly had more work for her scrubbing sheets.

Mite sighed. He understood well enough the burden of returning to the Hide empty-handed. "Come, let's have dinner in *Fat Fish*. I want to talk to Bill to make certain he'll cause you no trouble."

"I'm out of coin. And Penny didn't yet give me my share of the loot."

He reached into one of his many hidden pockets and pulled out three coppers. "Here, pay me back when you get it."

"I will," she said and shoved the coins into her trouser leg.

Mite followed her gaze to the smoke haze on the northern horizon. "Do not hope," he said, as if reading her mind. He was chillingly uncanny like that. "There's no hiding from the truth. They can't stop it. Do you know why so many died in Drasdark?"

"They didn't flee fast enough?"

He was looking at her steadily. "Aye. Most left it too late. Hope felled them in the end. The prince kept telling them they only needed to burn the Echoes to stop it. So they did, and still the Blight kept coming. But what if it's not the Echoes that are feeding the Blight?"

"What else can it be?" she asked, exasperated. Mite questioned everything. Why couldn't he just accept the world as it was, as men said it was?

"I've been thinking about it. I don't know. It just feels ... wrong. I don't mean just the Blight, rather the reason for it ... the Deadlands ... all of it." He breathed out his frustration in one long breath. "None of this makes sense."

"The Blight is magic's revenge for banishing it to the Deadlands. There's nothing more to it than that. It's magic's last strike against men in the Sundering War. Maybe it's what the Blight means to do for us. Push us all into the chasm."

Mite looked unconvinced, his gaze back on the northern horizon where red smoke was blanketing the land and sky alike.

"Magic is treacherous. Everyone knows that, Mite. It's self-serving and grasping and vengeful ..."

"Like men," he said blandly.

She started. He was close to sounding like a magic sympathizer ... a traitor. "No ... not like men. Magic is mindless and meaningless ... and it hates us."

He looked down at her. "It doesn't matter, anymore. None of it matters."

There was something behind his gaze that made her nervous, some decision brewing in his heart she recognized but did not want to acknowledge. "Just tell me what's on your mind."

"I'm trying to make you see that there's nothing, nothing at all men can do to stop the Blight. You must be ready to make the choice. If you leave it too late ..." He did not finish.

The Deadlands in the distance drew her gaze; the other half of their world beyond the chasm. The very thought of that choice made her stomach plunge sickeningly, as if she had stepped off the roof to her death.

"You've always been afraid of the unknown," Mite said softly. "Do you remember how you'd scream and fight and run away when we tried to take you to the edge of the chasm to look into it?"

"Perhaps I thought you wanted to throw me into it," she snapped.

He flinched and she felt a stab of guilt about bringing up what none of them ever spoke about. What had happened all those years ago when Penny and Mite threw one of their own into it. They never mentioned Lucky Lick. But when the winds from the chasm grew shrill, they all thought of him, she was certain.

"Let's go and speak to Bill," she said after a silence.

Fat Fish was a dingy old tavern overlooking the remains of the muddy harbor. It was dank and dreary. It was also the quietest tavern in Terren. It sold the sourest and most watered-down ale you could buy, which sometimes did not sit well in her stomach. But it cost only a single piece of copper for a whole tankard.

The tavern lay in an abandoned street of rotting fishermen's huts, which only the sick and the dying made use of. The crooked building stood facing what once was the vast shoreline of a great sea. It was a dust bowl now. Except when it rained. Then it turned to mudflats. The fishing ships from long ago lay tilted on their sides, rotting like unburied corpses. The kingdom of the sea was once ruled by Tsarin Ilikan, and his emblem of a fish riding a wave still hung over the door of the tavern.

Old, craggy Bill Fisher was said to be the last man alive who had seen the sea before the last of it had poured away into the chasm. His was the blue boat tilted away from them with a single sail mast. It was where he made his home to this day. He spent his days on the boat with his mending work, but his evenings were devoted to the *Fat Fish* tavern where he liked to nurse a tankard of sour ale whilst telling his stories to anyone who'd listen.

He had sworn he would rather throw himself into the chasm than try crossing the bridge. No one with any sense threw themselves into the chasm. But then men questioned how much sense Bill had left at his age. It was said that those who fell into it would plummet for eternity through the darkness, kept alive by the magic trapped within.

Mite stooped through the low doorway and nodded to the innkeeper behind the bar. The tavern was ancient and its walls were seven types of crooked. It was mostly empty, save for Bill in his corner, and a few regulars such as Green Silk Harry and Cross-eyed Abe, and Toothless Jake sipping his soup alone at his table. The fireplace was dark, even in the depths of winter.

Tinky, the young tavern maid, winked at Mite as soon as he entered.

Mite blushed like a fool.

Elika nudged him. "Stop grinning like an idiot, she only wants your coin."

He looked down at her and turned redder. "Just go and sit over there with Bill. You shouldn't be in a place like this, anyway." There was an embarrassed gruffness in his voice that amused her. She had been in places such as these since she was old enough to stalk death-walkers. But only recently did Mite seem to take an exception to it. Here at least, the ale was cheap and the patrons left her alone, for they knew the sight of her well enough.

Bill sat at his usual table. When she saw him trepidation went through her. He had seen her stab the bridge. Such information could make him a rich man. If Bill thought her a mage, he might just call the city guards on her here and now. She studied him closely, but there was nothing different about his manner. His shoulders were slumped over his ale, his eyes distant, as if he had retreated to another time.

Mite also appeared relaxed—striding to the bar in his alert yet oddly dignified way, his attention on Tinky. He always said that those who believed themselves to be indestructible became indestructible. She was not so certain that was true. Still, she thought to heed his advice. Pushing back her shoulders, she tried to walk with the same confidence as he did.

Bill saw her then and waved her over to his table with his crooked fingers. Elika had never in her life seen skin as weathered and leathery as his, or as wrinkled. His eyes were dark blue like the sea was said to be. There was also a sharpness in his gaze of one who never missed the smallest detail. His eyes glistened with sly amusement when she approached. "Haven't seen ye in here in a while, El. Thought you'd grown bored of me stories."

She sat across from him, trying to appear as if she had not fled from him last night. "Just been busy, that's all. How are you keeping, Bill?" The usual question came out awkwardly.

"Still breathing, which is as good as I can hope for at my age." He appeared to be his usual self. Perhaps he had indeed forgotten everything from the day before. Bill often forgot things. Might be there was nothing for her to fret over, as Bill himself would often say.

Mite returned from the bar with three tankards of steaming-hot, sour ale. He put one before Bill.

"Mighty generous of you, Lil' Mit'," Bill said as he wrapped his bony fingers around the warm mug. "Now what brings you both to see me like this and buying me ale so generously?" he asked with a note of mischief, as if he already knew the answer.

Mite sat back looking relaxed. "Been thinking of those stories of yours, Bill. I used to love them as a kid. Remembered every one of them."

"Aye, I remember when you were a mite in truth and used to sneak into my boat to sleep at night. You didn't know that I knew, now did ye?"

Mite shrugged and drank his ale. "I figured a man knows what happens on his boat. So I figured you didn't care whether I slept there, as long as I didn't steal from you, or leave muddy footprints on your deck."

Bill's eyes twinkled. "Always a smart lad you were. If the king had half your brain ..." He waved his hand. "Bah, what does it matter? The king's a fool, like all of them have been since the day the tsaren abandoned us. But then you'd know all about that, wouldn't you, Mitey boy? Aye, I remember the first time I saw you, all muddy and teary and angry, nursing a nose bleed and a broken wrist. And I remember that ring you had on you, too. Caught my eye, it did. The one you said you stole. I reckon you must have sold it for quite a penny ... or did you? I might have been tempted to keep it myself."

Mite continued to stare at him steadily, but his lips pursed more tightly. Elika began to feel uneasy. It was as if something was passing between them that she did not understand, as if they were speaking in some secret way beyond her ability to hear.

Mite tapped his fingers on the table. "Might be we're as smart as each other, hey Bill? Both of us know that there's things we might know about each other which we wouldn't want others to know."

Bill narrowed his eyes. "Are ye saying I talk too much?"

"I'm saying it's easy to let something slip especially when one's in the cups. Say, for example, me knowing you to be at least six hundred years old; might be something men would pay good coin to learn."

Bill started at that. "What did your brain conjure up, now then? Might be you need to forget what I said about you being a clever lad ..."

"But then, I wouldn't want to go about saying such things. Not when you've always been good to us," Mite said the last rather blandly.

Was this his plan to save her? A ridiculous accusation with which to sway Bill to keep quiet about her secret? "What are you doing?" she whispered furiously to Mite.

He threw her a shushing glance, which did not reassure her. "It's those tales of yours, Bill, that got me curious. See?"

"I don't see," Bill replied irritably.

Mite drank his ale leisurely. "The last of the sea poured away into the rift a hundred years ago, as you say. And aye, that's true. But you always said you watched it retreat from our shores, which is a funny thing to say ... since that was four hundred years ago." He smiled smugly. "It's in the priests' records. Undeniable, as they say. And your boat hasn't moved since then. There's other things you told us as if you were there. Things that I read about, which happened centuries ago."

Elika's mouth fell open. She closed it quickly. "You can read?"

"And how did the priests let you in to look at their records?" Bill asked.

"They didn't, but I looked anyway," Mite replied with a dismissive shrug. "Then there was that story of the sea-witch with a funny way of talking, so only you could understand her. And you boasted about how the priests paid you a full gold coin for repeating what she said. It's how you got your boat fixed up after that storm. Except that witch lived over three hundred years ago. And the *green storm*, as you called it, happened three hundred and seventy years ago. It's all in the records ... including a craggy old man named Bill Fisher, with the scar of a broken blade on his shoulder. It wouldn't be hard to check for it, now would it? See where I'm going with this?"

Bill's face changed. He looked dark and menacing, like those sea storms he often reminisced about. "Clever fools die young, Lil' Mit'."

Elika leaned in and whispered in awe. "It's true, isn't it? What are you ... a mage?"

Bill Fisher laughed and pulled out a heart-shaped, blood-salt from around his neck. "'Tis me charm. Infused with the blood of the witch I once married. Her gift to me, it was, when she still loved me."

"He's not a mage," Mite said slowly, as if he was chewing it in his mind. "He's a Scab. They used to brand Scabs in the old days with a burn of a broken blade. It was a way of keeping track of them when they outlived men. And you don't need that charm, Bill. Scabs have a resistance to magic."

"We prefer to be called tanes," Bill quipped. "And we don't have a resistance to magic. Only that magic doesn't like us. See? It ignores us as if we aren't even there."

"Then why the charm?" Mite asked.

"Ah, 'tis naught but a love-pendant she gave me, so I'd think of her always, and aye, I keep thinking of her. Feels more like a curse-pendant, if you ask me."

"You are a tane! One of the immortal men," Elika said with breathless wonder. "Children the tsaren fathered on mortal women. I thought all tanes were killed in the Sundering War."

Bill turned his beady, sharp eyes on her. "Now, princess, do I look immortal to you? I'm seven hundred years old and I'm dying as all men die. And all this talk of tsaren wearies me senseless. No one alive understands what it is they are. And what you should be asking is what it is *you* are. For you, me girl, have always been ripe with magic. It's pouring out of you like water out of a leaky vessel."

Elika hugged herself, feeling as if something was crawling over her flesh. "No need to say such cruel things, Bill. You make me want to scrub myself clean with a blacksmith's wire brush."

Bill chuckled.

But Mite was incensed. "Watch what you're saying, Bill," he hissed and glanced around to make doubly certain no one overheard them. "Do you know what men do to tanes when they find one hiding amongst them?"

"Spare me your threats, boy. I've no argument with magic or those who harbor it. Think I didn't know what was inside her all these years?" Bill tapped on his nose. "I may have no magic in me, but I can smell it well enough. 'Tis how I found her all those years ago hiding under the sail." He turned back to her. "I smelled you out, princess. I've not smelled magic that strong since that day I got a whiff of the mighty Tsarin Ravel and his beautiful Arala when they rode past one day. Aye, I knew you were tainted with it for as long as I've known you."

Elika started at that. "Why didn't you say anything before?"

"'Cause it makes no difference what you are or aren't. Not to me. But it does to them others who took it in their heads that magic is evil. And they'll be looking for you. Why did you have to go and hurt the bridge, El?" He shook his head sadly and pushed the bone-handled knife she had left buried in the bridge toward her.

She stared at it. Bill had washed the dark blood from it. Still, she dared not touch it, lest there was some lingering magic on it. "Why did you follow me, and hide like that and frighten me?"

"'Cause I'm curious as to what you are. And scratch me head as I might, I've no damned idea. Except … only that you must be one of *them* …" He stopped as the maid brought them two bowls of vegetable stew and a slice of stale bread with butter on the side.

Tinky placed one in front of Mite, winking at him as she did so, and one before Elika, then left with an exaggerated sway of her hips.

Elika was too hungry to pay her much notice. She took her half of the bread, buttered it thickly and ate quickly, following each bite with a gulp of ale.

"Oha ooom?" she asked with a mouthful.

"What?" Bill asked.

"She said, *one of whom?*" Mite said as he buttered his bread.

Bill scratched his head as if he had forgotten. "Oh, well, never mind that now. Pay me no mind, child. See, this is what you get." He waved his hand at her as she stuffed her mouth full with the vegetable stew. "'Tis the way with using magic. Makes you damned hungry it does. 'Tis why the tsaren and their mages were always feasting."

Elika swallowed. "I didn't mean to use it."

"As if you could stop it. Magic won't be contained, princess. It does what it wants." He leaned forward toward her. "Unless you're a tsarin who can command it. Then it'll listen to you."

Mite was chewing his bread thoughtfully, as if what Bill said made perfect sense. "If you're a true tane, then you'll know how to be rid of it."

Bill's eyes glistened with secret amusement. "Why don't you ask them priestesses about that?"

"Might be I don't like them," Mite said.

"Ah, a proper clever boy. See, that's the thing. There's no purging the magic from inside her. But you suspect as much yourself, else you wouldn't be here threatening me."

Mite regarded him with a thoughtful frown. "Tell you what, Bill. How about you don't speak to anyone of what you've seen and I'll tell no one of what I know about you."

Bill sat back in his chair. "Thing is, if they come for me, no doubt they'll make me tell 'em what I know about the bridge and how a knife had gotten into it. I'm not one to put up with pain ..."

"Tanes don't feel pain," Mite said dryly.

"They don't?" Elika stared at Bill's dry wrinkly skin in wonderment.

Bill waved that away. "Regardless, it's still rather grim and unpleasant to watch one's own flesh torn or cut open; to watch one's bones be broken and limbs hang askew. Pain or not, we bleed as any man. And it brings all manner of talk to my lips ..."

Mite ran his hand through his hair. "What do you want, Bill?"

"How about you bring me that ring of yours, Lil' Mit' and I'll keep your secrets—all the way to me grave."

Mite's face turned dark and thunderous. "The ring is mine. I ... I did not steal it."

"Is it?" Bill asked slyly. "Then why are you still here ... in filthy Riftside?" He spread his arms and looked around.

Elika was watching them closely, trying to understand what was passing between them. Where else would Mite be?

Mite's gaze darted to her and back again to Bill. "Why?" he asked quietly. "The ring means nothing to you."

"And there you be wrong, boy. I know who wore it long ago. The same man who imprisoned and tortured Arala. The same man whose wicked deeds began the Sundering War. I dare say the king would pay more for that ring than he would for our little princess here."

Elika could see Mite was torn about something. "Mite? What ring does he speak of? What man?"

Mite drank deeply of his ale instead of replying.

"Your ring for my silence," Bill repeated when Mite remained silent, staring into his mug. Bill rose to his feet and patted Mite's shoulder. "I'll let you ponder on it, boy." He nodded to her. "Come and see me sometime, princess, and might be we'll talk some more." He downed the last of his ale and left the tavern.

"I can't give him the ring," Mite said quietly without meeting her eyes. "Don't ask me more about it … at least not yet. I don't trust him, Eli, and neither should you. Tanes are not men. At least not like us. If it suits his purpose, he'll betray you to protect the magic inside you. He'll betray us both regardless of whether or not I give him what he wants. He asked me for one thing I cannot give him. And he knows it, too."

"You don't have the ring …" she began.

"I have it." He pursed his lips as if to stop himself from saying more.

She could not ask him to give up what he clearly treasured as payment for her stupid mistake. "Then you keep it," she said firmly. "I never thought Bill was the type of man to sell me to the king. He's never asked before for more than what he had. Why do you think he wants riches, all of a sudden? Might be I'll talk to him again and see whether I can convince him to stay silent."

Mite raised his eyes to her and said nothing. She suspected he had his own ideas about Bill's strange demand.

It was late by the time they left the tavern and by then neither she nor Mite had any coin left. On the way out, Tinky whispered something in Mite's ear that made him grin like a fool.

Elika hunched her shoulders and turned away. She knew what the tavern maid hankered after. Once, she had found a way to earn an easy coin as a messenger between the wealthy, lecherous gentry and the mistresses they hid away from their wives. She had been to whorehouses and knew what went on between men and women. And now she saw Mite torn between seeing her home safely and joining Tinky at the back of the tavern.

Men were idiots, she thought and strode away. The Deadlands on the other side of the chasm glowed eerily as if in moonlight, except there was no moon out tonight.

Mite ran after her. "I'll see you home," he said quickly, guiltily.

"No need, I know my way. Go and bed your Tinky." She cringed inside at her sour tone. Why did she care anyway?

He cuffed her on the head. "Don't speak like that. It's not fitting for a lady."

She punched him on the shoulder. "I'm not a lady. Else you wouldn't cuff me."

He chuckled and rubbed his shoulder. "I'll still come with you. Not safe for a girl alone this time of night."

"No one knows I'm a girl," she mumbled a little drunkenly.

"Even so." There was bizarre chivalry about Mite which often annoyed her for no reason she could fathom.

The streets were never empty and eyes watched them from the shadows. She had another knife tucked into her belt, clearly visible to ward off those who might think her an easy target. She'd not need it tonight. Everyone around here recognized Mite on sight, even in the dark. Some acknowledged him with a curt nod as he passed. Mite had earned their respect, and with some, their fear.

When they were alone again and out of anyone's earshot, he spoke. "Whatever else, Bill is right, you cannot go to the priestesses. Keep out of sight, just for a few days while I try to figure this out."

She stopped and spun round. "There is no figuring this out. Not this time. I'm an Echo and only the priestesses know how to purge it from me. The echoes of magic are driving the Blight, and there's a large echo inside me. What if I'm the reason the Blight is marching faster now than before? What if the magic in me was the reason Drasdark was destroyed so quickly? Don't you see? They must purge it from me. I just ... I can't face the bridge." Her chest tightened and she could not speak, could not breathe for the fear of it. What if they could not purge the magic from her?

Inside her, she harbored their enemy. She was a traitor to her kind. She had to destroy the magic before it destroyed them all. Bill was wrong, she had to give herself up to the priestesses. But her feet would not move toward the temple. She thought of Arala sacrificing herself for mankind and felt wretched for being too much of a coward to do the same.

"We'll think of something," he promised again. "Just give me a few days."

Desperately, she wanted to believe him. She shoved her hands in her pockets and turned to walk.

When they returned to the Hide, everything was as it was meant to be. It was late and everyone was asleep, except Penny, who was sewing by the low glowing embers of the fire. Rosy Rose slept by her feet, her hair sheared off close to the scalp, and the fluffy stubble left behind looked shiny and clean. The faint smell of burned hair lingered in the air.

Elika went straight to her bedroll and burrowed into her pile of blankets. She was exhausted and wanted nothing more than to fade away, but restlessness besieged her. She closed her eyes, but something told her that Mite was still awake and watching her from his side of the room. Then she heard him move. Through narrow slits, she watched him slip out again without a backward glance. She turned on her side, feeling oddly hurt and annoyed. She knew where he was going, though why she should care was beyond her.

For a long time, she just lay there, trying to fall asleep, but every sound disturbed her, every thought filled her with sick anxiety. And she could not stop thinking of Mite and Tinky.

Through half-open eyelids, she watched Pit the Picker return from his watch. With a big yawn, he sat next to Penny, who was still mending the little trousers of the young ones. They started whispering, then their voices rose, and her ears snagged on what Pit the Picker was saying. "... not like the other Echoes, but a mage."

Bad Penny stopped sewing in disbelief. "There's no magic left in our world. It's all on the other side ..." She motioned with her needle to the covered windows. "And there's been no mages for six hundred years. They aren't born but made by the tsaren."

"It's what they say," Pit insisted in a fierce whisper. "What if one was hidden here all this time? They say mages live forever unless you burn them. And only magic can hurt the bridge. Everyone knows that. It would explain why the Blight is advancing rather than retreating. It's 'cause they thought they'd killed all the magic, but seems some has been hiding all along and no one knew. So, whoever it was that as likely killed the bridge can command magic to do his bidding. Why else would the king offer a chest of gold for his capture? Just think, we'd be rich if we found him. Just imagine, a whole chest of gold. They'd let us live in the Silver Circle. And we'd never go hungry, and we'd wear nice clothes ..."

Penny resumed her sewing. "I've already sent Tommy and Vale to scout the streets and see what they can learn about this Echo. And Echo he is, mark my words. All the gangs are looking for him. If he's any sense, he'll take the bridge before they find him."

Elika felt sick in her stomach. She could not stay here. A chest of gold would feed their pack for years ... or until the Blight reached them. She looked around and saw what the rest of them refused to see. Only half the pack wore blood-salt crystals. No one would ask why the others did not. No one ever wanted to admit to being an Echo, and the others would not point a finger at their own. Loyalty was all they had left in this world, and they valued it above life itself, as Lucky Lick had learned to his demise.

How could so many of them be infected? Had it always been thus? Then a darker, sinister thought intruded—*what if it was you who infected them?* Bill had said magic poured out of her. She did not know what it meant, but once the thought occurred to her, it was impossible to shake it.

It grew late, and Penny put her mending aside and went to her own bedroll. By then Pit was snoring softly. It was a frosty night and only the dying glow of the cooking embers was giving off any heat.

She was still awake hours later when Mite sneaked back to his bed, his hair mussed, a grin playing on his face. He glanced only once her way to check she was asleep and did not see her slightly open eyes watching him in the dark.

Hurt rose in her chest sharper than ever. Only yesterday he was with Pretty Bessy, who everyone knew was his favorite ladylove. Had he forgotten her so quickly for Tinky? And what about giggling Pearl, or Dana whose oldest son was Mite's own age? He did not know Elika knew about them. But she had followed him, had seen him with them in dark alcoves, hiking up their skirts ... ugh. He was a rotten letch who could not keep his breeches on whenever a woman winked at him in passing. Elika would not mind so much, but whilst he was pumping the queans in the back alleys, who was keeping an eye on the young ones in the streets? Might be if he'd been watching, Fast Flint would never have had his finger cut off. He nearly died from the fever afterwards.

She stared at Mite's blanket and allowed anger to build inside her until she felt it crawl out like some invisible snake and make its way toward him. Then she watched his blanket grow roots and branches, and she knew herself to be asleep and dreaming, for this could not be happening in their world that had no magic left in it. It was a strange dream, and aye, she was angry with Mite. She could punish him in her dream and would feel better for it in the morning. She smiled and urged the roots to wrap around him.

He startled awake and cried out. He tried to throw aside the blanket, but the roots enveloped his arms and legs, whilst the branches scratched his face.

More screams came from around the Hide, shrill and terrified, as the younger children woke up, their eyes wide with horror. Elika sat upright and watched her dream morph into a living nightmare.

This cannot be real.

Penny was there, beside Mite, pulling and tearing the grasping blanket from him. Together they threw it aside, but it crawled back toward Mite. One of the older kids ran toward it with burning wood pieces and tried to set it alight. She felt the heat of the fire and recoiled from the pain, pulling away from it.

This is a dream. Just a dream.

She looked down and faced the sight that filled her with equal horror and disgust. The dark tendrils of magic had emerged from her hands, but as she stared, they receded and faded. She felt that strange, vital force coiling contentedly back inside her, like a snake in her gut, and she felt its ravenous hunger for food.

This is a nightmare. It is not real.

She met Mite's shocked gaze. For an eternity he just stared at her. Then his face twisted with anger and disgust as he finally saw the monster she was. He turned away, as if the very sight of her revolted him. And that was more dreadful than the creeping, chilling sense of the magic nesting inside her.

It was then that she finally realized it was not a dream, that the magic had claimed her, and it was ruthless and self-serving.

They were all looking at her, the whole pack. The young ones were cowering away. Little Rosy Rose was crying and clutching her feather to her chest. The older ones were tense, weapons in hand at the ready, held back only by the fear of what else she might do to them. Between them and her stood Bad Penny, sharp daggers drawn, her gaze icy, her face stern and angry and filled with the hurt of deep, deep betrayal.

Elika's eyes filled with tears and she could see nothing more. Before they found their wits and attacked her as one, she jumped up, grabbed her scant possessions, her blanket, and fled the Hide, knowing there was no going back.

CHAPTER FOUR

The Blight

"History records Maramera as being the first city to fall to the Blight, one hundred and fifty years after the sundering of our world. This event also marks the first recorded sighting of the Blight. Having combed the old records, I believe the Blight appeared in our world during the early years of the Sundering War. Long before the ocean city fell to this invisible, silent horror, the northernmost village of Fireslay was likely its first victim. Though other scholars claim magic alone killed those folk, witness records and stories are consistent with the advent of the Blight and its effects."

History of Men, Gods and Magic,
By Priest Oderrin

The pack was on the hunt for her—led by Mite. Their footsteps bounded on the roof overhead, their demanding voices called out to each other. She lay curled up between the rafters, her back pressed tightly against the warm chimney. She refused to think of how much she missed the pack, how alone she was. The nights were the worst. There had always been others around her, shrouding her in a feeling of safety. Now she slept fitfully, startled by every sound.

You could not survive alone in the city. The fools learned that the hard way. The smart ones found a gang to join; even a dog-gang was better than being alone. For her, joining another gang was not a choice. Switching gangs had to be agreed upon by both parties; a transaction of sorts, for no one trusted a traitor. They were usually found with their throats cut as a warning to others. Besides, eventually, they would find out she was an Echo. Or worse, a mage, for magic had a way of causing mischief when it could. She could not control it, and it would betray her.

When she had ventured into the streets, she heard no talk or rumor of what she had done in the Hide that night. That did not surprise her. The pack always dealt with their troubles without going to the guards and they punished their own. Mite and Bad Penny had kept that night secret and what they did not want known, the pack did not speak of.

That's how it had been with Lucky Lick. They did not speak of him, but they all remembered the wiry boy with a burned cheek and a sly glint in his eyes. At the time, Elika was too young to understand much of what had transpired between the older kids. After Red Tom left, a few of them vied for the leadership. Penny took over, but Lick betrayed her. He gave her over to the city guards, thinking to take over the Hide and the pack. But he misjudged Little Mite and his loyalty to Penny.

Elika was there, with the rest of the pack when Bad Penny and Mite dragged Lick to the chasm. He had been bound and gagged, but his eyes pleaded with them, begged for help from everyone who watched. Penny's face was stony. Mite's was fierce, relentless. Together they threw him into the chasm. No one ever spoke of Lick again. No one ever crossed Bad Penny.

The night that magic had escaped her and threatened Mite, Elika saw how Penny had looked at her. Penny had looked at Lick the same way just before they pushed him into that chasm. They would do the same to her.

No, not Mite. He was her friend; he had always protected her and stood by her ...

She remembered how he had laughed with Lick. They, too, had been close. They played cards together, drank together. And it was Lick who took Mite to his first whorehouse. She knew because she had not been asleep when Lick convinced Mite he needed to become a man if he wanted to take care of the pack like one. Mite had laughed. He loved a good lark like the rest of them, and they left together.

She followed them in secret, watched them disappear into *Sultry Sally's*. And she remembered how stony Mite's face had been when Lick went over the side into the bottomless chasm, screaming against his gag.

Long after that, when the winds howled, she thought she could still hear Lick screaming.

No, she must not think of Mite as a friend anymore. She had seen his disgust, his horror as he finally understood what she was—a mage. It choked her to admit it, even to herself. She was not like the other Echoes; she knew that now. She was a mage, or something else men had no name for. She did not know how it could have happened, but it had. Bad Penny would show her no mercy. And Mite would be there, too, as they pushed her over the edge of the chasm, his face stony, his eyes cold.

Her stomach rumbled. The chimney at her back had grown cold. That meant it was late morning and the old woman who lived below had moved to another room in the house.

Mite was not a fool, it was why the pack was so close overhead. There was only one place to hide in the city if you needed warmth and food without being seen, and it was in the Silver Circle. Here, you could count on the fire never going out. The gentry had enough coin to pay for the precious coal from Blackhill Mine to the east. They did not need to burn furniture or rags or floorboards, or dead cats. The only thing Elika could do was be more silent than a mouse, lest they send a servant up to the attic to set traps. Although she was silent as a mouse, the rats around her were not so cautious.

It had taken her days to find the perfect hideout. She had watched the old woman and knew she was half-deaf and prone to chills, so there was always a warm chimney to sleep beside. And her servants were lazy and contemptuous when their mistress was out of sight. So they never troubled themselves to investigate the occasional noises coming from the attic. To get there, Elika crawled a long way through a maze of interconnected attics, all the way from the burned-out roof in Meiser's Alley into the heart of the Silver Circle. It was not an easy path, as many attics had been blocked off.

Later, she had found another way down to the streets below, through an old, unused smuggler's vent in the tiles. She rarely used it, though, and only at night under the cover of darkness, when the gentry slept in their beds.

The cold from the outside seeped into her blankets. She shuddered. It was tempting to curl up against another chimney nearby, but she could not lie about all day. She was hungry and today was her wash day. If she was not careful, Mite would find her by the stench of her clothes.

With a sigh, she uncurled and gathered her things, in case the old woman imagined that she heard a mouse and sent her servants up to get rid of it. Soundlessly, she crawled along the rafters under the roof to the fourth house along from the old woman's.

The clerk's chimney was still warm. She did not come here until she was certain he had left. He was a young man, his ears keen and alert. She knew his routine. He left early each day—except on the fifth day when he left mid-morning—and came home late. He did not keep a servant, but a housekeeper came every other day. Today she would not be there. Still, it was best to be cautious. Elika pried open the hatch door to the house and peered through the crack.

Silence.

Days ago, she had scouted this house, picked the lock at the back, and explored its possibilities. It was perfect. Silent, empty, and his larder and kitchen cupboards were stocked with food. She had unlocked the hatch to the roof from the inside, before leaving again. No one ever noticed such tiny details, unless something was clearly amiss. Elika was careful not to leave anything amiss.

The house was narrow, with only one or two rooms per floor. It was more of a servants' quarter, a mere extension to the opulence on either side of it. Satisfied no one was about, she took off her shoes, lowered the stair and climbed down, carefully placing each foot so as not to make a whisper of sound.

The attic opened to the third floor of the house. There was a prettily decorated nursery with a crib in the center of the room and a chair beside it. The first time she had come here, the nursery looked so ready for a child she could almost hear echoing laughter. She had tiptoed to the crib and peeked inside ... Empty, save for a beautiful, crocheted blanket and a small doll. A sense of tragedy hung about the room. And Elika had a strong sense that the nursery was now a shrine. Ever since, she had avoided it, merely slipping past without glancing inside. Still, her skin chilled each time she passed the open door.

The floor below was where the clerk slept. There was a tousled, unkempt bedroom and a studiously neat study, as if a different man occupied each room. She had explored both rooms to learn more about the man she stole from. He fell asleep with a whisky bottle and a half-filled glass on his bedside table. His worn clothes were thrown on the floor with despondent abandon. The mirror on the dresser was shattered. There were no women's clothes in the wardrobe, no scent bottles, no delicate shoes. But beside the broken mirror lay a brush with long, golden hair wrapped in its bristles.

It was his study, however, that disturbed her the most. It was meticulous. Not a piece of paper was out of place, not an ink pot or quill misaligned. Books and ledgers on shelves were perfectly arranged. A man with such an eye for pristine order would surely notice if anything in his house was amiss, would know that another had been there. That knowledge chipped away at her courage each time she came here. He was a dangerous target. *Walk away.*

Just one more time, a bone-weary voice inside her whispered. *Then I will find another.*

She tiptoed to the floor below, past the large guestroom. There was nothing there but dusty, old furniture, damp, chilly air, and echoes of loneliness. It was hard not to pity the clerk, but hunger was a selfish, savage beast. So she proceeded down the narrow stair to the street level, past the front door and the parlor room, into the kitchen.

She rushed to the larder first, took out her small knife and shaved a single wafer of ham and a sliver of cheese so that neither the clerk nor his housekeeper might notice the theft. The food melted in her mouth and disappeared into her stomach, making no impression on her hunger, save that it intensified.

Her stomach ached and demanded she cut a larger piece of both. But if she took too much, she'd never be able to return. Too many were looking for her, and with the city's winter stores running low it was harder and harder to find food to steal. She quickly sliced another piece of cheese and closed the door before she was tempted to take more. She forced herself to chew slowly this time, to savor each bite.

That done, she went to the small alcove beside the back door where there was a barrel of fresh water connected to the gutter pipes. She took a bowl from its hook, filled it with icy water from the melted snow, and bracing herself, quickly wiped down her body using her own cloth. She gritted her teeth to stop them from chattering. Bad Penny allowed no one in the pack to go around dirty. They had learned early on to wash in rain or snow and to bear it without complaint.

Afterwards, Elika washed the clothes she had been wearing in the leftover water. She wrung them out and wrestled them on again, cringing as she did so. Later, she would dry them over the chimney.

She poured the water into the drain in the floor, wiped the bowl, hung it up again, and checked the floor to make certain she did not leave behind any whisper of her presence; no footprints, no fallen hair, not a drop of water or a speck of dust. She was about to walk out when she noticed the door to the adjoining parlor was ajar. The warmth seeping through it stopped her in her tracks.

Her hands were frozen, her clothes wet, and cold water chilled her to the bones. The warmth of the dying coal fire was much too achingly enticing. She had time. The housekeeper would not return until tomorrow and the clerk always worked late. She would just dry herself a little, draw the chill out of her bones and then she would leave.

She peeked through the slightly open door.

No one was inside. The grate covered the glowing coals.

She slipped through the gap and was awash with the heat. It infused her body, forcing out the cold. If only it could do the same with the magic inside her.

She came closer to the fire.

On the mantelpiece, there was a miniature portrait of a woman. She was not pretty, but she held Elika's gaze as if she was sunlight itself. There was such gentle kindness in her face ... and unhappiness. Her smile was sad, the eyes distant as if she gazed into another, better life ...

The front door banged shut.

Elika started and froze.

Heavy footsteps resounded through the hallway, drawing closer, closer. She judged the distance to the kitchen ... too far. Without thinking, she darted to the window.

The door opened.

She slipped behind a heavy curtain and stilled. Her heartbeat filled her ears. He was home early. The footsteps entered, paused, then walked ahead. There was a masculine sigh, and then he fell into the chair by the fireplace. His booted legs stretched out into her sightline.

Then silence. An awful silence, in which she was certain he could hear her strangled breath.

He shifted in his chair. Another sigh. Then, "You can come out. I won't hurt you."

Elika began to shake. If she was fast and agile, she might dart past him before he caught her. He was sitting with his legs stretched out and would be slow to give chase.

"Come out from behind there, I said. I know you've been coming round. Let's have a look at my thief, then."

Elika took a deep breath and emerged to face the clerk.

He sat with his head resting on the back of his chair, watching her. The few times she had seen him on the street, he seemed haggard and clumsy. He looked no different sitting down. There was nothing remarkable about him. His face was unmemorable, and his brown-woolen suit was much like those worn by every man in his trade. His hair was dark and graying at the edges. The only distinct feature about him was his long, beaked nose.

He took off his spectacles and rubbed his eyes, before putting them on again. "You were clumsy today, kid, to be caught like this. Thought you were smarter than that."

"If you knew I was around, why didn't you call the guard?"

He shrugged one shoulder. "What's the point? Of any of it?" He motioned to the chair. "Take a seat, I won't bite." He closed his eyes as if wearied by life itself, and Elika saw it, his readiness to leave it.

She approached cautiously and perched on the edge of the seat. Often men wanted to talk in their last hours, to unburden themselves for that last journey.

"I wasn't careless. You are back early," she said.

He looked at her and might have smiled but for the weight of his enshrouding malaise. "Lost my last client today," he said flatly.

She glanced at his chest and knew. "You are an Echo."

"Men no longer want to do business with you unless you wear the blood-salt pendant. Until ten days ago, I wore it, slept in it, bathed in it."

Ten days ago ... that was when Elika had come to his house for the first time. A coincidence, nothing more, she chided herself silently. But Bill's words continued to haunt her. *Magic is pouring out of you.*

"Thing is," he continued, staring at the dying embers of his fire. "I've had it before and been purged of it. Ever heard of a man getting it twice?"

"I ... I don't know," she said carefully.

He flicked his gaze to her neck and chest. "Looks like magic got you too."

"Might be I just couldn't find a blood-salt crystal to wear," she said, trying to sound nonchalant.

He reached into his pocket, pulled out the blood-salt wrapped in a handkerchief, and threw it to her. It was so fast, she caught it instinctively. Pain shot up her arms from her hand. She cried out and dropped it.

A small smile played on his lips. She flushed and berated herself for falling for his ruse like an untried urchin.

"You going to the temple?" she asked, trying to deflect his attention from herself.

"I repeat, what's the point? You know what comes for us. We are the last. The end is here."

"You could take the bridge," she said.

He flinched and his eyes rose to the picture of the woman on the mantelpiece. Again, he rubbed his eyes then his head fell back and he stared at the ceiling. "I've thought about it. What man doesn't? Loana took it. And she took our baby girl. I ran after her, but she was already on the bridge. I pleaded with her not to go, not to take my little Rosa. She was just a babe. The Blight was still far away. There was hope. With each step I took toward her, she took one away. Then she turned and walked and I watched my baby Rosa turn to dust in her mother's arms. Loana just kept walking, still carrying the ghost of our daughter. Then she reached the other side and just stood there, an unmoving shadow. Each day I went there, grieving and angry. Each day she faded further away. I thought about joining her there, many a time. But I find I cannot forgive her, cannot bear the thought of seeing her again."

Elika said nothing. A part of her that wanted to survive felt regret that he was not a death-walker. She felt ashamed of that feral, mercenary part of her. But it was hard to keep it at bay when each day she lived with the fear of what the next would bring.

"What will you do?" she asked at length.

He was silent for a long time, staring ahead at nothing. "Die, I guess," he said, finally. He waved at the kitchen. "Have as much food as will fill your stomach. I have enough to last me till the Blight gets here."

"They say it'll be some years yet. And the king sent the priests …"

His lips upturned cynically. "Seen any smoke on the horizon recently?"

"I haven't looked," she said with a stab of dread. She had been hiding in the roof from Mite and the pack for many days, emerging only at night.

"Then go and look," he said with a wave at the window.

And in that instant, as if this unimposing clerk had summoned the Blight upon them, dozens of war-bells rang throughout the city, a terrible chorus tolling their doom. A certain sickness of understanding rose in her. Even then, denial was quick on the heels of her shock.

No, it was something else. It had to be something else … it was too soon … But who would attack the city? No one was left in their world save the last, relentless enemy of man. Magic.

And then, amidst the furious ringing of the bells and the indiscernible calls of alarm, she heard the shouts she had feared to hear all her life.

"Blight! Blight!"

She had once fallen from the roof, and the instant her fingers had lost their grip on the jagged gutter, there was a sickening sensation of being weightless and heavy at once, of the ground rushing toward her and the brief knowledge that soon she would hit the hard stone and die and there was nothing she could do to stop it. She had that same sensation now.

Bile rose in her throat. Terren was alone, the last in the path of the Blight. There was no other city to run to. No place in the world left to hide, only the chasm at their back.

The clerk was watching her with a look of pity in his eyes, and a small cynical smile on his lips. "Go, have all you can eat. Take what you want from this tomb." He waved his hand.

Elika did not think she would ever feel hungry again. She felt sick in her stomach, in her body, in the very depths of her soul.

They said the Blight would not be seen from the walls of their city for years yet to come. Purging magic from the infected was supposed to slow it down. How could they be so wrong?

She remembered the distressed priest racing into the city and toward the palace. She had thought little of it at the time. But the priests who went out to halt the Blight never returned. Men said the Blight had caught them unawares. Else they discovered that nothing would ever stop it, just as Mite had told her. Many had tried before. All had failed.

"Blight!" The cries continued in the streets outside.

Those shouts filled her ears, her mind—until she wanted to curl up under the weight of the inevitable fate high upon them. That choice was meant to be years away, which was as good as an eternity. She was not ready for it, could never be ready for it. She did not want to face the Blight, did not want to face the Bridge, did not want their world to end.

Elika found her feet and walked to the window, unsteady and shaky. Outside, men raced toward the city wall to see the truth for themselves, to confirm that the invisible force of death and destruction was finally upon them. And inside her, she harbored the merciless magic that drove it toward them.

CHAPTER FIVE

Mite's Decision

"As long as our history can peer back with any clarity, four royal houses have ruled the earthly realm of Seramight: Northwind, Southfire, Eastrise and Westwater. The heads of the houses were known as the Kings of the Sacred Crowns. They were granted their inviolate right to rule the world of men by the gods themselves, three thousand years ago, when the celestial realm brushed the earthly and the gods crossed into our world as honored guests. Since then, the rule of the sacred kings has never been disputed, for every first son born of the Sacred Crown was long lived, larger than most men, and possessed unnatural strength. But it was their innate resistance to Magic that marked them as true heirs. When Tsarin Reval destroyed the houses of the Sacred Crowns and slaughtered the four kings, he did so not with magic, but with a sword driven by the might of hatred."

History of Men, Gods and Magic,
By Priest Oderrin

For a long time, Elika stood numbly by the window in the clerk's parlor, watching the folk outside race about like frightened mice. When she turned back, the clerk's eyes were closed and he held a glass of amber port in his hand. She had not heard him get up or pour it.

"I'm going out ... to look," she said, and her voice sounded oddly distant to her ears. Why was she telling him this? Save that she needed to say something mundane.

He waved with his glass. "Go, look. Do what you want, savor the days left to us."

She raced upstairs into the attic. But many feet drummed overhead. Gangs called out to each other. "Look! There! I see it," boys shouted.

Despite her curiosity, Elika shrank back. Every one of her pack would be up there, beside many others, seeing with their own eyes magic driving the Blight towards them. If they didn't blame her before, they would surely do so now. She sat with her back against the clerk's warm chimney, closed her eyes and waited.

It was dark when the roofs finally quieted. So it was not until the following dawn that she finally emerged to face the fading world.

She gazed out over the city wall to the rolling farmlands beyond, the chimney pleasantly warm at her back.

It was a strange sort of day, in that it was completely ordinary. The morning skies were clear. The low sun was warming, gentle, and laced with false hope. The last of the snow had gone. Spring was here, and frost had finally released its hold on the land. It was time to plant the first of the summer crops. The farmers were still tilling the loamy dark fields with their plough horses, hoping to sow early seed, hoping the weather stayed mild. It seemed like any other spring, joyous and filled with yearnings for the bountiful future. Except, there would be no harvest this year.

From high on the roofs, she could see the truth those farmers must know in their hearts. But men had to feed hope as well as their stomachs.

Her gaze moved past the fields, toward the last remaining forest. The trees were still deep in their slumber and did not yet have their first flush of growth. The only green came from the pines. And it was these that drew and held her gaze. There, in the farthest trees, she could just make out the rusting of dying leaves, the yellowing tips of the trees.

The Blight was here.

The signs were unmistakable. It spread over the land, an invisible wall of vile power, causing wilt and decay, killing everything in its path, insects, birds, horses and men. It turned fertile land to dust, trees to lifeless, gray wood. Those touched by it died from a decaying sickness of body and mind. The lucky ones simply fell asleep and never woke up. Nothing and no one survived the Blight. All her life, she had dreaded and feared this day. So how could it seem so ordinary?

On the road, a long, winding caravan of wagons made its way toward Terren. It could only have come from the last remaining village of Loamfield, not ten miles away, which grew most of the food for their city. Her gaze returned to the fallow fields with a sinking sensation. The hunger of the city would soon turn to starvation.

All the animals were kept enclosed in guarded grazing fields, behind a fortress wall, along with the last of the herds of cattle, deer, and mountain sheep the survivors of Drasdark had driven to Terren. Most were destined for the plates of the Golden Circle. But did it matter? Any of it? As the clerk said. It was tempting to accept his offer, eat his food and drink his whisky, and wait for the Blight to smother them in their sleep.

Elika wrapped her arms around her knees. Around her, the rooftop world of slate and chimneys was quiet. In the distance, youths raced across the roofs toward the spring markets, following the bustling crowds in the streets below. Instinctively, she searched for Mite's large form amongst them. Then, as if she had summoned him, he lowered himself next to her, appearing out of nowhere like a god of old.

She was not surprised to see him. A part of her wanted him to find her, come what may.

They sat there for a while, looking out at the land. She was tense, fearful of what he would say, what he might do. But he just sat there, as if she had never used magic on him, as if this was one of those many times when they looked over their world in just the same silence.

"I'm sorry," she blurted out, unable to bear the unspoken between them any longer. "I didn't mean to … I don't know how it happened."

"The priests say nothing they did slowed it," he said, as if he had not heard her. "They can't understand why it's moving so much faster as it nears Terren. Some say it's the bridge calling to it."

"Or a rogue mage," she added wryly what he was careful not to voice. "Magic calls to magic." It was an old saying, but perhaps there was some truth in it.

Mite glanced at her. "Why'd you run? I told you I'd look after you."

She stared at him, incredulous. "I used magic on you. I was afraid you'd throw me into the chasm … you and Penny."

He seemed startled by that. Then, abruptly, he looked aside. But she caught a flash of rueful torment in his eyes. "As we did with Lick," he said quietly.

They never spoke of it, and now she understood why. It haunted them still, the shame, the guilt, the disgrace. It stained them all. Even her, though she'd been too young and helpless to do anything but watch and learn the price of betrayal. Aye, she was part of it. By her silence, she had as good as pushed Lick into the chasm herself. They had all pushed him into it, not just Mite and Penny. They should have made him take the bridge instead. It would have been less cruel for everyone.

"He only tried to take power from Penny. What I did was worse."

Mite sighed and shook his head. "You were too young to know what it was that he did. He didn't seek power, only coin …" His lips firmed as if he could not bring himself to tell her. Then he ran his hand through his hair. "He sold girls … young ones, older ones," he mumbled "He betrayed Penny for coin, nothing more. Sold her to the guards. What they did to her …" His jaw clenched. "For some time, the girls in the pack were going missing. At first, we thought they'd ran off, or got foul of someone on the streets. Then Penny went missing and I searched for her. Days … it took me days to find her. I traded all the coin the pack had for information from Peter Pockets. That was when I discovered what Lick was doing." He shook his head again. "The chasm was too good for him."

Elika could not meet his eyes. "I didn't know."

"We'd never do to you what we did to him. Even if you were a mage. It's not your fault magic got you. Penny is beside herself with worry for you."

In his voice, she heard his own worry, too. "The Blight is here," she said blandly as if it explained something.

He stared ahead at the distant forest. "They think it'll reach the city by autumn," he said.

"Unless all the Echoes give themselves for the purging," Elika added.

He did not reply and his silence cut her deeper than his condemnation might have done. She wanted him to forbid her to go to the temple, to promise her that he would think of something. But he said nothing.

"Is that why you're here, to tell me to go to the Temple of Mercy?" she asked without feeling. "I know it well enough myself."

He turned his head to look at her with something that might have been tenderness. "I'm here to say goodbye."

Her heart skipped a beat painfully. "What do you mean?" she demanded, suddenly angry at him.

His lips curled in mild amusement. "Asks the girl who can read men's minds better than anyone I know."

She shook her head in denial. "The Blight has slowed again. I heard them talking about it. The purges are working. I'll give myself up to the priestesses. If enough Echoes get purged …"

He covered her hand with his. "It's no good, Eli. I'm infected too. We all are in the Hide. For every man purged of magic, ten more are taking his place. It's sweeping the streets. No one knows why so many are becoming mired with it. The priests say it's been like that for fifteen years. And in that time, the Blight has advanced more than in the two hundred years before it. It's why Drasdark was caught so unprepared. It's all linked somehow. Something has changed in our world. They don't know what or how to stop it. They need the tsaren back to make sense of it all."

She found it hard to breathe. Fifteen years ago—she was born then. *Magic is pouring out of you.*

Mite gave no sign of having made that connection. "It's time to make your choice. I've made mine."

She shook her head fiercely. "I'm not ready ... not yet."

"You fear the unknown too much. You always have. I dare say in the end, you'll be the last one left in the city." His smile was tender, rueful, too.

"Don't leave me, Mite," she whispered.

"Come with me," he said stubbornly.

She thought of the bridge and her throat closed up.

"We'll face whatever is on the other side together," he said.

"What if one of us doesn't make it ... what if neither of us does?"

He just kept looking at her. What could he say? That was the choice they all had to make. That was the fear men faced when they stood before the bridge.

Elika turned away. At the city gate, the king was riding out toward the Blight. The high priest in his red robes rode beside him, with the procession of Red Guards at his back. They passed the stream of grim, tired migrants on the road, paying them no mind. The gaze of the king and his priests was fixed on the invisible wall of poisonous magic ahead as they rode to meet it.

Men had always warred against the destructive nature of magic. Why follow it across the bridge, to the land which itself looked as if the Blight had swept through it?

"I'll cross tonight," Mite said firmly and rose to his feet. "Only Penny knows. She'll tell the others after I'm gone."

"Mite?" she said, and he looked down at her, pale and grim. "What's your first memory? Where did your story begin?"

His eyes roamed over her face. They never spoke of the past, of where they came from. "The day my father took me to see the bridge that first time," he said at length. "He thought it was time I learned the truth about our world, what it is we fight, what lies ahead of us. I think he wanted me to know why he was going to do what he did. We rode from the Golden Circle on fine horses, with Red Guards in tow. I thought it a grand adventure. But afterwards, I feared to fall asleep, for each time I dreamt, the dark bridge unraveled beneath my feet, and I fell into the chasm, screaming and screaming."

"You were the son of a nobleman?" Elika asked dully. There had always been something about Mite that made him seem so much more than others.

"Only for the first six years of my life. After my father led the rebellion against the king, he was stripped of his titles and property and we were banished from the Golden Circle. But the imposter king was not satisfied. He sent assassins to our hideout. They killed my mother and sister. Father fought them off before they got to me. Having lost everything but me, Father took the bridge. He asked if I wanted to go with him, but I was too afraid and refused. He told me that when I was ready, he would be waiting for me. He did not reach the other side."

"Your father was Lord Silvering, the one who wanted to be king?" She felt oddly hurt that she'd never known this about Mite, and now he was leaving. And she would never know anything else about him. They were parting as little more than strangers, despite knowing each other almost all their lives.

He must have guessed her thoughts, for he smiled sadly. "Look after yourself, Eli Spider. When you find your courage, I will be waiting on the other side."

The same lie his father gave him, she thought miserably.

He began to walk away, then halted, staring at something in his hand, deliberating. He spun back and held out a gold ring with an emblem of four crowns linked together. "Take it," he said gruffly.

She did, but only because she had never seen anything so fine and dazzling. One of the engraved crowns was larger than the rest, it held a dark-blue gem. A real gem at that, she was certain. Even a glass gem as pretty as that would have fed their pack for a year. The ring itself must have been worth more than the whole of Riftside, more even than a chest of …

"This is the ring Bill wanted," she said with sudden understanding.

"My father gave it to me before he left. It's yours now … to borrow. Give it to Bill to buy his silence, if you must. But be sure to steal it back before you cross. Bring it back to me, Eli."

And then he left.

She gaped at him, her thoughts scrambled. After she could no longer see him on the rooftops, she hugged her knees to her chest and fought the choking lump in her throat. But beneath it lay only hollowness.

She hid the ring inside one of her most secret pockets stitched into the hem of her shirt. She caught sight of the brass button on her collar which marked her as one of Penny's pack. She ripped it off and shoved it into her trouser pocket. As she did so, her fingers brushed the wooden carving of an eye. She took it out.

The ward drew the gazes of the celestial gods so that they would watch over her. It was strange that though men no longer cared for the old gods who had abandoned them, many still carried such wards. The Priests of Nerabyss taught that the celestial sphere was cold and empty, and the gods long dead. But sometimes she wondered whether the old gods were still up there amongst the stars, watching the folly of men and magic.

She wrapped her fingers around the carving and left the rooftops by sliding one-handed down the iron gutter pipe. A moment later she merged into life on the dank, busy streets.

Without thought, she picked the pocket of a passing man wearing a feathered hat. It was not her hunting ground. But then, she did not have one anymore. She had not eaten in two days and her stomach was aching. With the two coppers she stole, she bought a spiced potato pie and chewed it as she ambled toward Crow Side in the western quarter.

Despite the pervading sense of tension blanketing the city, life on the streets went on, as if the Blight was not right on their doorstep. Folk went about their business as they did each day. They bartered over goods as if such things still mattered. The blacksmith's hammer came down again and again in the same ageless rhythm. Old men still mended shoes and leather on street corners. The young ones picked pockets. The beggars still begged. The whores still teased and goaded.

Hope. There was always hope. Why did Mite have to seek his across the Bridge? No, she would not think of him. He had made his choice.

At the public notice board, a city crier in red livery was shouting the king's new decree. The citizens of Terren must put bags with every grain of salt they possessed outside their doors for the salt collectors. No animal blood was to be wasted. All Echoes were to go to the temple for purging or face the bridge without mercy.

Someone threw a stone at him. "Tell the king there's only men left in the city to take blood from."

"Don't give him daft ideas, you idiot," someone else shouted.

Another stone hit the crier. He ducked and ran off the stage. The city guards nearby laughed as they watched him flee. One of them was busy trying to pull a whore into the doorway of her cottage. She would probably not have minded, but the guards never paid for what they took.

In the distance, Elika saw a Sachi priest in brown robes carrying a string with many little wooden wards. Compelled by some whim, she began to follow him.

She had often been told that she had the look of a Sachi, and her blood must be tinged with theirs. She had gone to Crow Side one day, seeking the truth of it. The Sachi looked after their own and would have taken her in. But they took one look at her and shook their heads. She was not one of them, they said and chased her away.

When she had come to their temple, however, the priests were kind and gave her food. They told her about the celestial gods and the power of prayer. So she took the Eye of God prayer token as her ward. The Sachi might have rejected her, but it was not so easy for her to reject them.

The Sachi priest turned a corner and she dashed forward to catch up with him …

"Hey … El?" a whispered hiss came from the side alley.

Her hand was instantly on the knife tucked into her trousers.

Blue-eye Billy's face poked out from behind a rain barrel. Like everyone from Peter Pockets' gang, he was dressed in a fancy suit, polished boots and a long leather coat. It looked ridiculous on his boyish frame. Billy had not yet grown his first set of whiskers. His hair was oiled, brushed and shiny, as if he was a nobleman's son. He glanced around furtively and waved her over, then ducked behind the barrel again.

The alley was narrow, dark and empty, and seemed to have no other purpose to it than for men and cats to piss in. A brick wall cut it off not ten paces away.

She swallowed the last bite of her pie and approached the barrel, glancing around to see whether anyone else from Peter Pockets' gang was watching.

"What do you want?" she asked guardedly. "Did Rory send you?"

"No. Get down here, before anyone sees us," he hissed from behind the water barrel.

She glanced about again, before sitting on the ground beside him.

"Look, El, I ain't a traitor, you know that," he said.

"Never said you were," she replied, wondering why he was acting strangely.

"It's just that I owe you, see?"

She sighed. "No, you don't."

She had come upon Rimley's thugs beating him for no reason other than it was what they did if they took it into their head it needed doing. There had been three of them, Gerin, Fist and Whitedog, all bigger than Billy. She stuck her knife in the closest one who happened to be Fist. He fell to his knees, squealing like a pig in a slaughterhouse. Billy didn't know their names, but she did and they knew it, too. She politely reminded them of the Code, and that Peter Pockets might not like them beating one of his for no good reason. So they ran off. There was nothing more to it than that. Why Billy felt indebted was beyond her.

Billy's face hardened. "Peter Pockets says we aren't allowed to owe debts to anyone. And aye, I owe you one, which I must pay back. It's the way with the Code. But I've got nothing but information. It's not being a traitor. 'Cause I ain't telling you what's a secret, see? Just making sure you know what's what. And I can't bring you in myself, anyway, you being meaner and bigger than me."

Elika held back a smile. "Just say what you want to tell me and we're even."

"Well, it's like this. They know you're the mage everyone's looking for."

Her stomach lurched, and it was all she could do not to betray how much this shook her. "What have you been drinking, Billy?" she said smoothly.

"Just listen, El. I don't care about it right now, even if you are. Just paying back what I owe you. You see, guards talk when they're in their cups. And there was talk coming out of the *Barrack's Dunk*, where captain's men take their ale and whores. Seems one of the guards had seen who it was that stabbed the bridge. So Rory tracked him down and brought him to Peter Pockets for the questioning. He squealed and wept and pissed himself and told them every little detail. Then they cut his throat."

Mite had warned her about the guard who had seen her. She now wished Mite had caught him first, then and there.

"What did the guard tell them?" she asked, warily.

"Nothing useful. He didn't see the face of the mage and couldn't put a name to 'im. Only that the mage was a ragamuffin. So they didn't know where to look for him. But then, Bad Penny's pack turn skittish. We see them out on the hunt, though no one says for who. So, we know something's afoot, and Pockets thinks it may be to do with the mage. So, he takes one of yours, Pit the Picker, and asks him a few questions ..."

"He has Pit?"

"He didn't hurt him," Billy said quickly. "It's against the Code now, ain't it? Besides, he didn't need to. Pockets does well for us. None of us go hungry or thirsty. We wear nice clothes. And he buys his men pretty, clean whores as reward. So, Pockets invited Pit to dinner, and puts a roast chicken before him, with potatoes and bread and wine. And he sprinkled it all with some promises. Pit ate and drank as if it was his last meal and babbled everything he knew."

Oh, Pit, you traitor, she thought. *Penny will never forgive you.* Nor would Peter Pockets. Once a traitor, you'd always be branded as one.

"What's Pockets going to do with him?" she asked with a pang of fear for Pit.

Billy looked aside with a grim shrug. Traitors rarely lived out a year. Those who did had their right ear cut off so the others would know them for what they were. "So far, Peter's keeping his word. Pit's one of us now. As long as he doesn't stray."

Pit the Picker always strayed. She wished now she had beaten it out of him, or let Penny and Mite do it.

"But there's talk," Billy continued. "They're thinking of flushing you out, see?"

"No, I don't," she said with alarm.

"Pit said that you and Penny are close. Says you might be a girl, too. Though he's not certain." Billy stared at her, his eyes dropping to her chest, her groin. "Are ye?" He seemed more fascinated by that notion than that she might be a mage.

"What does Pockets want with me?"

"Well, here's why I'm not a traitor to him. He told us to go out and try to bring you in. Nice like. He doesn't want to hurt you, or to sell you to the king. Only to have your magic, as it were. You'd be treated well, be you girl or boy. He'd make you his top man, even above Rory. It's what he promises if you come to us."

"He wants to use my magic," she said slowly, incredulously.

Billy nodded eagerly. "Think of what we can do with real, true magic. We can take apart the walls of the Golden Circle and take the grain for the folk in the streets. And maybe strong magic can dispel the Blight ..."

"No. Magic can't be contained or commanded by humankind. Everyone knows that. It does what it wants when it wants to do it. I must get rid of it," she blurted out and instantly regretted it. If Pockets was looking for her, they'd be watching the temple now as well.

Billy shrugged, as if he had not noticed her blunder. But she knew he would store this knowledge to deliver it back to Peter Pockets. "Well, now that I warned you, I owe you nothing. Right?" He looked at her questioningly.

"As you say, your debt is settled," she replied with a sigh, then sprang to her feet and walked away.

"Just don't tell anyone what we spoke about," he shouted.

This was even worse than she had feared. She lowered her face. Too many knew her by sight. And if Peter Pockets suspected she was a girl, donning a dress would not keep her safe either. Did Penny know Pit had betrayed them? *Oh Pit, you fool.* Did Mite know? Did he know Peter Pockets now watched their pack? How could Mite leave at a time like this, when Penny needed him more than ever?

As Elika walked, she glanced about her often, but saw no sign of pursuit. She kept away from Pockets' hunting ground, where she was most likely to be recognized. This took her the long way round to her destination.

So it was well past midday when she came to Crow Side, one of the oldest parts of the city. Here, the streets were narrow, and stone cottages pressed tightly against each other. The Sachi migrants had arrived here hundreds of years ago, after their kingdom fell. They were a stubborn folk, unshakeable in their beliefs. Even after thousands of years had passed without a single visit from the celestial gods, the Sachi continued to worship them. Their descendants were no less stubborn today and continued to cling to the beliefs of their forefathers.

All around her, strange wards hung on windows and doors. Some elaborate, like woven metal wreaths. Others simple and inexplicable like a withered apple hanging from the beam above a door or a string of rusty nails. Whilst here and there, wooden eyes carved into lintels watched all who passed. But these were not even the strangest things about the Sachi.

Each house had its own crow, a sacred bird believed to be the messenger of the old gods. The Sachi believed that if you wished for the celestial gods to hear your prayer, you needed only to whisper it to a crow. The crows perched on windowsills, beside their cups of water and grain, watching her with those inquisitive yellow eyes that made Elika nervous.

Overhead, a crow with white-tipped wings gave a startling, raucous call and flew ahead, as if leading the way. It perched on the gutter above and continued to watch her. Elika's hand tightened around the wooden eye.

Like most, she did not truly believe in the old gods and thought that the sky held nothing but the stars. But here, in Crow Side, surrounded by superstitions, she could not shake a creeping sensation that the gods of old were watching her.

As Elika turned into Crownest Alley, the white-tipped crow cried overhead again, as if warning the gods of her approach. Foolish thoughts. But whenever she was here, such thoughts did not seem foolish at all.

The alley ended at a small, gray-stone temple, which was not much larger than the cottages around it. The doors stood wide open. Ivy climbed its walls and moss grew over its roof and spire. Inside, worshippers were kneeling by the stone feet of the five celestial gods, whispering their prayers.

Unlike the tsaren, the old gods looked nothing like men. The statue of Kisha, the God of Fire, had a serpent's head and scaled flesh. Anav, the Sea God, had tentacles instead of legs. Dran had muscled arms that ended with stone boulders instead of hands and he stooped as if they weighed him down. And Neka, the Goddess of Life and mother of all, had roots instead of legs, hair of grass and a dress of leaves.

But it was the shrine to Moreg, deep in the shadows of the temple, that always drew her eyes. The God of Death was a hooded figure of a man with eight thick limbs like spider's legs emerging from his body. In his hands, he held a webbed sphere. It chilled her, though she did not know why, other than it pulled at some long-forgotten memory inside her.

"And which god are you here to pay homage to, child?"

She turned to face a priest in hessian robes. Elika thought the Sachi a beautiful race, with black hair and exotic, upturned eyes and sun-darkened skin. "I … I am not here to pay homage to any god," she replied.

"Then why are you here?" asked the Sachi priest.

Elika searched for the answer inside herself. She uncurled her fingers and regarded the wooden eye, polished and stained from all the times she had held it. She had come here seeking hope from the gods, for her own was fading. Who else was left to save them?

"Why don't the gods stop the Blight?" she asked.

"Because men and magic brought it upon themselves and they are the ones who must stop it. This war was never theirs. But they watch over us still, as they always have."

Except it was not the gods who had watched over her, but Mite. At the thought, something hardened inside her.

"The gods have abandoned us," she said. *Just like Mite.* "Else they are dead, just like the priests tell it."

He lowered his face to hers. "Three spheres eternally circle each other, in a cycle as old as time, and when they brush, the fates of our worlds intertwine. Until the pattern returns and our spheres touch again, the gods cannot cross into our world. But they are still up there, child. They watch us and grant prayers to those they favor."

Elika studied the rows of boxes holding different stone and wood carvings. There were many prayer tokens. So many, she could not count them all. The hand represented gods' guidance, the wreath of leaves, their wisdom. A horse granted you an easy road. A hammer helped you achieve a hard task. There was a fish, the moon and sun, a flower, a baby for fertility, and countless other carvings representing every small wish one might conceive.

What good were men's prayers, when they went unanswered? Elika placed the wooden eye into the box with the others. No one was watching over her, and with Mite gone, she had to look after herself.

"What is your prayer, child?" the priest asked kindly. "Ask the gods and they may grant you your wish."

"Make the Blight stop," she said sardonically and looked the Sachi priest in the eyes. "Which token should I take to make it happen?"

"Test not the patience of the gods with false prayer," he scolded gently. "But I see what it is you seek." He picked up a token from one of the boxes and placed it in her palm. "Fear not death, for when we die, we are brought to stand before three paths. One leads us home."

She stared at a wooden bird, the prayer token for guiding the lost back home. "Which path do I take?"

"You must seek your own homeward path," he replied. "There are three spheres of life: the celestial, ethereal and earthly. Where do you belong? With gods, with magic or with men?"

"With men," she replied without thought.

He motioned to the statue of a man-like being with boulders for hands. "Then Dran is the one you should send your prayers to, the God of Earth and Stone. For it is he who gave men the earthly sphere we live in."

Elika turned her gaze on the gods who looked nothing like men. The gods who either abandoned them or had long ago perished. Since the beginning of time, men had fought unbridled magic with blood-salt and fire and prayers to the old gods. But the old gods never answered. Instead, another dark power replied—Syn'Moreg, Lord of the Abyss, who had sundered their world, giving half to men and half to magic, before vanishing again. So why add her voice to the cacophony of unheard prayers?

"They are not my gods," she said and walked out, pocketing the prayer token of a bird.

Late that day, when the streets grew dark and most folk had retreated to their homes, the king returned with his guards and the priests to the city. They rode under the fire of torches. Both the king and the high priest looked somber.

Elika had been waiting for their return with those ridiculous wings of hope fluttering inside her. But when she read their faces, those wings stilled and there was only the one place she wanted to go.

She ran over the roofs toward the chasm. She had to see Mite one last time, had to witness his fate, to know what became of him when he crossed, or she'd forever torment herself wondering.

She climbed through the hole into the abandoned building facing the bridge. The door below was loose on its hinges and creaked in the wind. The plaster on the walls was crumbling, the furniture long ago plundered for firewood. Cobwebs hung in every corner and small creatures scurried in the shadows. Now and then, the house groaned like a dying old beast. Outside, the relentless winds rose from the chasm, wild and fierce, and filled with those terrible screams.

Elika strained her ears for any sound that did not belong, whilst making her silent way to the window. Centuries of decay and grime had rotted away most of its timber. She peered out. The bridge was dark and still. Rift Street was empty. Night shrouded the lifeless lands beyond, but there were no stars in the sky over the Deadlands. No moon, either. Only a strange moon-like glow coming from nowhere she could fathom. Dimly, it illuminated the endless plains and the dark shadows of men who had crossed the bridge since the Blight had been sighted.

There were many more of them now. More than she had ever seen before. Dozens of motionless shades facing the Deadlands. Desperately, she searched for Mite's form amongst them. Was she too late? She searched, but no form seemed right. Had he perished on the bridge?

A tall shape detached from the ruinous wall of the building below. Mite. Relief flooded her and her legs grew shaky. He was alone. He turned slowly around as if searching for someone. There were other watchers about. There were always watchers about. No one approached him, though. A man had to face that fate alone.

He stuffed his hands in his pockets, hunched his shoulders against the bitter wind and strode toward the bridge. Elika's heart jolted all over again. She had to stop him ... had to go with him ... had to do something. She had sworn never to interfere, but this was Mite. She had to say goodbye, but her feet would not allow her to do that.

She could see in the set of his shoulders and in the firmness of his step that he had made up his mind to cross the bridge. He was not drunk, did not hesitate, but approached with calm, steely resolve and no fear. Aye, that was Mite. He would not tremble in the face of the unknown. He stopped at the blood-salt line, then after a pause, took a wide step across it.

Elika's feet moved of their own accord, down the crumbling steps, leaping over the missing floorboards. She burst through the door and ran for the bridge, calling out his name, shouting for him not to step onto the bridge. But Mite's feet were already there.

He turned around and froze. "Eli?" he said, a gentle question.

"Don't go. Wait ... just for a little while," she pleaded.

But it was too late. Those who stepped onto the bridge never returned. It was as if some foul magic held them there.

Sadness filled his eyes, sadness for her and not himself. "Come with me. We will cross together. I will hold your hand."

She shook her head. "There is still hope ... please, Mite, wait a few days. I'll purge myself. I'll kill the magic inside me and stop the Blight. I'll make everything right."

For a moment he looked like he might smile. "What can you do alone that countless powerful men before you could not do? We lost. Men lost the war. This is the end. Magic has won."

Her heart shrank back on itself. "No! You always told me to fight to the end. You lied."

He grew serious. "You still do not understand. Long ago, men made a terrible mistake when they destroyed magic and sent those who could command it to the Deadlands. *Men* started the Sundering War, not the tsaren and not the magic. And what is left of magic is now destroying men as we destroyed it. Do you not see? There is nothing left but Terren. And soon there will be nothing left but the echoes of magic. There is not enough blood or salt in the world to destroy every echo. Eli ... you do not want to be here when men lose hope. They will do terrible, desperate things ... come with me." He held out his hand to her, large and solid.

She stared at it and felt something inside her break. She would have taken it. Any other place, she would have taken his hand. Would have trusted him enough to jump off a roof with him, would have walked through fire with him. But here, by the bridge ... she could not move.

"Together," he said softly. "We will face the unknown together, hand in hand. Just you and me. Please, Eli," he whispered the last with such anguish, her gaze snapped up to his.

He was watching her intently, as if he willed her to understand what he was asking, seeking some answer she did not have. Then her gaze shifted to the bridge. The wound where her knife had struck continued to bleed. And all the while, the restless roots searched for her, the one who had stabbed it, as if the bridge knew she was near. And the roots would drag her over the side into the chasm. They crept toward her, touched the blood-salt line, and recoiled.

She took an instinctive step back. "I cannot," she whispered, for she dared not step onto that monstrosity.

He lowered his hand and gave her a sad smile. "Then I will wait for you on the other side." And with those words, he turned away.

But what if you don't make it? hung on her lips to say. But she dared not utter it, lest she somehow made it come true.

He walked into the night, solid, unwavering, as if he marched into battle. And she watched with bated breath as he neared the apex. She could run now and catch him …

Without warning, his foot fell through the bridge.

"Mite!" Elika screamed.

He grabbed the railing and clung to it with all he had, staring in horror at the pitch-dark chasm below his feet which battled to find purchase, whilst the wailing winds ripped at his cloak, trying to drag him down.

Then she saw something that chilled her. The bridge was unravelling. Its once fleshy railing was shriveling. The branches that once formed the solid path were wilting. What had she done? Had she destroyed man's only escape from the Blight?

Mite pulled himself up, straightened, and moved onward more carefully, holding on to the railing with one hand. And as she watched him leave their world, she thought no more of the bridge or the Blight, only of the ache growing in her chest with each step he took. And all too soon, he reached the apex. One more step and she would never see him again.

Elika's tears were hot on her face. She had not realized how much Mite had meant to her; how alone she would be without him in this world. One more step and he might die. Her chest constricted and she held her breath. But he did not hesitate, fearless and certain to the last, no matter what lay in his heart. He walked on and on and did not turn to dust. Instead, he grew shapeless, distant, fading away as he reached the other side. And then he was there, like so many others. Just standing there, unmoving.

For a long time, Elika stood there, waiting for a sign from him that all was well. It never came.

CHAPTER SIX

The hunt for the Mage

"Long have I pondered the true nature of mages and why the tsaren thought to bring them into existence. Many, rightfully, call them abominations, belonging neither in the ethereal domain nor the earthly. They are an unnatural, ugly unity of magic and man. Mages served and spoke for the tsaren who created them. They commanded magic in their name and served as tsaren's ambassadors to the human kings of the Sacred Crowns. Perhaps the tsaren sought peace between the joined ethereal and earthly spheres. After all, the mages brought wondrous things into the world of man, and for some centuries, men and magic had begun to accept each other. Trade flourished across Seramight, driven largely by magic woven items. The tsaren and the kings of the Sacred Crown dined in the same halls. And for a brief time, peace brought prosperity and wealth. Still, it chills me to recall King Northwind's private warning to the other kings of the Sacred Crown: 'The mages are multiplying, their numbers are growing faster than ever before. Why would so many of our people who hate and fear magic offer themselves so willingly to this irrevocable merging?'"

History of Men, Gods and Magic,
By Priest Oderrin

Bill Fisher's boat in the mudflats leaned on its side like a sick animal, groaning and creaking whenever anyone moved around inside. A faint light flickered in one window. Elika waded through the sticky mud toward it. The ground was no longer frozen, even at night, and silt clung to her boots, weighing her feet. Under the light of the moon, she could see the mud crabs scattering in all directions from beneath her feet.

She used to catch them with Mite when she was little. He showed her places to find food around the city. The crabs were small and there was little flesh to them, but they'd keep her alive long enough to find something better. Mite was gone now and without him, Terren seemed emptier, grimmer, and more menacing. The houses grew larger, the shadows darker, the eyes that watched her more malign.

When she reached Bill's blue ship, she scraped her shoe on a metal rack to remove the mud and climbed the rope ladder to the deck. Much of the ship had rotted away, but here and there Bill had added new boards he had scavenged from around the city. He had used black tar to seal the gaps.

Elika sat down and pulled off her boots before going inside. There was little Bill hated more than muddy footprints on his boat.

She carefully descended the crooked stairs, gripping the railing with both hands.

"Bill," she called out. "It's me … Eli."

"I know who it is," he called back. "I recognize you clomping and stomping on my deck overhead. And for a small lass like you, too. Now Mite is quiet as a thief. You'd never know he was there."

He was mending again. If anyone in Riftside needed anything mended, Bill Fisher was the one they came to. He charged a mere copper for his work, no matter how long it took him. At his age, he had told her, he needed nothing more. And better to have some work than none, else his fingers seized up. It was all the stranger that he wanted Mite's ring. But then, perhaps he'd forgotten all about it, she thought with a pang of hope.

"You'd better not be bringing mud in here," he said without glancing at her.

"Took off my shoes above." She stuck out a foot to show him. Her toe poked through a hole in the knitted gray sock.

"Then take a seat." He put aside the leather coat he was stitching and limped over to his small kitchen. He peered inside two mugs, then poured hot, watered-down whisky into them.

Bill brewed and distilled his whisky below deck from the bark and seed of a cedar tree. It had a pleasant odor, which put her in mind of tilled, peaty earth. But she had never gotten used to its acrid taste.

He handed her a steaming mug. "This cursed winter will never end. It gets into my bones, it does."

Elika reclined in an old rocking chair with a sigh.

Bill lowered himself across from her into his favorite chair made from driftwood. His knees cracked as he sat. He pulled a blanket over his lap and cradled the steaming mug in his bluing fingers. "So, Lil' Mit' took the bridge. Brave lad. Might be cleverer than I thought him."

It did not surprise her that he knew. "You've been following me again, Bill," she said with a pang of annoyance. She did not like being followed. Liked it even less that she did not see him. It was just the thing that got you killed in the streets.

He shrugged. "I've always followed you, princess. 'Tis the magic in you that draws me."

She leaned forward in her seat. "Are you truly seven hundred years old, or were you just gulling Mite?"

"What do you think?" he asked with a sly smile.

She considered him. She knew a liar when she saw one. "You might spin tales, but I've never known you to lie."

"Magic curses liars, and I have more than me fair share of curses."

"Then who was your father?"

"Tsarin Ilikan."

"The one who commanded the magic of ice and water?"

"Aye. Fickle and wild as the sea he was. But long before he seeded me, he was a Fisher ... of a sort. You see, he was found as a babe a thousand years ago by my great-great ... many times over great-grandfather."

Elika frowned. "Everyone on the street seems to have a great-great—many greats—grandfather who found a tsarin somewhere or other."

"But mine's a true story," he quipped back irritably. "It was my great, great, many greats-grandfather who raised him. He was a fisherman by the name of Fisher. One day he went out, threw in his nets as he always did, and brought out from the bottom of the ocean a net full of fish the like he had never seen before, golden and shimmering with eyes like jewels. And amongst the fish there was a baby boy. The old fool thought the boy was a child of the gods. Treated him better than he treated his own sons. When the fisherman died of old age, Ilikan left home and traveled to the Maysea Islands."

"To the city of Maramera," Elika said. Like all children, she had been curious about the terrifying tsaren who could command magic to do anything they wanted it to do. Even raise whole mountains then destroy them again, when the mood took them.

Bill rocked back and forth in his chair. "He *fashioned* the city of Maramera from ice and water."

Elika could not imagine a whole city built from water and ice, no matter how hard she tried. "I'm not certain it's true, Bill. If there was such a city, it's people would always be wet."

"No! No! No! That's not it at all. That's not how tsaren's magic works. It's not *wet* water, but water without being wet. It's *imagined* water, which means it can be anything a tsaren wants it to be. Do you see? No, of course, you don't. But never mind that. That's another tale. So, generations of Fishers passed after Ilikan left. My ma was the daughter of another Bill Fisher—I was named after her pa, you see—and she was a striking beauty at that. One day, Ilikan saw her on the beach from atop the wave he rode on his way to the mainland. He instantly wanted her. And tsaren took what tsaren wanted. He claimed her and seeded me in her. But he didn't want me, see? The tsaren never cared for their half-earthly children. Thought us some kind of perversion, or a corruption of natural order. As soon as he knew me inside my ma's belly, he left and never returned. Ma was heartbroken. Spent her whole life waiting for him, and whispered his name with her last breath."

That was the way with the rich and the poor, Elika thought. A tsarin, like a human king, was not likely to take a fisherman's daughter to wife, nor care for his lowly bastards.

Still, if Bill was unusual before, she thought him fascinating now. "You were truly there ... in the Sundering War? You saw Syn'Moreg sunder the world?"

His face darkened. "Lord of the Abyss sundered much more than the world, princess," he said, and his gaze was drawn to the window. In the land drenched by moonlight, the chasm was a terrible, pitch black scar.

"What happened to the people and the city on the other side?" she asked, with a chilling sense of dread.

"Syn'Moreg claimed that land for magic. What he did with the men trapped there, no one knows. We watched the other half of the city crumble to dust. Watched the mountain fade and the sea boil away until nothing but dust was left. Whilst here, men hunted and burned what was left of magic." His face twisted with regret, and his eye grew glassy. "I watched them leave … the tsaren, their mages, and what magic they could take with them. They reached the Deadlands and vanished. And our world grew silent and still, and a little empty, too. Men rejoiced. They had won the war. But I grieved." He drank deeply of his whisky. "It's a dry, empty world without magic in it. Men forgot, but I remember how much brighter the world used to be, full of vigor and color. Now, it's dull and gray, like a rotting corpse." His gaze drifted away, far into the past.

She shifted in her seat. She did not want to upset Bill. He had a way of falling silent and not speaking again, no matter that you were still there, asking him questions. He'd just stare into nowhere and say nothing.

"Why is magic in me, Bill?" she blurted out before he fell into one of those silences.

He looked up, opened his mouth to speak, then clamped it shut, as if afraid the truth might sneak out. "How about I tell you a tale of how the tsaren came to be," he said at last.

"You've told me those before, Bill. They were found as babes. I'd rather you told me about the magic hiding inside me."

"'Tis what I am trying to do, princess. Now shush and listen." He shifted and adjusted the blanket in his lap. "'Tis a story of how they came to be in their world, not ours."

From her pocket, she withdrew the carving of the bird and studied it. "The priests say the old gods formed the world and men and magic in it."

He huffed and crossed his arms. "It's because the priests don't know any better. When Arala died, Reval went mad with grief and burned down their temples, along with their libraries and the priests. No one was left to remember the old stories." He leaned forward in his seat. "The tsaren were forged from magic ... by the Great Web itself. The tsaren *are* magic in man's form."

Magic walking amongst them, disguised as men. Elika shuddered at the thought. "Then who made the Great Web?" She crossed her arms. "Might be the gods did?"

"No one made the web. It has always been there."

She thought of Moreg, the old God of Death with his spider legs. "Might there be a spider in the web?" she asked, with a pinch of humor. She liked to tease Bill on occasion, for he often teased her.

"What? No! There are no spiders in the Great Web. Now put away your cheeky smile and pay attention to what I am saying. The Great Web is made from the strings of silky essence of life, what men call Magic. And the droplets of dew on the strings are the life around you. See? Humans, trees, grass, birds, are all clinging to the web. One day, those strings of the Great Web rolled themselves into four balls. And like bubbles, they popped the tsaren into existence. Just like so. Pop!" He demonstrated with his fingers. "You see what I am saying, precious?"

She thought about it; scratched her head. "Maybe if you just came out and said what you want me to hear."

"I am trying to tell you how the tsaren came to be."

"But what has that to do with the magic hiding in me?"

Bill looked exasperated. "What I'm saying is that the web formed a tsarin before, and it can do it again. See what I'm saying?"

Elika did not, but did not want him to scold her again for not understanding. "But there is no magic left in our world, only the echoes of it. Or rather … no *dew* left?"

"Threads! Threads of magic, broken and flailing." He waved his arms to show flailing threads. "And what happens when those threads form another ball?" He cupped his hands as if he held a mouse.

She sighed. Bill rarely said anything that made simple sense. "Another tsarin?" she said, only to appease him.

He smiled, nodding vigorously. "Aye, another tsarin."

There was no sense in trying to wheedle sense from Bill, she decided and finished the last of the hot, watery whisky. She felt warm inside and out. "Bill, what are you going to do when the Blight gets here? Will you take the bridge?" she asked, yawning.

Something akin to grief touched his face. "There is no bridge for the likes of me, princess. I'd not reach the other side. Magic has abandoned me, you see, as if I was some abomination of life, as if I should never have been. And damned if I'll throw myself into that chasm. No, 'tis the Blight for me. Not a cruel death as deaths go."

"I'm sorry, Bill," she said, feeling drowsy with sleepiness.

"And what have you to be sorry for, precious?"

"For harboring the magic inside me," she whispered. "Can I sleep in your storage cupboard again, just for tonight?"

She did not want to be alone again tonight, not after having lost Mite. And she could not return to the Hide and her pack.

He looked distant and she wondered whether he had heard her, when he absently waved a hand in that direction. "Go, sleep, child. And don't fret about anything. Magic will keep you safe."

She knew better than that. Magic never kept anyone safe but itself. She put aside the empty cup and went to a small door at the end of the cabin.

The cupboard was snug and warm, even in the gray depths of winter. It was next to a small boiler, which he stoked with chips of wood and small lumps of coal just to keep his ship dry and free from rot. Bill was one of those men whom cold did not seem to touch. He never wore gloves or a scarf, and dressed the same in winter as he did in summer, in his shirt, gray knitted vest and an oiled tan-leather coat.

She lay down on top of the moth-eaten blankets, surrounded by rags Bill meant to get round to mending one day.

For a long time, she lay awake, staring into the dark, afraid to close her eyes, for behind her eyelids Mite crossed the bridge again and again. And beneath his feet, the bubbles of magic rose from the chasm and formed the angry gods. Bill was there too, sitting in his chair, waiting for the Blight as it advanced ever closer, ever faster. And inside her, she nurtured the ball of magic, which grew and churned like an invisible worm made of threads as black as death. And the snaking roots of the bridge were reaching for her, trying to grasp her and throw her into the chasm. The bridge unraveled into shreds, and Mite fell into the eternal chasm, his screams turning to wind. And in the shadow, the God of Death, an awful giant spider, was laughing, laughing … laughing like a crow.

She awoke with a start, beads of sweat on her brow, the sound of a crow's caw dying in her ears.

She thought of Mite, and her heart ached all over again. The thought of facing another day in this shrinking world without Mite made her want to burrow deeper into her blankets and sleep until the Blight reached her. She shook herself, angry with such useless musings. Mite was beyond the cares of their world. She was not. The Blight was within sight of the city and Terren had to stand against it. Mite had always told her to fight to the end. And yet, when the enemy was at their walls, he fled.

She flung the blankets aside and the chill on the air wove its way through her clothing. She gave only a passing thought to Bill's tales of the night before. In daylight, they seemed fanciful and mythical. And none were any use, besides, against the enemy approaching Terren. Mite had made his choice. It was time she made hers. Faced with the three paths toward the celestial, the ethereal, and the earthly, she would always take the path that led her back to men. And she knew what she had to do to save the city from the Blight.

Oh, Mite, if only you had waited.

Bill was still asleep in his rocking chair when she tiptoed past him. Just as she reached the door to the stairs, his voice stopped her. "I believe Mite gave you something for me, princess. I would have it."

She turned around slowly. His eyes were open, watching her. "I thought you were my friend," she said a little sulkily.

"That I am, which is why I'll take the ring." He held out his leathery hand.

"How do you know he gave it to me? Bill, have you been up on the roofs?" she asked, incredulous. Old Bill was slow to climb the stairs and grunted when he did.

His eyes twinkled with amusement. "I know 'cause I can see things about men and their hearts that you can't. No doubt he asked you to bring it to him when you crossed."

She shifted on the spot, unsettled by his uncanny perception. "Mite's gone. Why would you want his ring? Do you need coin? I can get you some."

"The ring, girl," he insisted more forcefully. "I don't need coin, just that ring."

She took it out of her hidden pocket and put it brusquely into his hand.

He wrapped his fingers around it. "Do not stare daggers at me, princess. 'Tis for your own good and the good of magic that I take it. This ring must never find its way back into Mite's hands."

"Mite is in the Deadlands," she reminded him. "Little good the ring would do him there."

"If you say so, princess," he mumbled, and his eyes slowly shut.

Elika sighed. She could not bring herself to be angry with Bill. He was strange and his mind wandered. And aside from this sudden, odd obsession with Mite's gold ring, he never bemoaned lacking anything in his life, except magic. She left him there, asleep, Mite's ring clasped in his hand.

Outside, the air was crisp. In the mudflats, a young girl was gathering crabs into her basket. Elika sat down on the deck to pull on her boots. A crow gave a loud caw overhead. Her gaze snapped up. From atop the mast, the crow with white-tipped wings was peering at her with its yellow eyes. It cocked its head and gave out a quizzing, rattling sound. Elika was certain it was the same bird that had followed her in Crow Side. She leapt to her feet and quickly climbed over the side to get away from its unnerving gaze. Might be the crow was spying on her for the old gods.

The crow gave another loud caw, as if laughing at her thoughts.

Overnight, pools of water had formed in the mudflats, which told her it must have rained again. The mud stuck to her shoes, and with each step, her feet had to fight against its pull. She waded toward the city. Its roofs and white-washed buildings were tinged with the cool pink hue of the early morning sun.

She climbed over the harbor wall onto the solid footing of Rift Street. Ahead, in the distance, the bridge was dark and menacing. She could not bear to see Mite as a lifeless phantom. So she turned away from the chasm, shoved her hands into her pocket and walked up Wharf Street, past the *Fat Fish* tavern, keeping the chasm at her back.

Soon, she was strolling through the heart of Riftside. Away from the chasm, the crooked, empty buildings gave way to well-kept cottages with small gardens backing onto narrow alleyways. Here and there, drunks slept against garden walls and gates. She spied Eyeless Joe amongst them, his gray beard stained with ale and crumbs of bread. His blanket had fallen off again and as she passed, she stooped to cover him. Many a drunk had slipped into an endless slumber on a cold winter's night. Joe might be a drunk, but he never said a bad word to anyone, never begged, and never complained of the vagaries of fate that gave him eye-rot sickness.

His hand shot out and grabbed the hem of her cloak. "El, is that you?"

She crouched beside him. "Aye. Thought you were sleeping." It was hard to tell, for the lids of his hollow sockets were sewn shut.

He sat up with the help of her arm. "Been hoping you pass this way." His breath reeked of gin. "They're saying there's a mage on the run."

"I wouldn't be believing everything they say, Joe."

"Garlic, will keep you safe," he said drunkenly. "Find some garlic and wear it. Keeps magic away, it does. My Nan told me that when I was a wee lad. And she learned it from her Nan. Magic hates the smell of garlic." He patted her hand and lay down again.

"As you say, Joe," she replied and rose to her feet.

As she strolled, she was struck by scents of spring drifting from the gardens: the sappy scent of leafy growth, the delicate sweetness of apple trees in bloom, the budding snowbells growing from between the stones. The air was warm, and the intoxicating fragrance of fresh life filled her head. She loved spring above all other seasons. It put her in mind of survival. She had survived another winter. All in their pack had, this year. And soon, fresh food would fill the empty market stalls—apples and strawberries, potatoes and corn. Pies would be bursting with flavor. Jars of jam would once again fill the shelves of tea shops in Market Square. Penny, too, would make jam from the foraged fruits and berries the orphans brought home.

Potter Ned called out a greeting from his garden. Elika waved back in reply. He was sowing vegetables in orderly rows. In the summer she helped him weed his patch for a bowl of his wife's hearty vegetable stew. He allowed her to keep the weeds, too, which she took back to the Hide.

Penny used the good ones in her stews. The rest, Red-faced Roby used in his tonics. He had been the son of a herb-witch and could turn any weed into a healing tonic. He sold those on the street and earned a fair penny for their pack.

Over the garden wall, she heard One-thumb Will and his brother arguing again over where they should plant the tomatoes this year.

"The rot will get them again if you plant them in that corner," Will was saying. "We dig next to Ned's wall. What say you, Ned?" he called over the low stone wall.

Potter Ned put down his shovel and looked over the side, rubbing his chin. "If you've gotten rot over there, likely its everywhere. Ain't that so, El?"

Elika wandered over to them. Aside from helping Ned weed, she knew nothing of growing things. But she often heard things about rot. "It's what they say. Why not plant in both patches?"

One-thumb Will threw his hands in the air. "And get half a crop?"

"Better than none," his brother cut in. "It's what I've been trying to tell him."

"Mary Lidle at the end of the street says blood-salt kills the rot dead out," Elika said. "Says it shows that rot is caused by the echoes of magic hiding in the soil."

Ned shook his head. "Mary has a funny way of thinking. Just plain old salt will kill rot, but you need to do it one year for the planting the next year, so the rains have time to wash the salt out."

Will turned on his brother. "'Tis what I told you to do last year."

And so they continued to argue, with Ned joining the debate. None of them noticed when she left.

Across the alley, seamstress Tayna was in her herb garden, glancing at Will from the corner of her eye whenever she thought he was not looking. All the while, he watched Tayna whenever her back was turned, blushing if she caught him staring.

Elika knew every face, every story in Riftside. Mary Lidle's dog barked as Elika passed her cottage. Toothless Jake, sleeping beside Mary's gate, grumbled incoherently, rolled over and covered his head with his coat. Lusty Lucy hung her washing on the line outside. Whenever Elika walked by, she could not help but stare at the strange and frivolous underclothes of lace and netting hanging on the wash line.

Lucy caught her staring and winked. "Let me know when you're ready for your beard to grow, El. One night with me, and you'll have the stubble the next morning."

Elika's face grew hot. "You are a terrible tease, Luce. Besides, I've not enough coin for you."

Lucy laughed. "Might be I'll give you a special price."

"I'll think about it," Elika lied and turned the corner.

Aye, the streets were cruel and hard and grimy, but Terren was all they had. This was her home, and these folk her people. Mite had given up on them. She never would.

Her step grew more certain as the decision she should have made the instant she discovered the magic hiding inside her, firmed in her mind.

She joined Market Street with its many eateries. The baker had opened his doors, and a warm aroma of fresh bread drifted toward her. She had no coin left, and her stomach rumbled with hunger. Her possessions were still hidden in the roof space above the clerk's home. She'd go back for them after she had faced her sole task that day— purge herself of magic.

Everyone was looking for the mage, but she need not reveal herself. She would cleanse herself, then she would go back to Bad Penny and her pack. And might be by nightfall, she'd be sleeping again in the Hide. She would save Terren. And perhaps the Blight would retreat and men would reclaim the lost lands. Aye, she would save them. There was no going back from it now.

Market Street joined the wide, straight City Gate Parade, which led past the barricades to the Silver Circle and toward Temple Square. Blue Guards grabbed everyone they could at checkpoints and tested them with blood-salt. Along the road, prison wagons were filling up with the infected.

She took in the scene. Something was wrong. Things were changing. She felt it in the air. She blended with the others on the street, strolling with calm purpose, trying to appear unafraid by peering into shop windows.

As she approached one of the prison wagons, she heard the guard tell the driver. "Take this one to the temple. The rest are for the bridge. Captain's orders."

The driver nodded and spurred the horses into motion. The wagon destined for the temple was filled with gentrified folk. The others, headed for the bridge, were crammed with the sick, the old and the beggarly. It seemed that Captain Daiger had once again taken it upon himself to rid the city of some pestilence or other.

Upon learning this, Elika left the City Gate Parade and followed a more meandering route to the Temple of Mercy. Even in the alleyways she knew well, the sense of pervading tension and distrust thickened the air. The folk regarded each other closely, watching for the proof that they were not tainted with magic. She hunched her shoulders and kept walking without meeting any eye, keenly aware that she was not wearing a blood-salt crystal.

As she drew closer to the temple, the streets grew busier. Cutpurses and dippers were out in force. She ducked between bodies, nimbly evading the city guards milling about on the streets. Amidst the crowds, she spied the watchers, dressed in fine clothes of the gentry, but with the look of ruffians. Peter Pockets' gang, out in force, intent and alert as they studied the crowds. If Blue-eye Billy had not warned her they were looking for her, she might have walked straight into their net without realizing. As it was, the temple was two streets away, and they hovered on every corner and patrolled the rooftops overhead.

Beside the door to *Bessy's Pies*, she spied One-eyed Rory. A young lad stood next to him, wearing a fancy, red-velvet suit, his hands shoved into his pockets, his shoulders slumped. His head was bandaged, else she would have recognized him more quickly. Pit the Picker. He was looking grim, frightened. Blood seeped through the bandages where his right ear should have been. *Oh, Pit, you fool. You knew the punishment for treachery.*

Pit's gaze roamed the street, but he appeared to see little. She must have stared too long, for his eyes met hers. His jaw dropped, closed, dropped again. He looked like he might raise the alarm, but then his gaze slid to the ground, his shoulders slumping even more. He gave her but a moment, nothing more. If Pit saw her, Rory's keen, seeking eye would soon find her, too.

There was no way to sneak past them to the temple. She turned into the nearest alley and strode away, keeping her pace steady and light. Here too, from up high, Pockets' men were scanning the streets.

She should not have looked up. No one in the streets looked up. Someone pointed in her direction, yelling out to the watchers on the street. She ducked into another alley and ran.

Like a pack of dogs, they gave chase; up above on the roofs, down in the streets behind her. Two stepped out across her path. She swerved into bustling Baker's Way, nimbly slipping between milling folk. The chasers ploughed into the crowd, colliding with everyone in their path. She glanced back to see them falling behind, but the roof runners were hard on her heels.

There was only one place to hide from them. But first, she had to make them lose sight of her, if only for a moment. She ran into the first tavern she came to. There were at least three ways out of any tavern, one at the front, one at the back, and one through the tavern keeper's home at the top. She raced up the stairs, and finding the door unlocked into the tavern keeper's abode, ran through it and jumped out the window into the alley below. She climbed through another window into a house across the road. A woman with a babe in arms spun about in shock. She was about to scream, but Elika sprinted past her through the door, bounded down another set of steps, and out through the back door into the tiny courtyard. She swept her gaze across the roofs. No one was there.

She leapt over the low garden wall and ran into the narrow alley she had been looking for. Under the cover of an arched passage, she caught her breath and carefully picked the lock to a low door which led to the back of *Ruby's* whorehouse. She slipped in and closed the door quietly behind her.

In the morning, the whorehouses were silent, stale places. She could hear faint voices of the women and their movements through the ceiling overhead. She paid them no mind, tuning instead to go down the dingy, worn stairs into the cellar. This was one of many ways sisters Ell and Mill used to get into the sewers. The cellar was dank and rainwater seeped into it from the streets above, pooling on the floor and flowing out in a gentle stream through a hole in the wall. Only a sliver of light came through a narrow air grate overhead. The cellar was empty, with only a few broken barrels and rusted ironwork in the corner.

She searched for a drainage hole in the muddy wall. There was always one, seeing as autumn brought endless rains, and cellars around the city would often flood. She found the stone-lined opening behind one of the barrels and squeezed through it. It was barely large enough for her slim shoulders to pass. The hole led straight into the cavernous sewer. She fell into foul-smelling mud and water, using her hands to break the fall.

It was pitch dark, the type of dark you only ever found in sleep and death. The dark of dreamless slumber and of memories lost. It crushed your chest just to look at it. That eternal dark of the bottomless chasm and endless screams within it. She closed her eyes, for she could not bear to look at it. Her breath grew heavy.

She shook herself. She had been here before with Mite. He had carried a lantern. There was nothing here but arching stone walls and a stream of water and sewage beneath her feet. Not even rats. They had been hunted to the edge of existence by the swineherds as food for their pigs. But all sewers ran to the edge of the chasm, and if she was not careful, she might just step into that abyss. Her hand flew outwards, groping in the darkness until her fingers found the stone wall: cool, slimy and solid.

If she ran her left hand along the sewer wall, carefully placing each foot with each step, she would come to another turning. And near that intersection, there were stairs up to the city. Pockets did not have enough men to watch every street. No doubt they would be combing the last place they saw her, thinking she was hiding somewhere nearby.

She began to walk, keeping her eyes closed, for the darkness behind her eyelids was not as oppressive and terrible as the darkness beyond. The sound of flowing water steadied her. Even the stench of the sewer was a welcome reassurance. Ell and Mill had been to the edge of the sewers, had looked into the chasm ...

Do not think of the chasm, she told herself sternly—of the men and women and children, dead and alive, all falling and falling and falling. Her breath quickened. She tried to empty her mind, but the tales of wicked magic burrowed their way into her. Magic lurked in dark places. Long ago, men feared to go out at night, feared to ride alone through the magic-infested forests. Many a time the ground had swallowed an innocent traveler on the dark road ...

A frightening thought struck her. She was not alone in the sewer, after all. Magic was with her. What if it sent her astray, tricked her into going the wrong way? Her feet shook beneath her. She halted and caught her breath. Would it do that? Could it make her walk off the edge into the rift?

She took another careful step, probing the wet ground beneath her foot before she placed it, as her hand probed the wall ahead. How many steps had she taken? It seemed an eternity had passed since she had begun to walk. It didn't matter, she told herself to calm her ragged nerves; if she kept her hand on the wall, she'd find her way back.

She heard a sudden scurrying sound near her feet that sent chills through her. A rat. It must be a rat. She remembered the tendrils of magic that attacked Mite. Were they out there now, causing some mischief ahead, for her to walk into? She stopped and listened, barely breathing. The scurrying sound was farther away. Then, nothing, but the sound of trickling water. She moved on.

The wall ended abruptly under her fingertips. She came to a halt, imagining the chasm at her feet. There was no wind. Surely there'd be wind if she was facing the chasm … but magic was deceptive, treacherous.

She stood there breathing, trying to gather her scattered, frantic thoughts. This was the intersection. It had to be. She had to cross to the other side of the tunnel. From there, she had to run her right hand along the wall to reach the stairs out of this wretched place.

She released her hold on the solid, stone wall, and the world fell away. It was just her and magic, inside the endless chasm, falling and falling. Her chest constricted, and she wanted to scream and curl up and call for Mite to come and save her. But he was gone. Mite was gone. A sob escaped her, and echoed.

She put out her hands probing the air for the wall which should be there, nearby. She took a careful, probing step forward. At her fingertips, there was nothing but darkness so thick she could feel it. She wobbled, her balance precarious, though her feet were on solid ground. She took another step forward and her foot sank deep into the mud and flowing water. She fell forward, her hands and knees sinking into foulness she did not want to name, but which her nose could not deny. Panic built in her chest, choked her, numbed her. All thoughts left her. She began to crawl through the slushy grime, faster and faster, as if Moreg himself chased her …

Her head hit a brick wall, light exploded in her eyes and her hands crumbled beneath her. She lay there, her head spinning and spinning, and falling through the endless darkness. The type of darkness that never released you. It crushed her chest until she could not breathe …

She must have lost consciousness, for awareness crept up on her from somewhere else. There was damp ground beneath her cheek, her body was sprawled on the ground, water flowed over her legs. She opened her eyes and for a moment thought she was blind. Then she remembered where she was.

She pushed herself up from the ground and holding on to the wall, came to her feet. Something wet trickled down her face. She touched the cut on her forehead. It throbbed fiercely. It took her another moment to remember to keep her right hand on the wall. She took an uncertain step forward, then another, probing her way along the wall until it ended beneath her hand. She looked up and there, high above she saw a glimmer of light falling on a stone step.

She ran and staggered up the steps, toward the sliver of sunlight. She had just enough sense to stop herself from bursting through the metal door out of this cavern to snatch a breath of fresh air. It might have been the clash of swords outside that brought her to her senses.

She took a deep, steadying breath. Peter Pockets was hunting her. Captain Daiger had now gotten it into his head to send every infected pauper across the bridge rather than the temple. The guards outside would just as likely stick her with a sword than ask questions. She took another calming breath and peered through the crack in the metal door. The training ground of the barracks was filled with city guards at their daily practice drills.

One night, Mite had brought her here, to show her the way into the Blue Guards' lair and more importantly, a way out. "If you were caught and they brought you here," he had said, glancing at her in a strange, discomfited way.

"I can climb to the high-way," she had pointed out.

"And what if you couldn't?" he'd snapped. "Anything might happen. Head for this door and the sewers."

She had thought he was acting peculiar at the time but paid it little mind. Mite had his reasons for doing what he did. But since he had told her about Penny's abduction, she wondered whether this was where the bastards had kept her.

Years ago, not long after they threw Lick over the side into the chasm, the old barracks had burned down. Since then, a new stone building had been erected in its place. She studied it through the crack in the door and marked her path up the drainpipes to the rooftiles. Then, she fell back against the wall and settled in for the long wait.

It was deep into the slumber hours of the night when she finally left the sewers. She crept out into the guards' training yard, and keeping close to the outer wall, tiptoed to the back of the garrison. From there, it was easy to climb up the gutter pipe to the low roof of the armory, up to the garrison and from there across to the Silver Circle.

The moon was out, and her way was clear. She raced to her hideout in the attic above the clerk's home. There, she grabbed her spare shirt and trousers, which had long since dried beside the chimney, and crawled to the hatch.

She peered into the sleeping house. Silence.

Carefully, quietly, she lowered the stairs and climbed down. She crept through the house, placing each foot soundlessly in front of the other, until she came to the kitchen. Only the faint glow of the dying fire in the adjoining room gave any light.

She took off her filthy clothes and washed quickly, then donned the new ones. As she gathered the pile of soiled clothing, a door opened and the clerk came in, carrying an oil lamp. He wore a night robe and his hair was tousled.

She froze.

He did not appear surprised to see her. "You have left quite a stink through my house. It woke me up."

"I'm sorry ... I'll clean it ... I ..."

He turned away and strode into the parlor, taking the lamp with him. She heard him pour a drink into his glass and sit back in his armchair.

Elika returned to the attic, dropped off her filthy clothes, then went back to the clerk's house to clean the footprints she had left behind. After she poured away the dirty water, she peered into the parlor. He was sitting in front of an enlivened fire, a book in one hand and a glass of amber port in the other.

"Grab a drink and take a seat." He waved his glass at the bar without turning around.

She ignored the side table with bottles on it and perched on the edge of the seat.

He was wearing a pair of round spectacles over his beaked nose. He lifted the book to show her. "*Sonnets of Mage Wildfire*. There is no finer minstrel. I don't suppose you know him."

Elika shook her head.

He returned his gaze to the page he was reading and began to recite,

> *"Shed not your tears as the spring rain,*
> *Vent not your anger on the winds,*
> *Still all the waves of glory past,*
> *Sleep, magic boy, and dream no more.*
>
> *Let not your woes call fire's breath,*
> *Nor vengeance put into the rock,*
> *Spare all and hide your folly's heart*
> *Sleep, magic girl, and dream no more."*

He raised his eyes to her. "Have you ever wondered whether men got their ideas about magic all wrong?"

She shook her head again. "Bad Penny says that men are not what they say but what they do. Wicked men have smooth tongues, just as good men have crude ones."

He smiled. "Bad Penny? The fabled gang leader in Riftside, who is whispered to have cut the throats of twenty Blue Guards in their sleep, before setting the whole bar-racks on fire. Have they not hanged her yet?"

"They have to catch her first," Elika said darkly. She might not be part of the pack anymore, but she was still loyal to Penny and always would be. She had heard those rumors, but had given them no credence, for she could never imagine Penny cutting the throats of sleeping men. Now, she could not help but wonder.

He shrugged. His gaze fixed on the cut on her forehead. "Want to tell me who's been chasing you and why?"

"No," she replied stiffly.

He adjusted his spectacles and turned back to his book,

"Fair blow the winds as magic roams the lands it wove in ages past,
Through man's domain, it flies unhindered …"

"I need clothes," Elika interrupted.

He looked at her over his spectacles. "I don't think my clothes will fit you. I have nothing for boys …"

"Can I borrow a … dress? One of your wife's maybe. Something old, nothing shining or expensive … maybe a servant's skirt …?" The rabble of words faded away on her tongue.

"Dress." He continued to look at her, quizzically this time. "I see. That's how it is, is it?" His eyes flicked up and down over her. "They won't fit. You are too short and too skinny. But if you are handy with a needle …"

"I am. Somewhat," she lied. She was handier with a knife than a needle. Though Penny had taught her how to mend her clothes and stitch a new hem.

He waved with his glass toward the door. "Then take what you want. I burned most of what my darling wife left behind. But there is a trunk with a few dresses in the nursery cupboard. I assume you know where that is? Shred them, defile them if you have to, and drag them through the sewers if it pleases you." He drank deeply and returned to reciting out of his book.

Elika left him there and went up to the nursery. Moonlight cast unfriendly shadows on the wall and the crib was cold and desolate. She crossed the room straight to the cupboard, opened the trunk inside it, and breathed out in frustration. These dresses were utterly unsuitable. They were expensive, richly decorated and very much what the well-to-do gentry would wear. She'd look absurd in such fine things. Peter Pockets' men would spot her from three streets away.

She rummaged through the trunk and pulled out the plainest frock. If she removed the fancy sleeves, the stitched-on flowers, the silver lace, she'd have something that an impoverished lady's maid might wear. There was only one bonnet in the trunk, and it did not match the dress. She took that too.

It did not take her long to find a needle and thread. She had looted many a home and knew folk tended to keep their things in the same place as each other. There was a pattern of sorts they all followed. She lit a lamp, sat at the top of the stairs with it and began slicing off all the frills with her knife. The clerk's wife must have been a tall

woman, and Elika had to cut the hem before turning it up.
She had no patience for such things, and despite Penny's
patient teachings, her stitching was dreadful.

At some late hour of the night, she could no longer hear
the clerk's poetic voice. Nor did she hear him climb the
stairs to bed. He must have fallen asleep in his chair.

It was dawn by the time she finished the dress. By then,
her eyes and fingers were raw, and she could not stop
herself from yawning. She examined the dress. It was as far
from being a lady's dress as she was from being a lady. The
few false patches she added to it gave the appearance of a
looted item. She was pleased with the result. Pockets' thugs
would not recognize her. Or so she hoped. As Pit had told
them she might be a girl, they might just look doubly hard.
Still, there was no other way for her to get into the temple
for the purging.

And once she was free of magic, Peter Pockets would
want nothing more from her.

CHAPTER SEVEN

The Temple of Mercy

"What we call the ethereal sphere of life is the realm called Alafraysia. It is impossible for us to conceive or understand it, for it bears no likeness to our earthly realm. During his drunken reminiscences, Tsarin Draygan described it as a world without a true sense of up and down, a world of sky and floating mountains, of water and fire, strange animals and plants, all moving and changing, guided not by physical laws, but the mood of their creators, the tsaren. The tsaren are the guardians of Alafraysia, who imagine all the physical manifestations of their realm into existence. These manifestations are as real as a dream you find yourself in. The tsaren are the shapers of their world. The concept is bewildering to our human minds, bound by the solid chains of the possible, the true and real. Alafraysia's inhabitants, the Laifae—the beings we collectively call Magic for we have no other way to comprehend them—live free and unbound and bow only to the tsaren who they revere as their world-shapers and guardians. The Laifae are both one being and many. They merge and break apart. They have no defined form or even clear substance, as we understand it. Their sentience is ever changing and fleeting, like their world. What must they think of our unshakable one?"

History of Men, Gods and Magic,
By Priest Oderrin

The salt collectors' carts made their daily rounds through the city, picking up bags of salt left on doorsteps. The king's Red Guard on horses guarded the carts. Growing fear permeated the streets. Men were saying there was not enough salt to cure everyone or to stop the Blight. Some said salt was now more expensive than gold. And where did they get enough blood, save from the men themselves? There were whispers on the street that Rimley's gang were selling barrels of blood to the priests, with no one asking which animals it came from. Elika thought it best not to wonder.

The Blight had slowed since it had been sighted, and men took it to mean the purges were working. Others praised Captain Daiger's resolve to send half the Echoes straight across the bridge. And good riddance too, they said, as the food carts grew bare on every street. Elika had walked past two bakeries, which were dark and empty, with the baker nowhere in sight. Impatient crowds were forming around eateries and food stalls. The sight of them made her uneasy. How much food was left and what would they do when it ran out?

Elika adjusted her bonnet and once again reminded herself that she was a young woman and not a street orphan. She pushed back her shoulders, softened her facial expression, and schooled her features to look both pleasant and prim at once. The dress sat awkwardly on her. It was loose around her chest and waist, and the hem dragged in the mud. She had hung a string around her neck and used a woolen shawl to hide the absence of the blood-salt pendant. So far, no one had tried to accost her.

There was a trick to hiding in plain sight and it required you to be plain and in sight. Show no fear and they would not see you as prey. So, she took the bustling City Gate

Parade to the temple, strolling with unhurried purpose, keeping her gait light, not looking up, not glancing around.

From the corner of her eye, she noted Pockets' watchers on street corners and roofs. She stopped to gaze through the window of a milliner's shop whilst playing with the strands of her bonnet before continuing on her way past one of Pockets' roughs.

This one was dressed in a dark silk shirt and a green velvet vest. If not for the sly, watchful glint in his eyes, she might have mistaken him for a fat pouch from the Silver Circle. He noted her, too, in that brief, measuring way men noted all women, before his gaze drifted aside, back to the street.

As she drew closer to the temple, she joined the increasing throng of people heading in the same direction.

She spied Rory at a distance and quickly lowered her head to hide her face. He was the only one in Peter Pockets' gang who might recognize her, despite her disguise. He might have only one eye, but it was sharp and quick. Pit with his bandaged head was once again standing beside him, miserable and broody. She was certain they would see her.

Behind her, she heard shouts to clear the street, followed by the rumble of carriage wheels, and the slow clip-clop of a horse's hooves. Elika stepped aside and quickened her pace as it rode past, keeping the carriage between her and Rory.

She stared ahead but from the corner of her eye, she noted the occupant of the carriage—an ancient, white-haired, old woman, wearing the white robe of a priestess. Something about the woman felt oddly familiar, unsettlingly so. A frightening memory tickled at the edges of her mind, one she could not grasp. She could not explain the sense of recognition, for she was certain she had never seen the woman before.

She glanced sideways, to look closer, and found that the old woman was staring back at her with shock and surprise. Then she banged her cane on the roof of the carriage. "Stop the carriage! I said stop, you big oaf of a fool."

The driver pulled sharply on the reigns. The horse, startled by the abruptness, reared and neighed. Men rushed forward to calm it.

It was all Elika could do not to run. She kept walking, as if she had not noticed, lengthening her stride. Behind her, she heard the old woman berate the driver for being too slow. Then the carriage wheels rolled again.

Elika quickened her pace, yanked off her bonnet, lest the woman recognize her by it, and merged into the masses in the Temple Square.

As she did, all thought flew out of her mind. Ahead, dense crowds had gathered on the temple steps. Young and old, rich and poor, pushed and shoved their way toward the giant doors whilst the guards hauled those who did not come willingly.

So many ... she thought in alarm. Just as Mite had told her. Could they purge so many before the Blight reached the city? She suddenly felt very small and foolish. Did she think that by purging herself she would save them all when there were still so many echoes of magic left in their world?

"I've been purged already, I tell you," a scraggy man cried as the guards dragged him to the temple. "Please, not again, not again," he pleaded piteously.

"Stop your squealing. 'Tis the temple or the bridge," the guard grumbled in reply.

Elika froze in trepidation. It was said nothing was more painful than the purging, for magic was a cruel foe that clung to your soul. It was how Bitey had described it to Bad Penny once—like ripping your soul out of you. *And what if it does not release its hold on you?* a voice whispered in Elika's head.

She would do whatever it took to be rid of magic, she reminded herself firmly. Mite was wrong to despair. Men had defeated magic before and they could do it again.

But did they? It is still here, is it not, hiding inside you?

Firm, bony fingers wound around her arm. Her heart jolted. "No, princess. 'Tis not the place for you," Bill Fisher whispered into her ear. "Not in there. What friend would I be if I allowed you to go there?"

She gathered her wits and snatched back her arm. "I must."

"Listen to me, girl. 'Tis no good, I tell you. Long ago the web was broken. Only its strands now flail in the winds of the Abyss. And the wind pushes those strands like so." He wiggled his fingers and hands. "You see what I'm saying? No, of course, you don't. Suffice to say, all your purgings are a waste of time. Magic's got nowhere to go. It will leave of its own accord, or not. But these fools are determined to burn it all down. You see, they're caught in the fishnet, but as they've gotten rid of the fishermen, there's no one looking after the net. The fish think they're clever and burn holes in the fishnet to get out. But the net is what keeps them all living and breathing. So now the fish are falling through it and dying in the barren sand."

Elika sighed and placed her hand on his arm. "Your mind's wandering again, Bill. There are no more fish left in the sea to catch ... because there's no more sea left. See?" She breathed out. "No, of course, you don't."

But his eyes were sharp and shrewd. "If you say so, princess. Heed my warning nevertheless and stay away from the priestesses, no matter what they make you believe. They don't understand magic half as much as they think. Got it all upside down, you see? Now come away with me, or the damned witch I married will never forgive me. Saw her not a moment ago." He grabbed her arm and began to drag her away, his bony fingers biting into her flesh.

She tried to yank herself away, but his grip was iron. "You told me your wife was dead."

He continued to drag her away from the temple. "I told you she left *me* for dead, after beating me over the head with a frying pan and calling all manner of curses upon my head. Some of which might have stuck. Damn her icy heart." His face softened with the recollection and he sighed wistfully.

Elika dug in her heels, then stomped on Bill's foot. That surprised and unbalanced him, and she used the moment of his weakened grip to yank her arm from him. "I'm going. Don't try to stop me."

"'Tis for your own good I do this." He tried to grab her again.

She jumped back, out of his reach. Chilly prickles of awareness ran over her skin. She looked aside and met One-eyed Rory's gaze, hard and intent on her. He pushed away from the wall.

Without thinking, she dashed into the crowd and was engulfed by the masses. Behind her, Bill cursed something foul, and then she heard him no more.

The river of bodies carried her along, hustling and jostling toward the temple doors. She snatched a glance over her shoulder. Rory was pushing his way toward her. She ducked in front of a towering, fur-clad Drasdane. The crowds grew tighter and tighter, shuffling and bumping. She pushed her way through the throng, then stood on tiptoes to peer over another man's shoulder. The doors to the temple were close.

Behind her, Rory shoved a woman with a child in her arms out of his way to the outrage of the onlookers. When he tried to do the same to the Drasdane twice his size, the fur-clad brute shoved him back. "Mind your manners and wait your bloody turn, you greedy bastard."

Rory threw a punch. The giant Drasdane staggered back. Another man came at Rory. Elika turned and squeezed her way to the front of the jostling crowd.

At the temple doors, the priestess wearing a wreath of leaves on her head and a strained smile on her face urged everyone to keep back. As they waited, one by one green-robed priestesses hurried forward to take charge of the next Echo.

Behind her, Elika heard the shouts and whistles of the guards. Many turned to look at the commotion, and she took advantage of their distraction to slip in front of a young woman, right into the path of a round-faced priestess. The priestess could not have been older than her.

"Oh! Eager, are you?" the priestess said chirpily. "Well, look at you, all dirty and frightened. Come, don't be afraid. We'll cure you of this vile infestation in no time." She led the way into the enormous temple.

With a flood of relief, Elika followed. She glanced back only once to see the temple guards breaking up the fight in the crowd and Rory slinking away.

"Will it hurt?" Elika asked distractedly.

"Only a little," the priestess lied. "You look like an orphan. I can tell. I was one, too, after my ma and pa took the bridge. They came from Willowpond. Have you heard of it? It lay on the edges of Bellen River in the Serafae Plains." Elika had not, but the young priestess did not wait for a reply. "They fled the Blight, but lost everything, except the clothes on their backs and two goats. Thieves robbed them of those, too. So, they decided the bridge was for them. They wanted me to go with them, but I heard children rarely made it across. I think they simply wanted an easy end for me," she added in confidence. "Pa tried to drag me, but I ran away."

Elika was only half listening. It was an altogether familiar tale. Her attention was fixed on the giant statue in the heart of the vast hall, of a beautiful woman with flowers braided into her hair. Elika's jaw dropped. Only magic could have fashioned such a statue of marble and gold flowing seamlessly over each other. It rose to the roof and appeared so lifelike, it might have been a goddess standing before them.

The round-faced priestess chuckled. "That's Arala. She was beautiful, was she not?"

She was breathtaking, thought Elika.

"Everyone stares when they see her for the first time," the priestess said. "Tsarin Draygan built that statue using the magic of stone and earth. It was a courting gift to Arala. All the tsaren courted her, but she fell in love with Reval. Your eyes are like hers, a little exotic, large and upturned, like the Sachi's. Except yours are too pale." She leaned in to peer more closely. "And strange, too. Icy green, like frost-colored leaves. You have the Sachi's hair too, black, like midnight. Very rarely do Sachi come to us. They say the old gods protect them ..."

And so she talked, cheerful and bright, whilst Elika followed wordlessly, trying not to pay attention to the fear that stalked the edges of her mind. She took care to study her surroundings. Mite had taught her to check for escape routes and boltholes wherever she went.

Behind the enormous statue, wide stairs rose to the upper balcony encircling the hall, and higher still to the upper levels of the temple. There were many doors, each guarded by stony-faced temple guards, with pikes in hand and swords on their belts. She did not like her chances of dashing past them. Then again, if she did, Pockets' men would be waiting.

Hundreds of people filled the great hall. Young acolytes ran underfoot, carrying towels and buckets of water and mops. Some scrubbed blood from the floor on their knees. Echoes sat on stools and benches, waiting. The priestesses fetched each a cup filled to the brim with blood and salt from the large silver jug by Arala's marble feet. All too quickly the jug was emptied, and two priestesses carried it away. Another was hurriedly brought out to replace it.

"You should have come to us when your parents left you," the round-faced priestess was saying beside her. "We take many orphaned girls, as long as they are humble and hardworking. Arala was kind and gentle and so we strive to be in her image." The priestess led her to a spare stool. "Sit there, and I will bring you the purgative. And there is no need to be frightened. No one has died from it yet. It may hurt a little, but you'll be cured in no time. You'll see." She gave Elika a bright smile and walked away, toward the jug by the statue's feet, her green robes swaying cheerfully against the stone.

Whilst Elika waited, she watched others take a drink and sick fear grew in her stomach. Some shut their eyes and downed their blood-salt concoction. Others regarded the cup with dread, sipping it, then shaking their heads in refusal as their priestesses urged them on. She saw a young, brawny man scream as if he was being cut open, clutch his stomach and writhe on the ground. Another one panted and groaned through gritted teeth. Even now, her body recoiled with the memory of the sudden crippling pain when she had stepped onto the blood-salt by the bridge.

She took a steadying breath, taking her courage from the others around her. She could bear it. If only to purge the magic from her body. It was likely she'd be out again before nightfall, cleansed and free. Perhaps tonight, she would sleep once again in the Hide, surrounded by her pack.

Across the hall, a woman screamed and screamed and screamed for what seemed like an eternity, before falling abruptly silent. Elika grew hot. She wiped her sticky hands on her dress. Just a little pain and she would be free of magic …

"There you are." The priestess returned, carrying a wooden cup. "Just one drink and you will be cured." She placed the cup in Elika's hands.

She blinked at it. It was as large as a mug of ale. "Must I drink it all?"

"Anything less will not work. Go ahead, drink. And afterwards, if you wish, you can stay here and join the acolytes. With so many coming through our doors …"

The priestess' voice retreated into the surrounding hum. In her hands the warm cup filled with blood and salt grew large and menacing. The blood steamed faintly in the cold air of the great hall, and the foul smell burned her nose and throat as if it was fire itself. Her stomach flipped sickeningly, and she wanted to gag. And deep inside her, she felt something recoil in fear and curl up tight. She was certain it was her courage.

Her hands trembled. *Drink it and you will be free. You can stop the Blight.* One drink and she would destroy the magic inside her.

Mite chose the bridge. But surely this was better than the Deadlands. What was there but death and emptiness in the lands ruled by magic? He stood there now, neither living nor dead, eternally cursed to wander those endless plains as a phantom. That would not be her fate. The pain of the purge was preferable.

"Go ahead, drink." The priestess put her hands over Elika's and gently urged her to raise the cup to her lips. "It will be easier if you drink it all at once."

Elika looked around and saw men, women and children rise to their feet, pale and shaky, but alive, and cleansed of their vile affliction. Unsteady, dazed, but walking. The priestesses hung blood-stone pendants around their necks and smiling with approval, guided them out of the temple. Just one drink was all it took. She could do it, too. She thought of Mite and Penny, and her pack—Rosy Rose, Lazy Eye, Silky Song, Rusty Pipe, Clever Kit, Ell and Mill and others. They were her family. For them, she could do it. For Terren, for the folk she passed on the street.

The cup touched her lips. She took a deep breath and drank every vile drop as quickly as she could before she gagged. The blood was warm and foul, and she dared not ponder what animal it came from. It was sickeningly salty, and right at the end, there was more salt at the bottom of the cup. She drank every sticky drop, swallowed every grain, and stared at the empty cup in her hands …

It hit her immediately. Her throat constricted. The agony was unlike anything she had ever felt before. Light exploded in her eyes, fire spread through her body. Everything, her skin, her gut, her head hurt as if afire, and as if a thousand daggers stabbed her at once. A piercing scream filled her ears. She fell to her knees, clutching her belly. And through the white, blinding pain, she saw Mite's hand stretched out to her, asking her to go with him. She should have taken the bridge, should have thrown herself into the chasm, should have died instead, for nothing was worth this. Nothing. Her body shook, and with violent heaves, she threw up the blood and the salt until there was nothing left in her stomach.

Slowly, the pain retreated. She lay curled up on the floor, exhausted. Above her stood the young priestess, covered in blood which Elika had retched. Her round face was stony, her mouth tight and disapproving.

An older priestess appeared by her side. "The magic is strong in this one. It is fighting back. Take her to the dormitory, Grisla. She will need multiple purges to cleanse her."

Elika could not move, could only shake her head. "No ..." she managed to utter. *The bridge* ... she would rather face the bridge. But the thought could not voice itself. Rough hands gripped and lifted her and placed her on a hessian stretcher. She was covered with a blanket and brusquely carried away, deeper into the temple. She reached out to take Mite's outstretched hand, but it faded away and she grasped only air.

CHAPTER EIGHT

The Purge

"Where there were two worlds, now there are one. Some scholars claim the ethereal realm was destroyed in the collision with our own, and thus Seramight belongs to men alone and magic is the invader. The tsaren insist they still live in their realm of Alafraysia, which overlaps now with Seramight. Their proof was that they could dream new rivers into existence and change their flow at will. They dreamt the sand that buried a human city which sought to defy Magic's claim to their united realms. They raised and destroyed mountains … but only those they dreamt into existence. They had no power over the earthly rivers, seas or mountains. Their powers were contained within their own realm. Those they imagined into our world had fleeting existence and quickly faded. The drain on their strength was extreme and required long years of recuperation. The damage they caused, however, was real, and felt by men long after."

History of Men, Gods and Magic,
By Priest Oderrin

There were six of them, to whose souls echoes of magic clung like a parasite.

They followed the high priestess through the cold, stone corridors in a solemn line, each with a guiding priestess by their side. They marched silently, pretending to ignore the temple guards at every door, pretending to ignore the fact that they were prisoners. No one said so. No one spoke of it. But there were only two ways for them to leave the temple—purged of magic and free, or in the back of the prison wagon headed for the bridge. And this day was the third and final day of Elika's trials. If she could not find the strength to expel the magic from within her today, she would face the bridge come nightfall.

For two days, she had tried. Days of relentless purges and torment. She limped as she walked, each step filled with pain and despair. She had done everything expected of her and more. Nothing had worked.

They stopped beside the bronze metal door of the first ritual chamber and her hand slipped into her trouser pocket where she kept the wooden bird. She clutched it in her hand, reminding herself that her sacred path would always lead her back to the world of men. She had to fight and defeat the magic inside her.

There were five types of magic, High Priestess Herra had told them, and there was no way to know which echo had infected you. The daily rituals were intended to strengthen you against them all. Three days they were granted to wrest magic from their body or be exiled to the Deadlands.

"No need to look so grim, Lika." Her guide, the chubby Grisla, smiled benignly. "New dawn, new hope, as my ma used to say."

"Your ma took the bridge," she could not help biting back.

"Oh, well, you will too, if we can't get you purged today," Grisla replied cheerfully.

Elika gritted her teeth before she said something that might draw the high priestess' discerning eye toward her. She was careful not to draw attention to herself, remaining silent and subdued. The talk at meal times was about the ever-desperate hunt through the city for the rogue mage as the Blight bore down on them. Whilst outside, Peter Pockets' men stalked the temple from the roofs and streets, waiting for her emergence. She had to be invisible. So she kept to herself at the back, behind the others.

They were a strange group, the six of them. Rummy was a fat merchant from the Silver Circle, who repeatedly dabbed his face with a handkerchief. Chilla, the shoemaker's daughter, was the youngest of them. She cradled a sock-doll and kept close to Tix, who was a head taller than her, though he was a child himself. He was the son of a nobleman and dressed in a silken shirt, with silver threaded flourishes. His hands were soft as a babe's. Elika had often imagined children of noble houses were spoilt, demanding and arrogant. But Tix was timid and never uttered a word. At night, she heard him weeping quietly in his bed. From the priestesses talk, she had learned that his parents had been through the trials and failed, and had since taken the bridge. Soon afterwards, Tix's aunt, who had the care of him, brought him to the temple for the purging.

The worst of their group was Blood-dog, a greasy, mean-eyed ruffian. She paid him no mind, for it was Pretty Bessy, the buxom tavern maid, who drew her secret ire. Bessy was more beautiful than pretty. She did not know Elika, and they had never spoken, but Elika knew her. She was the one Mite had taken a special liking to, the one who fed him and bedded him at every chance. More than once Elika had spied her kissing Mite in the streets.

The high priestess clasped her hands and recited the same tale they heard each day. "Long ago, the Priests of Nerabyss lit a great ceremonial fire in honor of the celestial gods. On their knees, they prayed before it, begging the old gods to help them fight the foe corrupting our world. When the fire died and cooled, in the hot ashes, the priests found a baby boy. And they hailed the mercy of the gods for the gift and raised the babe born of flame ..."

Blood-dog yawned loudly.

"And Reval grew to tame and command the magic of fire and air ..."

"Aye, and the bloodiest bastard he was of them all," Blood-dog said. "Let's get on with it. I tire of your ceaseless sermons." He rolled up his trousers and pulled off his cracked leather boots.

"Deaf is the man who cannot listen to the truth and blind is he who fears to see it," the priestess replied sagely and thrust open the door to a dark, narrow room.

The heat hit Elika, and her dread grew a little more. The floor was a bed of burning coals. They cast the only light in the room. It took six excruciating steps to reach the door on the other side.

"One day I might like to watch you walk through them coals and see if your robe catches fire," Blood-dog said to the high priestess as he strode inside.

The priestess snapped the door shut behind him. A moment later, foul curses came from inside the chamber.

There was an answering glint of satisfaction in the high priestess' eyes. "Fire could not hurt Reval," she continued. "And to defeat the magic of fire, you must not fear it burning you. You must stand strong against it."

"But fire hurts us," Chilla wailed and her guiding priestess silenced her with a whispered admonition.

Blood-dog limped from around the corner, red and wet with sweat. He spat on the floor by the high priestess' feet. "Your turn will come, you ugly shrew."

"And when it does, I will bear it with grace and strength you do not possess."

Blood-dog sat down, mumbling more curses. His feet were raw and charred. He grimaced as he pulled on each boot.

Her own feet were still blistered from the trials of the previous days. And today it would hurt even more.

"Tix, you may go next," said the high priestess.

Tix took off his shining leather boots with gold clasps and his guiding priestess urged him forward. Shortly afterwards, yelps came from the chamber. Tears streaked his face when he emerged.

One by one, they went through the chamber, all under the watchful eye of the temple guards. Chilla was wailing when she came out.

Then it was her turn. Elika took off her shoes and socks and caught sight of the raw soles of her feet. The skin was peeling where the blisters had popped.

"Lika, proceed," the high priestess commanded. "Do not delay us."

Elika lowered her head and mumbled an apology. She took a deep, steadying breath and walked into the ritual chamber. Instantly, she was engulfed by the searing heat.

The metal door closed behind her.

All around, the floor glowed red with the angry fires of the old gods, threatening to burn her and her magic alive. The other side seemed impossibly distant. Six quick steps over the coals was all it took to reach it. Sweat beads formed on her skin. Each breath burned her lungs, yet her feet refused to move.

You must not fear it burning you, the high priestess had said.

If only her skin was made of hard leather. She closed her eyes and imagined just that—the skin on the soles of her feet was thick and leathery, like the hide of a bull.

Fire cannot touch me, she chanted, desperate to believe it with all her heart.

Her skin was leather, it could not burn. She forced that belief onto herself and the heat retreated. At the same time, her skin felt strangely heavy. She took the first, probing step onto the glowing coals, readying herself to sprint across ... there was no burning pain, only slight warmth on her feet.

She snatched back her foot and examined the sole. Her soft, human skin was gone, and in its place was dark, unfamiliar leather. She looked at her hands and gasped in horror. Her skin had turned to hide. There was no time to think or be afraid. In six long strides, she skipped across the coals to the other side and stopped abruptly by the door. Her hands were still made of hide. She could not go out there like that. Panic gripped her chest. How did she make it go away?

Instinctively, she strained to reign in the outpouring magic. As she did, the heat grew more and more fierce, and the true skin of her hands returned. Her body felt lighter, too. She touched her face, feeling her own skin beneath her fingers.

She burst through the door with relief, forgetting to cry out. But no one noticed. Outside, she found herself amidst commotion and cries of pain. The guiding priestesses were yanking off the blood-salt crystals from around their necks and throwing them onto the floor.

"Calm yourselves!" The high priestess' firm voice rose above the wails, though she also looked shaken. She, too, had cast off her pendant. "This is not the first time magic has struck out against us."

"But never all of us at once," shrieked one priestess.

Blood-dog laughed. "Serves you witches right. How's about you take your turn in the flames?"

"This is a curse," cried another.

Elika stared at them in mute, wordless horror, her mind racing. It was just the same as what had happened in the Hide. She had infected them all when she used her magic ... no, when it escaped her. She hadn't meant to use it.

"I said calm yourselves," the high priestess repeated sternly. "Let us all proceed to the purging hall at once and rid ourselves of this vileness."

Elika lowered her face, and grimacing as if in pain, limped toward her shoes. It was a feigned limp, for her feet were no longer sore, but no one was paying her any attention.

She sat on the floor and quickly pulled on her socks. As she did, she caught sight of her feet. The skin was unmarked, and neither raw nor painful. There was no loose skin, no oozing blisters. The magic had healed her. She gritted her teeth. She would not be grateful. Everyone knew magic was self-serving. It needed her alive and healthy, else it would need to find a new host.

At that moment, ravenous, dizzying hunger hit her like a blow to the stomach. It was the type of hunger that made men kill each other for a piece of bread.

Bread. Do not think of bread, or Penny's mushroom stew, or ...

"Well, are you coming, Lika?" Grisla asked pertly. She looked up. Everyone had walked ahead. Her stomach rumbled. But there was nowhere to go, no food to steal or beg. Two more trials lay ahead before they took their luncheon. And even that was a meagre affair. Inside her, she felt the magic coil up tighter, as if it knew her thoughts. There was nothing to do but follow Grisla and the others.

When she entered the purging room, sick fear tied her stomach into knots. She had come to this antechamber each morning and evening for two days, and it had not grown easier. Her gaze settled on the stone cup filled to the brim with a dark viscid mixture of blood and salt. An empty bowl lay beside each goblet. Everything in her recoiled and tightened.

"But we already had our purge this morning," Pretty Bessy said with horror.

The high priestess' face was stern and unyielding. "Everyone will take the purge. The longer you allow the magic to fester, the harder it clings."

Elika's feet moved forward.

High Priestess Herra stood at the head of the table, hands clasped together. "Life is made from blood and salt, and magic hates life, so blood and salt hurt it, weaken it and destroy it. But blood-salt is not enough, you must wrestle and fight the magic within you."

Around the table, the others, too, were pale and sickly. Rummy, the fat merchant, wiped his brow as he stared at his cup with disgust and dread. Blood-dog stood there with his arms crossed, glaring at his cup. Pretty Bessy looked ready to retch.

"Now drink." The high priestess' voice was soft, but beneath it lay steely command.

As one, they picked up their cups. Elika's hands shook. Chilla began to cry. No one offered her comfort. There was none to be had. The guiding priestesses gazed upon them without pity, their own cups in hands and fear etched in their faces.

Elika stared at her cup. At the back of her mind scratched those niggling rumors of Rimley's gang trading in barrels of blood, though they had no animals to slaughter. Her stomach churned, but her hands moved up, raising the cup to her lips. She drank quickly, in rapid gulps.

As before, the blood and salt burned a path into her body, setting it afire. All sense left her. She bent over, clutching her stomach. She could feel the ball of magic pushing away the purgative, its will fighting her own. It did not want to die. She pushed back. It must die. She would not retch. She would hold on to the blood-salt and let it burn the intruder within her. The enemy of man.

Somewhere in the distance, Chilla screamed. Elika fought not to give her own voice to the cacophony of agony.

The magic pushed back harder, refusing to yield, forcing her to heave, to retch, to expel the poison from her body. She grabbed the bowl and lost the battle. Dizzy, disorientated, she fell to the floor and curled on her side. Then there was nothing but darkness. But she was not alone in that darkness, a giant spider watched her from his web …

Voices penetrated her mind, then the light. She opened her eyes and found herself lying where she had fallen. The vile taste of blood and salt still clung to her mouth. Around her, there was joy and excitement. How could there be happiness when she was dying?

She pushed herself up with shaking arms. The priestesses once again wore the blood-salt pendants. Everyone had surrounded Chilla, who was both laughing and crying with joy. Around her neck hung a gleaming blood-salt pendant.

Envy and wretchedness cut through Elika. She hated herself for it. Hated that in the moment of joy for the child, she could not find it in herself to feel gracious and happy. Hated that she could not see Chilla's success as a candle of hope for herself. She wanted to be pleased for the little girl, but as cramps shook her body, she felt nothing but deep, bitter resentment and welling tears.

The high priestess smiled down at the girl. "Chilla, you have made us all proud. You have shown that even a small child can have the strength and courage to defeat the most formidable of foes. You have faced magic, fought it, and now you stand victorious."

Elika hardened her heart against her own failures and roughly wiped her tears aside before anyone saw them.

After Chilla was led away by the hand, the high priestess' face turned stony again. "The rest of you have failed, but there is still time. Let us proceed to the ritual chamber of Ilikan's trial." She marched out, serene and composed.

They formed an orderly line and followed.

"You are the worst of them," Grisla whispered as they walked. "Why do you always have to make such a big fuss over the purges and faint like that?"

Elika did not reply. Her head was spinning from hunger and pain. The purges were weakening *her* rather than the magic within her. Each day the fight in her faded a little more.

"Every priestess here is once again free of magic. See how easy it is?" Grisla continued blithely.

Elika said nothing, though Grisla's words were cutting.

They entered a bare chamber lined with large barrels of ice and water, and all thoughts of magic and hunger flew out of her mind.

The high priestess was already reciting Ilikan's tale. "...
the fisherman threw in his net and pulled from the bottom
of the ocean a baby boy ..."

Grisla rushed to stand beside one barrel. Elika followed
more slowly.

"... and he tamed the magic of ice and water ..."

Her chest tightened and each breath became labored
and precious. Could she use magic to help her again? She
shook off those treacherous thoughts. That's how it
corrupted you, with sweet promises, like a shameless bawd.

"... to vanquish the magic of water and ice, you must
strengthen yourself against those elements and learn not
to fear them."

"Take off your clothes," Grisla whispered.

Elika's cheeks grew hot but she undressed until she
stood only in her undergarments. She hugged herself,
trying not to look at anyone else. But she felt Blood-dog's
shameless gaze on her and sensed his feral smile.

"Come along, Lika. This trial is much easier than the
last," Grisla chirped.

"Have you ever tried to drown yourself?" she hissed back.

"Oh, I never needed to. A simple blood-salt purge
always cured me. Now come along. This is the last time
you'll need to do this, after all."

That in itself was more frightening than the trial.

With another failed purge, the bridge loomed ever
closer. The dark creature knew she had stabbed it. Its roots
had tried to grasp her, so that it might throw her into the
chasm, just like in her darkest dreams. It would never let
her cross.

Elika caught her breath and climbed into the barrel of
icy water. Waiting would only make this harder. The cold

was like a thousand shards of glass on her skin, cutting all the heat out of her body down to her bones. She began to shiver uncontrollably. She inhaled as deeply as she could and ducked beneath the water.

Grisla covered the barrel with the lid, thrusting her into the cold, fathomless darkness. The wheel above turned, locking her inside. The sound of that filled her chest with primal terror. She fought it and refused to think of the lid blocking her escape. She must not panic, must not allow her heart to race. Grisla had told her stories of those who had drowned, mostly children who had grown too frightened and fought to escape.

Her lungs burned, and still there was no mercy from above, no way to reach the air. Her chest tightened and strained with the need to breathe. Flashes of light appeared under her eyelids. She must not faint, for she would surely take a desperate breath and drown. And then she heard the sound that filled her with relief. Overhead, the wheel screeched and the lid ground open.

She burst out, gasping, coughing and breathing, just breathing.

Grisla held out a drying cloth to her. "There, see? Nothing to it. Just holding your breath a little."

She wanted to dunk the happy, chatty priestess in the barrel and lock her in it until …

Inside her, the magic stirred and began to uncoil, as if answering her summons. Elika startled and quickly pushed aside those murderous thoughts. The magic retreated. It was no longer a small ball from a few days ago. With each purge, with each trial, as Elika weakened, the coiled magic grew larger, bolder, more assertive.

Without meeting Grisla's gaze, she climbed out of the barrel, shivering violently as she did so. She dried herself and dressed with numb, clumsy fingers, wrestling with each button.

"Must you be so slow?" Grisla said with her hands on her hips as the others left the room. "The high priestess hates tardiness. It implies a loose mind. And a loose mind has loose morals."

Elika might have given her a suitable reply if her teeth were not chattering uncontrollably.

In the ritual chamber of Draygan's trial, the high priestess was droning the history. "... a small, wailing voice behind the rock wall, deep inside the mountain. The miners used picks to break apart the rock and they came upon a small hollow with a baby boy inside it, with eyes as gray as the stone from which he was born ..."

Elika joined them at the back, hugging herself to stop her body from shivering. Her fingers were blue from the cold. And she wished she was back in the chamber with hot coals.

"The boy grew to love stone and earth, and thus was the magic he commanded ..."

Her gaze fixed with dread on the large, rough-cut rocks of different sizes in the center of the floor.

"Pick up your rock," the high priestess instructed.

Tix had a smaller rock. Blood-dog was given the largest.

Elika's hands were still numb and her rock today was even larger than the day before. She cradled it in her arms and began to walk in a circle around the room, trailing after the others. She had not walked two circles when her arms began to ache under the strain and her legs grew shaky, threatening to give way beneath her. She focused on one step at a time, refusing to look at the others, focusing only on not being the first to drop the stone. The first of them to drop it had to pick it up and carry it another twelve circles.

So, they kept walking until the weakest one amongst them was found. Yesterday it had been Chilla, who was now purged of magic.

Elika took another labored step and her knees trembled. She could no longer feel her fingers. Pain shot through her back as if she had been struck with arrows. From the corner of her eye, she tried to see which of them would be the weakest. To her horror, she realized it was her, for even now the rock was slipping from her grip. She could not stop it, could not grasp it. With all her strength, she tried to hold it, but her arms would not obey. The rock slipped away and hit the floor with a loud thud. She fell to her knees beside it. Sighs of relief went around as the others dropped their burdens.

Grisla stood over her with crossed arms. "I expected better of you today. If you keep failing, the other priestesses will blame me. They'll say I'm a bad guide, and they'll send me back to laundry duty, or worse, cleaning out the chamber pots."

Elika had no strength to reply. She was ravenous. She wanted nothing more in the world than food.

"Everyone may proceed to the feast hall," the high priestess said. As she strode past Grisla, she added. "Twelve circles, for her. Not one less."

"I will make sure she does them," Grisla replied with a bowed head.

When everyone had left, Grisla adjusted the wreath of leaves on her head and gave her a stern look. "Tix is younger than you and the pampered son of a nobleman. Yet even he carried his rock without dropping it first."

"His rock was smaller," Elika bit back. "Mine was almost as large as Rummy's."

Grisla remained unmoved. "This is your last day of trials. Each day, they must get harder to strengthen you more."

Elika nodded mutely.

"Well, get up. You'd better hurry if you don't want to miss the midday meal. I am famished, and it would be cruel for me to miss my main meal of the day because *you* couldn't hold your rock for just a little longer."

Elika pushed herself up to her feet. There was feeling again in her arms and she instantly wished it had not returned. The pain was crippling and the rock might as well have been a mountain she had to carry. But she lifted it. And emptying her mind of everything but her hatred of magic, she walked and walked and walked.

And Grisla chatted and chatted.

Elika did not hear a word. Her mind simmered with anger. Anger at Mite for abandoning her. Anger at herself for being too weak to destroy the magic hiding inside her. But it was the hatred that drove her on, until she felt nothing but its fire coursing through her body. Hatred of the tsaren, the Blight, the bridge, which linked their cursed lands, and above all else, hatred of Syn'Moreg, who had broken their world and brought this wretchedness upon them.

A sudden clapping of hands cut through her awareness.

"Twelve! You did it!" Grisla chirped.

Elika dropped the stone and realized her face was wet with tears. She was not sad, however. She was angry. Magic was the cause of all that was wrong with their broken world, and she would destroy it. With that promise, she pushed her shoulders back and stood tall, refusing to feel the pain in her body.

"Let's hurry before all the food is gone," Grisla said and rushed ahead.

They took their meals in a small room with two rows of wooden tables. The guide priestesses sat at their own table and Grisla rushed to join them. Elika approached the other Echoes and sat next to Tix. To her dismay, she found the platters were mostly empty. She snatched a wedge of cheese and the last of the bread. The fruit bowl was bare. And only a few drops of goat's milk were left in the jug.

She stuffed her mouth with bread, heedless of the smirk on Blood-dog's gaunt face as he watched her. "Weak little duckling, ain't ye? All hungry and skinny. Might be I'll give you this prune for the taste of your cunny."

Tix, gasped in shock. Bessy giggled, and Elika found it hard not to give in to that twinge of resentment at the golden-haired beauty who had claimed Mite's interest.

Elika's hand covered the knife beside her plate. "Might be I'll cut off some of your flesh, Dog, and feed it to the pigs on Swine Corner. And earn me a copper for doing it, too." The city's swineherds took anything they could feed to their animals, including the dead, when no one was about to see it.

"Suit ye self." He shrugged and threw the prune into his mouth.

She took a bite of her cheese. It did nothing but taunt her hunger.

The high priestess stood up. "Two more trials are ahead of you before the final purge of the day. For the three of you, this is your last chance to find the strength to destroy the magic inside you."

Her gaze fell on Blood-dog, moved to Tix, and finally came to rest on Elika.

Blood-dog smirked and shrugged dismissively. Tix looked sickly pale. Elika's food lodged in her throat. For them, the bridge was now a certain end.

"How arrogant we were, believing we had vanquished a potent foe like magic," the high priestess continued. "But the war will never be over until every echo of it is destroyed. And in you it seeks refuge. Understand your enemy, then fight it. Let us proceed to the next trial. The trial of Syn'Moreg."

They rose and followed her out.

Elika felt faint and dizzy, and chills spread over her body. On the way out, she grabbed a half-eaten slice of buttered bread from one of the priestess' plates and gobbled it down as she followed behind the rest.

They were led into a dark, windowless chamber. It stank of death. It was not enough to dispel her aching hunger. The stench came from the large urns, which held rotting animals; probably the rats they had caught in the temple's larder.

In the light of red fire torches, the high priestess' face was forbidding. "Behold the dark heart of magic." She swept her hand at the urns. "We shall not speak of Syn'Moreg, Lord of the Abyss. He rules the dark realm of death where magic is born. No one knows why he sundered our world, except that he sought to save magic from its final destruction. Magic is death. This test will remind you of that."

They were blindfolded, bound, and made to kneel on the hard stone, surrounded by the stench of death. Her body tensed. She knew what was to come. Still, when the whip hissed and found her back, she cried out in surprise and pain, and fell forward. Today was her last day, and the high priestess did not spare her. The whip tore into her flesh, and blood trickled down her back. When she refused to rise again, Grisla was there, pulling her up to her knees. "Fight the magic," she whispered furiously. "You must be strong."

The whip rang out, and Elika flinched and trembled. But it was Rummy who grunted in pain.

"Death, pain, fear," the high priestess chanted. "This is what magic brings us. By harboring it inside you, by allowing it to prosper and send its destructive tendrils from within your body, you are condemning us all to die. Fight it! Repel it. Drink the blood and salt and kill the beast in you."

Another crack of the whip, and she fell forward from the blow, faint with pain and horror. The whip rang out again and Tix screamed.

"You must fight to reclaim your body and your soul from the foul magic, no matter the pain."

The whip found Elika's back again and again until she could no longer rise. Then it was over, and her arms were untied and the blindfold removed. She lay there, wanting to fade away into blissful oblivion, wanting to weep, but no tears came to her eyes.

"It's the magic that does this to you," Grisla whispered. "The high priestess only tries to give you strength to fight it."

But she felt worn and broken. She had no strength left to fight, no strength left to face the last trial. She was not alone. Whimpers came from around her.

Only Blood-dog remained defiant, snapping at his priestess when she took off his blind. "What an ugly cow of a sight ye are. I'd rather have the whip than look at you." He laughed. It was a strained laugh and the bite was gone from his insults.

"'Tis the bridge for you, dog," she hissed back.

Grisla examined Elika's back. "The cuts are not too deep, but they'll scar a little. It's a good sign. The magic will flow out with the blood. Here, you can wear this old robe. Your dress is too torn and bloodied." Grisla helped Elika to her feet and gave her the robe to pull over her dress. "Chew this, it will help with the pain." She placed a piece of willow bark in Elika's hand. It had a bitter taste, but it eased the whip burn. "You are stronger today than you were yesterday. I am certain today you will be purged. See, I have your blood-salt crystal ready." She pulled out a piece of string from which dangled the red crystal.

Elika could only stare at her. Every part of her body hurt. Her back bled. Worst of all, she could not find a single copper-worth of hope to hold on to.

Each day, as she grew weaker, the magic within her grew stronger. It used those moments of weariness to firm its grip on her, to solidify into a creature that threatened to consume her soul. More and more, it demanded her attention. Elika refused to listen, closing her mind to it. Yet, each day the blood-salt was harder to drink and hold down. And at the end of each day of torment and failure, she had barely enough strength to stagger to her straw bed and sleep. And in those moments of exhaustion, she felt magic reassert its clasp on her pitiful soul. It would never release her.

The high priestess returned the whip to its hook on the wall. "And now, the final trial," she said serenely.

The Trial of Arala was the most merciful, where they were forced to kneel on the bed of thorny roses before the statue of the goddess whose sacrifice had purged the world of magic.

Except it hadn't, had it? Elika thought bitterly as she followed the others. The old gods had abandoned them and magic was still destroying them. Arala died for nothing.

Only one more trial with the blood-salt purge to follow remained between her and the bridge. Be cured or face the fate she dreaded most. The thought sent a note of terror through her. But inside her lay bone-deep weariness and relief that this torment would soon end, that the choice of crossing the bridge would be taken from her.

They turned a corner and instead of being led to the statue, they climbed up a wide staircase to another part of the temple.

On the uppermost level, they came to a bright and spacious garden under a glass-domed roof and translucent walls. With the sun overhead, it felt like summer here. The floor was soil, and all around grew fruit trees in early bloom. Butterflies fluttered from flower to flower, and crickets chirped in the grass. Under an apple tree, in an enclosed pen, five goats were chewing leaves off the lower branches. And in the distance, young acolytes tended vegetable beds.

"Long ago, before the tsaren came, we worshipped the old goddess of life, Neka," the high priestess was saying. "Then Arala Lai'Neka came to us. Old scripture tells us she was a demi-goddess, daughter of the goddess Neka and a tsarin named Orian. Blood of the old gods ran in her veins, and their grace and mercy she lived by. When Arala came to us, we knew that Neka must have sent her to save us from magic. This is the exact spot where the babe was found …"

"No, she was not!" a cranky old voice interrupted. "What nonsense are you teaching these fools?"

The voice was familiar, but for a moment Elika did not know why. Then an ancient priestess appeared between the trees, and instantly she recognized the cranky woman from the carriage. The same woman who looked like a face from a distant dream. Her face was so wrinkly there was not a piece of smooth skin upon it. Her hair was white, her fingers knobbly. She shuffled along with the help of a white cane, which looked like it might have been made from bone.

Before the old woman noticed her, Elika slipped behind Blood-dog.

"Priestess Igla ... you have returned from your solitude," said the high priestess with surprise. Then, as if catching herself, she inclined her head. "We were not expecting you for some days yet. If you wish, we will leave, so as not to disturb you."

Igla tapped her cane on the ground. "Arala was found in the old wood," she said as if she had not heard the high priestess. "Where the Priestesses of Mercy were gathered for the spring celebration of life and fertility. They planted seeds in the ground and danced and ate bright mushrooms and ... Well never mind about the rest. Let us say they were not as chaste as you would have these novices believe. As dawn approached, those seeds they planted sprouted and grew, and inside one giant flower there lay a baby girl, her eyes green as spring leaves ..."

"It matters not where she was found," the high priestess said stiffly. "Only that *we* raised her and she grew beautiful and joyous and all men loved her."

"Aye, all *men* loved her and therein lay the problem," Igla replied slyly. "What are ye doing here with your novices? I don't teach until summer."

"These are not novices, but Echoes we seek to help," the high priestess replied. "We are here to remind them of Arala's mercy, her love of life and why she had died protecting us all from the destructive magic."

"Ha! You are still peddling that lie. Arala died not for men but magic." The old Priestess Igla stamped her cane again. "You are as ignorant as your predecessor. Arala was like the rest of them. The tsaren cared more for magic than they ever did for men. And she was not kind and gracious but shrewd and vain. If anyone should know her true nature, it is me."

The high priestess' lips firmed in disagreement, but she only bowed her head. "As you say. We will take our trial to the lower temple and leave you to rest." She bowed gently, as if showing reverence to a higher power. Yet there was no higher power in the temple than the high priestess herself. Elika's sense of disquiet intensified and she tried to shrink back even more behind Blood-dog.

"And take your rabble of fools with you." Igla waved her cane and those shrewd, sunken eyes, found Elika. They stared deep into her face and appeared like sharp pinholes. And those pinholes grew sharper, as if she knew the secret Elika was trying hard to hide.

The old woman shuffled toward her, digging her bone cane into the ground. Elika's every instinct told her to run. Then, when she was close, Priestess Igla sniffed her, and her eyes grew wide and knowing and menacing, too.

Elika took a step back.

The woman's bony hand darted out and she grabbed her by the arm. "You, my dear, will stay here with me."

The high priestess stopped in her tracks and spun around. "She must come with us, for she is an Echo. Once we purge her, you may have her. We must complete Arala's trial."

Elika tried to pull her arm from the grasping, wrinkly hand. But those frail-looking fingers were strong and dug deeper into her skin, like bony talons.

"Must you, now? How about I give you the true test of Arala? Then you may go and leave me this girl."

The high priestess opened her mouth to object, but seemed to think better of it. "As you wish," she said coolly. "Would you like them to tend your garden? Maybe do some chores which strain your back."

"Not today. Today, I have another test for them."

The bony fingers released Elika at last, and she staggered away from the old hag.

"Follow me," Priestess Igla commanded and led the way into the garden.

Deep in the orchard, they came to a strange abode. In the middle of the grass, shaded by the wide-spreading branches of an elm, was a home without walls. There was a straw bed, a kitchen, a fireplace with a chimney rising high, and a table with two chairs beside it—all arranged as if invisible walls divided the rooms. The old woman shuffled to a bookshelf and took a covered basket from it. She returned with it to the kitchen table and fumbled with the catch on the lid. From inside she withdrew a green snake with a red stripe running down the length of its body. It coiled around her wrinkly arm, hissing and rearing.

The high priestess raised an eyebrow. "It is spring. The moss-fire serpent is at his most temperamental and his most venomous."

As if to give credence to her words the snake's head darted forward with a hiss at Tix, who had strayed too close. He jumped back with a startled cry.

"This is the test of Arala's mercy," Priestess Igla said. "Today you will learn the bite of nature when it is angered.

Come forward and put your arm out for Forran to bite. If he favors you, he will not release his venom. If he sees darkness in your heart, he will kill you."

"Surely spring is not the time to test Forran's generosity. He is hungry and irritable." The high priestess held her composure. But Elika saw uncertainty and fear in her face. And it was not wholly the fear of the serpent, but of the old woman, too. It made Elika even more anxious. Did the serpent know Elika was a mage? Was this the way for the old woman to test her or kill her?

"You wanted to test this pathetic pack and a test you will have," Priestess Igla snapped. "You, with fat ankles, come forward." She pointed at Rummy.

He looked around, as if expecting to find another fat man beside him, then wiped his forehead with a handkerchief. "Now, mistress, this is not the same as the other tests. I know this here beast, and he's as likely to kill you as look at you. One bit my horse once. The poor brute was dead by the time he hit the ground."

Igla's eyes narrowed. As if the snake sensed her mood, his head darted toward the merchant with a hiss and a snap. "I said come forward. This is the trial of Arala, one you must complete if you do not wish to face the bridge come nightfall."

Rummy wiped his forehead again, looking around for help where none was to be had. Staring with horror at the serpent, he edged forward and held out his shaking arm. More sweat beaded on his face and neck.

Forran's teeth sank into the merchant. Rummy cried out and snatched back his arm. There were two puncture marks, but no sign of the green venom under his skin. He looked as if he might faint with relief.

"Now you," the old woman pointed at Tix.

The boy shook his head, backing away. Blood-dog blocked his retreat. He placed a hand on the boy's shoulder, bent down and whispered something in his ear that none of them could hear. Whatever it was, Tix seemed to take courage from it. The boy lifted his chin and took a bold step forward. There was terror in his eyes, but he raised his arm. When the snake bit into it, the boy yelped. But he too had been spared the venom.

Next, the crooked finger pointed at Blood-dog. There was plenty of darkness in his heart, and if anyone was to die from the moss-fire serpent's vengeance, it would be him. They all thought so, including Blood-dog himself.

He stepped forward and thrust out his arm. "Alright, you old hag. Get this done with. 'Tis time I faced the celestial paths and the guardians. Might be I'll take the path to the gods this time."

But no, he too survived the test, as once again no venom came forth.

Then it was Pretty Bessy's turn. The buxom maid looked ready to faint with fear.

Elika could not look at those large blue eyes of hers, or at those plush lips, without remembering Mite's idiotic grin as his hands roamed over Bessy's body. She had followed him one night, curious to know what it was he did and who he saw and why he slept in so late. She saw him with Bessy behind *God's Water* tavern, kissing her as if she was precious food he could not get enough of. With a dreamy gaze, he mumbled things that made Bessy giggle in reply. Mite never looked at anyone else like that and Elika had been certain he was in love. When he hiked up Bessy's skirts, Elika ran away, feeling oddly cold and furious at once.

She could not blame him either. Bessy was beautiful in a way Elika was not. Pretty Bessy had long hair and a curvy body, and no one would ever mistake her for a boy, no matter how short she cut her hair. A dark, unkind part of Elika secretly wanted the snake to dislike her too. It was a wicked thought, for it was not her fault Mite was such a wretched rascal. Tomorrow, Bessy would likely cross the bridge, and if she made it ... Elika's mind stuttered on an awful thought. If Bessy made it, she would be with Mite. The thought was unbearable and jealousy reared its head ...

The serpent's head darted out. Bessy cried out and cradled her arm. She looked down and her eyes widened. "No ..." She shook her head in denial. Then looked up pleadingly, as if begging that this was all a mistake.

Green venom oozed from the wound. It ran through her veins under the skin and reached her face. Before anyone could breathe out, Bessy's blue eyes grew empty and she fell lifeless to the ground.

Horror and guilt cut through Elika. She had thought it, but she had not wanted it to happen. She did not truly wish the serpent to bite Bessy. It was just a meaningless, harmless thought, like any other which men nurtured in their hearts but never gave voice to. Foolish jealousy. That was all it was. She did not even like Mite. He had left her, abandoned her and their pack. This could not be her fault. How could it be? But as she stared into Bessy's now sightless eyes, they seemed accusing. *It was your fault for wishing this on me*, they said. *You wished me dead, and the magic in you replied.*

The high priestess paled, but her expression grew more closed. "Take her away. She has failed the test."

The other priestesses ran forward and carried Bessy away.

The old woman's merciless gaze shifted to Elika. "Now you." She pointed her finger and there was a sly glint in those eyes, as if once again she knew all Elika's grimy secrets.

Did the snake know her secrets too? How she had used magic, the lies and deceits, and being too afraid to do what was needed to save their city? Could it see the magic hiding inside her? Had it heard her wicked thoughts about Bessy?

Elika stepped forward and met the serpent's scaly eyes. They looked into her heart and she was certain they saw the darkness in it. She was the mage everyone was searching for.

She put out her arm. Let the serpent judge her.

The snake's head moved forward in the strangest way. Its long tri-pronged tongue darted out to taste the air.

"Closer," the old woman commanded.

Elika took another step toward the serpent. Its head reared back, and it coiled itself tightly around the ancient woman's arm.

So she stepped closer until she was eye to eye with the shriveled, old woman, still holding out her arm for the snake to bite. But Forran only hissed and slithered away up the bony arm, onto the table and into its basket.

An involuntary laugh escaped Elika, a bubble of hysteria. It was not funny, nothing was funny, save that the deadly moss-fire serpent was afraid of her. She laughed again and petted its head in the basket. It unwrapped and crawled onto her arm, winding gently around it, as if showing obedience and deference to a master's summons.

It took her a moment to notice the deep silence surrounding her. All eyes were on her and no gaze was more potent than Igla's.

"This one has Arala's magic inside her," the old priestess announced. "It is strong in her. Your tests and trials are useless, as are your purges. She will remain here with me. This one is mine."

The ground seemed to sink beneath her feet. The tests, the purges were useless on her. Bill, too, had told her as much.

"Then we must take her to the bridge," the high priestess said with rising authority.

"Not yet," the old priestess replied. "Arala's magic is merciful and not to be feared. Besides, I did not say there is no hope for her. Only that I want her. Take the others away and do not bring them again."

The high priestess nodded, but there was disapproval in the set of her lips. As they left, Elika wondered who this old woman was, and why the high priestess heeded her wishes.

Once they were alone, Igla turned her shrewd beady eyes on Elika and said coolly, "So, Arala, you have returned."

CHAPTER NINE

The King's Decree

"Historians and scholars of the lore of the three realms rarely mention another entity: The Great Web binding the spheres. In the Sachi lore of the celestial gods, there are whispers of a great spider who guards it. He is a half-blood son of the god Moreg and a human princess. He is the Lord of the Abyss, whom the gods cast out from the celestial sphere. His name is Syn'Moreg."

History of Men, Gods and Magic,
By Priest Oderrin

There were times in Elika's life when she felt as if her world faded away, and she was spun into another mythical one. Often, those times were during one of Bill's tales of the old days, when their world was awash with magic.

Standing there, under the old priestess' probing gaze, she felt as if she was once again cast into that strange place of magical lies and illusions. A place where she could not trust her ears or eyes. Where her mind was twisted in knots and reality became an impossible, unfamiliar thing. In her mind, she groped for something solid and true to cling on to.

"Name's Eli," she said with as much conviction as she could muster.

"So you say," Igla retorted. "Instead of glaring at me with your tsarin's gaze, why don't you do something more useful and make me a herbal tea over there." She pointed irritably toward the kitchen. "My joints are stiff as stone today. And seeing you here doesn't brighten my mood either." The old priestess lowered herself into a rocking chair, very much like the one Bill had on his boat. Except, her rocking chair was under an olive tree, in a meadow of small spring flowers and tiny butterflies.

"If you think I'm the demi-goddess Arala, shouldn't you be fetching me the tea instead."

"Ha! Look at you, drab and scrawny, like a drowned rat, half-eaten by fleas. Where's your might and majesty, where's your wisdom and grace? You, my dear, are no goddess. At least not yet. So if you don't want to know what my cane feels like on your backside, you'll be fetching me that tea and quick about it, too."

Elika was acutely conscious of two things at once. The old woman was mad. And it might have been that same madness, which had saved Elika from facing the bridge that night. So she did what the mad old priestess demanded.

The kitchen was nestled under a large apple tree, as were the table and two chairs beside it. Every surface of the kitchen, and the grass beneath her feet, was covered in small petals from the apple blossoms. There was a bed by the rose bushes, a chest carved out of an old tree stump and shelves made of branches. The old woman's strange home was reminiscent of Bill's tales of mages and their unusual abodes.

On the shelf in the kitchen, there were many jars filled with different grains, flour, dried pieces of fruit and flowers.

The only thing she knew of herbal teas was that they involved steeping weeds in hot water. That was how Penny made them when anyone in their pack was sick.

"What's taking you so long, girl?" the cranky voice demanded.

"I'm looking for some weeds."

"Weeds! I said herbal tea, not weed."

"What's the difference?" Elika asked over her shoulder.

The old woman narrowed her eyes. "Are you ignorant, girl? Have you been living on the streets all your life?"

"Aye," she replied slowly, thinking it should have been obvious.

That startled the old woman. "But 'tis not where I left you." Then she waved her hand in the air as if swatting away an annoying fly. "Well, never mind that now. Just pick some of those herbs drying beside the chimney. No more than three in a brew. Put them in that silver pot and pour in the hot water."

Beside the cooking fire's chimney, tens of strings hung from a low apple branch, each held a bunch of wilted herbs and flowers. She picked what she recognized from Penny's brews: mint, dried daisy heads and a few rosemary sprigs. She put a pinch of each into the silver pot. Nearby, Forran lay curled up in his basket watching her.

"Have a cup yourself too, Arala," the old woman called out.

She regarded the old priestess from the corner of her eyes. Igla was rocking gently in her chair with her eyes closed. There was something strange about her that seemed less than human. It was as if Elika was looking at a lifelike picture of a woman rather than the actual woman; as if some essence of truth was missing. It was starkly reminiscent of Bill. And she had only ever seen that many wrinkles on one other person, and that was Bill, too.

A thought struck her. "You're a tane," she said blandly. "How many of you are there?"

Igla huffed. "So, you've met more of us?"

Elika picked up a cloth and with it took the black pot off its hook above the hot coals. "Bill Fisher is one," she said.

The old woman's eyes flew open. "That rotten scoundrel, curse his cold heart. Don't you go talking to me about that wretch."

Elika poured the hot water as her mind raced to connect the pieces. "You must be the *damned witch* who married Bill and left him for dead?" She poured herself a cup, too.

Igla perked up and her eyes glistened. "He speaks about me, does he?"

Elika replaced the black pot on its hook. "Bill speaks about a lot of things."

"Aye, that he does," Igla said a little wistfully.

Elika handed the old priestess the steaming cup and went back for her own. When she inhaled the scent of mint, rosemary and daisy upon the steam, her soul sang in reply. It had been a hard day of trials. With the promise of respite, her body felt heavy and sluggish.

Igla waved at the other rocking chair. "Sit. Else you'll give me a crick in my neck." She sipped her tea and sighed. "Why did you kill that poor girl, Arala, setting Forran on her like that?"

Elika lowered herself into the chair and grimaced at the pain in her back, even though it had been dulled by the willow bark. "I didn't kill Pretty Bessy. You and your snake did that." To her dismay, she tasted the lie on her tongue. Her unkind thoughts had brought about Bessy's death. "And my name's not Arala, but Eli Spider."

The old tane's eyes narrowed and she stamped her cane. "We will not get on well, girl, if you keep trying to deceive me. I can smell what you are from here. And who do you think found you as a babe? Me, that's who. 'Twas I who wrapped you in your first blanket and found a home for you."

Elika sighed. Aye, she was as daft as Bill. "My ma and pa took the bridge when I was young. No one found me. After they abandoned me, an old woman took me in."

She remembered the firm hand that held her back from running after her parents. The stranger who seemed as ancient as time and limped as she walked had taken Elika to a warm cottage. She had been fed and allowed to cry in peace until no tears were left. She had slept by the fire and was given small chores. And each day the old woman had told her stories of the tsaren and the Sundering War, and a great many tales which Elika no longer recalled.

Igla tipped her head in interest. "Who was she, the woman who took you in?"

An echo of grief went through Elika. "I never learned her name. One day, I woke up and she was blue and cold. Dead in her bed. The snowdrifts had come that night, and the window blew open ..."

She fell silent and recalled with startling clarity the moment she had seen the old woman strangely still and limp in her bed, and Elika's heart had raced with the fear of some ungraspable doom. She was alone in the world filled with wickedness and formless terrors that stalked her mind in the night. She had nowhere to go and no one to ask for help or mercy.

The days that followed had grown vague in her mind. Though young, she knew enough of their world to know not to trust the city guards. So she told no one of the woman's death, merely covering her with a blanket and leaving her where she was. For some days, she hid in the desolate house, until the food ran out and she was forced to venture out in search of more.

Someone must have marked her. For that same night, the door creaked open and two youths crept in, holding dim lanterns. They covered their noses with scarves, looked at the dead body with disgust, and ignoring Elika rummaged through the house, taking anything and everything their hearts desired.

In the following days, more men invaded her home. They paid her no mind and took what they could carry. The last thing they took away was the old woman's body, which they likely threw into the chasm, or sold on Swine Corner, to be fed to the pigs. The same men returned shortly after, threw Elika out into the street, growled a warning not to return, and shut the door behind her, taking the cottage for their own.

Igla scratched the mole with a hair poking out of it on her jaw. "And did she take you to a little cottage with yellow curtains?"

There was such certainty in the question it stumbled Elika. She gaped at the old woman before catching herself. "Aye," she replied suspiciously. "How did you know?"

"Ha! So, it was that old hag, Nora, the daughter of Draygan, who smelled you out. She always fancied herself to be noble-born, just 'cause he got her on some nobleman's daughter. Nora might have been born in the silk sheets, but she was raised in the sewers like the rest of us."

"She was a tane, too?" Elika said with resignation. She remembered little of the withered old woman who had cared for her for a time, only the impressions of patient kindness and worldliness, and she was glad to finally learn her name.

"Listen to me, girl. I found you and I gave you to the folk you believe to be your parents."

"Where did you find me?" she asked uncertainly.

Discomforted, the old woman shifted in her seat. "In the bridge."

"Which bridge?" Elika asked, though she feared she already knew the answer.

"*The* bridge. The only one worth speaking of—the Bridge to Magic."

"Then someone must have left me there." Elika shrugged and sipped her tea.

"*In* the bridge, I said, not beside it. And 'tis a tale I will tell you. Just as I told it to a white-tipped crow once, so it could carry it across the chasm and let the tsaren know of your return. Each century, on the same day and the same hour that I watched you die, I go to the bridge to morn you. You were never a mother to me, Arala, but I was a daughter to you, whether or not you wanted it. And I grieved. I am not ashamed to say it. At the bridge I spoke my heart to you. Just as I tried to do to you as a child. Do you remember? And I was met with the same cold silence from you in death as in life."

Elika shifted in her seat. Grief turns clear minds to mud, Penny always said. And there was no sense in trying to make men see through the murkiness until the mud settled.

"Fifteen years ago, I stood there again. Then, when the wind quietened, I heard a strange whimpering. I followed the sound and it led me closer to the bridge. And there, beneath its skin, I saw a lump moving. I reached out and touched it and I felt you, Arala, stirring and calling to me. The black strands parted to reveal a hollow. And there you were, curled up inside—a naked babe, bound to the bridge with a cord, like a babe to its mother.

Elika shuddered at the awful tale made of nightmares. "Tane Igla … are you telling me this to scare me? If so, you should know I don't scare easily. Your tale is as fantastical as Bill's about a three-headed whale eating a fleet of warships."

"Scare you? Aren't you listening, girl? I am telling you what a marvel you are. That you are born of Arala's magic." Oddly, her eyes glistened as if with tears. "You may look different to how I remember you, but I see parts of her in your face. Your magic fashioned the bridge and your magic reformed you."

The horror of what she was saying was too dreadful to contemplate. "Even if what you say is true, how can you be certain it was me you found?"

"I'd know you anywhere. Your eyes put me in mind of a frosty spring morning on the Moss Moors. Were I to look, I'd not find their like. And your smell I'd know anywhere, for you smell like magic. Besides, I suspect you still have that mark of a burning butterfly upon your lower back."

Elika hugged herself. How could the old woman know about the inky mark on her back? No one, not even Penny, knew.

To believe that she had been spawned by the bridge was inconceivable. What manner of being was she if that was true? Perhaps someone had abandoned her beside the bridge, and maybe it took her. Or the old woman might simply be mad and had dreamt up the whole story. Then how could she know about the birthmark?

Elika's mind churned. Try as she might, she could not deny there must be some truth in the old woman's tale.

Their paths must have crossed long ago. Could it be that the people she thought her parents were hapless strangers upon whom Elika had been thrust? Was that why it was easy for them to leave her behind? She recalled her mother's tears, the tight embrace, and the anguish in her whispered words before she walked onto the bridge, and once again doubts sank their roots deep into Elika's mind.

"Then why didn't you keep me? Why give me away?" she asked with a rising sense of hurt and resentment. Hurt that perhaps her parents cared little for her beyond some drive of duty.

She imagined what it might have been like living here with Igla in the comfort and safety of the temple—never knowing hunger or fear—or the biting cold of winter, which buried itself into your bones, so deeply, it did not melt away till summer.

The old woman huffed and crossed her arms. "And why should I look after you when you never looked after me? You never cared for any of your babes. Like the rest of the worthless tsaren, you cast us all aside. Whilst all the while, you roamed the lands caring for the human children. I never did understand that strange nature of yours. Cold and unforgiving to your own babes, yet like a mother to another's. Besides, I couldn't bring you here, now could I? The priestesses might show reverence to a harmless Tane-daughter of Arala, but the return of a tsarin is quite another matter. They'd have thrown you on the fire before I could stop them. I had to hide you. So I left you on the doorstep of a seamstress and her husband. Good, honest folk, they were. I knew they'd look after you. But then they and you vanished, and I haven't seen you since."

Elika's mind spun. Nothing felt right, and all the terrible and wondrous possibilities opened wide before her like deep traps. One wrong step and she would never find her way back to her own life and the world she thought she knew. So she clung to the only certainty she had. Whatever link she had to magic, or the bridge, or this tane, she knew without doubt that she was not Arala.

The daughter of the gods commanded the magic of life, whilst Elika could barely stop it from escaping her and acting out her every mean thought.

"Why did you come here, anyway?" Igla snapped. "I can't keep you safe now, can I, when you're dancing around the temple casting magic this way and that?"

"I came to be purged of magic."

The old woman blinked and burst out laughing—a choking, hoarse cackle. Then she grew calm and scowled. "Bill let you do that? He'll be feeling my cane when I see him next, you can be sure of that. What was he thinking?"

"It wasn't his choice but mine," Elika said feeling the need to defend Bill against the woman who had already left him for dead once.

"We'll see about that. For now, you shall stay here with me." The old, knobbly hand held out the empty teacup. "Take this and wash it. There's water in the barrel."

Elika rose to her feet; her back was throbbing. She took the cup and limped to the kitchen. Sitting down, even for a moment, brought out every ache from days of trials. She leaned on the table for a moment, waiting for the pain to subside.

Igla was quickly beside her. "What's happened to you? You're bleeding." She said it accusingly, as if it was Elika's fault her back had been whipped raw.

"The trial of Syn'Moreg," Elika replied bitterly. "It taught us that magic is pain and death." A lesson she knew all too well without the whip.

"Well, why don't you heal yourself, foolish girl?"

"I'm not one of Arala's mages. I cannot heal myself."

"You are Arala, and it was one thing you were good at, healing yourself and others. Until you spent your magic, that is, and needed to replenish it. Have you spent your magic heedlessly?"

"Perhaps," she said, if only to make the old tane leave her be in peace. She was too wearied to argue, and it was often best to allow people to believe what they would.

The priestess' wrinkly face softened. "Take off your dress and lie here on my bed. I will bandage your wounds. Damned priestesses and their worthless trials. Whatever possessed you to do this to yourself? Why don't you just cross the bridge? Reval is there, waiting for you, I dare say."

Elika lay face down on the straw bed beside the rose bush. "Reval scorched the world with his fires. I am only sorry he didn't burn himself along with all the folk he murdered."

"He only burned it after what the four kings did to you. Try to remember! They abducted you, tortured you, and King Northwind raped you. They meant to kill you, for nothing more than their own ambitions. Trouble was, they didn't know how to kill a demi-goddess who could heal herself, and they tried many ways to end you. Is it any wonder Reval burned their lands and cities when he'd learned of their betrayal ... of what they had done to you? He saved you from them, and then you went and killed yourself regardless. It broke him. 'Tis why I sent the crow to him, to tell him the glorious news. But the damned bird refuses to fly across the bridge."

Elika listened and though she tried, she could not stop her eyes from closing. The crackly voice grew distant. Then there was nothing, not even dreams.

She was shaken awake again what seemed like mere moments later, but all the light had gone from the day and stars peered through the branches of the apple tree.

"Get up! Time to go to the bridge," a crackly old voice said.

For a moment, Elika could not recall where she was. Her head was pounding. She moved and found her back was bandaged with a cooling poultice numbing the pain. She rolled to her side and sat on the edge of the bed. It was dark but for a small lantern nearby.

"Here, put this on." Igla thrust an acolyte's robe at her.

The old woman's words pierced her dulled mind and she came wide awake. "The bridge … I'm yet to take another purgative." She was still owed one more chance to vanquish the magic in her.

The tane turned away abruptly. "Foolish girl, I do not mean you. We go to see the other worthless members of your group that Herra brought up here."

Relief washed through Elika. She was not being forced to take the bridge yet. Then shame crept in. There'd be no such mercy for young Tix. It was she who should be sent to the Deadlands above all others.

Elika looked at the dark windows and hesitated. "I can't leave the temple. There are … men looking for me."

"Men, the guards, the king. Aye, I know. Do not fret, they'll not see you. Now dress."

She pulled on the robe and a hooded woolen cloak the priestess gave her. Then she followed the old woman down a small dark stairway and outside through a low door. In a small courtyard at the back of the temple a coach waited for them. The coachman held open the door.

Igla climbed in first. Once seated, she banged her cane on the floor. "Well, come along girl unless you wish to walk."

As she climbed inside, Elika fought the urge to look up and around. Instead, she lowered her head and pulled the hood to cover more of her face from the watchers in the night.

The coachman closed the door behind her.

The seats were plush and there were curtains covering the windows. At their feet, a coal pan warmed the carriage. If only Mite could see her now. The thought sent waves of loneliness through her.

The driver spurred the horses onward and the carriage jerked into motion. Igla arranged a blanket over her lap and stared out the window with casual disinterest.

Elika sank back into the shadowy corner of the carriage and scanned the streets and the roofs. No one appeared to be following them. She kept her senses sharp for sounds of pursuit, for alerting whistles and stalkers in the night. Here and there, children huddled in the doorways, despondent, world-weary. The sight was a blow to her senses. She remembered her pack and what she owed them, what she owed Penny, and she felt as if she had awoken from a dreadful dream. During the last few days she had not thought about them at all.

For the first time in her life, since she had arrived at the temple, she did not need to worry about finding food and coin, whether she brought her share to the pack, or whether the young ones were safe. A thousand daily worries had vanished, replaced with only one—purging herself of magic. Until now, she had not realized what a deep relief it was to care for just yourself. To know that each day she would be fed and the only price was to subject herself to their cruel trials. Perhaps this was why Mite had left, to reclaim his life for himself.

Either through need or death, everyone left eventually—her parents, the old woman, Nora, who cared for her, and now Mite. She had no one but herself to rely on.

With that thought, her street instincts sharpened instantly. When had she become so careless, so trusting? There was no reason for the tane to take her to the bridge. The old woman had another purpose. She appeared relaxed, but she was not. She gazed out the window, stiff as her cane, not looking at the city, but merely avoiding looking at Elika.

Everything felt wrong. Elika assessed the door. Only the driver and the coachman accompanied them. She could jump and run and be up on the roofs before they pulled their horses to a stop. Still, try as she might, she could not convince herself the old woman meant her harm. Surely, if the tane wanted her to cross the bridge, Elika would now be riding at the back of a prison wagon. Might be she'd wait and see where this journey led them.

Absently, Elika's fingers brushed a gilded button on the seat. She scratched the surface … paint, but beneath it was metal. A metal button like this could be traded for a slice of bread and there were a hundred such buttons stuck to the seats. No one would notice one missing. Her fingers slipped under her robe, found a button and when the carriage turned a corner, she moved with it and plucked the button from the seat. Aye, she must never forget where she belonged, must never forget her pack. She slipped the loot into the pocket of her robe as the carriage came to a stop.

Igla turned her dark eyes on her. "We are here."

They stopped across the street from the bridge and the wailing of the eternal wind filled her ears like a long-forgotten song. And out there, dark and forlorn, lay the Bridge to Magic. It was the color of the night sky. The color of the deep chasm beneath it. They merged into each other seamlessly, so that you could not tell where one began and the other ended. It seemed as if an age had passed since she had last laid eyes upon the bridge, and it was almost a relief to behold it again.

On the other side, the shadows of those who had recently crossed haunted the Deadlands, swathed in an unnatural ghostly light. She could not help but uselessly search the far side for Mite's form amongst them, even though she knew he'd be long gone by now.

Aside from their carriage, Rift Street was empty. Few crossed at night, for in those dark hours, dark thoughts and images filled men's minds.

"Where are they?" she asked, watching the tane closely.

Igla shifted and began to straighten the perfectly flat blanket. "The prison wagon will arrive shortly."

Elika gauged the distance to the door. "Why did you bring me here?"

"Since you ask, I think it's time we discussed your future …" And there was that betraying glance toward the bridge that Elika had been waiting for.

She leapt for the door, just as it burst open and a man jumped in, colliding with her. She fell back into her seat and wrestled to right herself, but the man filled the carriage. Curses flew, and Igla's cane was everywhere at once. It caught Elika on the shoulder and she rolled to avoid another blow. Then the man fell on top of her, crushing her beneath his wiry body and a stream of foul curses.

Igla's voice cut through the mayhem. "You filthy rascal, dammed letch; get out of my carriage."

"Ow, woman! Damn it! Peace. Peace." There was more wrestling and cursing, and then he fell back into the seat beside Elika. In his hand, he held Igla's cane. He tried to snap it against his knee but gave up moments later with an exasperated sigh. "Damned whalebone. Why did I ever make this for you?"

Elika tried to gather her wits. "Bill?"

But neither he nor Igla paid her any mind.

Igla was glaring at him. "Bill Fisher, son of Ilikan, how dare you show your face to me?"

"Why must you always hit me with your damned cane each time you see me?" He rubbed his head.

"'Cause you're a rotten rake. And I don't want you here. So, go away."

"Unforgiving witch. Can a man not make one little mistake?"

"One! I counted eighteen of them since we wed."

Bill looked taken aback. "You knew about them, too? But they meant nothing to me. Only for Lidia did I have any real hankering, and that was 'cause she was a mute."

"She'd need to be deaf and blind too, to run off with a wretch like you," Igla said with a huff.

"My love, 'twas never a need for you to be jealous. She was only a human, and you knew I'd come back. 'Tis you I married, after all. The wench meant nothing to me. I just liked her … silences." He sighed.

"Ha! You mean she had no choice but to suffer through your endless blather. What are you doing here anyway, you old cod? I hope you're here to say your farewells before you throw yourself into that chasm."

He grinned. "Still got a fishwife's tongue on you, hey my love?"

Elika watched in disbelief as testy old Igla blushed. "I have not been a fisher's wife in three centuries. Since you absconded with that mute dairymaid of yours and left me cold and dry on your rotten boat. So quit your quibbling and tell me why you allowed Arala to go to the temple, and why she still believes this nonsense about being purged of magic."

"Arala?"

They both looked at Elika.

She shrank into her seat. "I'm Eli," she reminded them. Though little good it appeared to do.

Bill turned to Igla. "Has your mind addled, up there in your temple? 'Tis not Arala."

"Who else can it be?" Igla asked in shocked disbelief as if Bill was mad to suggest otherwise. "Besides, doesn't matter what you call her. She thinks she's human."

"Ah, well. The girl's not ready to know. And who are you to force on her what's not her time to learn? 'Tis not how magic works. It takes centuries to grow. You start with a small bubble and feed it." He cupped his hands as if holding a butterfly. "Then it morphs and puff." His hands opened again as if releasing that butterfly. "How old was Reval when he learned what he was?"

"I don't know. I wasn't there, was I?" she replied sulkily. "I'm not that old and don't you dare say I look it."

Elika did not think it was possible to look older.

"'Tis in the old scripture, as you well know. Spent two hundred years thinking he was a child of some god or other as the priests taught him to believe. And she's what, nary fifteen years. Besides, I tried to stop her. But she's magic itself. What would you have me do, tie her to me boat mast? Besides, where were you all these years when I've been keeping an eye on her?"

"Ha! You can't keep an eye on yourself beside a mirror," Igla snapped back.

"Well, you have her now. Is she still hankering to be rid of her magic?" Bill chuckled at that. "She's like a little fish what thinks it's a seaweed."

"I'll get rid of it if it kills me," Elika cut in.

Igla threw her a rueful glance. "She's as difficult as Arala ever was."

"Then send her to Reval to fuss over. Make her take the bridge." Bill waved in its direction.

"'Tis what I'm here to do."

Elika grew cold and eyed the door again. "No. I won't go. Not today. I'm owed one more purge." It was a feeble excuse, but she clung to it, nonetheless.

She was spared a reply by the sound of wagon wheels rolling past them on the cobbles. A prison wagon pulled up beside the bridge. There were only two prisoners in the back, Blood-dog and Tix. Side by side, they made a startling contrast. Blood-dog was filthy and bored-looking. He was no stranger to death, she thought, and must have dealt it out many a time in his life. His dirty, long hair was loose over his eyes, his clothes old and stained.

Tix was small beside him and pale as the dead. His fair hair was neat, his face clean. *Never show them fear.* She wished she could force that thought onto him. The guards unlocked the door, and Blood-dog pushed the boy out first. "Stop your weeping. What are you, a woman? It's just a damned bridge. Nothing to it but to walk across it."

Tix stumbled out and fell to the ground. When he found his feet again, his eyes frantically searched the empty streets. For whom, Elika did not know.

For a moment, Tix looked numb with shock, then he looked at the bridge and retched. Blood-dog straightened him by the scruff of his neck then bent down to say something in his ear. The boy wiped his eyes and stood a little taller, finding some morsel of courage, or perhaps pride.

The guards untied the prisoners' hands and removed the chains that bound their feet. The head guard took out his sword and pointed at the bridge with a bark of command.

Blood-dog spat on the ground and marched ahead, insolent and cocky. At the bridge, he turned to the guards, gave them a mock bow, followed by a rude gesture, and laughed. He waved the boy over but did not wait to see if he followed.

Tix swallowed and glanced at the guards.

One of them had lost his patience and advanced on him. "Right. That's it. 'Tis the chasm for you, you coward."

Tix screeched and ran onto the bridge. The guards laughed. Painfully slowly, watching each of his chary steps, Tix followed Blood-dog.

Elika held her breath. Children rarely made it across and she dreaded what was to come. The boy gripped the fleshy, black railing, placing each step as if it was his last, whilst Blood-dog jumped lightly over the newly formed gaps in the unravelling bridge. When he reached the apex, he stopped a mere step from the deciding fate and looked back at Tix.

Then Blood-dog did what she had never seen anyone do before; he turned around and walked back toward the boy. When he reached Tix, he picked him up and carried him. The boy clung to him as if the ruffian was his savior. Blood-dog marched across the apex without pause. Neither of them vanished, neither turned to dust. On the other side, they became motionless shadows, man and boy, side by side.

"Arala, I bring you here to give you freedom," Igla said kindly. "There's nothing left for you in this world. The web is unravelling and only one thread holds it to the other side and it's the bridge you fashioned. It's there that you'll find your own kind."

"My kind," she echoed, her gaze still on the bridge and the Deadlands beyond.

"The magic, child. 'Tis what you are. You were not born of a woman's womb. You are not of the earthly domain, but the ethereal. The woman I gave you to had a burn on her cheek. Her name was Estilla, her husband was Rollen."

"Aye," Elika replied breathlessly. She had forgotten. But as Igla spoke, she remembered touching the scarred cheek. Her mother's name was Estilla. She had a beautiful voice and sang to Elika each night to keep the dark dreams at bay.

To remember her parents now only to lose them again to this old woman's yarn was more than Elika could bear. She did not want to believe any of it, but simply wanting never got you anything. She imagined letting go of everything she ever knew and becoming someone else—Arala or some other being born of magic. Could you stop being what you were, abandon all you had come to believe and assume a new way of being as if the past did not matter? Such things were impossible, of course.

"It matters not where I came from," she said and faced Igla. Those were the laws of their pack. The past did not matter, only where they were now and survival. Loyalty mattered above all else. "It's men who raised me. It is they who cared for me, and I lived amongst them. They are my people, my kind and my family. It's them I pledge my loyalty to, not magic, and not to the tsaren."

"Then go to the other side and be amongst the men who went there."

Elika stared at the bridge to nowhere. Magic was vengeful. It had tried to grasp her with its roots. Were she to step on it, she was certain it would throw her into the chasm.

"There's nothing but death there," she said at length. "It's the same as what's behind us. Deadlands. That's what magic makes of the world."

Bill crossed his arms and stretched his legs, looking smug. "'Tis not so easy ordering a tsarin about, is it, my love?"

Igla's face turned mulish. "What is it you want, *Elika* girl?" She said Elika's name as if it tasted foul on her tongue.

"To purge magic from inside me."

The old woman's beady eyes twinkled with amusement. "Is that so?" Then something akin to mischief touched her lips. She leaned forward. "Well, if it's what you want, princess, then it's what we shall try to do. So, what will it be, blood-salt drinks, walks through fire?"

Elika did not trust the sly glint in those old eyes. "The trials don't help. You said so yourself. I'll drink the blood and salt. I've seen men purged with it. It kills the magic in you."

"Oh, well, if you are so clever, then we shall do as you say."

She had a strong feeling the old priestess was laughing at her. Well, she could laugh all she wanted. Elika would do anything to purge her magic.

Bill leaned forward and grabbed Igla's hands. "You've always been a daft, stubborn woman. But now you must listen. 'Tis the warning I came here to bring you. I might talk a lot, but I also know how to listen. And I hear whispers on the street. There are things afoot. Drasdanes have been stirring fear, saying the priestesses serve magic. They say the purges are useless and fire's the only way to kill it. Their blacksmiths are working through the night making weapons and giving them out for naught but a penny. Whilst the priests have been whispering in the king's ear, saying there's too many Echoes to push across the bridge. They're feeding him poison from the old scripts. You see what I'm telling you?"

Igla tried to withdraw her hands, but he held them firm. "I'm not a fool, Bill. Never have been. The king is merciful and he looks to us for guidance."

"Curse it, woman, you don't understand the minds of men. You've been spending too much time with them women. When you go back, you must close the temple doors to the Echoes ... to everyone. Barricade yourself inside."

Igla snatched back her cane from his lap. "You've delivered your message. Arala is being stubborn, as you can see. It's time we returned to the temple."

"I'm Elika," she mumbled.

"I'd wish you well, Bill, but truth is I'd rather you threw yourself into the chasm." The note of humor in Igla's voice belied her harsh words.

Bill chuckled. "If I did, I dare say you'd be jumping after me just to be certain I hit the bottom."

Igla huffed and turned away, but a small smile played on her lips.

Bill opened the door and jumped down. "Heed my warning, woman. I don't want to bury you. It'd kill me, love."

Igla rearranged the blanket over her legs, trying not to look at him, then she banged on the roof with her cane. "Take us back."

They rode to the temple in silence.

Here and there, shadows stirred in the streets; thieves and gangs stalking the depths of the night for their next prey. It was a great relief to return to the quiet refuge of the temple.

Igla limped to her bed, stopping only to point at the chest where she kept spare blankets, and instructing Elika to make her own bed on the ground by the cooking fire.

Late into the night, Elika lay on her pile of blankets waiting for sleep. In the incense-heavy silence of the temple, her mind churned with useless thoughts of all that had transpired that day. She longed to speak with Mite and hear him say he had found a way to fix all her problems. She wished for Penny's quiet council, and ached for the comforting hum and laughter of her pack.

Despite her exhausting day, when it finally came, it was not a restful sleep. Her dreams were haunted by the unravelling bridge and a giant web choking the world. She was a tiny spider, lost in the web, scurrying this way and that, looking for a way out. She ran to the edge of the sundered web to look across the enormous chasm. There, in the other web, sat a giant spider as large as the sky, his terrible, glowing eyes trained on her. They pinned her to the spot and she trembled with fear, for surely he would leap across and eat her.

She backed away. He darted forward and would have been upon her in a flash, but for the chasm between them. She scurried away, fleeing from him, from his gaze upon her. But there was nowhere to hide. The web around her was breaking and the strands were flailing in the wind. In her terror, she heedlessly ran onto a flailing strand. The wind whipped and swung her over the edge of their world, threatening to rip her off it. She held on to the strand with all her might, suspended over a dark nothingness, more frightening even than the dreadful spider. Then she began to slip, and slip, falling into darkness ...

She was startled awake with a scream lodged in her throat. The dream had been nothing like her other dreams. It felt as potent and palpable as a memory. *It's just a dream,* she told herself firmly and tried to shake off the lingering sense of panic it left behind.

The pale light spilt through the glass roof of the dome. Igla was asleep in her small bed. In the distance, goats bleated. Elika arose and put the blankets back into the chest carved from an old tree stump. Her body was stiff and aching from the trials of the day before, and her back was still painful, but she paid it little mind. Knowing that no more trials awaited her, lightened her mood.

She strolled around the garden, following the well-trodden paths between the orchard trees. As she did, she plucked a strange red fruit from a tree beside the goat pen and ate it. She drank out of a water barrel and meandered past the vegetable patch, toward the glass walls of the dome.

When she gazed over the city's roofs below, a pang of nostalgia went through her for the freedom they once offered. She wanted to run over them again, stopping only to gaze at the lands in the distance, and dream of bold adventures and faraway places she would visit one day ...

Her gaze shifted to those lands beyond the city and her heart stuttered.

Fresh shoots of summer crops had turned the land surrounding their city verdant and fresh. Herds of cattle grazed in guarded fields to the west, basking in the early morning sun. But it was the long train of coal wagons that gripped her attention.

They raced along Coal Mine Road from the east toward the city. Tens and tens of loaded wagons, driven by frantic miners, spurring their horses onward, glancing behind as they fled. Her gaze moved along the road. As she watched, the farthest wagons came to a sudden stop as the horses fell to the ground and the men slumped in their seats.

"What do you see, girl?" said the crackly voice behind her.

"Death," she replied with a strange numbness in her heart. "The Blight is moving toward the city again. Blackhill Mine is lost."

Strange how she could not find emotion to attach to that knowledge and the fate that now lay ahead of them all.

The last coal mine that kept the city warm had been cut off by the Blight. If they lived through the summer to the next winter, they'd have nothing left to heat their homes or stoke the cooking fires.

"Tell me, why does the Blight keep marching toward us?" Igla asked.

"Because magic wills it," Elika muttered.

"Is that so?" The old woman's voice was mocking.

Elika turned to face the tane. "I'm ready for my blood-salt purge."

"Then take it." The old woman said bitingly. She strode off and rang a bell hanging off a branch.

A moment later an acolyte girl ran in.

"Bring me the purgative," Igla commanded.

The girl curtsied and ran off. She returned shortly with the jug of blood and a goblet. Elika's throat constricted. The girl placed them on the table and Igla waved her away.

"There you go." The old woman waved at the goblet. "Drink as much as you can stomach." She sat in her rocking chair, clasped her hands over her stomach and closed her eyes. "The bowl for you to retch in is beside the barrel."

With a firm resolve, Elika strode to the table, poured the blood into the goblet and drank it in one gulp. It never became easier. The agony never lessened. The fires that consumed her body, her very soul, never subsided. She groaned and writhed on the ground whilst trying to push away the ball of magic inside her. *Get out, get out. Die!*

With just as much determination it pushed back, and Elika sensed its anger and determination to live ... and she sensed its fear.

Die! she screamed at the magic inside her.

But she did not want to die ... no, *it* did not want to die. It fought back. And once again she lost the battle.

When she opened her eyes again, the old tane stood above her. "Did you feel it fight against the poison, *Elika* girl?" Again, the old priestess said her name as if it was a curse.

She could only nod in reply, for her stomach was still cramping.

"Why is it fighting, tell me?"

"Because it's wicked." Elika groaned.

"Do only wicked men fight? No." She thumped her bone cane on the ground. "So, why is it fighting?" she demanded again.

"It doesn't want to die."

"Who does?" the old woman replied and her face softened.

"It doesn't matter what it wants. I want it to leave me be."

"Do you still not understand? Your magic cannot flee, for you *are* your magic. You are not two but one. To destroy it, you must destroy yourself. The blood-salt purge cannot kill a human, but it can kill you, for magic cannot unbind from you."

What if what the old woman said was true and she did find Elika in the bridge? What if the bridge somehow took her as a babe and turned her into a mage? Might be everyone was right about her.

"Am I mage?" Elika choked out.

"You are a tsarin," Igla repeated relentlessly.

Elika shook her head, refusing to believe it. She might be a mage, and perhaps the bridge had indeed taken her and changed her. But she would never believe she was a tsarin. She was human. There was no other way for her to be. But Igla was a tane, her heart bound to magic.

Elika rose to her feet, holding on to the table for support. "You don't know. You can't know this."

The tane looked on her without pity. "Then take another drink." She filled the goblet to the top and handed it to Elika.

In that instant, Elika hated the old hag. But she hated magic even more. She snatched the goblet from the old woman's hand and was about to down it, when High Priestess Herra strode in, disheveled and frantic.

"I couldn't change his mind!" she cried out. "You must speak with him, Tane. You might still have some sway with the king."

Igla turned to face her. "What's happened, Herra? Why are you so flustered?"

"He came to see me. He was angry ... no, he was furious. He accused us of deceiving him and cursed us as liars and threatened to send us all across the bridge ..."

"Stop your rambling. Who have we deceived?"

"The king! The priests showed him old scripture, which said the blood-salt purges did not kill the echoes of magic but sent them fleeing to another host. They told him it was why more and more of his subjects became infected, despite the purges. Only blood-salt combined with fire can destroy it."

"But I told you this years ago," Igla said calmly. "And you argued."

Herra did not appear to have heard her. "The high priest told the king it's too late to send every Echo across the bridge. And the bridge itself is unravelling. There was only one path left to them … I begged him not to do it, but he was angry. 'Let us hope we are not too late to undo this,' he said to me. But it did not save Drasdark, and it will not save us … it would make us no better than magic. It's the mage's fault, I'm certain," she cried. "We need to find him …"

Igla stamped her cane. "Calm yourself. You are not some foolish acolyte. Tell me what has happened without this blabbering."

The high priestess composed herself, though Elika could see it took a great effort. She gripped the table for support; her eyes were wild. "The king has passed a decree. All Echoes are to be burned alive on the pyres around the city."

The cup of blood fell from Elika's hand. In a daze, she looked toward the skies above the city, where columns of red smoke began to rise. This couldn't be happening. Not to Terren. There had to be another way.

"Seal the doors to the temple," said Igla in a lifeless voice.

CHAPTER TEN

The Destruction of Mercy

"When the dust settled after the sundering of our world, it took decades for men to gather knowledge of what had happened at the end of the Sundering Wars and why. Namely who Syn'Moreg was and where he had come from. Throughout history, old royal records of the Sacred Crowns mention his name, though there is much secrecy and fear about it. What we know is that the four kings knew of him since the days the celestial gods came as guests into our world. None has understood the reason the last war enraged him and drove him to sunder our world."

History of Men, Gods and Magic,
By Priest Oderrin

There was nothing men would not do to survive. Mite had warned her.

She should have listened, thought Elika as she gazed out at the city shrouded in blood-stained smoke. The pyres had died overnight, but soon they would start again. As soon as the blood-red fog blanketing the city dissipated with the rising sun. *It should be you out there on the pyre*, a mean little voice whispered inside her mind. *This is all your fault.*

She had failed her pack, failed Terren and man. She had wanted to save them. Instead, she now hid behind stone walls whilst the Blight bore down on them and death ruled the streets. And each morning she awoke to the taste of acrid smoke that made her sick to her stomach.

Today, the fog was thicker than normal and hid the lands beyond the city wall. It did not hide the sounds of savagery that now gripped Terren. Day and night, shouts, fighting and screams came from the streets. Whilst below, the mob clamored at the temple doors, shouting abuse and vile promises of pyres and the chasm.

Elika refused to count how many days had passed since the king's decree. To do so was to count the suffering, the dead, the tears and grief. She wanted to hate the king, but so much hatred already filled her heart, she felt cold in the face of more.

There were no more purges for the masses. The priests had declared that magic could only be killed with blood-salt if it was combined with fire. That was how Tsarin Reval had been defeated, by men throwing blood-salt into the magical fire he had sent against them.

A forbidding sense of waiting had descended on the temple. Elika was kept busy with endless chores: weeding, cooking, cleaning and sewing. She kept her head low and did as Igla instructed, all the while ignoring the futility of these little tasks. She could not hide here forever. If the mob did not get them, then the Blight would.

Nor could she leave. The doors to the temple had been sealed, the guards were tense and watchful, the priestesses and acolytes terrified. Outside, no one without a blood-salt crystal could walk the streets. Neighbor turned against neighbor. The infected were dragged from their beds onto the pyres by the wild mob. Neither the old nor the young were spared the fire laced with blood-salt. Were she to run, they'd catch her and burn her with the rest.

Since the burnings had begun, she had suffered with fever, which came in the night more oft than not. It was morning again and her fever had subsided, so she steeled herself for her daily purge. Despite what the priests had said, she refused to give up. A part of her looked forward to the punishing pain, for it offered some relief against the guilt she nursed inside her chest. She turned away from the window and returned to the kitchen beneath the apple tree.

Igla watched her with a disapproving expression, saying nothing.

The jug of blood-salt awaited Elika, a wooden cup beside it. She did not think but poured and drank. And when she faded into darkness, she was a tiny spider in a giant shining web, surrounded by dark red flames. They licked at her skin, drove her toward the edge, toward the bridge and onto it. The roots wound around her legs and dangled her over the chasm. And then they let go. She fell and fell, and the fires chased her, burned her skin, her eyes, her face.

Her scream filled her ears, and she came to.

An old, gentle hand stroked her hair whilst a crackly voice chided. "Why do you keep doing this to yourself, Arala?"

Elika bolted upright and stared at her arms for she was still burning. There was no fire, no burns, and yet the echoes of the fierce flame still lingered on her skin.

"You feel it, don't you?" the tane whispered. "The fires."

She frowned at the old tane. "How …?" The question died on her tongue, for she feared the answer.

The old woman replied, nonetheless, to the unasked question. "You are bound to the web, and its burning is what you feel."

"I want it gone. I want to be me again. Tell me how to be rid of it."

"Foolish girl. You want the impossible. Why do you hate the magic so?"

"It's wicked and destructive."

"Might be it's not as evil as men fear it to be."

"It infests," Elika cried. "It's growing inside me, consuming me."

"It doesn't infest but seeks refuge."

"It hurts me."

"No, child, you are hurting it. It's not your own pain you are feeling but the magic's."

"No! You twist everything I say. I'm hurting. *My* body."

Igla struck her on the back with the cane. The shock of it wrenched a cry from her lips.

"This is the pain of your earthly body. When you drink blood-salt, you feel the pain of your ethereal soul. Damn it, girl, we don't have time for your ignorance. The Blight is nearing and we have little time to save you."

"Then give me another goblet of blood. It's the magic in me that's feeding the Blight. I must banish it or we'll all die."

"Enough of this! I'll not indulge you a moment longer. Rest, Arala, and we'll make plans to smuggle you to the bridge."

"I'm not Arala!" she cried. "I'm Elika. Eli Spider of Bad Penny's pack. I'm a human. My parents were human."

"You're not human, but magic that formed itself in man's image so it could walk amongst us. You're a tsarina. In seeking to purge your magic, you seek to unravel yourself. I won't stand by any longer and watch you do this to yourself." She stamped her cane. "Magic is fleeing to you for protection, seeking refuge from death and persecution. And there you are, torturing it and yourself with blood-salt. Shame on you, foolish girl."

Elika shook her head to clear it. The old woman was twisting her mind, filling her with doubts. She had to get away from the mad old tane. She was not a tsarina. She was not Arala. She hated magic with every fragment of her soul.

She scrambled to her feet and realization hit her. "You are a tane, rejected by the tsaren and magic. You want magic to accept you ... Mite said tanes can't be trusted. It's not me you want to save but the magic inside me."

"Damn it, girl, you're delirious with pain. I'm trying to keep you alive, for you are my queen and I live to serve you. Even though you abandoned me as a babe, you are still my mother."

Elika wanted to close her ears and her heart to Igla's words. But somehow the old tane kept her imprisoned in this strange world, making Elika doubt everything she knew was true. She had to get away.

She staggered toward the glass wall and made her way to the door. As she did, she glanced outside.

The fog had dissipated and the red smoke rose once again in straight columns.

Her gaze moved on. Past the outlying farms and pasture, the green gave way to wilt. Farther still, where King's Forest once carpeted the land, the trees were gray and leafless, the ground fallow. Birds rotted on the ground where they fell. Along the road, a caravan of wagons stood motionless, as if frozen in time, the bodies of men and women slumped where they sat in their seats or lying where they had fallen when they had tried to run. The horses and animals they had brought with them fared no better. She might try not to look, but there was no hiding from the stench of death staining the spring air.

For six hundred years, the Blight had marched across their world, turning life to death, turning fertile soil to dust.

Only a sliver of their world was left standing in its path. They were surrounded, with nothing but the chasm at their backs. Had she believed once that she could stop it?

Her gaze shifted and she saw a sight that was a death toll for their city. The Blight had reached the outlying farms. The seedlings, those fresh shoots of life, were wilting. Even if by some miracle they could stop the Blight, the city would be starving by autumn. And by winter, men would turn to eating their own dead. They had done that in Tulston, seven hundred years ago, after a magic snowstorm had cut off the roads in the middle of summer. For years, no one could reach the city. Until one day, the snow melted of its own accord. It was a cautionary tale of the wickedness of magic that all children knew.

She sank with her back against the glass wall. There was nowhere to run. Outside, screams filled the air as pyres were lit in the temple square. She put her hands over her ears. Perhaps it was not magic, but men who deserved to be vanquished. Magic did not burn magic. Was magic worse than the terror men inflicted on their own kind?

Magic brought storms, killed cattle, burned down forests and broke apart city walls with lightning. It was fickle and wild and vengeful. Yet none of that seemed to matter anymore. Nothing men had ever blamed on magic was worse than the dying screams of honest folk and the stench of burning flesh.

A white cane appeared in her view. "Are you going to sit there all day? I want my tea and I want you to fetch it."

Elika rose and went to the kitchen. On the table lay warm bread and boiled ham. She sliced the bread, placed it on two plates and began to cut the ham.

"How much food is left in the temple?" she asked, trying to focus her mind on what needed to be done rather than surrendering to despair.

"We have stores of seeds in the cellars, and we grow food in our gardens come summer or winter."

Elika put the slices of ham beside the bread. She was not hungry, but such an ordinary movement of her hands made it easier to ignore the distant screams and the red smoke rising into clear skies.

"'Tis hate of magic that does this," Igla said with a sigh.

Elika poured the tea into two cups without speaking.

"It's the way of things that we remember wrongs more keenly than rights. For five centuries, Bill and I were happy together. We have loved each other since the day we met. Then one day, I found him under the tree with a young dairymaid. He returned days later, crawling into our boat like a bashful crab. But it was too late. One small injustice had shaken my world apart. Mere days of pain and misery overrode all we'd shared. So, I left him. For centuries that followed, I recalled not the love and joy we shared, but my husband atop another woman with his pants around his ankles. Should I have purged the world of him, thrown him into the chasm? Aye, and it'd be too good for that letch, were you to ask me. But would it be just? Was it a crime that he had hankered for a beautiful lass after hundreds of years of living with a dour old woman? Would you call him wicked and evil, Elika girl?"

"A man straying with a dairymaid isn't the same as the Blight destroying our world," she replied.

"True, if the Blight is the work of magic and not men themselves. Ever men blame another for their folly."

"How could men cause the Blight?" Elika asked incredulously, sliding into the seat across the table from the tane.

"Didn't that ignorant fool Bill Fisher tell you about the Great Web?"

Elika stared sightlessly at the food she did not want to touch. "He told me about webs and nets and the fish caught in them that want to go back into the sea."

It was reassuring that even Igla looked puzzled at that. Bill had a way of talking as if he spoke sense. And when you did not understand him, he had a way of looking at you that made you feel stupid for not understanding.

"Damn Bill with his fishy tales and nets. Everything you see about you … trees, birds, fish and man, all are bound to the Great Web. What happens when you take away the web?"

"The fish fall out?" Elika replied.

Igla stamped her cane against the stone floor. "The Blight happens. Soon you'll know that all I've told you is true. For you're born of magic and you're bound to it. And you'll know the fires burning it down as surely as if you were inside them yourself."

The old woman must have truly wished it upon her, for that night, as Elika slept, her fever was worse than ever. The flames engulfed her, trapped her. And inside them, she heard not the screams of dying men and women, but the call of dying magic.

Then voices emerged from the darkness.

"We are all infected. As soon as we purge one, another falls foul of magic. It is fighting back … it's the burnings."

"Magic is not fighting but fleeing. I told you this before, Herra. The more men they burn, the fewer places there are for the echoes of it to hide. It's too late to worry about it now. Are the doors holding?"

"For now. But the temple is surrounded, the lower gardens are overrun, and there is no help from the king. The Temple of Reval has fallen. The priests are being burned on the pyre as we speak."

"Then you must ready yourself to fight."

The voices faded. A wet cloth touched Elika's brow, her arms, her legs; a mild relief from the fire engulfing her body.

Cold water trickled over her lips and tongue, and there was a voice, soft and kind. "Shush, 'tis but a bad dream. 'Tis morning and it will fade." Then the voice became angry. "What did I tell you? But you would not listen, would you? 'Tis your task to take what magic you can save to the other side."

More water touched her lips. She swallowed. "It's killing me, Igla. The magic is killing me."

"Men are killing you. They are burning from this world all that you are. Don't speak. It can't last. The fires are subsiding. The people are rising against their own savagery. For it's their fathers and sons, wives and daughters they're burning. Else they've run out of trees to burn. Chopped down most of the King's Wood for these pyres, they did. Fools! Sit up, take a drink of water."

Igla's arm slipped around her shoulders and helped her up.

Elika drank deeply. Every breath was a struggle. Her lungs were raw with smoke and on it she tasted burning flesh, blood and salt, and the pain of all who had perished. But there was more in that smoke. It was thick with fear. Elika followed that fear and it led inside her.

The ball of power had grown even larger overnight. Yet it held itself tight, as it tried to hide, to stay very still and not spill out.

"I want to get up … I need to see."

"Might be best that you don't," Igla said grimly.

Elika wrestled with her weakness as she stood up and wobbled on her feet.

"There, let me help you if you insist on being stubborn." Igla held her arm and led her to the windows. "The fires are dying out. There'll be some respite for you."

The sky was gray and tinged with red. Beyond the wall, only a thin green strip of grass remained between the Blight and Terren. What wasn't cut down of the King's Wood, the last of the woodlands, was now wilted and gray. Everything beyond the city wall was dead, decaying and ashen. The color was fading from their world.

"The Blight is almost here …" Elika choked out. "They've been burning the Echoes, but the Blight hasn't slowed. How can that be?"

Igla was grim and there was a resigned dimness in her eyes, a hopeless wisdom in the face of endless cycles of destruction. "How indeed? Haven't you worked it out yet? But you will before the end is here."

"If you know, then you can stop it," she pleaded.

"I tried, centuries ago. I spoke with one king after another. No one can stop the Blight, for the hatred and fear in men's hearts is a deep river. It runs strong and true to its preordained course. Syn'Moreg knew this, and 'tis why he sundered the web and gave half to men. Let them learn the lesson the hard way, he thought."

Despair ripped through Elika. "When will it end?"

"When everyone is dead."

She shook her head. "No." She could not accept that. Else why take another breath?

"Get dressed, girl."

On the chair lay a neatly folded pile of clothes fit for a street urchin.

"Where are we going?" Elika asked in alarm.

Igla threw a cloak over her robe. "The priests are dead. We are next. There is no time to waste. I must get you out of here. Be quick, now."

Elika pulled on the trousers and threw on the shirt. The familiar attire made her feel as if she was finally going home. It filled her with restless energy, the need to move and be on her way. She hated being confined and the feeling of helplessness that came with it.

As she was buttoning her shirt, an acolyte ran into the room, her eyes wild. "Priestess Igla, they're breaking through our barricade ... they're attacking the temple."

"Find a place to hide, child," Igla replied calmly. "Come with me, Elika girl." She walked ahead, leading the way with her cane.

Elika pulled on her boots and ran after her.

Priestesses and acolytes were running along the corridors, hiding inside rooms and barricading the doors. The shouts outside were growing louder. Deep booms rang out through the hall, coming from the giant temple doors. Igla strode determinedly ahead, her cane banging in step against the stone floor. They came out onto the sweeping balcony high above the great hall. The head of Arala's statue was just below them.

Another great boom reverberated through the air. Elika looked down over the railing. The guards raced toward the doors to reinforce them with wooden beams and their bodies. The priestesses prayed on their knees before Arala's stone feet. Some acolytes beside them were barely old enough to recite a prayer. Grisla was there, too, praying and crying, seeking help from the cold statue of the demi-goddess who had perished long ago.

With another strike of the battering ram, the giant doors shuddered and groaned.

"Why aren't they fleeing?" asked Elika.

"There's nowhere for them to flee. Now come along, there's no time to waste." Igla tried to pull her by the arm.

Elika resisted. "Then where are you taking me?"

"To a safe place where we can hide until this is over."

Hide whilst they die? The thought was abhorrent. "No. Not without them."

"There's only enough room for two where I'm taking you. Where the fire will not burn us when they set the temple alight. There is no secret pass, no other way out, save past the mob. If you don't want to live, then choose another to take your place." There was a touch of biting smugness in her voice, as if she was daring Elika to refuse the offer of life over death.

Again, Elika looked below. The temple guards formed a scant line between the mob breaking through the doors and the priestesses they were trying to protect. Hide, whilst they fight and die.

Her hand slipped into her pocket and found the wooden bird. The doors thundered again, and their shudder went through her. She wanted to run and hide, in truth. Wanted to live. But her path lay with men. And beside them, she had sworn to fight to the last. Except, this enemy they now faced was not magic but other men.

"Chose, Elika girl," Igla demanded with a stamp of her cane. "Life or death?"

Elika met her gaze. "I chose to fight." And with that she raced down the stairs.

"Arala!" Igla shouted after her.

Elika took out her small knife. She had been in brawls before, had been attacked and challenged, and on occasion had cut boys and men, though she had never killed one. Still, she could take care of herself.

When she reached the great hall, Grisla ran up to her and grabbed her arm. Her round cheeks were streaked with tears. "We are lost. There are too many of them. We have no more blood to purge ourselves. They'll burn us!"

Elika saw then that none of the priestesses wore blood-salt crystals. Her own fear thundered in her chest. There were not enough of them to fight off the mob. But she could not show the young priestess her fear. "Fight, Grisla. You must fight and when you have a chance, run for the streets."

Another loud thud reverberated through the hall and they heard the crack of the timber doors.

"We are out of time. Sweet Arala, give us your strength and mercy," cried the high priestess.

Elika's hand on her knife grew damp. The guards in front of her were armed with swords and shields. She knew nothing of wielding a sword and her knife now seemed as paltry as a cub's claw against a bear.

Oh, Mite, how could you leave us? It was her last coherent thought before a loud crash and screams filled the hall.

The attackers poured in to the temple. Axe-wielding Drasdanes, side by side with Terrenians, brandishing knives and daggers and short swords, and any manner of a weapon they had found.

Elika stared at them in horror. This invading army was dressed in the garb of common men. Street merchants and cobblers, tavern keepers and stonemasons, farmers, weavers, chandlers and brewers. Amidst them, she saw Green Silk Harry and Cross-eyed Abe, and the miller's young son. Simple folk whose names she knew, whom she had spoken to and shared an ale with and lived beside all her life. They were not their enemy. How could they be?

But the wall of guards rushed forward. There was a fierce clash of weapons and grunts and cries of pain, and blood flowed over the stone floor. Men shouted commands she could not understand. Mesmerized by the fury, she stood there benumbed, watching as the temple guards slew the folk of Terren. But where one man fell, five more took his place, their faces savage.

Swords severed limbs. A giant Drasdane with antlers on his helm buried an axe in the head of a guard. Another young guard nearby was overwhelmed by three men using an assortment of tools as weapons. She took a step forward to help him, but a scythe found his neck. He fell to the floor, his body jerking.

Elika began to shake, her hands slippery on the small knife she clutched. This was evil. This was wickedness. Yet these were men, not magic. Nor were they driven by it. They all wore blood-salt crystals around their necks, like emblems.

Nothing felt real. It had to be a nightmare. Men did not do this, magic did this. And as in those nightmares, where she was surrounded by fire, her leaden legs were frozen in place. She wanted to run. But where could she run where men or magic would not catch her?

More and more attackers poured through the broken temple doors. And then there were no more guards between her and the mob. The attackers rushed past her at the priestesses. And she realized, dressed in street urchin garb as she was, they had mistaken her for one of them.

"Magic lovers," they shouted in rage.

"Kill them!" shouted a Drasdane as he grabbed an old priestess by her hair and sliced her throat with his butcher's cleaver. Before she hit the ground, he turned and grabbed a screaming acolyte and laughed. He lifted her off her feet and began to drag her away.

Without thinking, Elika darted toward the dead guard, snatched the sword from his limp hand, and with a cry on her lips, ran the murdering bastard through the back. The Drasdane released the acolyte in surprise. Elika pulled out the sword. He turned, and she slashed it down his chest and stomach before he could take another step. He crumpled to the floor, and all fight left her. She stared at him in shock. She had killed a man.

Then she felt a dark gaze on her. She looked up. A bearded Drasdane was glaring at her, his face contorted with rage. He charged at her with a farmer's scythe and she scrambled to raise her sword in time to block him. The force of his strike knocked her to the floor. Then the scythe above her filled her vision, and everything vanished but the silvery sharp tip falling toward her.

Suddenly he stumbled forward, unbalanced, and she saw a flash of a white cane retreat from his back. She rolled out the way of his scythe and bounced to her feet. Once more the cane crashed against his back. He cried out, arched his back, and Elika rushed at him with her sword and a shriek of fury. The sword drove deep into his stomach. The Drasdane stared at the sword in his gut. And she saw not an inhuman savage but a frightened farmer, his face twisted with pain and the realization he was about to die.

Elika staggered back, leaving the sword behind.

The Drasdane farmer tried to pull it out, groaned with pain and the seeming impossibility of it, and fell to his knees. He looked up at her, silently pleading for something she could not give him. And then he died.

Her hands shook. She stared at the blood on them without feeling. On the floor, she saw her knife. She reclaimed it and found herself standing at the base of the main stair. Dimly, she was aware of Igla's panicked voice, and an urgent tugging at her arm. The tane hit her on the leg with the cane. "Snap out of it, girl, and run."

In a daze, she took in the scene. One by one, the guards were falling. More attackers flowed from the passages at the back of the great hall. And Elika could only watch as priestess after priestess was slaughtered. Acolytes ran past her up the stairs, chased by a pack of youths. A group of men stripped the high priestess of her robes. Herra screamed and fought, but they fell upon her, tearing at her like a pack of feral dogs. They dragged her outside where the mob was shouting and jeering. And Elika smelled the smoke on the air as the high priestess' screams filled her ears.

Then Elika heard a shout. "Find the mage! The bastard's here somewhere."

And those words finally spurred her feet into motion. She ran up the stairs, forgetting everything but the need to survive and to reach the rooftops that had always kept her safe.

A desperate scream for help cut through her panic. She spun around at the top of the stairs and saw Grisla running toward her, terror in her face.

A Drasdane man grabbed her and plunged the knife into her back, his eyes aglow with savage joy. "You think you could hide the mage from us, you cow," he growled and stabbed her again.

Grisla jerked, gasped, and her gaze locked with Elika's. Her lips moved, but instead of words, blood emerged.

Elika choked out a hoarse scream, as realization struck her. This butchery was her fault. They were here for the mage, for *her*.

Then the mob parted. Through the broken doors strode a lean man with a silver-tipped cane, dressed impeccably in black velvet and wearing a long leather coat. Elika instantly knew him, though she had never laid eyes on Peter Pockets before. But she knew that man could be no other. Everywhere upon his coat and trousers, on the sleeves and hem, were countless pockets, both small and large. Each one bulging with some weapon or token. He walked with the air of nobility and slow consideration.

One-eyed Rory was close beside him. Instantly, his gaze found Elika, and he pointed toward her. Peter Pockets lifted his face and his eyes glistened, as if she was a chest of treasure he had come to plunder.

He took a step forward, but the giant Drasdane with antlers on his head blocked his path. The giant's grin was wide, and he gestured wildly with his axe to boast of their victory. And in that moment, Elika understood the chilling truth. This was not just a mindless mob attack on the temple, but an alliance between Drasdanes and Peter Pockets. And it was her magic he had come here to seize.

He flicked his gloved hand and a pack of his men ran toward her.

Elika remembered who she was—Eli Spider of Bad Penny's gang. She turned to run down the corridor, took three steps, and a hand grabbed her by the hair. From the corner of her eye, she could see it was not one of Pockets' men. In his thick hand, he held a butcher's meat cleaver. Unthinking, she yanked out her knife, spun in his grip and cut him across his face. He released her and clutched his bleeding cheek.

Out of nowhere, Igla charged at him with her cane. He shook off his surprise, roared, and his fist flew out. The old tane fell to the floor in a daze. His eyes settled on Elika. She turned to run, but he grabbed and yanked her back. His rage-filled eyes were before her, merciless and mindless. His fingers wrapped around her neck. He shoved her against the wall. The back of her head hit the stone. His other hand tore at her shirt and his rough, calloused hand crushed her breast. His body blocked out everything but his vileness. She beat at him with her fists as his fingers tightened around her throat until she could not breathe.

Everything grew dark, but a powerful impulse kept her anchored to the vestiges of consciousness. She did not want to die. She grabbed at the meaty hand around her throat, clawed his face, his eyes, then scraped the cut she'd given him.

He roared in pain and once again smashed her against the wall. He moved his hand and fumbled with his trousers, his breath hot and foul on her face ...

Then he was gone and she could breathe again. She slumped against the wall, coughing and choking.

"Not her," Rory said calmly, his dagger at the butcher's throat.

"But she cut me face," he complained and dropped his cleaver.

Rory looked at her, took in her torn shirt and drew his dagger across the man's throat.

Elika recovered enough to dart toward Igla and help her quickly to her feet. Together they ran through the nearest door. They slammed it shut and Elika pulled a side table to block it.

The door rattled. "Come out, Spit. We'll not hurt you."

"This way," Igla called out, limping toward the other door in the room, banging her cane as she went.

They came out into another corridor. Behind them they heard the crash of the side table.

"Run ahead, child. It's not me they're after," Igla said urgently with a backward glance.

Elika looked behind her, and there was Rory and more of Pockets' men with Peter Pockets strolling behind them.

"Barricade the way behind us," Igla shouted, as she limped along, leaning heavily on her cane.

"With what?" Elika asked bewildered. "There's nothing here ..."

"Your magic. Use your magic!"

"I don't know how."

"Just trust the magic inside you. It will help you."

Pockets' men rushed toward them.

Elika wished for a web across the hall, wished it with all her heart as Rory bore down on her.

As if on command, black tendrils emerged from the walls and the floor, growing like dark strands of fungus across the hallway. Rory came to an abrupt stop, and his men recoiled in fear. Then rage filled their eyes.

They slashed at the web with their daggers. Elika cried out in pain, for she felt every cut to the black web as keenly as a cut to her skin.

"Stop," she shouted, wanting only for them to stop hurting her. The loose strands of the web wound around the necks of the nearest men, strangling them, breaking the necks, throwing them aside. More men joined the battle against her magic.

"Enough," said a deep, cultured voice and his men fell away as one from the black web she had spun.

Peter Pockets stepped forward, his dark eyes on her.

"Run, Arala. The magic won't hold for long," Igla whispered.

But Elika's gaze snagged on a flash of blue in Pockets' fingers. He lifted his hand, showing her a feather she instantly recognized. Rosy Rose's blue feather.

"Where is she?" Elika demanded hoarsely. "If you hurt her ..."

Peter Pockets' smile was cunning. "Your pack is gone. But little Rose is safe ... for now."

The words cut her deeper than any knife could have done.

Gone? Dead? Disbanded? Lost? And Penny?

The memory of the red smoke blanketing the city rose in her mind, and every vile fear of what might have befallen them crept into her heart. She felt cold and broken and it was all she could do not to crumble to the ground and weep. Her gaze fixed on the feather, and it anchored her strength. Rosy Rose was alive, and she needed Elika now. She was one of the oldest in her pack, and if Penny was gone, she was all they had. As long as any of them lived, they would be a pack.

"Where is she?" Elika repeated.

Instead of answering, Pockets looked over the web she had spun across the hall. He brushed it with his fingers in wonderment. She felt that touch. It made her skin crawl with disgust.

"Amazing. So, it is true. You are a mage and a wonder. Who made you? How did you come to be?" he asked absently as if he did not expect an answer. Then his eyes fell on her. "I mean you no harm, Eli Spider. Come with us and you'll see your little Rose." His voice was soft and lofty, as if he was a lord in truth.

She crossed her arms, trying hard not to show fear, though her heart thundered with it. "Bring her to me, and I'll trade myself for her." She said it nonchalantly, adding a shrug to her demand. "Else, how do I know you won't kill her when you have me?"

He seemed amused. "Very well," he said and indolently waved the fingers of his gloved hand.

One-eyed Rory disappeared instantly back through the broken doors.

"No, Arala, you cannot," Igla whispered and pulled on her arm. "They'll kill you."

Elika covered the old knobbly hand with her own. "Tane Igla, you must know by now that I'm not Arala. I'm Elika, and my place is here in Terren. I have to help my pack. Please, you must help me save her. Take her to the hiding place with you. When I can, I'll find you both."

"Don't you know what they'll do to you?"

"They'll burn me," she said, feeling oddly calm. What was she, after all, without her pack? She had no answer to that, for there was no Eli Spider without Bad Penny and their pack.

Rory returned with Rosy Rose beside him, her face streaked with tears. Elika's heart filled with relief and she dashed toward the web that separated them.

"Give her back the feather," Elika said harshly to Peter Pockets.

He twirled the blue feather in his fingers. "What a fierce, honorable creature you are. We'll deal well together." With an exaggerated swagger, he bowed before Rosy Rose and presented her with the feather. "For you, my lady, may it bring you luck and joy."

Rosy Rose snatched it out of his hand with a pout. He placed a possessive hand on her shoulder. "You for her, as we agreed."

"I want one more thing. Spare the priestesses and their temple."

He tilted his head, considering it. She knew that she had overstepped the boundaries of their agreement. But she also knew that what he wanted was worth far more than the lives of a few women. His gaze roamed over the tendrils of the black web once again. "Very well. I make this gesture as a token of our alliance." He cast but one glance at his men and four of them ran off, back the way they had come. "The temple will be spared. Now come and step out."

Elika crouched beside the web. "Listen to me, Rosy. You must go with the old woman behind me. She's a kind priestess and she'll keep you safe until I find you again."

Rosy Rose peered around Elika's shoulder and frowned. "She look mean and angry."

"She might look it and she might sound it ... and sometimes she might act it a little. But she's got a good heart in her chest. You'll be safe with her. Safer than with these men."

That decided it for her. Rosy Rose nodded.

Elika stood up and faced Peter Pockets. "I'll walk through first. If you betray me, I'll kill every one of your men with my magic."

It was a hollow threat for she could feel the magic in her waning and weakening. Before long the web would fade of its own accord.

But Pockets could not know that. He stepped back, with a wide-armed bow. "I await eagerly our new *alliance*."

She stepped through the web, grabbed Rosy Rose and quickly pushed her through it before Pockets thought to betray her. Igla took charge of Rosy and hurried her away.

Elika waited until they were out of sight, then waited some more until the magic and the web faded. She was dizzyingly, ravenously hungry and her whole body wanted to sink to the floor.

Do not show them weakness. She heard Mite's voice in her mind. So she turned on her heel and walked past Peter Pockets and his toughs. They surrounded her and marched her through the great hall, past the bodies of the fallen, the priestesses, the young acolytes, past the dead guards, and out through the broken temple doors, past the pyre and the screaming High Priestess Herra tied to the pole, as the red blood-salt flames engulfed her.

The mob cheered and shouted vile abuse, whilst inside her, the magic curled tightly in fright. And it grew harder and harder to remember who her enemy truly was.

CHAPTER ELEVEN

The Peter Pockets' Ambition

"When Syn'Moreg sundered the world of Seramight, giving half to men and half to magic, the great catastrophe was greeted with a strange mix of terror and relief. Magic was driven out and banished. Else it fled of its own accord, following the tsaren across the bridge to the Deadlands. Half the world was restored to men. Only the echoes of magic were left behind. Those echoes, I would hazard to say, are akin to lost babes. They show no clear sentience nor possess any reason above the primitive and instinctive need to feed and hide. I do not hold to the common belief that they are driving the Blight, for they do not show the capacity to organize themselves into the force of such power as would be needed to do so. Another power is behind it. Could it be Syn'Moreg himself?"

History of Men, Gods and Magic,
By Priest Oderrin

The table was perfectly arranged. The servants stood nearby in their trim liveries. There were three jugs of wine, four types of meat, golden potatoes, shining dishes of carrots and sprouts, onions in a dark syrup. And beside Elika's plate lay an odd assortment of spoons and knives and five different types of forks.

Yet for all its lavishness, there was a subtle sense of absurdity about the whole feast. It might have been the gaudy, gold candle holders. Or that there was enough food to feed twenty men, yet only two of them were seated at the table. Or perhaps it was Peter Pockets himself. Though impeccably dressed in the finest attire, his every article of clothing was studded with countless pockets. They drew her gaze and she could not help but try to guess what secret was hidden in each one of them.

Peter Pockets' home was another surprise. Whenever she had imagined his abode, it was always in some dark tavern cellar, with many exits and rabbit holes. Instead, she found herself deep in the Silver Circle, inside one of the large mansions on King's Parade, surrounded by impeccable gardens and enclosed by a tall, stone wall. There was even a gatehouse with guards, a stable, and an army of servants to tend to his every wish. The butler took his coat and cane when he entered, and footmen rushed to obey his softly spoken commands. Four of them stood to attention now, staring ahead like statues.

He shook out his napkin and placed it in his lap. "Do begin, my dear. You must be famished after that spectacular piece of magic you threw at my men." His teeth flashed white as he smiled. "I'm told magic needs to feed, like us."

The smell of all this food was making her lightheaded. She wanted nothing more than to eat everything laid out before her. A servant had placed a bowl of parsnip soup in front of her and the sweetness of it filled her nose. But she remembered what happened to Pit the Picker; how he was tricked into betraying her and their pack.

She put her hands in her lap before they snatched something from the table of their own accord. "Might be you just come out and tell me what it is you want from me."

He picked up a spoon. "I hate talking business on an empty stomach. I find it makes one unreasonable." He took a sip of his soup. "My dear, do eat, I insist. This food is free, I assure you. Your freedom, however, is not. So, don't hold back from this little indulgence. You will remain here until we come to an arrangement that benefits us both."

She very much doubted any arrangement between them would benefit her. What did Pockets have that she could possibly want or need?

She looked at the food and felt near sick with hunger. There was no sense in starving herself. Besides, she would need all her wits to escape. So she snatched a piece of bread from the side plate, buttered it thickly and dipped it into her soup. As soon as it hit her mouth, she forgot everything but the feast in front of her. When she had finished the soup, the bread and the hot pastries in the basket beside her, a servant was instantly there, placing a leg of goose on her plate followed by potatoes and sticky onions.

She was about to pick up her knife and fork when Peter Pockets' oddly sultry voice halted her. "You are a pretty little thing, aren't you, beneath that rough?"

She raised her gaze, prickles of alarm running down her spine.

He sipped his wine as he watched her eat, his own plate empty. "Aye, I can see that you'll grow into a beautiful woman, fit to wed a king."

She didn't think he could have said a more absurd thing. Neither did she like the interest shining in his eyes. She picked up the greasy goose leg, shrugged and tore into it with her teeth. "If you shay shoo, m'lord," she replied with her mouth full, then ripped off another piece of meat and followed it with a large gulp of wine, which she spilt over her shirt.

Smiling, he sipped his wine again. "After, perhaps a little polish."

She finished the goose leg. "There's plenty of beautiful ladies out there, m'lord, all ready and polished. I'm sure you aren't lacking the choice of 'em," she said and stabbed a potato with her fork.

It was a strange sort of hunger, thought Elika; she must have eaten enough for five men. Her stomach was full to bursting and tight against her waistband. Yet she still craved something more that wasn't on this table. It was as if no amount of food could abate the deeper hunger of her magic.

From one of his many pockets, Peter Pockets took out a watch and glanced at it. Aside from his bizarre beehive of pockets, he might have passed for a true lord. Every pocket held something. She saw a handkerchief, the hilt of a throwing knife, a gold chain holding another watch, a white flower and many more secrets. Mite had once told her that Pockets carried enough gems and gold on him to buy an army and enough weapons to arm one. Until now, she had not believed him.

The door opened, and the servants brought pears in syrup, plums in cream and a cake with layer upon layer of jam. As she stared at the food she regretted her anger at Pit's betrayal. At that moment, she was certain she would have told Peter Pockets anything he wanted to know had he asked it. The thought was irksome. It brought her to her senses. With deep regret, she lowered her hands back into her lap before they leapt at the cake. "What do you want from me, Pockets?"

"I wish to discuss the terms of our alliance."

"We have no alliance. You took me prisoner in exchange for Rosy."

He spread his hands. "This prison, I dare say, is better than what you used to call home. Wouldn't you agree?"

"You can't buy me. I still belong to Bad Penny. My loyalty is to my pack. You're the one who set the Code for everyone to follow."

His eyes flashed. "My dear, the Code is dead."

Elika's breath caught in her throat. For twenty-five years his Code had ruled the streets of Terren. Before Peter Pockets, they used to fight in the streets and murder each other in their beds. They'd invade each other's hideouts, steal from each other and take what they wanted, when they wanted it. She had not been born then, but she had heard from the old hands what it had been like in those days.

"Why?" she asked. It made no sense that he would unravel his world and his rules without a flicker of doubt or regret.

"The end is here, my dear. The city is falling. No rule of law can contain a dying beast. Men seek only the one thing now—survival at any cost. Which is why your pack is no more. Your loyalty no longer matters."

"You attacked them ..." she said furiously.

He patted his mouth with a napkin. "And why would I trouble myself and my men with a pack of hungry raga-muffins?"

"Then who did? Rimley?"

"Korl Hammer."

"Who?" Elika raked her mind, but the name was not familiar.

"He's the Drasdane warlord who sacked the temple."

She recalled the giant man with antlers and an axe who had been speaking to Peter Pockets.

"It was he who revealed that the purges were useless against magic," he continued. "And the priestesses knew all along."

She shook her head. "They didn't know ..."

He leaned forward, his eyes intent. "They knew. They were simply too weak to do what was needed to purge the world of the last vestiges of magic. When Hammer realized this, he gathered his men. They went from street to street and grabbed every Echo they could find. Then someone whispered into his ear—before you ask, it wasn't one of my men—that Bad Penny's entire gang was infected. So he took his men to flush them out. My men followed, keeping their distance. That's how we caught your little feather girl. The rest ..." He shrugged.

Elika lowered her gaze, trying hard not to feel. She must not show this man any weakness. "You're allied with Korl Hammer."

"Naturally. We are of the same mind after all—saving mankind. He speaks for Drasdanes, and I for the people of Terren. It wouldn't do for us to work against each other, not when our true enemy hides behind the gilded gate."

"Our enemy is magic, not men."

"But there, you are deeply mistaken. This world is lost. I have no illusions about saving it. Only mankind. And you, my dear, will help me save our people and make me their king."

A bubble of laughter burst from her. "You want to be king? The Blight is here. What does it matter whether you die as king?"

His face soured. "I have no intention of dying. But I have every intention of being the savior of Terrenians. When the old order falls, the new shall rise. And for that, I need your magic. You see, the city is hungry. The king has stolen our food, animals and coal, and hidden them inside the impenetrable Golden Circle. Captain Daiger distributes rations once a day, but most go to those with gold-lined pockets."

Elika looked pointedly at the half-eaten feast before them, enough to feed twenty hungry men.

He spread his hands. "Neither I nor mine will ever go without. And I have decided to make all men in this city mine. So, I must kill the king and return everything he hoards for his nobility back to the people of Terren."

"It's impossible. You'd need an army," she said in disbelief.

"I have an army. I have the Terrenians, the Drasdanes, the Islanders, all eager to follow me. Korl Hammer had every blacksmith under his command work day and night to forge weapons for us all. The only thing we need is a dash of magic."

It was hard not to admire the man before her and his ambition. Elika had been hungry her whole life. Like many Terrenians, she knew what it was to fear the coming winter and hope for the early spring. They scraped by, ate simply, shared what they could, stole when need demanded it. And like them, she resented the nobility and their worthless, idle lives of plenty. She might not trust Peter Pockets, but his words embraced her own desires for the people of Terren. Aye, she wanted it for them. Wanted to feed and save them. Especially now that the Blight had destroyed any hope for a harvest this summer.

Then, as if he was near, she heard the clerk's despondent voice in her mind. *What's the point of any of it?*

"You might get the food, and you might live until winter; but to what end? How will you save them when the food runs out and the Blight is upon you?"

He raised his eyebrows. "Winter? We shall not be here when the snow returns. First, I will feed them. Then I will lead them." He picked up a piece of lamb with the tip of his knife and twirled it in front of his face. "Food is a powerful banner men will follow and die for. Once they are fed, and the old order that failed them is destroyed, I'll take them across the bridge to the new world as their savior and king."

Elika's heart fell. A dream. He was offering them a false dream in exchange for a breath of true power. Perhaps he truly believed there was a world beyond the bridge where he could be king. Might be he even cared enough for the people on the streets to lie to them and himself. But a lie it was, nonetheless. She wanted no more false hopes and dreams. It was better to accept the soul-destroying truth than to have your heart crushed again and again.

"I can't help you," she said with a pang of regret. For the briefest moment she had almost believed he could save them. She would have stood beside him had she believed it too. "Magic does what it wants. I have no power over it."

"But I saw you, my dear, doing just that, telling magic what to do."

She shook her head. "You were chasing me. It tried to save itself by saving me. In that moment we were merely of the same mind." At least that's what she had come to believe.

His expression darkened. "Then perhaps I can convince the two of you to unite your minds once again."

"You don't need me. If you have the men, you can storm the gilded gates yourself."

He scoffed at that. "Like ants trying to bite through the hide of a bear. Untrained men with axes against arrows and fire. We have no archers. And we cannot climb those walls. We'd lay siege to the nobles, but they would grow fat on the food they stole from us, whilst my army would starve beneath their gates. With magic, we can break those gates open and drown those hiding behind them with our men. By next dawn, every man left standing will have food, and their faith in me will be unshakable. And you, my dear, will be their hero. I'll make certain they know who had helped them in our hour of need. You'll never again be hunted or feared. Open those gates for us. That is the price of your freedom."

His passion carried her along with it. She was there, saving Terrenians, as she had always wanted to do, and they cheered when they saw her. And it was not Peter Pockets but *her* they crowned as their queen. Aye, a wonderful dream indeed, and foolish in equal measure.

Then she saw another version of that tale. Her magic refusing to obey, whilst the arrows rained on the desperate attackers below and burning tar poured on their heads. The Red Guards charging on horses at the hungry mob, slaying everyone with swords and flails and long pikes. The vision shifted and she saw the priestesses slaughtered before her eyes, and Grisla's mouth filled with blood, her eyes dimming. And in the flames, the high priestesses screamed and screamed. Elika had seen enough useless slaughter. She had killed and almost died. No more. There had to be another way.

She met Pockets' gaze. "This city has seen enough blood. I won't be an instrument of your ambition, for that is what you care about most and not the people."

He tapped his fingers on the table as he chewed her bitter reply. "You know, my dear, Rory was certain you could be swayed to our cause. I have never known him to be wrong about anyone before. But you have had a rather tiring day. Perhaps sleep will clear your mind and revive your wisdom. After all, what will I tell Korl Hammer now after I convinced him we needed the mage *alive*? Indeed, it is the only thing we disagreed upon—whether one throws a mage into the chasm or burns him in the red flames."

"Seems that you might do that to me anyway, whether I help you or not," she said sullenly.

"On the contrary, I would take you with me to the other lands ..."

"The *dead* lands," she filled in pointedly.

"A mage in the land where magic roams wild is a powerful ally. You could find yourself in the king's favor. That is to say, *my* favor."

The look he gave her brooked no question as to his meaning. Though he was not overly unhandsome, the thought of being in Pockets' bed made her stomach churn.

She did not hide her disgust well enough, for his lips firmed in annoyance. He barely lifted his hand to motion a silent command, when a servant sprang to life and opened the double doors. One-eyed Rory walked in with two men in tow.

"Take our guest to her chamber, so she may rest and ponder my generous offer." He rose and bowed to her with cynical amusement before Rory led her away.

The mansion was enormous. They must have walked half the length of King's Parade, she thought, before they came to a dark, narrow stair leading down.

She halted. "Where are you taking me?"

The sharp tip of a blade poked her back. "Don't make this hard, Spit," Rory said. "You won't be hurt. Peter Pockets always keeps his word. Besides, not everyone from your pack is dead."

She followed his gaze and saw Pit the Picker at the end of the hall, pale and wide-eyed, staring at her. She looked aside and walked on, down the stairs where the only light was cast by the lantern in Rory's hand.

They emerged into a dank cellar. Immediately, her skin prickled in that charged way, as if lightning was near. An oil lamp hung on a hook in the wall. And in its light, she saw a vision of horror. The walls were dark red, nearly black, and at one end of the cellar, metal bars glistened with dried blood-salt. Rory held open the prison door, and the guards behind her ushered her inside.

Without another word, they left her alone inside the bloodied cellar, where only the flickering oil lamp kept the darkness at bay.

She moved away from the bars and the blood-stained walls until she stood in the center of the cell. But even here, her skin prickled uncomfortably as if a million mites were biting her. There was a chamber pot in the corner, a jug with water on a small table, and a bed beside one wall. When she moved toward it, her skin charged and the prickling sensation increased. She wrapped her arms around herself and sat on the cold, damp ground.

From the silent shadows, the horrors of the day assailed her. Again and again, she saw the priestesses slaughtered by the ravening mob, the bloodied bodies lying beneath Arala's stone feet. Again and again, she watched the dark tendrils of magic form a web and strangle Pockets' men. She had killed two men with her own hands, and as she sat there, she killed them over and over again. She began to shake uncontrollably, her arms tightening around herself. Mite had killed many more than that, as had Penny. It was nothing to boast about, nor dwell upon. Then why could she not stop shaking? Why could she not close her eyes for fear of what lay in that inner darkness?

For a long time, she sat there, fighting memories and the enveloping sleep. But there was no escaping dark dreams. Her body demanded its rest and her mind soon followed.

When she opened her eyes again, a small figure sat huddled in the corner outside her cell. She could just make out his face in the low glow of the lantern.

"Pit?" she asked hoarsely.

She wondered how long she had slept. There was no window and she could not tell whether it was still night or morning.

He wiped his nose with the back of his hand. "It's all your fault."

His head was no longer bandaged. There was nothing left of his right ear, except a hole and an ugly scar. He hugged his knees and lowered his face as if afraid to meet her eyes.

"I'm sorry, Pit," she said and meant it. "I didn't mean for any of this to happen."

He wiped his eyes, angry and bitter. "Don't matter now, does it?"

"How are they treating you?"

He met her gaze and there was such desolation there, her heart tightened. "I just want to go home. I want it to be the way it was, with Penny and the pack ..." A sob choked him into silence.

"I can take you home. As soon as I escape ..."

His face grew angry again. "They're all dead!" he shouted. "There is no home for us anymore. And it's all your fault."

"They're not all dead. I saw Rosy Rose with my own eyes."

"She's just a useless kid, not anyone who matters. Rory took me there, back to the Hide, to make me believe him. I saw them, those who've been left to rot. Pipe, Tick, Lazy

Eye, Mill, Clever Kit ... dead, just lying there like discarded bloody meat."

"And Penny? Was she there, too?" Elika whispered, her own tears rising.

He shook his head. "Didn't see her, or Fast Flint, or Tiny Timmy, or some of the younger ones. Rory said they likely threw those they could catch into the chasm. It's quicker than building a pyre for them."

"Or might be they escaped. Pit, as long as there are any of us still alive, we are a pack. No matter what happened."

He jumped to his feet. "No! Not anymore. Why would I go back? There's nothing there. No food left on the street. A whole bag of gold can't buy you bread. Were I to go out there, they'd catch me and burn me, 'cause I'm an Echo, too. But Peter Pockets keeps us fed and safe and he don't care whether I'm infected. He won't let anyone kill us. Might be you'd do better to join him. He'd give you a nice room to sleep in and food to eat ..."

"Pit?" she said softly to stop him. "Did he send you here to sway me?"

He shook his head. "Didn't need to. I figured if he sent you down here, you weren't being good to him. Why are you being so stubborn? The pack is gone. Penny's dead. They all are. There's nothing out there for you."

There is Rosy Rose, she thought. And if she had survived, then perhaps the others had too. Who'd be looking after them if she sided with Peter Pockets? If only she could help Pit, too. Or might be he was better off with Peter Pockets than with her. What more could she offer him out there?

"Take care of yourself, Pit," she said sadly.

He stared at her, his lips trembling, then turned and fled.

Finding herself once again alone in the dark cell was like being doused in ice water. The ugly memories crept out like slimy serpents. Memories of the battle at the temple and the vile dreams that had haunted her sleep. She wondered how many hours she had been here. It was disconcerting not to know. Would the Blight sneak up on her without her realizing? Was this to be her final tomb?

A desperate part of her thought about using magic to escape this prison. She sought the magic inside her, hating herself for reaching toward it as if it was a friend. When she found it, however, it was curled tight, unwilling, still hungry and afraid of the surrounding blood-salt.

"Can't you dig us out of here?" she mumbled. But the magic only curled tighter.

She heard the door creak open at the top of the stairs, followed by heavy footfalls. A guard appeared, clad in a velvet suit and silver-trimmed vest. In his hand he held a tray with food. Behind him walked Peter Pockets.

The guard pushed the tray under the bars and left.

There was cold chicken, bacon, boiled potatoes, boiled eggs and leavened bread with jam, and a cup of milk. Her stomach rumbled, and she wondered whether this was breakfast. Or perhaps she had slept all day and this was dinner.

Peter Pockets leaned on the blood-covered wall with one shoulder, idly swinging the key to her cell. "Did you sleep well, my dear? The maids have readied your chambers upstairs, with a feather bed and silk sheets, and a hot bath. I instructed them to keep the room warm with a coal fire."

Elika stared at him mutinously, hating him for making her crave everything he offered with mindless ferocity.

He smiled, flashing his white teeth. "I understand pride, my dear, better than anyone. You don't need to say anything.

Just one nod to let me know you wish to improve your ..."
He cast a glance over the cell. "... situation."

One little nod and she need never worry about anything
but how to make her magic do what Pockets wanted it to
do. One nod and she need never fear starvation on the
streets or being alone without a pack. She had seen Pockets'
men. They were fiercely loyal, devoted, and proud. Might
be she was a fool and Pit the Picker had the right of it, but
even now she could not abandon Bad Penny or her pack.
Whether Penny was dead or alive, as long as one of their
pack was still breathing, she could not leave them behind.

"I'm Eli Spider of Bad Penny's pack, and I'll always be
one of them. And if I could get magic to do what I wanted,
I'd get it to break apart this prison and free me."

Peter Pockets pushed himself from the wall. "Think on
it some more, my dear. But don't take too long. I fear we
are rapidly running out of time. With or without you, we
will storm those gates. And if you are not one of us, you
are one of them." He turned on his heel and left.

Elika looked down at the laden tray but could not find
her appetite. She sat on the dirt floor and lowered her head
to her knees. Then the oil lamp went out, and she was cast
into pitch darkness.

Everything in her tightened, and it became difficult to
breathe. She hated pitch darkness. From its depths all those
nightmares emerged, where there lurked a giant spider,
watching her with those terrible yellow eyes. She curled
into a ball on the ground and lay as still as she could. If she
did not make a sound, nothing would find her in this dark.
In the silence, however, every faint sound became acute—
the drumming of her heart, her ragged breath, a sob
threatening to break out through the tightness in her
throat. She wanted to scream and beg and plead to be

allowed out. She'd do anything Peter Pockets wanted, even use her magic. But her magic was curled up even tighter than she and would not listen.

She felt as if she had lain there for an eternity, staring into the fathomless abyss, when a faint glow of yellow light appeared in its depths. For a moment, she thought it was a dream. Then she heard soft steps.

With trembling arms, she pushed herself up. A hooded shadow moved forward, silent and menacing.

"Who's there?" she called out, but it came out as a breathless whisper.

In the dim light, she saw a hollowed socket where an eye should be. The other eye was in shadow.

"What do you want, Rory?" she asked in a shaking voice, naming the horror that came from the dark.

He turned his head to see her better with his one eye, and she saw something in his gaze that she had never seen there before—uncertainty.

It was so strange that for a moment she forgot to be afraid.

"Came to talk to you, Spit," he said in that menacing way of his. But the apprehension in his voice took the edge off it.

"What about?" she asked wearily.

"Always liked you, Eli Spider."

She stared. He had never used her name before. Not ever.

"Peter Pockets would have been good to you if you'd joined us."

"Never liked Pockets. Nor you either, so just say what you want to say and leave me alone." It was the last thing she wanted, to be left alone again in the dark. But she could not give her fear voice, for it might just beg Rory to let her join them.

"Still angry about me cutting the finger of one of your little mice. I'd be the same for my lot." He gave an indifferent shrug that grated. "But I'm not here for me. Wouldn't ask for a favor for myself, but another ... one of mine." He shifted on the spot awkwardly.

"You want a favor ... from *me*?" she asked incredulously.

He sighed. "It's like this. I've got a son. One who means a lot to me, that is ... not by a whore, but a real son."

"Why would it matter if he was by a whore?"

"'Cause I raised this one as best I could. Loved his ma, see?"

She shook her head in disbelief. "Can't picture you in love, Rory."

"Well, I was. Then she died. Some years back. I've been looking after Chelik ever since. He's a good kid. Not a thief or a killer. Not like one of us."

She blinked in surprise. "How's that possible?"

"I didn't want him to be like me. Wanted more for him, like his ma would have wanted. I let her down. Wasn't there when she needed me. Too busy doing things for Pockets. Didn't want to let my son down, too. I've got plenty of coin stashed away. Peter Pockets is generous to those who do well by him. I did everything Pockets wanted and didn't drink or whore away the coin. So I paid a nurse to look after Chelik. Sour old cow, she is, but she's strict and won't take no nonsense from him. She came from the Silver Circle. He's a clever lad and knows how to read and write and knows all manner of things the priests taught him. Well-spoken, too. But with all that's happening, the nurse fled and left Chelik alone. I suspect she took the bridge.

But there are things I have to do now, and I can't have my boy come with me where I'm going, see?"

"You don't want him anywhere near Peter Pockets," she said, understanding.

"If they have him, they'll be able to make me do anything they want. I might cut a finger or two off a sneaky thief, but I'm not a savage. I had a ma and pa once, and sisters too. They've been gone a long time now. But I remember them and always will."

She shifted in discomfort. "Why are you telling me this?"

"I want Chelik safe. He's all I got. He's only eight and a good kid, not like his pa." He looked aside as if ashamed. "I don't have anyone I can trust—except you."

"Me?" she blurted out in surprise. "What makes you think he'd be safe with me?"

"Been watching you, Spit. I always knew you were a girly mouse. You're prettier than you think and been getting more so these last few years. And not in a masculine way, either. Despite being a girly mouse, you're smarter than most. And you're loyal and more honest than anyone else I know. If you give me your word you'll look after him and get him across to the other side of the bridge, then I know I can die in peace without worrying about 'im."

She shrugged. "I might be able to help you, but I'm stuck in here, aren't I?"

He lifted a key hooked on the chain over his finger.

"Pockets will kill you," she said.

"I'll convince him it was likely your magic that freed you."

"You'd betray him for me?"

"No. For my son. I'd cut his throat for Chelik," he said softly. And she suspected that was a warning to her, too.

She stared at the key. "I'll look after him." Truth was, she wouldn't have abandoned the boy, Rory's threats or not. Penny had taught them better than that.

His whole body eased with relief and he inserted the key into the lock. "I'll bring him to Antway Alley tomorrow night. Give me your word you'll be there."

"I'll be there," she promised. "If I'm breathing, I'll be there."

He unlocked her cell. "You know that I'll find you, if you play me false."

She strode past him. "Aye, I know."

He stopped her at the base of the stairs. "Not that way. Too many guards. You'll find your way through the sewers."

She swallowed, peered into the dark. "I ... I can't. It's too dark."

He thrust a lantern into her hands. "'Tis but a short walk. There's not enough rats left to bother you. Never imagined you to be scared of something as harmless as a sewer."

His amusement irked her. "Not frightened, just can't see in the dark."

"If you say so."

He led her to a low door, which opened into a small hall with many rooms and alcoves stocked with fat barrels of grain and wine, hanging hams and cheese rolls. There were rows and rows of shelves stacked with jars of jams, pickles made from tomatoes, onions and many different vegetables. Meats in fat, salted ham and strings of dried fruits. Her jaw dropped. There was enough food to feed the whole city.

Rory chuckled at her amazement. "Pockets is smart. He spent decades storing food. To my way of thinking, he doesn't need magic to help him storm the gilded gates. He's got enough wits to do it himself." Rory opened another door to stone stairs leading deeper underground. "This is where we part ways. I'll see you tomorrow." He lit another lantern for himself.

Elika held up her light. Behind her, the door closed, the lock turned and Rory's steps faded away. She hovered on the edge of darkness. Even if she found her way to the streets, what was there left for her? She thought of Rosy Rose and Penny and her pack. She would find them. Slowly, she began to descend.

CHAPTER TWELVE

The Mage at the Bridge

*"Since the collision of the ethereal and earthly realms, men
and tsaren have sought dominion over their joined worlds. In
that time, the Sacred Crowns have sought to discover why their
worlds merged and how to break them apart. Why King
Northwind suspected Arala's involvement in this disaster has
never been revealed, nor how he subdued the powerful tsarina
and imprisoned her. What we have unearthed from that dark
time, is that Northwind grew more and more convinced that
Arala was the culprit, and that her death would undo the
collision and cleave the realms."*

History of Men, Gods and Magic,
By Priest Oderrin

When she emerged from the sewers, Elika squinted
against the bright light of day. Though the sun must
have been high, the city was eerily quiet. Many buildings
were nothing but charred shells. Others were abandoned,
their doors and windows broken. Folk hid in their homes,
peering from behind the shutters. Else they scurried about
the streets, keeping out the way of the marauding dog-
gangs.

Even Market Street, usually busy with shoppers, was
abandoned. The stalls were overturned and there was blood

on the cobblestones. Men had done this, not magic. And she could not help wondering whether magic truly was more evil than men.

Once, she had believed it with her whole heart. She had gone through torment to be rid of magic. Now, where once there was hatred, lay only numbness. Were she to look deeper, there lurked something else that was cold and hard. She hugged herself and lowering her face, walked past the cold pyres and gray piles of ashes and bones.

She had to find Rosy Rose and reunite her pack. She'd find others, too, she promised silently. Whatever fate awaited them, they'd meet it together.

Shouts came from behind her. Without turning to look, she ducked through a broken doorway into an abandoned shop and hid out of sight. When no one followed, she peeked out through a dusty window. A group of townsmen ran past, chased by a pack of young lordlings on horses, brandishing their swords as they rode. The slowest runner was brought down first, the others scattered in different directions. But the horses were swiftly upon them and swords fell on them from above. A moment later, the lordlings were riding away, laughing, leaving the bodies where they lay.

Elika crouched under the window before they saw her.

"Treacherous vermin," one was saying to the other as they rode past. "Think they can plot against our king. Well, there's some dead for them to eat. Let them pick each other's bones."

The others laughed.

It seemed the nobility had found a new way to amuse themselves and a part of her regretted not joining Pockets' war. But she had her pack to look after. They always came first.

Tane Igla had taken Rosy Rose and Elika had to find them. She would ask Bill for help. Cautiously, she emerged onto the street and hurried toward the old harbor and Bill Fisher's boat.

There were other edgy fools like her on the streets, frightened, watchful; driven out of their barricaded homes by some weighty need. But there were no city guards in sight. Somehow, that frightened her more than the feral packs of men on the prowl. What laws did men live by now?

She pressed ahead, alert and cautious, keeping to her old haunts, for she knew these streets better than anyone. Twice she ducked into an alley, when cold, hungry eyes turned toward her. She was but a few streets away from the harbor when she heard a child's scream. Her heart stuttered as she recognized that voice.

Ahead, a man wrapped his beefy arm around a young boy's throat. "You little bastard!" he roared. "I'll show you what you get for thieving."

Tiny Timmy struggled in his iron grip. He was alive! That meant others might be too.

"Didn't steal nothing, honest," he cried. "I was chasing a rat, and it ran into your house."

She almost laughed with relief. Tiny Timmy looked younger than he was, and a great liar to add. Still, the terror on his face was honest enough.

"You're the rat who snuck into my house. And where's your blood-salt, you filthy Echo?" The man raised his hunting knife in the other hand.

Timmy screamed again and wriggled harder.

Without thought, she strode forward, snatching the knife out of her belt as she went, and stabbed the man in the side of his back where it hurt the most. He bellowed and collapsed onto one knee.

Timmy staggered away and saw her. His jaw dropped. He paled in horror, still staring at her. And then, to her dismay, he turned and fled as fast as his feet could move.

Hurt pierced her chest. "Timmy wait!" she called after him, and sidestepping a weak swipe from the man's knife, chased after the boy.

She called out his name again and again, hating his fear of her. She'd never hurt him ... *But the magic in her might.* The thought stopped her in her tracks and she watched him disappear into a wall of bodies.

Before her, hundreds upon hundreds of people blocked her way. They were carrying bundles of their possessions, all moving in the same direction—all headed toward the bridge. She was back in Riftside and every street she turned into was filled with fleeing remnants of mankind.

Her way to Bill's boat was blocked, so she scurried up onto the roofs. Despite the crowded streets below, the thieves' high-way was empty. She looked around the empty roofs in wonder and a deepening sense of aloneness. With so many abandoning their homes, the looters must be out feasting on the possessions they had left behind. Or might be with the Blight nigh upon them, the thieves, too, saw no sense in staying behind.

From high up here, her gaze was drawn toward the gray lands beyond, where men now sought refuge. So this is the end, she thought and her feet moved toward the lands where nothing lived.

As she neared the chasm, the crowds below grew more and more dense.

From the roofs above Rift Street she surveyed the scene. Though she knew that thousands upon thousands of people lived in Terren, until that moment she had never grasped how great a number that truly was. As far as she could see, desperate folk shuffled and pushed their way to the bridge.

Her gaze shifted to it.

Once she had thought nothing was more frightening than the menacing, black bridge—a living monster that did not belong in their world. She was wrong. The sight that accosted her was worse. The slender bridge was sickly and shriveling like a winter apple, with countless black shreds flailing in the rising winds. The railing on one side was gone altogether. Despite that, folk piled onto the bridge and fought their way toward the Deadlands. But the path across the chasm was only wide enough for two men to cross it abreast. As they jostled and pushed each other, desperate to reach the other side, the screams of those plunging into the chasm filled the air.

She had done this. She had stabbed the bridge and in doing so she had taken their last hope of escaping the Blight. Each man and woman and child who fell over the side where the railing had unraveled was a death she had caused with her hatred of magic. And as she looked, she saw not just the bridge unravelling before her eyes, but her world.

Unable to turn away from the sight she sank to her knees and watched. One after another, men turned to dust at the apex. But not all. Some made it to the other side, and the Deadlands were filled with thousands of motionless shadows. What fate had they envisaged there, each one who took that path? *It is not death*, they surely tell themselves, *it is not Blight*.

As the light of the day began to fade, she remained there still, punishing herself, forcing herself to watch the unending stream. Despite so many turning to dust, they kept marching onward.

But it seemed her punishment would not end there. As she watched, she suddenly saw that which shattered all she had ever known was true, for the secret of the bridge was laid bare before her. How was it possible that no one, not even the worldly priests, had seen it?

She stared and stared, refusing to believe it, yet unable to deny it. Everyone who wore the blood-salt pendants perished. Every one of them who was not infected turned to dust—blown away by the rising winds. But it was not the blood-salt that stopped them from crossing. Some cast it aside before stepping onto the bridge. Her mind raced. She thought back. Mite was infected, and he had reached the other side. Blood-dog and Tix, too, had reached the Deadlands. They were all Echoes.

An incredulous laugh burst out of her. How could it be otherwise? Only the Echoes could cross. The truth was always right before them. This was the Bridge to Magic. It was never meant to save men. Arala had forged the bridge not to banish magic, but to allow it escape from death and destruction wrought upon it by men.

As another man turned to dust, Elika wanted to shout the truth from the rooftops, to tell them what they did not see. But there were too many of them and they would not listen. The mob was frantic. Were she to tell them only the Echoes could cross, and the rest had to face the Blight, she would likely be set upon.

She searched the crowds below for a familiar face, someone to whom she could whisper the truth. She spied Green Silk Harry and Cross-eyed Abe, inseparable friends to the last, pushing ahead toward the bridge. It was no good; she could not reach them. Then she watched two children, both wearing the blood-salt crystals and holding their mother's hands, step on to the bridge. It was why children rarely crossed. They were young and had not lived long enough to be infected. Further ahead, a mother and babe both turned to dust. Elika flinched.

She had to do something to save them. But what?

A thought struck her. She had used magic in the hide and infected everyone with it. And in the temple, when magic had escaped her during the Trial of Reval, it spread to the priestesses. She could not stop anyone from wanting to cross the bridge, but she could stop them from dying whilst doing so. If she used magic, everyone below would become tainted by it.

Another man, a child, an old woman all turned to dust, and still more rushed ahead. There was no time to waste. No time to ponder what awaited them across the chasm. Those folk below wanted to reach it, and she could grant them this much.

She closed her eyes and sought the ball of power inside her. Silently, she asked it for help. She felt it unfurl curiously, looking up at her with interest. *You can see me?* It might have whispered.

I know you are there, Elika replied.

But what magic could she do? She knew nothing about it.

She closed her eyes and thought of those slick, black tendrils, for it was the last thing she had conjured. She imagined those tendrils running over the roofs surrounding the folk below ...

There was a sudden terrible sound, like rolling thunder, and her eyes snapped open. Giant black tendrils were shooting out from her, racing over and through the roofs, tearing through tiles, breaking through windows, ripping through brick and stone. And as Elika watched in amazement and horror, one of the old, abandoned buildings collapsed on the crowd beneath it. The city filled with screams.

"Magic!" they shouted.

Folk stumbled over each other and trampled the fallen in their haste to flee.

"Magic!" they screamed as they ran.

In their panic, they fled back into the city or shoved their way onto the bridge.

Heedless of it all, the tendrils raced outwards and onward, and Elika felt herself unravelling and growing fainter and fainter, as if at any moment she would cease to be.

She tried to recall the magic, but the black tendrils just kept writhing joyfully on and on, as if they had waited for this moment of freedom and now that they had it, they would never return. She felt herself detach from the world, fading away like the shadows in the Deadlands.

"Stop! I command you to stop," Elika screamed.

The magic halted as if startled, hesitated, then ran back like a frightened child to its mother, coiling back into a tight ball inside her.

Elika looked toward the folk on the apex of the bridge. They were crossing. She had saved them by turning them to Echoes. She smiled and wobbled weakly on her feet.

Then she became aware of the strange silence. The type of silence that sent the same dark tendrils of fear through her heart, racing and tearing through her.

She looked down and met thousands of eyes looking up.

A man pointed a finger at her. "A mage! He's the one who's sent the Blight upon us."

"Burn him!" Rose the chorus of voices.

"Burn him!" Beat the drums of hate.

"Hey, that's Eli," someone else shouted. "I know 'im."

Groups of men detached from the crowd and raced into the building below her. Her feet moved, driven by feral, mindless fear. She darted into a bolthole, crawled through the hidden hole in the wall and climbed into a roof space, making herself still and small between the beams. Mite had shown her all the ways to outwit her pursuers. How to hide and sit still for hours, long past when she was certain the threat had gone.

"He's here somewhere," said a voice nearby. "Look for a bolthole."

"Got one here, see?" said another.

"Follow him. We can't let him escape."

Elika held her breath.

The voices and bounding steps faded.

Still, she dared not move. Even when the world went dark and she had heard no voices for a long time, she just lay there, ravenously hungry and sick, her whole body hurting.

The magic was killing her each time she used it, it left her shrunken and faded, as if she no longer lived in this world, as if she was becoming one of those phantoms in the Deadlands.

With great effort, she shook off sleep, for she was certain if she fell asleep she'd never wake again. She forced herself to move and crawl out the building.

It was night. The moon hung low in the sky. Rift Street was once again empty, and the bridge a sorrowful sight. Elika turned away and made her way toward Bill's boat, her legs weak and unsteady, her head spinning, and her hunger more ferocious than ever.

She walked past the piles of rubble, where houses had stood upright the day before. Here and there, she saw bodies buried beneath it, and she suddenly knew with unshakable certainty that she would never be rid of her magic.

CHAPTER THIRTEEN

The Pack

"Since the destruction of the Sacred Crowns and the end of the lineage of Northwind, Southfire, Eastrise and Westwater, there have been seven claimants to the old thrones. All have met with an untimely, furtive end. What hand works against them, none can say. I would not be alone in suspecting the tanes. Though common men believe tanes have been hunted to extinction, the priestesses and the priests have been aware of their secretive existence amongst us. They are a necessary evil in our world, for in our dark age they hold much knowledge from the time before, and thus we guard them and ask them questions."

History of Men, Gods and Magic,
By Priest Oderrin

"What have you done to yourself, foolish girl?" Igla grabbed her arm and helped her toward the chair.

The warmth of Bill's boat was dizzying. Bill was rocking in his chair, a cup of his warm whisky in hand.

Elika looked around the cabin. "Where's Rosy?"

Igla shifted before snapping. "She ran off."

"You lost her!" Elika said aghast and turned to go out again.

"She ran off, I said. I didn't lose her. And she's fast and lithe as a mouse. What was I to do, chase her through the streets and roofs?"

Elika's shoulders slumped. It was dark, she'd never find Rosy now. "Where did she go?"

"Didn't tell me, now did she? You can go running after her once you've rested and eaten something. Just look at you. Have you been using your magic again without feeding?"

"I ate … last night." She fell into a chair and the room spun and spun. She had never felt sicker.

"Here, eat this." Igla thrust a warm bowl into her hands.

"I can't," Elika mumbled.

Another hand was there, pouring warm, spiced whisky into her mouth. "Drink this then," said Bill's voice. "Cloves and cinnamon will revive your magic."

Elika drank and miraculously, the room stopped spinning. In her lap lay the bowl of soup. She picked up the spoon and caught sight of her emaciated arm. For a moment she just stared at it, an alien object attached to her, little more than bone and skin. This could not be her body. How could she have grown so thin so quickly?

"It's eating me from the inside. Magic is killing me," she said without feeling.

"You're not dying but wasting away," Igla said. "So eat."

Elika did as she was told, eating quickly without tasting much. When she finished the bowl of hot soup, another was placed in her lap. After nothing more was left, she stumbled to the cupboard, and mumbling about needing sleep, curled up inside.

It was late and still dark when Igla's raised voice pierced through Elika's dreamless slumber. "Bill, she's dying. She's been using magic, but she doesn't know how to feed. Only Reval can help her. I sent him the crow, but the damned bird is now perched atop your mast. He's refusing to fly across the bridge."

"Ah love, you worry too much, as ever," came Bill's muffled reply.

"Aren't you listening, you big oaf? There's hardly any flesh left on her ..."

"She'll work it out. They always do."

Igla harrumphed. "'Tis your answer to everything. Just ignore it and it'll set itself right."

"And more oft than not, it does."

"But what if this time is one of those when it doesn't? We need to force her across the bridge. Might be I'll drag her there myself. But I need your help. We can tie her up ..."

Elika stiffened where she lay.

But Bill chuckled. "It's a nice thought, but I fear we are too old to start another adventure. Were you to go, I'd not come with you."

"Don't talk like that, Bill. I'm not going anywhere, now am I? I was only thinking aloud."

Their voices dropped lower. For a while, Elika listened to the gentle hum of their love, the soft laughter, and whispered reminiscence of their lives long past. It seemed so normal, it made her want to weep for the life she had never known. And perhaps she did weep, before the soothing hum of humanity finally lulled her to sleep.

Her dreams were filled with blood, flowing from the bodies of the priestesses, down the temple steps, and drowning the streets. Whilst in the dark, awaiting her, calling to her, was the Bridge to Magic. And from the Great Web overhead, a giant spider watched her, waiting to pounce. It dashed toward her ...

Elika startled awake, her heart racing. The boat was silent. Sunlight sneaked in beneath the cupboard door.

Her first thought was of Rosy Rose. She was out there, alone and unprotected. Elika had to find her, Tiny Timmy, too, and the rest of her pack. She dared not hope that Penny was still alive, but could not accept she might be dead. Whatever had become of them, Elika would not abandon them.

Silently, she opened the cupboard door. Bill and Igla were asleep in each other's arms on a narrow bed beneath the round window. She grabbed her coat and tiptoed past them.

At the door, she paused. Mite had entrusted his ring to her. She could not leave it behind. Casting a glance at sleeping Bill, she tiptoed to the cabinet and opened each drawer as silently as she could until she found the ring with four crowns. She pocketed it, turned and met Bill's gaze.

Her cheeks grew hot, but she refused to give in to shame. The ring was Mite's. There was nothing wrong with stealing from a thief. So she lifted her head high. "The ring's not yours, Bill. I can't let you keep it."

He didn't move. "'Tis for your sake I keep it from him, princess."

"This ring is nothing to me."

"But there you be wrong. Look at the ring and tell me what you see."

She withdrew it from her pocket. "Four crowns. A blue gem inside the largest of them."

"It's the Ring of the Sacred Crowns. Long ago, the world was divided between four kings ..."

"The old kings are dead. Reval destroyed their houses six hundred years ago."

"Reval killed the kings, their wives, children and servants, but he did not kill all the sons. Mite is Northwind. He's the descendant of the king who abducted and tormented Arala.

And I swore upon my soul and hers that I would make certain no man would ever wear that ring again."

Elika shook her head. "Mite's father was Lord Silvering..."

"Lord Silvering is Northwind, the last true king of men. The ring is proof of that."

"His forefathers might have stolen it or found it."

"Damn it girl, 'tis more than just a ring." Igla shuffled on his shoulder in her sleep and he lowered his voice. "Mite's the spit of King Airling Northwind. Looks just like him. He's the heir. And he's got a reckoning with the tsaren, though he may not know it yet."

"Mite is just and fair," she objected.

Bill suddenly looked ancient and sage. "Mite will grow into all this ring expects of him. It's in their blood to conquer and destroy. The Sacred Crowns warred against magic, and it was their deeds that summoned Syn'Moreg from the depths of Nerabyss. Their crimes led to the Sundering Wars and the destruction of the Great Web. Let the old world die, El. Leave the ring behind."

Elika could not meet his impassioned gaze. "I'm sorry, Bill. I owe Mite too much. Might be he'd make a better king than his forefathers. Or might be he's already dead. But the ring is his."

Bill's lips thinned and there was deep disappointment on his face. "Then go, take it and do not return to this harbor, princess."

Hurt rose in her chest. But Bill was right, she could not steal from a man and claim his friendship. She nodded once and left his boat for the last time.

The day was fresh, warm and sunny, but it did nothing to ease her spirit. There was a hollowness in her which she didn't think would ever go away. She had grown old, she thought with regret. She had seen too much, and perhaps had finally understood too much.

Rift Street was again crowded with desperate folk, all headed for the bridge. Once, magic had been her enemy. Now, she regarded men with the same dread. Nothing made sense. Nothing felt right anymore.

The white-tipped crow cawed overhead. Elika looked up and saw it watching her with its probing yellow eyes. Ignoring it, she climbed over the side of Bill's boat and down the rope ladder to the mudflats. It had not rained in days, and the ground was solid all the way to the old harbor wall.

She walked away from the crowds, heading into the city. She had to find Rosy Rose. And she had promised to meet Rory later that night. Pockets' men must also be looking for her by now, so she kept her eyes sharp for them as she strode through the backstreets of Riftside. Everything around her had changed beyond recognition. Homes stood looted and abandoned. Signs of pyres were everywhere. The familiar faces were nowhere to be seen. Everything was broken. Her world was broken.

She scrambled to the nearest roof. In the distance, she saw a few youths wearing the red scarves of Rimley's gang. They were too far away to cause her any trouble and their attention was fixed on tracking someone below in the alley. After a while, they vanished from the roofs altogether.

Elika did not know what sense drew her gaze north; nor what sense had spurred her feet to race toward the city gate, just as the chorus bells tolled from every tower.

A hushed stillness descended on Terren. In the streets, men stopped, their gazes turned northwards. Beyond their city, the land was gray and fallow, the forests dead, the grass turned to dust.

Then somebody shouted, "Blight!"

As she raced northwards, the war bells grew louder, more urgent, and shouts of "Blight!" joined the chant.

"The Blight has breached the city!"

"Blight!"

And the bells tolled *Blight!*

She stopped on the edge of the gutter above King's Parade, from where she could see the city gate. It was closed and painted thickly with blood and salt. Beside the gate, the guards were slumped against the wall, their eyes vacant, their mouths slack. One guard's body jerked as if something was being ripped from inside him by an invisible foe.

Along the city wall, men lay dying, unable to move, unable to call out. No one approached to help them. The Blight had no smell, no sound, no other sign it was there save that all it touched fell and slowly wasted away. And now it was here, inside her city, relentless, unforgiving. Not even a blood-salt barrier was enough to stop it.

Only two deaths remained to them now, thought Elika, the Blight or the bridge.

In the streets, everyone stood silent, and she could almost hear their thoughts, for they mirrored her own. *This is the end. Magic has won.*

Bitterness welled up in her heart. It was not bitterness at the magic that had wrought this destruction, nor at the harrowing choice they must now face. She was bitter at Mite. He had left her to face this alone. He had left them all.

She spun away and went in search of her pack.

The day faded. She had found no sign of Rosy or her pack in any of their usual haunts. Tired and hungry, she now hid in the shadows of Antway Alley, where Rory had told her to meet him.

The city was once again silent, and a sense of waiting tension permeated its stones. With so many abandoned homes, the dog-gangs and looters paid little mind to those on the street. Even so, she started when a shadow formed itself into a man.

But it was only Rory stepping out from a dark doorway. "Hey, Spit."

She pushed away from the wall. "I thought Pockets might have caught you helping me."

"He caught another fool, after I whispered a name to him." He grinned humorlessly.

She shifted on the spot. No doubt it was someone who'd crossed Rory. "Are they looking for me?" she asked.

"Did you see anyone looking for you?" he countered. "I heard about your little caper at the bridge. Not very good at hiding, are you? Anyway, I whispered some rumors into the crowd, about how they'd caught the mage and thrown him into the chasm. Not long after, every man on the streets claimed to have seen it happen. Pockets thinks you're dead."

She hated to be grateful to One-eyed Rory, but she was. "Guess I owe you."

"Aye, you owe me and you'll pay me back." He pulled out a boy from the doorway behind him.

There was no denying the boy was Rory's, with that long face and dark eyes. He was wrapped in a plain-looking cloak and might have passed for a street orphan, save that there was a naïve, soft youthfulness about him. He clung to Rory whilst looking at her as if she was some horror made of blood and night. Unlike his father, the boy was not wearing a blood-salt crystal.

Rory held out two full sacks to her. "Here. This food should last you a while."

Elika took them, again feeling grateful. There was no food to be had on the streets, just as Pit had told her, not for all the gold in the land.

"I'll look after him," she said.

"Go on then, son," Rory gruffly urged the boy forward. "Eli will take care of you. I'll come and visit when I can," he lied. "Just stay with Eli and you'll be fine."

"Don't leave me, Pa," the boy begged. He had a softly spoken manner, and but for his likeness to Rory, she would have thought him to be the child of some fat pouch.

Rory crouched down in front of him. "Listen to me, son. You must do something for me. I love ye, you know that, aye?"

The boy nodded, tearfully.

"I just want ye to be safe. And right now, I can't come with ye. But soon. And if by some ill-luck I ..." He could not say it, but the boy understood. "I just want to know you're safe. That's all I want in the end. See? Promise me you'll do everything to be safe, else it would simply kill me."

The boy flung himself at Rory. "I don't want to go without you, Pa."

"If fate's kind, I'll see you soon. But for now, you must go with Eli. And don't wait for me to cross. I'll find ye on the other side." He pushed the boy away.

She could see how Rory wrestled to hide his own devastation. He knew he would not be crossing that bridge. His one eye roamed over Chelik's face, as if absorbing every line and detail. Then he rose to his feet, hardened his features and turned back to her. "You make sure he crosses. You swore you'd do that for me."

"I will, and not just 'cause I owe you. I discovered something, too. Only Echoes make it across. Chelik will reach the other side."

The harsh lines of Rory's face eased. "Well fancy that." He ruffled Chelik's hair and strode off into the night.

Elika turned to the boy, uncertainly. He was still regarding her with fright.

"Can you climb drainpipes?" she asked.

His jaw dropped. Catching himself, he closed it and shook his head.

Her uncertainty grew. What was she to do with him? She couldn't leave him alone, not even for a moment. It was likely he'd do something stupid and get himself killed. She considered him with a frown. He was an orphan now, so he'd have to learn how to be one. It was as simple as that.

"I'll teach you to climb another day. For now, we'll use the streets." She turned to walk. "Stay close and do as I tell you. Do you know how to run?"

He fell in step with her. "I'm not stupid."

"Then be sure to remember that when I tell you to run. And here, carry one of these." She shoved a sack of food into his hands. "I don't want to be caught with both hands tied up."

He stared at it, then up at her. "Pa gave the bags to *you* to carry."

She cuffed him. Not hard, just a mild warning. But the boy wailed like she'd beaten him near to death.

She cuffed him again, harder this time. "Stop that. Do you want to bring every dog on the street upon us? They'd cut you to pieces and eat you." She did not like scaring the young ones, but it was the quickest way to silence them.

He stopped wailing and looked around in fright. "You hit me. Pa never hits me."

"Never?" How was it possible the man who'd cut a man's throat in a blink never cuffed his own son?

Chelik glared at her defiantly. "Never. He said anyone who hits me will taste their own blood on his knife."

"Well, you ain't with your Pa now. And no one's going to do things for you anymore. I only promised to keep you safe, and not pamper you as if you're a princeling. You wash and feed yourself, and do your fair share. 'Tis the laws of the pack. And you share everything. Else you get cuffed … or worse."

"What's worse than getting cuffed?" he said with a sniffle.

She gaped at him. "Did your pa teach you nothing about the streets?"

"Aye. He taught me to avoid people like you." He took out a dainty white handkerchief and blew his nose. "Where are you taking me?"

She had been walking without a place in mind. But her feet, it seemed, knew where to take her. Home. She was back in Riftside, outside the Hide. The dark door hung loose on its hinges and swung in the wind.

She was home. She recalled those nights when they had sat around Penny's stew, the laughter, the familial anger, the easy friendships. Her pack was gone, and she knew that inside, only dark, cold rooms awaited her.

"Are we going in there?" Chelik whispered in alarm.

She hesitated, fearing to find more inside than the empty rooms. The bloodied bodies of her pack rose before her eyes.

"Let us go somewhere else," he said in a shaky voice.

She almost heeded his plea. But then she thought of Rosy Rose. As long as they were pack, the Hide was their home.

"This is where we live," she said firmly and strode in.

Chelik trailed close behind.

The Hide was not as she had left it. There was a sense of abandonment about it. No traps were set and the old ones had been destroyed. The stairs had lost more treads. The wind blew through the broken windows, and parts of the roof had caved in. Only the faint moonlight illuminated their way as they reached the top landing. But there, coming from the Hide, was the faint glow of a fire.

Elika's heart jolted with something akin to hope. But she dared not indulge that false organ. She fought the impulse to run and embrace whoever was there. Instead, she ushered Chelik into the nearest room and put a finger to her lips. After dropping the bag, she crept toward the glow and stopped outside the doorway. Silence.

The Hide had never been this silent, not even when they slept.

She peered into the room.

Her eyes fell on a shape in trousers staring out the window, hugging itself as if against the cold.

"Penny?" Elika whispered on a breath.

The woman spun around and stared at her without emotion. "You're back," she said dully, neither reproachful nor pleased.

Elika stepped out from behind the wall. She wanted to run to Penny and cling to her like she used to as a child, and weep into her shoulder. But she was not a child anymore. "You're alive," she replied, keeping her tone equally dull.

Penny's lips twitched into a reluctant smile. "For now."

Elika glanced around the Hide and relief swept through her. There was Tiny Timmy glaring at her, and Rosy Rose, huddled in the corner, the blue feather in her hand. And there was Silky Song curled up in bed, coughing roughly, and ...

And no one else. *Where is everyone?* was on the tip of her tongue to ask. But she met Penny's desolate gaze and could not bring herself to do so.

Elika forced a wobbly smile. "Pit is safe, too. And I found a new pup ... and food for us all," she added quickly when she saw Penny's face fall and her gaze dart to the empty stew pot beside the small fire.

Before she could say anything, Elika rushed off to fetch Chelik and the bags of food. She dropped the sacks by Penny's feet and opened them. Inside, she found bread, hard cheese, grain for the stew and dried meat strips.

"It'll last the six of us three days," said Elika.

And after that? said Penny's despondent expression.

Elika had never seen Penny despair, and it frightened her more than Penny's anger might have done. "I'll find more. I swear it," Elika promised. "You're not alone anymore, I'm here."

Penny's gaze shifted to the children. "Look what Eli brought back," she said with false cheerfulness.

It stung that even with this offer of food, the children were reluctant to come near her. So Elika stepped away from the food and strode to the fire, casually throwing a broken table leg into it. Only then did Rosy and Timmy approach.

Chelik regarded his new home with weariness. He seemed as daunted by the other orphans as they were by him. When Penny emptied the bag of food to share between them, Chelik glared at Elika as if she had betrayed him. Tears of helplessness flooded his eyes.

It was a harsh lesson they all learned, she thought, and Chelik would learn it, too. Only as a pack did any of them have any chance of survival. The food would have run out quickly, even if it was just the two of them, and Chelik would be little use in gaining more. Alone, she would never have been able to feed them both, and they would have starved soon after. Now, with Penny here, there was hope.

Tiny Timmy took Silky some bread. Only then did Elika see how sick the young girl was. She was deathly pale, her lips blue, her eyes sunken. Timmy tore small pieces of bread to feed her. But it was no good. Silky refused to eat. Elika had seen this many a time. For no reason they understood, some of them got sick and died. Night sickness, some called it, or else Moreg's Touch, for they often succumbed to it at night when the God of Death was on the prowl.

With a heavy heart, Elika took her own portion of bread and cheese.

They ate in somber silence. Chelik followed Rosy's lead and sat next to Penny. Timmy remained by Silky's side. Their eyes, once filled with joy, were lifeless now, as if the Blight itself had touched them.

Elika kept glancing at Penny, fearing the questions, the accusations, the unspoken that lay between them. But so much had happened since the night Elika had fled the Hide. What could they say to each other that would make any difference or lessen their grief?

"Mite left," Penny said suddenly, cutting through the tense silence.

Elika nodded. "He took the bridge. Made it across."

"So, he found you. Told me if he didn't, to tell you that he'll see you on the other side."

Strange how even now, speaking of Mite could still wound. "He should have been here. He left you ... and now everyone is dead. Whether he waits there or not, he's just as dead to me." The bitter words burst out of Elika before she could stop them. The empty Hide around them spoke of his abandonment louder than her words ever could.

Her outburst was greeted with shocked silence. Everyone left. It was the way of things they all accepted.

Bad Penny's face softened. "He asked us to go with him. Do not begrudge him his choice."

That only riled Elika more. *Just the two of us*, he had said. "Then he should have waited for you to be ready to cross."

Penny looked aside. "He was right to leave. We should have gone with him. I should have made us all go with him."

"You can still follow him, if you wish it."

Penny hugged herself. "I think I'll be one of those turned to dust."

"No, you won't. Echoes can cross. Only Echoes. I saw it myself, it's the truth. You'll make it."

Penny tilted her head at that. A small, cynical smile touched her lips. "Fancy that. Makes sense, that does. Always thought it was random, myself. But it makes sense."

"You can all make it across," Elika said.

Penny glanced at the young ones, eating sullenly beside the fire. "Cross to where? The Deadlands, with no food, no shelter. There's nothing there for us. My place is here, in Terren. Maybe it's kinder to let death sneak up on you in your sleep."

That was not Penny, thought Elika. Penny was never despondent. But then, this was not the fierce Bad Penny she had left behind in early spring. This young woman was worn down by grief and pain. Hunger had carved its way into her face. Deep shadows lay under her dull eyes. Her once glorious red hair was listless and brittle. Penny had always prided herself on cleanliness and a tidy appearance. Now, her clothes were stained and unkempt strands of hair fell out of her plait.

Penny had always been strong for them all. When their hearts were ready to give up, she gave them hope and a will to survive. Now, she looked broken. Perhaps it was time someone else was strong for her.

"We'll get through this," Elika promised her firmly. Tomorrow, she'd find a way to feed them all. "I've never seen so many houses ready to be looted," she added.

Later that evening, Penny sat beside Silky and told her the old tales in a soft voice. Chelik sat alone, eyeing them all with suspicion. When Rosy Rose tried to approach, he shied away barking at her to leave him alone. Hurt flashed on Rosy's face, and Elika wanted to cuff him again. But then she was distracted by Timmy on his bed roll, twiddling a stick.

She sat next to him and he looked like he might bolt. "Why did you run from me, Timmy? You know I'd never hurt you."

"You hurt Mite, didn't you?"

"I didn't mean to."

"Then that only makes it worse. What if you kill me with your magic without meaning to?"

She frowned, thinking about that. "I'm not sure I could."

"Rosy Rose said you killed Pockets' men with magic."

"They were trying to catch me."

He shrugged. "That's 'cause you're a mage."

"I'm not!"

"Then what are you? A tsarin?"

"No, of course not." She spoke harshly, for Bill and Igla had been trying to convince her of just that.

Her denials were hollow, however. Timmy did not trust her, and he was right not to. That was how they survived. She felt like an outcast all over again. She had found her pack, but they did not want or need her.

That night, Elika slept in her old spot, hoping to recall the comfort of her old life. But it was not the same. She was startled by every sound. There were no traps to warn them of an intruder, and not enough of her pack left to fight off an attack. She kept her knife under her pillow and for much of the night she watched the shadows and listened to the howling winds in the chasm.

When the bells rang at dawn, warning of the encroaching doom, Elika threw aside her blankets and dressed. She'd look after her pack and Penny. They would live through this.

Penny sat up and watched her.

"I'll return soon … with more food," Elika said brusquely.

"Don't go alone. Take Timmy with you. Gangs are picking each other off. And Captain Daiger's men are no longer guarding the streets but running an execution mob. They hang every beggar and thief they catch from the garrison wall."

"I heard the captain's handing out rations each morning," said Elika.

Penny sniffed at that. "They give a cup of grain to those who wear a blood-salt crystal. The crowds are large, so most go without."

Elika refused to be deterred. "I'll be back soon," she repeated and left the Hide.

The sun was barely peeking above the horizon, but the streets of Riftside were already crowded. Folk lumbered toward the bridge, carrying what possessions they could. Two city guards wrestled a goat from a man, ransacked his belongings and found stale bread and a string of cured sausages.

Looking outraged by the find, one of the guards beat the man about the head with the butt of his sword. "No one's to take food from the city. Them's the king's laws."

Further along, Rimley's thugs, with red kerchiefs around their necks and clutching bats, loitered at the edges of the crowd.

They stripped one man of his purse and shoes and beat him for good measure. Then two of them grabbed a well-dressed woman and dragged her away, screaming. No one intervened. Not even the greedy guards nearby, searching the bags of those fleeing the city.

In the next street, a group of noblemen and Red Guards forced their way through the crowds on horseback. Elika jumped into the nearest doorway out of their way. From there, she watched a line of carriages go past, carrying fine ladies and stiff lords toward the bridge. Many wore blood-salt around their necks. Except for a young child in a pretty lace dress. She alone would cross into the wasteland, to be at the mercy of magic or men. Once again, Elika made her heart numb to the cruelties of their world. She had her own pack to care for.

The procession passed and she made her way deeper into the city.

The streets grew quieter. The stench of death intensified. Shops had been plundered. The barracks had been burned down, but the guards still milled about in their training yard. Some had even taken it into their heads to rebuild parts of the wall.

In the Silver Circle, the barricades had been destroyed. Some mansions had been ransacked, but others had not been touched. The streets here were empty, the sentry guards long gone. On doors, residents had hung pieces of black ribbon or black lace wound around a wooden bird; a sign that the occupants inside were waiting to die. It was the old symbol of mercy, and any thief or looter who ignored it would face the wrath of the guides in the afterlife.

Elika walked up the steps to the clerk's house. Either side of the stairs, decorous stone statues of winged cats loomed over her. A torn black strip of cloth was tied to the brass knocker.

She ignored it and knocked. The sound reverberated through the street. It was met with silence. She felt watched and glanced over her shoulder. The drawn curtains moved in a house across the street.

She knocked again, harder this time.

Still, no one came to the door.

She picked the lock and slipped inside.

The chequered hallway was empty and silent. But the house did not have an abandoned feel to it. It was warm and dry and smelled of a recent coal fire. The door to the parlor was ajar. She peeked inside.

The clerk was sitting in his chair, just as she had last seen him, with his head bent over a book. Around him, more leather-bound tomes lay scattered on the floor.

"You are back," he said with only a slight turn of his head in her direction.

"You're still here."

"And where would I go?"

"Might be you changed your mind about the bridge."

He rolled his head on the back of his chair to look at her. "I have not."

"Death by Blight is slow," she said. "Some take days to die. Makes you sick and listless. Some say it hurts, too, for you can hear the dying moan."

"The other side doesn't look any quicker to me." He motioned at the empty chair. "Sit if you like. And there's wine on top of the cabinet."

She noticed he quite pointedly did not offer her the port he was drinking himself. Its sweet aroma was heady on the smoke-laced warmth of the fire. So she poured herself a small measure anyway, sat down and sipped it. It was the smoothest port she had ever tasted and not sour at all.

His gaze dropped to her glass. "Impudent, girl. That's my favorite, you thief." He did not sound angry. In his hand his own glass was full.

"You should bolt the door from the inside. Your lock is easy to pick," she warned him.

"But then I'd never get company," he replied wryly and sipped his drink. "My offer is still open. You can stay here if you want. It's far more depressing to die alone, or so I'm finding. More cheerful with the two of us here. And I've got enough food to last us the summer, so you won't starve in the meantime."

"Food's why I came here." She shifted, feeling oddly like a thief, which was ridiculous, for she had always been a thief. But facing her target and speaking to him about stealing from him made it seem wrong and grimy. "Got hungry kids. Orphans. Waiting, too, but starving as they wait."

There was a brief pause. "Like that, is it?" He drank deeper than before and waved his empty glass toward the kitchen. "Take what you can carry and come back for more." He returned to reading his book. "I dare say this *History of Men, Gods and Magic* will bore me to death long before the Blight gets me."

"Then why do you read it?" she asked curiously.

"Priest Oderrin is the most renowned historian of our age, and I always swore I would read this before I died. Seems I might have left it too late. There is a lot to read in the five volumes." He waved at the pile of books next to his chair.

Elika rose to her feet. "You're a kind man. I wish I could return the favor, but we've nothing."

"Name's Anten ... Anten Grey," he said irritably. "And I need nothing from a street urchin." As she made her way into his kitchen, he called out, "In case you are wondering, it's polite to give a man your name when he gives you his."

"Name's Eli," she replied.

She loaded her shirt with bread and ham and the last of the cheese in his larder. After she had stuffed all her pockets with biscuits, grain and dried beans, she returned to the guest room. "I'll be off now. I'll take the roofs. It'll be safer and quicker with this food than the streets."

He ran his hand through his hair. "Tell your orphans they can come here if they want," he said gruffly. "There's a bed and a warm fire, and any food you might have left behind," he added with a pointed glance at her bulging pockets. "I dare say it'll be more comfortable to await your end here than whatever damp, moldy corner you've found."

"I'll tell them," she said and made her way to the door.

There was an oppressive sense of melancholy about the house. The thick silence was haunted by the phantoms of a life once lived, the echoes of children's laughter and lovers' whispers. As she climbed the stairs toward the attic, she felt those phantoms follow her, leaving her only when she crawled out onto the roof.

Once again, the high-way was empty, which was just as well. Laden as she was with food, she moved awkwardly. Anyone who saw her would know she carried something worth killing for. So, she waddled ahead as fast as she could. She imagined those large, dull eyes on small sunken faces lighting up with joy. Might be even Timmy would trust her again. And surely all this food would give Penny hope and revive her spirits.

Ahead, she saw movement as three of Rimley's thugs climbed onto the roof. She stopped, cradling the ham beneath her shirt. They saw her at once. And all too keenly she remembered that the Code was dead. No law governed the streets or men. Except the laws of survival.

The red-scarved thugs took her in, their greedy eyes running over the lumps in her clothes with hungry interest. Then they advanced.

She turned and ran, limping and clutching the food.

"Get him!" came the shouts behind her.

"Cut him off at Pillwark," another shouted.

They ran parallel to her, widening the net then converging, narrowing her path of escape.

Panic fluttered in her chest. If she was not so laden, she could outrun them.

Drop it, save yourself, came the echo of Mite's voice of reason from her mind.

But the large hungry eyes of the young ones swam before her. She could not lose the food. Not when she was this close to Riftside. She lengthened her stride, sprinting now, their steps close behind and gaining.

Just ahead, there was a whorehouse, a refuge if only she could reach it. There was a balcony. She'd jump down to it and ...

She staggered to an abrupt halt, a single step from the plummet to the rubble of a building below. The whorehouse was gone. The burned-out corpse of the building was left in its place. She spun around. Three youths blocked her escape, bats and knives in hand.

"What have we 'ere, a fat little piggy?" one said with a sneer, and they laughed.

"Greedy little piggy's stolen all the food," said the other.

"Might be I fancy me some bacon."

They laughed.

"What say you to that, little piggy?"

"Methinks he's mute," the other said. "Have we cut out your tongue before? How about you give us all you're carrying, and we'll not cut off your hands to follow?"

Her feet shifted precariously close to the edge. "I'll give you half," she said, trying to sound unafraid. "This food's not for me but for my gang. Might be we can work together."

"There's only one gang in this city that matters," said one of them as he tapped his red kerchief with the tip of his knife. "Know what I'm saying, kid? I think you'll be wanting to give us *all* of it. If you fight, we'll cut you into small porky pieces."

Elika looked into their eyes and saw the lie in their cruel words. It was a small thing, really. Rimley's gang never pointed at their red scarves. They never bragged, never told you they'd cut you. They just did. They did not stand there and barter and laugh. They came at you, cut you, took what they wanted and cut you some more. These youths were not Rimley's gang, but imposters. They were trying to be tough and callous, but the thought of her blood on their knives repulsed them. If Rimley's men caught them posing as one of their own they'd make an example of them.

The realization was little comfort, for she also saw in their faces that feral desperation. They craved survival. There was no reasoning with them, no bargaining to be had. They had their own to feed. They would kill her and everyone in her pack for a piece of the bread she carried.

She could not fight this many … She could call on her magic.

Something of her thoughts must have escaped her. Without warning, the biggest of them barred his teeth and charged.

She tried to sidestep him, but laden with food she was heavy and slow. The bat hit her on the side of the head. She fell to her knees. The bat struck her back, her legs and arms … Pain shot through her, the world spun and the sky was everywhere at once. Then many hands were there, ripping at her clothes, eager to find every scrap of food she was hiding. She curled into a ball, hoping only that they would not kill her or push her off the roof.

And then, abruptly, they were gone.

Her head throbbed and spun and she threw up. In her pockets she found only crumbs instead of biscuits, and a few beans and grains. And yet she found herself bizarrely grateful to them for not pushing her over the side of the roof to her death.

She hugged her knees and wept. As her body shook, she felt the bruises, and the broken ribs. Her back hurt, and her head was bleeding. She had been stupid, reckless and arrogant to think she could look after them like Mite had once done.

It was dark when she returned empty-handed to the Hide.

"I'm sorry, Penny," she mumbled.

Without a word, Penny helped her down to her blankets and then silently washed the blood from her face.

CHAPTER FOURTEEN

The Fall of Terren

"The account of Tane Iglasina, eighth daughter of Arala, detailing the formation of the Bridge to Magic speaks of Arala's body morphing and breaking apart, spreading across the chasm to form the bridge across it. The same account speaks of Reval's grief and his race from the battlefield to reach Arala before she perished. That day he set Terren on fire. He fed the flames with the winds he conjured. As with all dramatic magic feats, he quickly drained himself of strength. His now much-weakened magic was no match for the blood-salt men threw into his magical fires. He was saved from death by his mages. They carried him across the bridge, a broken shell of what he once had been."

History of Men, Gods and Magic,
By Priest Oderrin

Another morning of senseless bell tolling. Unwilling to move from her pile of blankets, Elika lay listening to the bleak reminder of their coming end. Today, there were fewer bells than the day before. Tomorrow there would be fewer still. She should leave her bed, but to what purpose? She had lost the food meant for her pack ... no, not her pack, but what was left of it. Her pack was gone. Only the lonely stragglers, like her, were left behind.

Aye, she had been foolish. She should have listened to Penny and taken Timmy with her. She should have been smarter and taken only what she could run with. But she wanted to prove herself to Penny and the others.

The Hide was dark and desolate and awfully silent. Frail wisps of light found their way through the slats on the windows, and she could tell the day was gray and cloudy.

A sniffle reached her. Timmy was sobbing. Her heart remained numb, though she knew why he wept. She could hear it in his quiet anguish.

She did not want to look, but she did, just to punish herself for failing them, and to remind herself of the cost of that failure. She moved her head and gazed at Silky Song's bed. The child lay there, still and peaceful, her body covered with a single blanket.

Aye, she had failed them. She had failed Terren and its people. She had failed Mite, and Penny and her pack. She had failed Pit and Grisla, and herself, too. Was it any wonder Timmy now stared daggers at her?

Bad Penny knelt beside her and tried to place a torn piece of bread in her hand.

Elika rolled her fingers into a fist, refusing to take it. "Give it to them."

"They have enough. You need to heal."

Her body hurt, but it was her soul that hurt the most. And what cure was there for that?

"Don't give up on us, Eli," Penny whispered.

And her plea shamed Elika. There she was, curled up like a helpless mouse, whilst Penny once again carried the burden of their survival.

She forced herself to sit up. Her ribs were bandaged beneath her shirt, and the side of her head throbbed dully. She grimaced with pain and forced her mind to work.

They needed more food. Anten Grey had told her to return for more. He had enough to feed the young ones, a warm fire and soft beds.

She took the bread from Penny and chewed as she spoke. "There's more ... more food where I got the last lot ..."

Penny's face remained blank. Of course, she knew nothing of what had happened the day before, only that Elika had been set upon. So Elika told her about Anten and his offer.

As Penny listened, her lips firmed. "You know better than to trust a fat pouch. We have enough trouble without brewing more."

"He's not fat, and he's not like the other pouches. He had a wife and child once. He's alone and sad. I know people and he's kind."

Penny looked torn. She would not trust a stranger, and a man at that, but her gaze kept drifting to Silky's body. "I'll see him for myself," she said at last.

"I'll take you there," Elika said, rising shakily to her feet.

Penny helped her, frowning with worry as she did so. "We'll take the streets."

She shook her head. "I'm well enough. It'll be quicker along the roofs. I'll not slow you."

Despite her assertions, Elika did slow them down. Her footing was unsteady and each unbalanced step sent pain shooting through her ribs and back. Penny ran nimbly ahead, dressed in trousers and shirt. The hilts of two daggers stuck out from her belt.

No one was better than Penny at wielding them, for she had been taught by Eight Dagger Duggie himself. He was a legend on the streets in the old days, feared even by the city guards. It was said that half the thieving brats running in the streets were his get. Bad Penny was Duggie's daughter and a favorite of his bastards. And he had made it well known, too. He was likely dead now. Got blind drunk one night and disappeared. That was before Elika knew what was what on the street.

Like Duggie, Penny carried eight daggers on her, though you'd only ever see the two she wanted you to see. She could throw them as true and sharp as an arrow's flight. Penny would have killed the three thieving youths before they had gotten close. And her stark copper hair, said to be a spit of Duggie's, would have warned everyone for miles about who she was. So it was that no one accosted them now as they made their way toward the Silver Circle.

When Elika suggested they enter the house from the attic, Penny flashed her a disapproving frown. "And appear weak and timid before him? We have to show him we fear nothing."

Elika didn't think it would matter to the clerk whether they climbed through the window or strode like royalty through his front door. He'd probably wouldn't even raise his head from his books to look at them. But Penny's word was law.

They climbed down from the roofs two streets away from the clerk's home. Or rather, Elika lumbered down like a sore bear, grunting as she went.

They strode up to Anten's home and knocked loudly.

As she reached for her lock pick in anticipation of being ignored again, the door was flung open.

The clerk looked down at her. He was tall, Elika noted. Taller than she had imagined him to be, long and stretched thin. "Thought it might be you again," he said. "Didn't fancy picking a lock today, or sneaking in uninvited?" His gaze roamed over her face. "Dare I ask what happened to you?"

"Better you don't," she replied and glanced toward Penny.

His gaze followed hers and seemed to snag. His jaw dropped, closed, dropped again. Penny's lips firmed at his stunned perusal of her. Then his gaze returned to Elika. "I take it this is Bad Penny. Are you here to kill me?"

It was such a blandly spoken question, hopeful almost in its tone, that Elika could not hide a grin. "We just want to talk."

His gaze returned to Penny, dropped to her daggers and up again. "*You* are the notorious gang leader of Riftside." He rubbed his stubbled chin doubtfully.

"And why is that hard to believe?" asked Penny rather flatly.

"I thought you'd be ... hairier," he said lamely.

"Hairier?" she echoed with a raise of her brows.

He waved his hand irritably at her body. "How does a slight woman in breeches terrify murderous men on the street?"

There was a way Penny could look at you that would shrivel your insides. Elika never understood that look, save that it was potent, softly menacing, and chillingly unwavering. Penny looked at the clerk in that way now, the sky blue of her eyes turned icy.

He shifted on the spot in discomfort. "Never mind. I see." Then he grinned brashly. "And do you live up to your name, Bad Penny?"

Elika shoved past him. "Aye, she's bad luck to any man who crosses her."

He closed the door behind them. "Do come in," he said dryly.

In the hallway, Penny faced him. "You told Eli that the orphans can stay here, with you."

"Aye," he said, uncertainly. "I said that. You didn't take it as some kind of power challenge? It was not ... I just thought ..."

"What do you expect in return?" she interrupted him, before he made a bigger fool of himself, no doubt.

For a moment, he appeared taken aback. Then disappointment flashed across his face, as if Penny's completely reasonable question had insulted him. A cynical glint entered his eyes. "I want nothing from you or your pitiful pack of orphans." He turned on his heel and walked back into his guest room. A moment later, they heard him pouring a drink.

Penny strode after him, her back stiff. The clerk sat in his chair, a book in one hand, a drink in the other. She stopped in front of him, arms planted on her hips. "There are six of us ..." she began and flinched. Silky was dead. "Five. There are five of us, now," she said, and Elika heard the brittleness in her voice.

So did the clerk. He lowered his book and looked up. "That's a lot of mouths to feed."

"If you're still willing to offer us a place to sleep and what food you can spare, I'll clean your house and cook for you and mend your clothes. And share what food I bring back myself. I'll also make sure no looter bothers you."

His head fell back against his chair. "My house is at your disposal. Do as you wish. I ask only that you do not cut my throat whilst I sleep."

Penny's lips turned up with wry amusement. "As long as you give me no reason to cut it."

"I hope snoring is not one of those reasons."

To Elika's amazement, Penny chuckled, a warm, unfamiliar sound. "I'll fetch the children." She began to leave, but halted at the door. "Thank you ... Master Grey."

He turned back to his book. "Call me Anten. I'm nobody's master."

And Elika saw Penny's shoulder's ease, and cautious hope bring her eyes back to life.

~

The days that followed were strange indeed. If death was coming for them, there was no sign or mention of it in Anten's house. And it was hard to remember that the Blight still crept toward them. The atmosphere inside the clerk's home was almost festive. The children were clean and dressed in pretty dresses and smart trousers, and joy shone in their eyes. Even Chelik was chatty and eager to please.

Elika was the last one to wake up on the morning of their sixth day in their new home. She had been looting late into the night, though there was little to show for it. Cheerful voices rose toward her from the kitchen as she came downstairs.

Chelik, Rosy and Timmy sat around the table, eating porridge. Penny was at the stove. She looked radiant, shining like a penny in truth. Her hair was brushed and gleaming like copper down to her waist. Elika had never noticed that Bad Penny was beautiful. But then, she had never seen Penny dressed in such pretty clothes. In that blue satin dress, she might have passed for a lady, until she started waving the spoon about whilst scolding Timmy for stealing Rosy's food. "I'll clout you if I see you take what's not yours again, and you'll go without for a day."

"But I'm a thief," he objected. "Besides, she stole from me first."

Chelik nodded in support. "I saw her."

Penny huffed. "Well I didn't and that's good enough for me."

Rosy gave the boys a wicked grin and stuffed her mouth with a spoonful of porridge.

Penny saw Elika and filled another bowl. "Don't just stand there. Take this and sit."

Elika joined the children at the table. As she ate, vague memories surfaced in her mind of a warm kitchen, a woman's gentle voice, and a plate of honey drizzled over buckwheat in goat's milk. Was her mother still alive on the other side? Were the folk she thought her parents waiting for her? Foolish thoughts. Foolish longings and regrets.

It felt like a betrayal of Penny and her pack to think of the past, but these people before her seemed more and more like strangers. They were no longer a pack, but a farcical family in a normal house, living in a merry bubble, as if the world beyond went on as always.

Penny suddenly blushed and looked laughably shy, and with a pang of irritation, Elika knew who had come into the kitchen. The children, too, grew quiet.

Elika glanced over her shoulder at Anten.

He was smiling, his eyes fixed on Penny. "Any crumbs left for me?"

Penny tried and failed to look serious. She waved the spoon at the full bowl she had put aside just for him. "We won't eat you out of your own house."

Elika doubted that was true. In the few days they had been here, Anten's cupboards had grown depleted. Some were stripped bare altogether. Each day, she and Penny set out in search of food, but rarely brought enough for them all. Anten wanted to go with them, but they both refused him firmly. Elika thought he'd be nothing but a hindrance. After all, what did he know of looting and stealing. And every dog on the street would see him as easy game. Penny, however, seemed almost ashamed about their nocturnal ventures. Elika had no idea why. Penny was a master at finding what needed to be found and everyone respected her on the streets.

Anten picked up his bowl and lowered his head when he passed Penny, as if he was embarrassed to be in his own kitchen. As soon as he sat in his seat, Rosy Rose climbed into his lap.

He pulled out a velvet bag and placed it on the table. "Look what I found in the old attic."

Timmy was the fastest and had it in his hand before the others could grab it. He pulled out a handful of glass beads and wooden arches.

Rosy Rose giggled with delight. Elika took another mouthful of porridge and tried not to feel resentful.

Since they had arrived on his doorstep, Anten had drunk less, smiled more, and each day found a new game for the children to play. The day they had arrived, he had left home and returned with enough clean, tidy clothes to dress them all. Penny had been near to tears when, one by one, the children scrubbed off the grime and stood before her in their new attire. She had gazed at Anten with such intense gratitude, he had blushed, mumbled something about the fire needing to be tended and fled to another room.

As he ate his breakfast, he told them the rules of the new game he had brought them. A moment later, he halted in mid-telling, stared at their bowls and frowned. "I think you forgot something."

He was on his feet, opening a larder. After moving around some pots and jugs, he held up a jar that made Elika nearly weep with want.

"Honey," he said. "How can you eat porridge without honey?"

The children regarded it with blank expressions.

"Well, aren't you pleased?" he asked with a note of dejection.

Penny's lips twitched, but she refrained from laughing. "They've never had honey before."

He blinked, then turned red. "Sorry, wasn't thinking." He cleared his throat. "We'll just have to fix that, won't we?"

Outside, the bells rang in unison. *Blight!*

And it seemed as if a cold shadow fell over them. They grew silent and tense. Each morning, the bells tolled around the city, and each morning fewer bells could be heard as the Blight advanced a little more. One of the bells was only a few streets away, and Elika knew that each morning they all waited for it to ring. And when it did, they secretly breathed out with relief. Another day awaited them. Another absurd day of false joy, foolish games and hollow laughter, as they pretended they were not waiting to die.

They were not laughing now, Elika thought with almost savage satisfaction. They had not forgotten, no, merely chosen to ignore it. They never mentioned the Blight, never spoke about the bridge, or what they would do when the inevitable came for them. Would that she could find her own peace in the lie.

She finished the last of her breakfast, pushed away from the table, and grabbed her cloak. The brusque wind had turned cold in recent days and brought with it rain, and she had a long walk ahead of her.

"If you wait, I'll come with you," Penny said and sat at the table across from Anten.

"No need. I just want to see what's what," Elika mumbled lamely. "And before you object, I'll be careful." Then her eyes fell on the jar of honey and unreasonable anger filled her chest. It was a sweet lie they hid behind as they awaited their end. "In case you've forgotten, I was raised on the streets and not in a pretty little house with pretty little dolls," she added with fury.

Her outburst was greeted with tense silence. She faced them, feeling like an intruder in their newfound happiness.

"I've not forgotten," Penny replied, her gaze turning to ice. "Go. We'll speak later."

Elika looked aside. She had overstepped the boundary. Might be she was too old now to cuff, but there were worse things than being cuffed.

"I'll find us more food," she said as a pacifier and left the kitchen, conscious of everyone's eyes on her back.

Outside, she became instantly aware of a different air about the city. The streets had gone silent. It was an ominous, brooding type of silence. But in it, she heard the unspoken as loudly as if men had shouted their intent. Many had fled the city for the Deadlands, but many more remained behind and they had been abandoned by the king to their fate. Terrenians might be content to die from the Blight, but they would not stoop to die from hunger when there was food to be had. So they cursed the king who stole their food, and with the same breath praised Peter Pockets and whispered of revenge.

Unnerved by the surrounding silence, Elika took a different route through the city as she looked for a freshly abandoned house that showed no sign of having been plundered. You could always find jars with scraps of leftover pickles or jams, or dried grains for cooking or planting.

The day was gray, and the drizzly rain slowly seeped into her clothes.

She turned into Forger's Alley and came across a band of Drasdanes, giving out weapons from barrels to anyone who passed. No one bothered you anymore, whether you wore a blood-salt pendant or not. Pockets had convinced them to allow the Echoes to live, arguing that they would need every man to storm the gilded gates. Besides, the king who stole their food was their true enemy.

One of the Drasdanes saw her and waved her over. "Over here, boy." He held out a short sword. "Take this and be ready."

There was no way to refuse. She took the sword and examined it with feigned awe. "'Tis the best sword I've ever seen. But I've no coin or cookie to give you."

"Just be ready to use it. That'll be payment enough," the Drasdane said in his soft accent, looking pleased by the compliment. "And there'll be more reward for you, too, if you help us."

It was no secret that Peter Pockets was planning a rebellion. Every day, lordlings rode out as a hunting pack, chasing down dog-gangs and any one they suspected of brewing unrest, whilst along the walls of the Golden Circle, an army of archers awaited. Today, charged anticipation hung over the city, thick and heady.

"What's the signal to be, then?" she asked in a confidential whisper.

"The fires. We'll have smoke to hide us from the archers. They'll not see us well enough to hit us."

Elika stuffed the sword in her belt. "Well, that's something then," she replied and walked on.

Pockets' army had grown. It seemed every other man patrolling the streets was dressed in a bright, fancy suit. Today, they were handing out small bags of grain.

After watching them, she approached boldly. "Ma says I'm to get some grain if you have any to spare for me and my brothers." She leaned in and added with a proud nod. "We're waiting for the fires like we've been told."

He saw her sword and grinned. "Tell your brothers not to go to bed tonight, then. And here." He gave her a small bag of grain. "How many of you are there?"

"Six if you include my pa." She smiled cheekily. "But he's a useless drunk. So I'll not be giving him any grain. Ma's been feeding him stewed rats. Passed out on gin most of the time when he's not roaring for my ma to mount him."

The man chuckled. "Here's three bags. And tell your brothers there's more food coming if they join us come sunrise."

She stuffed the sacks into her coat. "Can't wait. Ma says it'll be better to leave Pa behind and go to the bridge. But she's afraid. Says if Peter Pockets goes, then she'll go, too."

"Then she'll get her wish soon," the man replied with a wink.

The rest of the day, Elika wandered the streets. She searched three houses but found only half a jar of dried peas. Close to dusk, she came to a tavern, nestled below street level, and largely hidden by a hedge beside the stairs. The tavern keeper was a red-eyed drunk. He was asleep at the bar when she entered and only roused himself to pour her a tankard, asking only for a handful of grain as payment.

The tavern was a dank cellar with low beams and wobbly tables. Aside from her, there were no other patrons. So she sat alone in the darkened corner and nursed her ale.

She had found her pack only to lose them again to Anten. Or might be she had lost them the day she used her magic on Mite. They were Anten's pack now. It was his house and he provided for them. He seemed to delight in the patter of feet running up and down the stairs, and the children being underfoot from dawn till dusk. Penny was different, too, her eyes always following the clerk. Rosy Rose doted on him. Timmy couldn't do enough to please him. And Chelik had grown close to Penny, whilst regarding Elika with much the same aloofness as before. She could not blame him, either. Tiny Timmy still did not trust her, and Rosy Rose kept her distance, too. They had formed a family, but she was left behind.

She did not begrudge them the food, the comforts, or the happiness they had found. She wished all this for them and more. But each day, she felt more and more like an outcast. Or might be she just could not pretend.

But what was she without her pack? She was alone, that's what. She downed the last of the ale, and seeing as it was late, returned to the clerk's house.

The children were already abed. Anten had given the nursery to them, taken away the cot and pulled out a treasure chest of toys for them to play with. He had dragged two wide beds up there for them to share. Proper beds with soft mattresses and pillows. Elika, however, continued to sleep in her blankets on the floor as she had always done. No use getting used to comforts. It would only make it harder when she lost them again.

On the way past, she glanced into the guest room. Penny and Anten sat by the fire, drinking wine and speaking in hushed tones. From their faces, she could tell they spoke of things close to their hearts, of their fears and the past, of the brief future that awaited. By some tacit agreement, they had decided this was their path, simply waiting to die in this house.

Anten said something that brought a smile to Penny's face and his own lit up when she laughed. Elika had never heard Penny laugh out loud. It was hoarse and uncertain, as if it did not sit right in her throat. There was a strange tension between them, an awkwardness that somehow seemed to encircle her and repel her at once.

"I've brought more grain," she said loudly, startling them both. She held up the bags. "'Pockets' men giving it out again. They are saying the rebellion's likely to be tonight. Thought you'd want to know. Might be smart to barricade the doors and windows."

Anten's gaze dropped to her short sword. "Thinking of joining them, are you?"

Penny was on her feet. "No. I forbid it."

Days ago, Bad Penny's command would have been law, unthinkable for her to disobey. But now, the command rang hollow. Her heart sank. Everyone left. Eventually, everyone grew up. Was this how it had been for Mite? And in that moment, Elika knew that she, too, was leaving. But she could not bear to show her true heart to Penny and see the echoing hurt in her face. Nor would she undermine Penny's authority before another.

"As you say, Penny. Just thought to be ready."

Penny was not a fool. Her gaze grew intent and probing. "I can't lose you, too," she said quietly.

She was lost already, didn't Penny see? Elika wanted to weep. Instead, she yawned widely, pretending not to understand Penny's plea. "I'll put these in the kitchen and then I'm for bed."

After she left them alone, she lingered in the hall outside long enough to confirm her suspicions about them. That night, Penny did not return to her bed in the nursery where they all slept.

Elika awoke to the smell of smoke and the sound of hammering coming from inside the house. From the streets, came shouts and sounds of fighting. She threw aside her blankets and looked out the window.

Smoke blanketed the city. Drowsy from sleep, her first thought was that they were burning the Echoes again. But these fires were not laced with blood-salt and the smoke was dark and gray.

Peter Pockets' rebellion had begun.

Men ran past, heading toward the Golden Circle, weapons in their hands and kerchiefs over their noses.

"Fight to the end," she muttered and felt her soul awaken.

What right had the king to hoard the food? What had the nobles done for them but ride out into the streets to hunt down the desperate? The Blight might kill them, but the proud folk of Terren deserved to die with dignity.

She turned away from the window. The nursery was empty for it was long past dawn. She dressed and went below, following the sound of banging.

Downstairs, Penny held the floorboards to the window, whilst Anten hammered nails into the wood. They were laughing together as if the rebellion outside was a big lark.

The children were looking out the window. Timmy's eyes were lit with excitement. Chelik was more circumspect, his expression a mix of doubt and fear. Rosy Rose was playing on the floor with a wooden horse.

No one noticed Elika standing in the doorway. So she grabbed her cloak and sword, and without a word raced up the stairs, toward the attic and the roofs.

The skies were gray, the air muggy with drizzling rain. Beyond the city, fields of churned earth remained fallow and spring seedlings had long wilted to dust. Might be this rebellion was the last stand of men against their cruel fate. But they would not starve whilst they awaited their end.

She raced toward the Golden Circle. Much of the city had been destroyed, and not by magic or the Blight. The roof of the Temple of Mercy had caved in, and its walls looked like broken shells. The Temple of Reval had been burned to the ground. Only the dark, crystal spire of the palace still loomed over the city; the last reminder that magic once roamed through their world.

As she drew closer to the Golden Circle and the fires, the roar of rage intensified. Men, women and even children strode out their homes and marched toward the gilded gates. Their numbers grew and grew until they became a dark, angry river flowing through the city. And she followed the course of that river, running above it along the roofs. She stopped on the edge of the building across the great square from the enormous, shimmering gates that hid the nobility from the heart of Terren, and the sight she beheld took her breath away.

So this is what the end of humanity looks like. The dark sea of bodies crashed against the gates whilst a rain of arrows fell upon their heads. Ripples of death ran through the water, but where men fell, more rushed in to take their place.

Tall ladders rose up from the welling mass and settled against the walls. Men raced up them, heedless of the burning tar the defenders poured over them. The shining army along the wall pushed back the ladders and threw those who reached the top back over the side to their deaths.

She searched the river and found the man who would be its king—Peter Pockets, mounted on a great black horse, and clad in a green velvet suit, with only a leather vest as his armor. He shouted commands, and men rushed to obey. Peter Pockets' ambition might have brought them here, but their own hunger and desperation drove the river of men to break uselessly against the gilded gates.

They would die fighting rather than as helpless victims of their fate. She shoved her hand into her pocket and clutched the wooden bird. She had failed her city and its people before. She would not fail them now.

Overhead, the white-tipped crow cawed and Elika imagined the gazes of the gods upon her. She took a deep breath and her lungs burned with the smoke. She closed her eyes and called upon the magic inside her. *If you want us to make peace, then do what I ask.* She spread out her arms and imagined the tendrils of magic rushing along underground, then rising before the gates …

A deep, rumbling came from below and the building beneath her feet shook. She opened her eyes and there was magic, alive and battling beside men and for men. Battling for Terren, for justice, and most of all, for her.

The river fell away from the gates, and the rain of arrows stopped in awed wonder. From the ground rose terrible black tendrils, and magic not seen in six hundred years was prying the gates apart. The defenders on the wall shouted curse upon curse and arrows rained upon the tendrils.

Elika cried out in pain. She felt every strike as if it pierced her body but fought the urge to withdraw and hide from the onslaught. But the arrows were too many and she could not hold on to the magic. Then a triumphant roar washed over her from the streets below. Men pointed up toward her and she was not a monster anymore but their savior. With renewed determination, she strained to clench her fists and the tendrils held on until the gates groaned and broke apart.

She pulled back her magic, breathless with pain from the arrows. Peter Pockets looked up and she met his gaze. Astride his great horse, he looked like a king in truth. He tipped his hat to her, then raised his sword and spurred his horse forward.

The river of men rushed forward and spilt into the Golden Circle. Red Guards and nobility rode their horses to meet the rising tide, their swords glistening in their hands. They formed a solid red wall, but the dark water surrounded them and drowned them stone by stone. And the torrent raced onward, flooding the parklands, the grass, the pristine roads. It swamped the brightly colored folk in its path and washed their blood-stained bodies upon its shores. And it raced onward toward the palace.

Once, it had been the home of the glorious Tsarin Reval. Long ago, he too had been swept away by the flood of hate and despair. As Elika watched, she thought of that long-ago time when it had all begun. For all their stories began and ended with the Bridge to Magic.

The Red Guard along the palace wall sent arrows toward the unstoppable force of nature, a force too large for mere men to fight. The river absorbed those arrows and crashed against the palace gates. The mighty hinges strained against the flow of anger and gave way.

The king rode out into the courtyard on his magnificent horse, clad in shining metal armor like a god of old, his giant sword high and eager to smite the foes. He charged at the swelling tide. A man in a green suit and leather vest emerged from it and rode to meet him. The battle was brief, like a wail of death, and like the tsaren had done long ago, King Tesman and his Red Guard fell to the wrath of mere men.

Elika stood there, on the roofs of the Silver Circle, and watched. King Tesman was dead. Their world was broken. The world of man was no more.

Or perhaps there was hope, after all. Peter Pockets atop his horse raised his sword in victory, glorious and fierce. And the men cheered and raised their swords to their new king. Their roar filled the city and startled a flock of birds. The birds rose high into the sky and as they rose, they circled and circled …

And one by one they fell to the ground, lifeless and limp.

From high above, Elika saw what the victorious river of men did not see—the birds falling out of the sky were right above them.

The new king, the man they called Peter Pockets, slumped in his saddle and fell with his horse to the ground. The dark river stilled. Those who saw men ahead falling mid-step, turned and fled, for the Blight was upon them. And she could do nothing but watch the old men, children and women with babes in their arms flee their homes then fall, never again to rise. And those poor fools, too, who turned back to help them. The smarter of those who had seen them fall dropped all they carried and ran as fast as they could from the invisible wall of that foulness born of magic.

Elika sank to her knees and lowered her head. She had not saved them, after all, but destroyed them. By opening those gates, she had killed them all.

Yet she had hoped … she had hoped. What a worthless thing, hope. There was no hope for mankind.

CHAPTER FIFTEEN

Life Between Two Deaths

*"Arala's sacrifice and death have never been explained. Why
did she destroy herself to form the Bridge to Magic? Surely the
reason is simple. She sought to save magic from destruction by
men. She gave it a path to the world across the chasm where it
had been exiled. Though such is my belief, I would not be a
true historian if I did not mention Priest Lesman's theory of
the Sundered Web. Lesman asserted that Syn'Moreg had not
merely sundered our world but also the Great Web of life.
What disaster did he truly inflict upon the three realms when
he sundered ours? Was Arala's sacrifice meant to hold the
Great Web together in the dark Abyss? What little we know
of the beings we call gods, is that they are the weavers of the
web, and its guardians. Above all else, they seek to preserve it
from destruction. Then why have they not sought to restore the
wrongs done by Syn'Moreg, a half-breed child of the God
Moreg? Perhaps the gods are truly dead, as we have come to
suspect."*

History of Men, Gods and Magic,
By Priest Oderrin

Elika remained standing where she was on the edge of
the roof. Death had imprinted itself upon her eyes,
invaded her mind and seeped into her bones. Death was

everywhere. In the Golden Circle and beyond, many lay motionless, some still moved, listless and confused, before surrendering to their end.

Panic raced ahead of the Blight, spread through the city. The bells rang furiously. Then one by one, began to still as the Blight continued its march. Below, in the square before the gilded gates, men fell as they fled. Frozen on the spot, Elika watched the Blight advance toward her.

"Destroy it," she whispered to the magic inside her, willing it with all her might to slay this beast of madness and destruction Magic had long ago unleashed upon mankind.

But in reply, she felt the creature inside her shy away from that thought.

Then let it take me, let it take us both. It is a just fate for you and me, she thought numbly.

The Blight moved onward, heedlessly killing the fleeing folk, the horses and bright flowers in the great square below. Then, abruptly, almost cruelly in its seeming mockery, it stopped not ten paces from where she stood.

Elika turned and walked away.

The dark clouds churned overhead. In the distance, the bells continued to ring. Shouts and screams filled the city.

"The king is dead!" they shouted.

"The Blight is coming!"

"The king is dead!"

Men fled their homes, running toward the chasm, toward the bridge, away from the cruel fate at their back.

It began to rain—cold, large drops that soaked her hair and clothes in moments. Elika hugged herself and allowed her feet to take her where they would. They led her back to Anten's house. It seemed an age had passed since she had left to join the rebellion. Another Elika returned, harder, colder, defeated.

She looked down from the edge of the roof at the doorway below. The stone statues of two winged cats rose up to meet her. From the roof she could step onto their heads and make her way down to the street. But her feet would not move.

For the first time since she had witnessed the Blight destroy the rebellion and the hopes it carried, an emotion stirred in her chest—sharp and piercing. It was her fault everyone was dead.

Her pack was gone, too. Penny and the children were Anten's family now. Yet she had promised One-eyed Rory to keep Chelik safe. The Blight was coming. Rory was dead. There was no King Peter Pockets to lead his people across the bridge. It was up to her to save Chelik. She had to keep her word.

At that moment, the door opened below, and Penny stepped outside. She stopped two men on the street rushing past. "What's happened?" she asked them.

They glanced behind with fear. "The Blight ... the king is dead," said one.

"The rebellion's gone, too," added the other. "The Blight's sweeping through the city. You must run if you don't want it to catch you."

They rushed off again.

Penny stood there for a moment, then strode inside. A moment later, Elika heard voices coming from the house, instructions shouted, questions asked. The patter of feet through the house and the door bust open again. Penny emerged, followed by the children and Anten. They carried bundles in their arms. It struck Elika how much they had changed, for none of them looked up to see her standing there. Mite had taught them to always check the roofs for watchers, enemies and spies. How quickly they had forgotten those lessons. With a pang of regret, she watched them follow Penny, the last of her pack, headed toward the chasm.

Chelik would be safe with Penny. Far safer than he would have been with her. And far happier, too. Elika let them go, knowing there was no home for her amongst them.

Then where was home?

She grasped the wooden bird in her pocket. The crow cawed overhead. And the answer came to Elika. *Where her memories began.*

~

Elika steeped dried mint leaves in hot water, poured herself a cup and put some beans to boil on the stove. She sat back on the creaky wooden chair and looked over the cottage with the yellow curtains where her memories began. The curtains still hung on the windows though they had faded with time.

She had few memories of the old woman, Nora, who had stopped her from crossing the bridge with her parents, saving her from an uncertain end. And for a time, she had thought of this cottage as her home. It was smaller than she remembered, nestled a few streets away from the chasm in a small alley of many such cottages. Its one room contained a kitchen, a rickety old table and a narrow bed.

She had returned there the day of the doomed rebellion to find the house abandoned. With no further thought, she fell on the bed and slept. During the days that followed, she busied herself with removing years of dust and neglect. She occupied her mind with fixing the broken furniture and restocking the empty cupboards. There were countless little chores and she tackled them all with fervor, for they stopped her thinking about Penny and Anten and her pack.

She had not gone back to see them, had kept herself hidden from them. They would be better off without her. Let them think her dead.

Penny would have guessed she had gone to the fateful rebellion from which no victor returned. No food was brought out to be shared amongst the people. No new king emerged to lead his subjects across the bridge. Only the Blight moved deeper into the city, as if drawn onward by the relentless death of men and magic.

The beans boiled. Elika drained them into a bowl and added the last of the goat's milk. As she ate, she waited for the bell to ring. It was a grim, daily habit, this, waiting for the bells to tell her how much closer the Blight had moved toward the last of the survivors clinging to this world. She used to count the remaining bells but for many days now, only the one bell still rang.

It was four streets away, in a tower above Pedlars' Square, in the heart of Riftside. Eyeless Joe manned it, saying he had nothing better to do. He swore he would keep ringing it until the Blight got him. Elika made certain he never ran out of food to eat nor warm blankets to sleep on. Today, she packed him a jar of strawberry jam which she had made from strawberries growing in the abandoned garden next door.

She finished her breakfast. Outside, the sun rose higher, and her sense of unease grew. Eyeless Joe always rang soon after dawn when he felt the warmth of the rising sun on his face. She lowered her head into her hands and waited, refusing to think, refusing to wonder. The sun rose higher and higher, but the last bell remained ominously silent.

She thought of Mite. Strange that she should. He had become vague in her mind, like a fading dream. She thought of him with neither affection nor resentment, neither sadness nor regret. He was simply an echo of another life. He had told her there was nothing she could do to stop the Blight. As always, he was right. Yet, she did not regret trying. Only her failure haunted her still.

She washed her bowl and went into her small garden. There were no voices outside, no sound of birds. The day was hot again, and the strangling stench of death from the unclaimed corpses smothered the city. It was hard to ignore, but there was nothing to be done about it.

Her garden was a disorganized tangle of green beans. She set to picking the ripest of them. She had watched Potter Ned grow seeds and had helped him weed many a time. So, in early summer, she had planted a handful of beans. She had never grown her own food before and was pleasantly surprised when they sprouted quickly. Since then, the beans had taken over her garden and gave her enough to eat and trade with the other survivors. She filled a bag with fat pods, left through the back gate and headed toward Pedlars' Square.

A strange, listless calm had descended on the city. The streets were silent, the last stragglers of humanity rarely seen. Homes stood dark and deserted. There were days when she could walk the last remaining streets and not encounter a single person. Those who had not fallen with the rebellion took the bridge instead. Now, Rift Street was once again empty.

Terren was empty.

Empty of its people, animals and gangs. Empty of hate, fear and suffering. Deep peace came with that absence.

There were others like her, the lingering remnants of mankind, trapped in a life between two deaths, refusing to accept one or the other.

How does one choose between two types of death? The waiting was worse. The hovering on the edge of the precipice, seeing the end, unable to escape it.

When she neared Pedlar's Square, others appeared on the street, also heading toward the bell tower to confirm what they already knew.

They acknowledged each other with weariness and curt nods. It occurred to her that there were no familiar faces anymore, merely strangers who had become a familiar sight. They had seen too much, done too much that none of them wished to remember. In their faces, she saw the same fear that lurked in her heart, fear of having their part in the fall of Terren discovered.

There were nights when she lay awake, wondering what would have happened had she not opened those gilded gates, or if she had taken the bridge instead of going to the temple. How many lives had she condemned with her choices?

As it was, the Red Guard and the gangs had fallen in the uprising. The Blue Guard were also no more. Once Captain Daiger had no more food to give out, the mob hung him from the beam of the empty grain shed. There was no law. Yet neither was there lawlessness.

The survivors had found themselves a small, peaceful corner to live in. Thievery seemed inconceivable. And what was there to steal, anyway? Coin was useless, whilst scavenging was plentiful.

She stopped at the edge of Pedlars' Square. The stalls stood empty. The courtyard, once bustling with folk of many different races, was silent. The bell tower was quiet. A man sat with his back against its wall, listless but still breathing. His head lolled to the side, his eyeless sockets staring vacantly at nothing, his mouth moving slowly, as if trying to speak. Eyeless Joe. Her heart constricted. She took a step toward him and stopped again.

The Blight was invisible. But if you looked closely, there were many signs of its presence—dead rats and birds, a rangy old cat twitching as he died. And there, an orb spider fell from her web in the corner of a stall. The blades of grass which were green yesterday had yellowed overnight. And just beyond the bell tower lay the lifeless bodies of those who did not read those signs, or simply walked into the Blight to find a quicker end.

Her feet moved toward the bitter temptation but halted again a few paces from that invisible boundary between life and death. If she put out her hand, she would touch it. One sure step and she would be inside it.

Once, she had prodded that boundary with a pike. There was no resistance, nothing of substance, no sign that she had touched anything at all. But this close to it, she could almost sense it on her skin.

It was not a sensation she could name, rather an absence of one. She could feel the rays of the sun on her skin, the movement of air. But just a pace away, it ceased to be. It felt as if the world beyond did not exist and only a reflection of it was left behind. Nothing existed beyond the Blight. One step, and she too, would cease to be.

Might be it was the innate arrogance of men to believe they could vanquish magic. Or perhaps it was always meant to be thus, that men were to be vanquished and magic would inherit the world.

What would it take to stop this destruction? What must they do to end this meaningless war? How did they atone for what men had done to the tsaren and magic?

"What do you want?" she shouted at the Blight, and her voice echoed off the empty houses.

What do you want? she asked the magic inside her. *Please, make it stop.* But the magic remained silent. The Blight would not stop until it pushed them all into the chasm.

Step into the Blight and it will all be over.

She turned and walked away. Another day awaited her and she would live it.

She strode toward the harbor.

Here and there, clumps of grass fought for life, growing between the bricks and the pavement. A tree had seeded itself in the crack of a brick wall. Wharf Street was quiet. It had rained the night before and water pooled in the endless mudflats where once there had been a sea. A seagull screeched from the roof, a sad lonely babble. His companions were rotting in the mudflats where once they sought crabs and worms.

Bill's blue ship drew her gaze. On the deck, Igla and Bill sat beside the old mast, holding onto each other. They looked peaceful, and when she passed, she pretended that they only slept. Or else she imagined Igla smiling contentedly whilst Bill told her one of his tales.

Elika turned aside into the *Fat Fish* tavern.

"Jake," she called out, "it's me, Eli. I brought you more beans, freshly picked today ... and strawberry jam."

"Ou' here," Toothless Jake called from the back.

She followed his voice out to the garden.

No one had seen the tavern keeper since the burnings began. No one knew what had become of him, nor of the other folk hereabouts. Tales of their fate varied depending on who told them, but it was either that they were burned alive or had taken the bridge.

Jake had taken up residence in the *Fat Fish*. It had always been his favorite haunt. He was outside with his goat, brushing its coat. Elika did not know where he found the poor, three-legged animal, and did not ask.

At the other end of Riftside, Fix-it Frances, the carpenter, had found himself a milking cow and traded milk for food. Some folk kept chickens, and Hober had two roosters he gave out to the chicken keepers in exchange for daily eggs and some grain to feed his noisy birds. Then there was Kreya on Mugger's Corner who owned three pigs and a sow heavy with a litter of piglets. Those who did not have an animal of their own, grew food instead and helped with the feeding of the hapless beasts when they could.

Elika placed the bag of beans and the jar of jam beside Jake's freshly filled jug of goat's milk. He also grew tomatoes and potatoes which he traded with her for corn. When a generous mood took him, he shared his secret stash of ale the tavern keeper left hidden in the cellar. There was enough there to last the summer, Jake had told her, if he was stingy with it. And after that ... well, they'd likely not live past autumn, he would often say.

"'O Bell," said Jake through his toothless mouth. It took Elika a while to learn to understand what it was he said. But once she did, she found him incessantly chatty.

"No bell today," she agreed. "The Blight's gotten Joe. It's moving again. Might be best if you move closer to the bridge. You can stay in the cottage next to mine."

They were surrounded now—a bubble of life between the Blight and the chasm. And for many days, the Blight might not move at all. There was no sense or reason to it that any of them could understand. Then, as if drawn by some power, it would march onward, relentless and determined. And when it did, the city grew a little quieter, a little emptier.

Jake shook his head, stubborn to the end. He'd lived here all his life and he'd not be chased out of his home now. He'd wait for it. What use was there in running?

Elika looked longingly at the goat. It would perish with him. "Might be, then, you give me the animal. I'll not take a drop of its milk without paying you for it."

He wagged a finger at her. "My goat, you likle 'hief."

"I'm not a thief anymore. No need for it, see? And aye, I know the goat's yours, which is why I say it's better for everyone if you don't lose yourself to the Blight."

He waved her concerns away. *What did she want with the goat anyway?* he said in his barely comprehensible way. *Might be better she follow the others across the damned bridge. Might be more there than here.*

"You can see there isn't," she replied.

He shrugged and went inside.

She helped him make cheese and earned herself half a mug of ale. As she drank it, she listened to him recount his recent foray into Riftside, where he had found a bag of gold hidden beneath some floorboards.

"What use is gold to you?" she asked in bewilderment.

He shrugged. "Nice 'o have. I'll die a rich man."

She smiled at that. "Might be I'll find me a crown and die a queen."

Jake chuckled.

It was late afternoon by the time she left him, taking the jug of milk with her.

She rarely walked along windy Rift Street anymore. The sight of the Deadlands and the bridge was too depressing. Besides, Elika suspected Penny had been looking for her.

Once, she had spied Penny and Anten standing hand in hand in front of the bridge. She thought they might cross but they walked away. She had followed them and discovered they now lived just behind Rift Street in a large house. They had taken over three gardens and were growing all manner of food, which they traded. She saw Chelik, Rosy and Timmy in the garden, looking well-fed and happy. Having satisfied herself that they were well, Elika had walked away.

She strode through the maze of alleys behind Rift Street. A young family now lived in Potter Ned's house. And there was no sign of Mary Lidle or her dog, or Joe Pitch who used to sleep beside her gate. Lusty Lucy's home had been taken by an old woman, Betty, who grew corn, spinach, and traded eggs from her small flock of chickens. Some days, Elika no longer recognized her city. Other times, she was grateful to have what was left.

She turned the corner and froze.

There was Penny, walking alone, her gaze sad and wistful. Elika did not know how much Penny had guessed about her part in the rebellion, but Elika could not face any of them with either the truth or a lie. She thought about leaping back behind the corner, but there was something in Penny's eyes that held her rooted to the spot. Her heart raced with recognition of what that look signified, of the way Penny's lips were pressed in that firm resolve.

Then Penny saw her, stopped and smiled with such honest relief that guilt flooded Elika. She dropped her gaze to the ground and waited for Penny to approach and embrace her. "I knew you were alive, Eli."

Elika wanted to weep, wanted to babble and beg for forgiveness, but guilt lodged in her throat kept her mute.

"How have you been?" Penny asked, pushing her gently away.

The question took her aback. How had she been? Numb, alone, afraid to live, afraid to die, trapped between two inevitable ends.

"Well enough," Elika replied at length. "And you?"

"As well as we can be. Rosy Rose never leaves Anten's side. Chelik and Timmy have grown as close as brothers. Chelik still asks about his father. He hasn't yet accepted he's likely dead." Penny looked aside, seemingly uncomfortable, almost nervous. "We've been looking for you ... me and Anten. We've made a decision ..."

"You want to wed." Elika pretended to misunderstand. "Might be hard with the temples burned down and the priestesses gone."

Penny blushed. "Now where did you get an idea like that from ... Oh! I'll not have your cheek, Eli Spider. This isn't what I meant, and you know it. We've decided to cross the bridge."

"All of you?" she asked and fear gripped her.

They were the last echoes of her old life. She realized now that having them near made her get out of bed each day and stopped her from taking that final step into the Blight. What would remain for her if they left?

"Echoes can cross," Penny said, misunderstanding her alarm. "I've seen the truth of it myself. We're all infected. None of us will perish."

Until you reach the other side, thought Elika.

"Come with us, Eli."

"You're a family," she replied, as if that somehow mattered.

"You are part of our family. There will always be a place for you with us."

"Penny ... I can't."

"We've had some fair weather, aye, but there's winter on the way. If the Blight doesn't get you before then, hunger will. Frances' cow's dead. The Blight got it overnight."

Elika realized that was how Penny knew she was alive. Frances was the only one with a cow. Everyone traded with him.

"What about Frances?" she asked.

"He's taken the bridge. Others are talking about doing the same. Forester, his wife and three children left yesterday, as have Jenny and her sister."

There were fewer than a hundred of them left, even before the Blight began to move again overnight.

"Do you truly want to die alone here?" Penny asked her.

"Rather here than there," she replied mulishly.

"Why? What does it matter?"

Elika had no answer to that, other than it mattered. She slipped her hand into her pocket and cupped the wooden bird. She could not abandon Terren or her world. It was all she had ever known and cared about. How could she give it up for an uncertain fate?

"Come with us," Penny said with more force.

Even if Elika wanted to leave, the bridge would likely throw her into the chasm in vengeance. "I don't think the bridge would let me," she said with quiet certainty.

Penny's face crumpled. "There's no future here. We are a pack. Whatever is on the other side, we'll be stronger together. We'll look after each other as we always have."

Elika's fingers moved past the bird and came to rest on Mite's ring.

She took it out and stared at it. Everyone left eventually. She had left the pack the night she fled from them, the day she discovered she harbored magic inside her. Mite had left her soon after.

She handed the ring to Penny. "Give this to Mite when you see him. It belongs to him. Tell him … tell him …" Words failed her.

What could she tell him, even if he was alive? He had left them to face their fate without him. He had faced his own fate without them. They were no longer a pack.

"I'll find him and might be I'll hit him for you," Penny said with a wry smile.

"When will you leave?"

"Tomorrow, after sunrise. Many are leaving today. They don't want to be caught by the Blight in their sleep. This is the end, Eli. And the bridge isn't likely to last much longer. Don't let the past imprison and condemn you. None of this is your fault."

The death of countless folk was her fault. Might be the Blight had killed the rebellion because she used her magic to help them. Might be she should have crossed that bridge long ago to save them.

They parted ways after that and Elika returned to her cottage. She sat alone by the window, watching the empty street. The end to her story was near. So she thought back to its beginning, the day her parents faced the bridge and left her behind. She tried to recall every detail, every word, every gesture and kiss they placed upon her cheek. But her memory was faint and insubstantial. She strained to remember whether they had made it across. It seemed some deep decision within her depended on that answer.

Were they waiting for her? Would they know her all these years later?

Why did they not take her with them? Why did they give her to the care of a stranger so readily? Might be Tane Igla spoke the truth and they were not her parents at all. Or might be they did not want her to perish.

Those thoughts churned endlessly in her mind without finding an answer to the one question that had haunted her all her life. Only the bridge had the answer to the fate of her parents.

The dark had fallen. Elika snatched up her lantern and went outside. Shortly afterwards, she stood before the bridge, her lantern held high. The winds whipped her face, just as they had the day of her earliest memory. She strained to recall the bridge as it was then, sinewy, frightening and awful. But all she saw now was a shriveled creature clinging desperately to the edge of their world.

She looked past it and recalled the teary eyes of her mother, recalled wanting to go with them and fighting against the dry hand holding her back. She recalled her fear … the ache in her chest, the tears, the loss … She focused on the pain she had sought to forget. The pain of grief, of knowing she would never see her parents again … Then she recalled the warm fire beside which she had wept.

Countless times, she had gazed upon the bridge and wondered. Had they crossed to become some strange phantasms or turned to dust? Now, amidst the rising echoes of the long-forgotten grief, she found herself too afraid to know. Might be it was as well she had forgotten.

As she was about to turn away, a recklessly summoned memory came from the dark—a scream—her own. Two shapes emerged from the buried depths of her mind, a man and a woman walking toward the apex, hand in hand.

Elika wanted to stop the memory, but they just walked on and on and …

And turned to dust.

Grief struck her all over again. No one waited for her. She was, in truth, an orphan.

All her life she had hoped they were somewhere in the land ruled by magic, waiting for her. A small, irrational part of her had clung to the belief that she was not an orphan but merely lost. Again and again, hope had turned to nothing but dust and tears. She would not hope again. Hope was the Blight that destroyed all it touched. There was nothing beyond the chasm but the cruelty of fate and magic.

She turned away and went back to her cottage along the empty streets.

The next dawn came too quickly, though she had not slept all night, kept awake by the deathly silence of the city. That silence was now brazenly shattered by the raucous call of a crow. The white-tipped crow had continued to haunt her, roosting on the chimney of her cottage. It sounded agitated this morning, but Elika paid it no mind. She knew she should rise. Penny, Anten, and the children might already be at the bridge. There was no reason for her to go to the bridge, no reason to see them cross to the Deadlands, save that she owed it to them to witness their fate.

The crow cawed again and its face appeared in the window. It pecked the glass with its beak. It had never done that before. Perhaps it was hungry.

Elika rolled out of bed. She would find no rest there from the damnable creature. Nothing had changed from the day before. She was still an orphan. The fate of her parents had been decided long ago. Hers was still uncertain.

She wiped herself with a damp cloth, dressed and left the cottage. As she closed the door behind her, she started. The Blight had marched overnight and stopped a mere few steps from her doorstep. The grass there was wilted, the roses had lost their petals. A few more moments and it might have claimed her, too. The crow had saved her, she realized with wonder.

It took to the wing, cawed loudly and flew toward Rift Street. Elika ran after it, away from the Blight. She glanced behind her and knew she could not return to the cottage.

When she came to Rift Street, many were once again gathered there, waiting their turn to cross. Judging from their numbers, by nightfall, there'd be not a dozen of them left behind. Or might be by tomorrow morning the Blight would have reached the chasm. Relentless winds blew from inside it, howling forlornly in those dark depths. But the bridge across it was more daunting than ever before. It was shriveled like a diseased vine, barely held together by the wilting black branches. Step on it and you would fall through.

Elika sat in her old spot and watched as the last of the folk of Terren abandoned their world for an uncertain fate. There went Clever Colin, who was once a priest, gripping the railing lest it give way beneath his feet. He grew carrots and cabbage and enough potatoes to feed most of the street. Then came Spotty Sam and Showy Inky. One after another, the last of mankind slipped away into the Deadlands. They all made it, for they were all Echoes. She watched their fleeting expressions as they neared the bridge—hope, fear, doubts, and above all else, resolve. They drew strength from each other. And they still indulged *hope*.

Elika imagined crossing with Mite, holding his hand …

To what fate? Came a treacherous whisper from inside her mind.

No, she would not cosset Hope—that shameless, cruel creature which struck from the edges of fear and death.

A shout came from around the corner. "The Blight's coming!" Betty ran onto Rift Street, holding two chickens under her arms and looking behind her with fright. "It's gotten Hober and his roosters and my chickens too." She hobbled toward the bridge and shoved her way toward it.

Something inside Elika stilled with dread. A whisper of terrible understanding crept into the edges of her mind. She scrambled to her feet and peered around the corner with an ominous premonition of what she would see.

Not two streets away, along Bridge Street, she saw the yellowing grass which grew from the cracks in the building, and the sudden wilting of a daisy flower. She watched the Blight advance a mere few steps more and stop.

Her mind reeled. It could not be.

She spun to face the bridge. An old man stepped on to it. She watched him cross. Then she glanced over her shoulder to see the Blight move again and halt.

She laughed, bitterly, for fate was a cruel jester.

Nobody ever understood the Blight or what drove it. Magic was blamed. What else could it be? What other power could create such a monster and drive it across their entire world? Men blamed the Echoes, the tsaren, the gods and vile fates. They blamed everything and everyone but men themselves.

But they were wrong. And yet, how could they have known? Only at the very end did the truth burn so brightly.

She watched another cross the bridge and the Blight advance in reply. And she understood what no one had fathomed in six hundred years. She understood the Blight

... too late—too late to save them—too late to make them see.

And she could do nothing but stare at the monstrosity men had created the day they destroyed magic. For it was not the magic driving it, but the absence of it. Men had brought this fate upon themselves when they sought to destroy magic.

The revelation was so sudden and crippling it choked her.

The Great Web was shrinking, just as Bill and Igla had tried to tell her. The tanes knew about the web, as had the tsaren. Men had been destroying it since the beginning of time. And when they did, they left the world a little emptier. With every echo of magic that fled across the bridge, with every Echo destroyed in the blood-salt fire, the web of life retreated, leaving behind an empty void.

The Blight was never the magic's revenge against man. It was not born of magic, but simply the end of it. There was no stopping the Blight. Not anymore.

Syn'Moreg had sundered the web, and Arala sacrificed herself to weave the sole path to save magic trapped in this dying world from the destructive force of *man*.

There was nothing Elika could have done to save the city or its people ...

Nothing, except remain behind in this world, for inside her, she held the largest piece of magic keeping the Blight at bay.

She recalled the firm hand of Tane Nora and her strange words. *Not your time, precious. I told them so. Told them you must stay behind to hold the world together for just a little longer.*

Were she to cross that bridge, she would destroy the last pocket of life clinging to the edges of the bottomless precipice.

So, she stood there, watching the last of the humanity leave one by one until no one was left and Rift Street was empty. The Blight had stopped a mere street away.

Then she saw Penny and Anten, Rosy and Timmy and Chelik. They carried bags packed with food, blanket rolls, and leather skins with water, flung over their shoulders. Chelik also had a fat purse on his belt, stuffed with coins his father had left him. Rose took her favorite doll which Anten had given her. And Timmy took the small pillow he would not be parted from.

They saw her and approached. Rose clung to Anten's hand, eyeing her suspiciously.

Penny frowned. "You're upset. Have you changed your mind?"

Elika shook her head. "Thought you never wanted to cross," she said to Anten somewhat accusingly.

He shrugged. "I guess I was wrong. Seems there is more to life than moping about the end of the world." His gaze darted to Penny and filled with tenderness.

Elika looked aside with a pang of envy for something she would never have.

"Come with us," he said.

She could not bring herself to tell them the crushing truth of what had befallen their world and why everything and everyone was dead. Nor that it was the folly of men and not magic that has done this. And why she alone could stop the Blight from destroying the last small pocket of their world. As long as she did not cross that bridge.

If she crossed, the last of their world would unravel and vanish. She'd be the one to destroy it.

So she mustered a wavering smile. "I think I'll stay behind just a little longer."

Let them enjoy the last of their blissful moments together. She could see that they still clung to hope which allowed them to believe beyond what their own eyes could see.

"Maybe it's not what it appears to be," Chelik said, his gaze following hers toward the Deadlands.

They were naive, she thought. There was no fear in the faces of the children. They had seen so much, lived through things no child should live through. Maybe death held little meaning to them. Only hope stirred their fluttering hearts. She would not be the one to crush it.

"Might be you're right," she replied with a shaky smile.

"Find us when you cross," said Penny.

She stood back from them. "Don't wait for me."

Then she watched them leave.

They reached the other side and stood there like so many others before them, mere shadows in the endless gray lands.

And the Blight advanced a little closer.

CHAPTER SIXTEEN

The Bridge to Magic

"Here I recount a tale the Sachi claim to have heard from the gods. Long ago, the ethereal realm touched the celestial. The brushing of the spheres allowed magic and gods to walk through each other's worlds. The goddess Neka fell in love with a tsarin whose name was Orian. Together they conceived a child of great beauty and power over the essence of life. The child's name was Arala. When the two realms began to drift apart again, Arala chose to remain in her father's world, for by then she had given her heart to Tsarin Reval. Orian, however, could not bear to be parted from goddess Neka, so he joined her in the celestial sphere. It is said he died there when the realms drifted apart once again, for he was not a god, and could not live in their domain."

History of Men, Gods and Magic,
By Priest Oderrin

Summer faded. The Blight had stopped behind Rift Street with the last man to leave the city. That was old Ned Nosy, who finally decided that he was curious to see what was in the Deadlands. He had sought Elika to say his farewells and suggest she go with him. She refused.

If she crossed, everything would cease to be. The Blight would not edge any closer, as long as she remained in this world. It was a small victory, but she claimed it. She had stopped the Blight from destroying the last of their world. Sometimes the thought made her laugh aloud. Else the loneliness did.

Autumn had come and gone, and winter arrived upon doleful winds.

She lived in the house across the street from the bridge. Each day she awoke to another cloudless, sunless day across the chasm in the Deadlands, no matter what the weather was overhead. Her home was stocked well enough with food and supplies she had scavenged to last her the winter. Come spring, she'd plant more beans and carrots, potatoes and tomatoes.

She did not think beyond that.

She sat on her doorstep, huddled in a cloak from the chill winds. The city was silent, save for the wind whistling through the empty buildings. Long ago, before the Sundering War, her city was the heart of their world, where the different races of the four kingdoms gathered to trade and settle disputes. It was the city of learning and wisdom, renowned for its great scholars and eminent artists. Now, it was the graveyard for the last vestiges of mankind.

She watched the bridge, for there was nothing else to do. She had gathered the last of the vegetables and fruits in late autumn, and preserved what she could not store. The ground was too cold for planting more. She had all she needed to survive the winter, except company.

She was alone in a city filled with corpses. Alone, but alive. What was there across the bridge for her, anyway?

Hope, came a whisper from her mind.

She stared at the Deadlands beyond, empty, bare, desolate. Though the sun had climbed overhead, its rays did not reach the gray lands beyond.

There was no hope there. Here she was alive.

Alive, but not living.

One of the bridge's roots lost its grip on the ground ... her heart shuddered. It occurred to her that even now, despite everything, the bridge was still her last thread of hope. Each day, she watched the bridge unravel more and more. Come spring, it would likely be gone and there would be no escape from this broken world.

The magic inside her might keep the Blight at bay, but to what end? What was left here but a bubble of life for her to grow old and die in? The buildings were going to ruin. The city was crumbling, stone by stone. But here and there, grass clumps still grew. And she had an apple tree that yielded plentiful harvest nearby. There were no birds, however, no animals, only her and the empty cobwebs.

A crow cawed overhead, as if protesting her thoughts.

"Aye, I know you are here, too," she said aloud. "Little good you are to me. I can't even catch you to eat you."

The white-tipped crow cackled, a mocking laughter.

Was this then to be her life, spending her days talking to the mad crow? She thought the gods were watching her and laughing too. Perhaps Penny was right, it was time to let go of the past and look to the future.

Her world was gone. The story of man had ended. Did it perhaps begin again across the chasm? Could she take that chance?

Maybe it's not what it appears to be.

She surveyed the Deadlands for any sign that somehow she could forge a new beginning on the other side. She looked for anything that she could grasp and feed to the starved hope inside her heart. But there was only the desolation. Might be hope and faith were intertwined. She needed to believe in order to hope. But she could not believe beyond what her eyes could see. The land there was gray and lifeless, a mirror of her hopes.

She jumped to her feet and walked back into her home. Home. The crumbling old building with missing floorboards and decaying furniture. Though she had boarded up the windows, the icy wind whistled through the holes in the walls and rattled the roof. She strode to the house next door to rip up another floorboard to start a fire. She tried to yank up the board with cold, numb hands, but it held firm.

Her life was not so bad, she told herself. The nights were frosty. But she had enough blankets and clothes to keep herself warm. And there was a good stock of dried beans, grains and even a bag of flour. She had harvested enough potatoes to last till spring. There was no meat ... but last night, she thought she heard a mouse in the wall ...

She wrestled the board until her hands were pierced with splinters and her fingers bled, but it would not come up. She screamed in anguish and rage and sank to her knees.

A mouse in the wall. She laughed through her tears. *Then she might eat the damned crow and see how the gods liked that.*

She shook her head. This was not life but barren existence. There was no life without mankind. And there could never be life without magic.

She wanted to live in truth, to wake up to another sunrise, to smell spring on the air and hear children's laughter. She wanted to feel fresh hope again that rode upon each dawn. She wished for life and all its whispered promises of things to come.

It would be a mercy to simply allow herself to freeze on this wintry night. Just let the fire die out deep in the night, throw aside the blankets, and she would never wake up. It would be peaceful, painless—a kind end. Far kinder than this existence she was trapped in.

The crow cawed outside, a lonely, rattling call.

Elika lifted her head and saw three paths before her, the path to gods, to magic, and to men. She could walk into the Blight and face the gods. She could remain here in the world once claimed by men and live with just her memories. Or, she could cross the Bridge to Magic.

Perhaps there had never been any path for her to take, save one. All stories began and ended at the Bridge to Magic and thus would be her end.

With that resolve, a great weight lifted from her soul, for in her heart, she knew there was no turning back. Despair was replaced with relief, dread with purpose. There was elation, too, and a rising sense of adventure. She would face whatever lay beyond the rift. Death or life, surely it was better than this gray, uncertain existence.

She passed her gaze over her crumbling home. There was nothing she wanted to take, save what she was wearing—a warm cloak, woolen trousers, a shirt and a pair of sturdy boots which fit snugly. On her belt hung a knife, an old habit she found comforting. In her pocket, she carried only the wooden bird. She would not burden herself with anything more for the crossing or the awaiting fate. Without looking back, she strode outside.

Overhead, the crow took wing. It circled and flew toward the bridge, as if it had been waiting all this time for Elika to accept her fate.

The crow landed on the bridge and waited for Elika to cross the street toward it. Then it cawed one last time and flew across the chasm to disappear into the Deadlands. Elika stared after it, wondering whether she had imagined the crow all along, for she could not see its shadow on the other side. Or perhaps it truly was the messenger of the gods, showing her the way home. Foolish thoughts, but she took courage from them. The bridge offered her the last refuge from the world that had lost its magic.

There was no blood-salt line. It had been washed away long ago by rain. The roots were wilted and shriveled. She took a step toward them and waited. Once, they had sought her eagerly. Now they were just lifeless fingers barely clinging to the ground. The blood still oozed in a sluggish trickle from the wound she had inflicted last winter.

On one side, the railing had unraveled, and black strands flailed listlessly on the rising winds. The once solid floor was a broken web, with barely a place to put a foot. The bridge looked as though it would crumble beneath her weight.

All her life, courage had failed her. Maybe that was why Mite had left her—to allow her to find her own courage to do what she was always meant to do.

She had faced the Blight, now it was time she faced the bridge. She would not look back anymore, only ahead. With that resolve, Elika pushed back her shoulders and stepped onto the Bridge to Magic.

Beneath her feet, it groaned and stirred. And with that first step she knew it was not magic that held men here and made it impossible for them to turn back, but their own hearts. With that first step, her heart released its grip upon her world, the past, and all her fears. It reached for the future, eager to grasp whatever lay ahead.

She took another cautious step. The roots did not move, did not grab her to dangle her over the edge as she had once feared. Emboldened, she moved onward and put her hand on to the black shreds of the last remaining railing.

The bridge was warm beneath her fingers and supple like skin.

With the next step, she left the ground and her world both, to be suspended over the endless chasm, with only the dying bridge between her and the eternity of the Abyss. The wind ripped at her cloak, screeching and howling like the screams of men and women it had claimed. It brought up the stench of death and threats of eternal darkness.

She looked down. It was a foolish thing to do, she knew.

Terror lodged in her throat. From below, darkness rushed up, gripped her and pulled. Her legs sank beneath her body, and her stomach plunged into those depths. She clung to the railing with all her might, staring into that rift. The darkness was not like the darkness of the black night, or the darkness of blindness. Instead, it was the darkness of death, of nothingness. And she finally understood Bill's words. Syn'Moreg had sundered not the land, but the very fabric of their world.

Her breath quickened. The other side of the chasm was an impossible distance away, whilst her legs were leaden and unable to move. She closed her eyes and felt herself sinking and falling into the Abyss. She had seen the bridge unravel beneath men's feet and watched them plunge into that chasm, falling sickeningly fast and disappearing.

Do not look down. Do not look back.

She opened her eyes. Ahead was land. The bridge had not given way. Only her fear was pushing her into the chasm. She took a steadying breath and her feet edged onward. But with each step, the black strands flexed under her weight and the bridge trembled and shook. Her stomach sank sickeningly.

Do not let me fall. Do not let me fall.

A thread unraveled under her feet. She yelped and wound her arms around the fleshy railing as her feet scrambled to regain their footing. The rising winds from the chasm screamed louder and louder, deafening now to her ears. They ripped at her clothes, like clasping hands trying to drag her down. She focused on the bridge. It was still there, solid and warm … and soft, like flesh. It smelled of loamy earth and grass and flowers. How could something so dark and frightening smell like spring itself?

She forced herself to look only ahead to the uncertain future in the Deadlands. She wanted with all her heart to reach it and to meet whatever fate it offered. Still gripping the railing, she stood tall and moved onward, carefully probing with each step.

Another step and the bridge groaned and shuddered.

The gaps grew wider where the criss-crossing branches had fallen away, and it became harder and harder to find a path that would not lead her into the chasm below. Then the path in front of her fell away altogether. The gap in the bridge opened wide, and the bottomless darkness rushed up.

Her heart trembled. The next step was too far to reach. The only path was one that took her away from the railing, where the winds threatened to push her over the side.

There was no choice. She had to let go and follow the narrow path in the center of the bridge with only the drop on either side.

Elika released the railing and wobbled. She put out her hands. Though the footing was solid, her legs felt as if they were sinking in quicksand. The winds whipped around and yanked her cloak this way and that, unbalancing her. She unfastened her cloak, and the winds ripped it from her hands. It spiraled away into oblivion, but her footing was steadier for it.

She had climbed roofs all her life and knew to focus her gaze ahead. Only the other side mattered, not what lay beneath her feet.

Nothing to it. It's just like leaping over missing floorboards. You have done it many times and you never once fell through, now did you?

She braced herself, hopped over a small gap and steadied herself against the gust of wind. There was no railing, only black shreds flailing back and forth. She pressed on, each step slow and uncertain. The bridge was far longer than it appeared from the land and it felt like an eternity before she reached the apex.

She stopped a mere step away from where so many had turned to dust. So many lives she had seen perish here. Despite knowing that the magic inside her would keep her safe, fear and doubt assailed her. But there was no turning back. Her fate had been decided the moment she stepped onto the bridge. She took a deep breath and strode across the apex.

Relief swept through her. She had survived.

In front of her, another piece of the bridge unraveled.

Her relief fled, replaced by an awful suspicion. Her mind raced as another black strand fell away and her folly rushed upon her. Her breath quickened and grew heavy with a terrible certainty of what was behind her.

I will not look back. Only ahead.

But she did. She looked back because she had to know, had to witness the end of her world and her story. Aye, she looked back because she suddenly knew that she could never cross the bridge. The Deadlands were still too far away, but the world behind her had ended, for she had taken the last piece of magic from it.

She looked back and the sight from nightmares accosted her eyes. A graveyard of life she had known and loved. The Blight had reached the chasm. Her world was gone. Nothing but the hollow, dry bones of Terren remained. And its lifeless beauty struck her in that moment, seeing it like this, beyond her reach. How had she never seen it before? Blinded by fears and anxiety, by squabbles of everyday life she had never stopped to take in the wonder of the world she lived in. The fine carvings of stone pillars, the bright sea of rooftops and spires against the blue sky and distant mountains brushed by the passage of clouds. The street fountains and flower urns and carefully laid cobbles for all to tread ...

Then her gaze moved to the bridge and her heart stuttered. As she watched, the roots of the bridge finally released their grasp on the cobbled stones and for a moment the bridge floated in the air upon the winds. Then it began to unravel toward her, the far end slowly falling into the chasm.

Her mind froze. The chasm seemed wider than ever before. Within moments the unravelling, falling strands would reach her and take her with them into the eternal depths ... Her feet spurred into motion. She raced onward, leaping over the gaps. The bridge was still bound to the other side. The Deadlands loomed ahead harsh and forbidding and she wanted nothing more than to reach them.

She did not want to die. She could not die. This could not be her end ...

Then the bridge was no longer beneath her feet, and for an eternal instant she felt weightless, not bound to the world, not bound to life. No, it could not be real ... and she was falling, falling and screaming. She reached out and grabbed the fleshy strands, gripped them with all her strength as if they had some power to save her from the fate that was always meant to be hers, the eternity of plunging through the Abyss like so many others. She screamed and screamed. The wind swallowed her screams and merged them with its own. The light was gone, the darkness blinding. She closed her eyes against it whilst clinging to the remnants of the bridge, plummeting into the rift, her screams growing hoarse as the air rushed past …

She hit something hard with a force that knocked all air out of her.

Sharp pain exploded in her shoulder, but somehow she managed to hold on. Her breath was erratic and rasping. Her throat was tight and raw. It took a long moment for the realization that she was no longer falling to permeate her mind. She opened her eyes and stared at the sheer rock face of the sundered world. Far overhead, where the bridge was still bound to the Deadlands, there was light.

Her feet scrambled to find purchase on the loose fleshy strands, but there was none to be had. Her hands grew wet with sweat and her grip became slippery, whilst the winds whipped around her legs, pulling her down, demanding their last victim.

"No!" she screamed, as her hands lost their grip.

Again, she began to fall, clawing uselessly at the strands of the bridge hanging limply against the chasm wall.

A black strand snapped out and wound around her wrist like a whip. It dangled her over the dark chasm, and every nightmare she'd ever had rushed into her mind. She had been here before, at the mercy of the bridge, at the mercy of magic, suspended above the chasm, before it released her to her doom.

Please ... she opened her mouth to plead, but no sound came out save a ragged breath.

This was to be her end, falling eternally in the darkness. Her mind seized. She thought of Mite and Penny and her pack, of Bill and Igla and Nora and her parents, and every face she had ever known. She thought of Lucky Lick, too, in the depths below. Might be this was justice.

She raised her eyes to the light overhead, filling her last memories with it. There was no light in the Abyss. There, she would be blind.

The strand holding her moved, and a sob escaped her throat. But instead of throwing her into the chasm, it yanked her up and pulled her back against the bridge. Elika gripped the black vine and her feet found purchase. She did not think, did not question, merely did what her body demanded she do to survive—scramble up and climb toward the light. It did not matter what fate it held, for there was nothing behind her.

As she climbed faster and faster, she grew more and more certain that the bridge would not allow her to fall. The fleshy strands wound around her protectively, pushed her up, urged her onward. The light above her grew brighter. Hope swelled in her chest.

With a last heave of her arms, she pulled herself over the edge onto solid ground. She crawled a little way and collapsed, breathing heavily, feeling nothing but the cool rock beneath her body.

She stared at the bridge for long moments. "I am sorry I hurt you," she whispered. Despite what she had done, it sought not to punish but to save her. "Thank you," she added.

As she watched, the black roots released their last, desperate hold on the stone, and with a groan, the bridge slipped away into the chasm.

Elika shook off an inexplicable pang of grief and rose to her feet.

Around her, the Deadlands were gone, replaced by an impenetrable fog. It swirled around her and she could see nothing beyond the stone ground at her feet ... no, not stone, but a cobbled path.

The mist was damp on her face and she took comfort from that, for it was real, and it was water. She had never seen mist in the Deadlands, and a small part of her mind, which was not numb with shock, was confounded by it.

She began to walk into the unseen and the unknown. The air was wintry and she hugged herself, missing her lost cloak. She could see nothing of what lay ahead, nothing of what lay behind. But each of her steps grew bolder.

All stories began and ended with the Bridge to Magic.

Was this to be the end of hers?

From somewhere near came an unfamiliar sound, like a thousand whispers rising and falling. She walked toward it through the fog. It grew louder. She could smell the salt, could taste it on the mist.

Suddenly, what lay beneath her feet changed and she stumbled forward in surprise. Her knees and hands sank into sand. From the mist, water washed over her hands and legs, then retreated. She scrambled away from it. Again, with a whisper, the water returned and yet again retreated.

A bird screeched nearby. And voices were near.

She staggered to her feet.

The mist cleared abruptly, as if it had never been there at all, revealing the world before her—bright and dazzling and filled with color the like of which she had never seen. As she beheld it, her eyes filled with tears, for the world that greeted her was nothing like the Deadlands.

Waves from a great sea, like something out of Bill's tales, washed over the sand and licked her boots. And there were boats, the same as Bill's, bobbing in the sparkling blue water. The sun was low, the air crisp, and frost covered the masts.

Then she turned and before her rose a city she knew so well, the city they had lost six hundred years ago when Syn'Moreg had sundered their world.

She wanted to laugh and weep. It was not true. The old saying was not true. All stories lay *beyond* the Bridge to Magic. And as she gazed upon the other half of Terren, vibrant and alive and filled with the voices of its folk, a sob escaped her throat.

Magic was treacherous, it lied to them all, for the deadlands beyond were not dead at all.

About the Author

Alex Thornbury

Alex Thornbury is an award-winning author. She grew up in Cheshire UK and developed deep love of history and fantasy thanks to the many castles she visited as a child. Though she grew up to be an Alchemist by trade, she never stopped fantasizing about other worlds, dragons and epic battles. She has abandoned her Alchemy and potion making career and is now a full-time author of high fantasy.

www.alexthornbury.com

ACKNOWLEDGEMENTS

Being an author is a lonely thing. We toil away until our hopes feel like a dusty landscape of our dreams unrealized. We tread the minefield of endless edits and reworkings. Yet in the end we are not alone on our journey.

I would like to thank the wonderful folk who have helped me along the way and made this book what it is today— Barbara Unkovic and Rob Bignell for their expertly edits, Alejandro Colucci for his artwork and cover design.

A thank you also to Simon Ward at Simon Says Web Design, Albert Griesmayr at Scribando for his marketing talents, and everyone at Smith Publicity who worked to promote my book, with a special thanks to Andrea Kiliany, Olivia McCoy and Kellie Rendina for bringing this story to the attention of the readers, bloggers, reviewers and editors out there.

And most of all, a special thank you to Brian Keaney who guided me through the dusty landscape of my hopes towards the meadows of my dreams fulfilled. His tireless insights, edits and comments have morphed me from a struggling writer into an author I am today. I would not be where I am today without his help and guidance and brutally honest feedback. I am forever in your debt, Brian.

Alex Thornbury

The Rogue Mage

Book 2 of the Sundered Web Trilogy

Elika crosses the Bridge to Magic to find the world ruled
by magic. Mages run the streets, whilst the tsaren, their
masters, hideaway in their great halls, indifferent to the
plight of men. Faced with the injustice of the mages,
Elika discovers her own untapped gifts that may yet shift
the balance of power back into the hands of men. But
her dabbling in the power she does not understand draws
the attention of the dreaded demi-god Syn'Moreg. Elika
must now outwit the shadow that hunts her, whilst
seeking a way to free men from their oppressors.

*"How could she live in a world where nothing was certain? Where
reality was as cutting as a sword and yet as waning as a dream?"*

Shadow Lore
PUBLISHING

The Sundered Web: Book II

The
ROGUE
MAGE

ALEX THORNBURY

A Sneak Peak:

The Rogue Mage
(Book 2)

A special preview of the next book in

Alex Thornbury's

The Sundered Web Series

A dark sequel to **The Bridge to Magic**

RELEASE DATE
DECEMBER 2023

CHAPTER ONE

Al-Terren

"We remember the day, We, the many, became one ... one creature inside this body. It was the day we woke up in the world of Seramight, the world from our dreams. We remember seeing through the strange eyes of a man. Seeing much that was wondrous ... and yet not seeing what must be there. Seramight is not beautiful as Alafraysia is beautiful. It is not as magnificent nor dazzling. And we grew uncertain. Then we, or rather the man who sheltered us, took a breath and touched his face and we Felt. We felt the smooth, warm skin beneath our fingers, we felt the air rush into our chest ... we smelt it in his nose. Upon it, we smelt the odor of the man and felt disgusted. Aye, we felt that emotion, so alien to us. We heard the sounds of the world that we so long desired to live in. A world made of stone and earth, water and air, and life. A solid, unchanging world which is more than a mere dream ... Then we saw our Tsarin Reval standing before us. 'Your task, Aeon-Bluelight is to write the history of our combined realms. 'Tis why I brought you to this world.'"

The History of Alafraysia and Seramight,
By Mage Aeon-Bluelight

They said all stories began and ended at the Bridge to Magic. The wise priests who knew such things, men who had listened to the tales of their forefathers, and old women who told them to their children.

They were wrong. Stories ended at the Bridge to Magic. And then began anew. At least for those who had survived the crossing.

Elika crouched down and brushed the shimmering water as the old sea rolled over her shoes and retreated again. Cold. Icy cold for it was winter. She brought her fingertip to her lips. Salty. Just as Bill Fisher had told her. He had seen the great sea that had once covered half of Seramight. That was before Syn'Moreg had sundered their world.

Her gaze ran over the sparkling water towards the dark chasm and beyond, to the grey landscape of the city she had left behind. Only this morning, she had stood on the other side of that dividing dark scar, gazing across at the vast, empty plains of rock and dust of the deadlands. All her life, she had stared at them from across the chasm and wondered.

She was the last to cross the bridge before it unraveled, walking towards that lifeless landscape. But magic was treacherous, and it lied to them all. Instead of the deadlands, she was greeted by a vibrant world of color and life and men's voices. A frightening feeling crept up on her; perhaps it was she who had lived in the deadlands all her life whilst life went on here, across the chasm.

Her city was now a broken rubble, dead, lifeless, abandoned. All the lands beyond it had been destroyed by the Blight. Death reigned there instead of man.

There was no sea on that side of the chasm. It had drained away long ago into the rift, leaving behind endless salt marshes and mud plains littered with carcasses of ancient ships.

Here, on this side of the divide, the sea ran up to the chasm and stopped abruptly, held back from spilling over the edge by some force ... by magic. The thought wormed its way into her mind. Magic. She was in the land to where it had been exiled, the land ruled by that untamed force, with no way back home. The bridge that had brought her here was gone. She had stabbed it and destroyed it. Some deep, secret knowledge of her soul suspected she might have made a terrible mistake.

Voices cut through the crisp air, shouts and calls of alarm. She spun and faced the tall city wall of the other half of Terren. For six hundred years, men believed this half of their city had perished in the great cataclysm. Yet, here it was, built from the same silver-veined grey stone, only larger and fiercer than before. The streets, which once joined with those on the other side, ran to the edge of the chasm. The houses which had once stood across Rift Street were a mirror of those she had left behind. But that was where the similarity ended.

Here, the residents had built an enormous outer wall between their city and the chasm, capped with towers and battlements. The wall had sprung up behind abandoned old buildings and rose high, as if against a giant enemy coming from the Abyss. It ran into the sea on the one side, and along the coast on the other, encircling a sprawling city. Even from here, she could see enough to know that it had grown and grown whilst her world had been shrinking.

There was a squat city gate in front of a circular stone courtyard, tall enough for a horse and rider to go through. The portcullis was raised, but it seemed unwelcoming. It faced the chasm across the courtyard. There, she saw the upturned cobbles and the gouges in the ground where the roots of the bridge had once held firm.

She beheld the empty courtyard. Turned to take in the empty beach and the old cobbled road along the other half of Rift Street beside the chasm. An ache arose in her chest. No one was waiting for her. Neither Mite, nor Penny, nor her parents. Her parents had died crossing the bridge. Penny likely thought her dead by now. And Mite … he had left her behind to find a new life without her. Did she truly expect him to be standing here waiting for her?

Aye, you did, a voice inside her mocked gently. Foolish that you are.

Bells began to ring.

"Dae-Terren!" Men shouted from atop the city wall.

Above her, the guards rushed to the parapet to stare and point at the city across the chasm.

Folk began to emerge from the gate into the empty courtyard. They were clad in loose clothes made of strange, brightly colored cloth. Some wore shimmering garb and plaited their hair with silver lace. No one was looking at her. Their gazes were fixed on the ruinous city from where she had come, as if they had never seen it before.

"'Tis Dae-Terren … So, it's real," said a boy in wonder, coming to stand beside her.

"'Course it's real, you fool. Where do you think all the Daes came from?" replied an old woman next to him.

They spoke in the common tongue of men, but with a soft accent unfamiliar to Elika's ears.

"Where did the fog go then, Nan? Do you think it's Ilikan who's up to no good again?"

"Now, how am I to know that? Besides, it's Reval who controls the clouds, and fog is like clouds, ain't it?"

More folk came to stand on the beach. "Hey, you, Dae, did you just cross?"

Elika felt eyes on her and turned.

"You, boy, aye. Did you just cross?" The man who spoke was looking straight at her.

She shook her head and walked into the crowd, away from his probing gaze.

More and more people piled out of the gate. "Where's the bridge?" she heard someone ask.

"What happened to the mist?"

Aye, there was a mist when she crossed. It disappeared soon after the bridge fell into the chasm.

"'Tis a Dae," someone said as she shoved past them towards the squat city gate.

The throng of folk grew thicker, and she walked against their flow. She needed to get away before more of them realized she did not belong. She had to find a quiet place to think. The guards at the gate walked out, too, their gazes fixed upon the newly exposed old street and crumbling houses.

Out of nowhere, a dark shadow fell over them, as if a thunderous cloud had blocked the sun. Elika looked up and gaped in horror. Up in the sky, a mountainous island of rock and gardens floated towards them. It spun and turned, as if it did not know which way was up or down. There was a crystalline palace in its heart, surrounded by lush gardens and bridges over flowing streams. And she grew certain that she must be asleep, dreaming one of Bill Fisher's old tales of things that could never be.

"Reval!" someone shouted and pointed at the sky island.

"Why is he here?"

"Guards to the wall!" a commanding voice shouted.

But his shout was drowned by another.

"ARALA!" A fierce roar of anguish boomed over the land like thunder and sent a wave of wind with it.

Elika covered her ears and ducked against the force of that wave.

Someone shoved past her and knocked her to the ground. Then all around her there were boots and legs and skirts, tripping over each other, fleeing back towards the city. She crawled to the stone wall and found her feet.

The deafening roar of wind filled her ears. Over the heads of the panicked crowd, she saw a vortex of dust and water heading for them.

Her feet spurred into motion, and she joined in with the pushing and shoving through the gate and the tunnel beneath the wall.

"Reval!" Men shouted the warning to the folk ahead who sought to see what the commotion was about. "He's sent the winds against us! Hide!"

"Close the gates!"

Elika emerged from the tunnel into a crowded square. Everywhere she looked, her way was blocked by fleeing bodies. She darted to the edges of the street before they trampled her to death.

Overhead, a roof blew off. She covered her head against the rain of stone debris and tiles and fled onwards. The winds intensified, and each step grew labored. She glanced behind. The whirlwind was upon them. A young woman screamed and was yanked into the sky, her screams swallowed by the winds.

The vortex advanced towards Elika, ripped at her clothes and limbs, made her feel light and weightless as it threatened to whisk her away. She pushed open the nearest door, threw herself inside, crawled into the corner and curled into a tight ball. Then there was nothing but darkness and the fierce roar of the wind, shattering of glass and screams.

It seemed an age passed before the rumbling noise of destruction faded to silence. Elika uncurled. Light had returned to the world. She took in her surroundings and found herself in a small shop. Its windows were broken. Shattered jars of herbs, dried flowers and berries lay beneath the empty shelves. A small boy peered at her with large eyes from under a table. A plump woman was hiding behind him under the same table. They emerged uncertainly, looking stunned. The shopkeeper rose to his feet from behind a counter, confused and dazed, wiping his bald head with his hand as he took in his ravaged shop.

A man dressed in a bright green suit emerged from behind the same counter. Though he trembled, he made a show of calmly brushing off the dust from his sleeves. The shimmering cloth was unlike anything Elika had ever seen. It was distractingly decorated with gold leaves and rippled with light under his touch.

Then their gazes snagged on her.

"It's a Dae," said the pouch in the green suit, halting mid-preen. "She's dressed like an Othersider." His voice was laced with that same strange, soft accent. It contrasted starkly with his disdainful gaze that raked her head to heel.

Elika could only stare at him in disbelief. A magical wind had just ripped through their city, and she was the oddity worthy of his notice?

"Magic hater," the shopkeeper sneered, dusting himself off.

"It's the magic you are all hiding from in here," she bit back and cringed at the rough sound of her own harsher tongue compared to his song-like lilt. "It's the magic that broke your shop."

"Not magic, but that damned Reval. He's as raving mad as a bull with busted ... ahem, pardon me, mistress." He bowed apologetically to the plump woman before turning back to Elika. "Nothing anyone can do about it when he gets into one of his moods. The archmage no doubt is on his way to calm him."

The shopkeeper bent down to pick up his broken jars, muttering to himself about insane Reval and the bloody tsaren with their endless squabbles.

"Did ye just cross, boy? Have you a master?" asked the woman in a kindly voice. Though she was also dressed in vibrant colors, her dress seemed plain compared to the man's gold-leafed coat.

"Been here a while," Elika lied. She could tell from their faces that they did not believe her. In her rough spun trousers and shirt, she must look like a beggar to them.

"Mummy, is that a barbarian from the other side?" the boy whispered to the woman.

"Aye, dear, 'tis one of them. He's from Dae-Terren."

"Where magic-haters live," he breathed, eyeing her with wonder.

"Shush. The old race has not been civilized like us."

"Pa says they're crude, simple-minded invaders who come to destroy our world, like they destroyed their own."

"Your pa's not wrong, boy," scoffed the man in the suit. "Get the guards before this one causes mischief."

Elika noted he did not step closer to her himself.

"Might be the guards are too busy cleaning up the mess," she snapped and pushed past them. The woman gripped the boy as if she thought this barbarian was going to kill him.

None of them followed her outside.

In the street, the destruction left by the vortex was reminiscent of a war. Men and women lay lifeless on the ground, looking like broken dolls in pretty dresses. Others were walking around, dazed. Roofs had been ripped off. Here and there, buildings lay in ruins. Nothing seemed real. Elika hugged herself and walked in the opposite direction to the folk rushing to help the injured. She needed to find a place where the eyes of these people did not follow her.

This was Terren, her home, yet she did not recognize any part of it. Soon, she was disorientated by the unfamiliar streets and unknown faces. Even the blue sky here was wrong. Everything was brighter, the colors more vivid. The air itself was thick with some vital force. She felt it deep in her bones. Even the familiar grey buildings of old Terren, which had survived the vagaries of time, were more vibrant somehow. She felt as if she had awoken from a dream into a stark and frightening reality.

She turned into a quiet, dead-end alley. A large plant pot with a small tree growing from it stood beside a closed door. She ducked behind the pot, crouching against the wall, trying to gather her scattered thoughts.

She had crossed the bridge—almost died crossing it. Instead of the deadlands, she had found herself here in Terren ... the other half of Terren they had thought destroyed. The folk here had not died six hundred years ago when Syn'Moreg sundered their world but lived on. These were the descendants of those who had long ago vanished. They must have known there was another world across the chasm, for many had crossed from it. Daes they had called her. The incomers from her world must have carried tales of another Terren. But why did no one cross from this one into hers? Might be because these descendants believed her kind to be uncivilized barbarians, she thought with rising bitterness.

Magic hater, the man had called her. His scorn-filled words did not sit easily in her mind.

Scarcely a moment ago, magic had torn the city apart and killed those poor fools who got in its way. Only in tales of long ago, when the tsaren still lived in their world, had she heard of such terrible things.

A terrible realization finally struck her. The tsaren, the enemies of mankind, the ones who had started the Sundering War—were here. They had not vanished or died, only crossed the bridge long ago. They were living here still. She had not merely stepped into another world, but another time which her own people had long ago resigned to history.

Was there a human king here also? But that thought was pushed aside by the cold from the stone at her back. It had crept into her body, chilling her inside and out. Overhead, clouds had gathered, threatening snow. She had lost her cloak and would not survive the night if she continued with these useless musings about kings and tsaren, instead of finding shelter for the night.

She caught sight of her trousers, ragged, dusty and torn. Her clothes betrayed her as a Dae and drew attention to her on the street. She needed new garb to blend in with the locals. Might be she'd find a gang of orphans to join, or an abandoned building for shelter. Either way, she could not sit and hide here all day.

She examined the closed door beside her. The lock was unlike any she had ever picked. Instead of a hole for the key, there was a brass insert for a medallion. She could not pick it and steal inside.

Magic hater. The man's voice echoed through her mind. Her doubts grew, but she made herself rise.

She gazed up and around at the buildings. The old, grey bones of this city reminded her of home. This was Terren. She knew this city, knew how to survive on its streets. She just needed to relearn the streets all over again, that was all. Surely its people could not have changed all that much. They were human, after all, and spoke in the same common tongue.

She emerged from the alley and chose a direction to follow. The clouds grew darker and darker and dropped their snow, thick, heavy flakes, the size of a babe's hand, larger than she had ever seen before. Unnaturally so, she thought darkly and hugged herself against the biting cold.

Everything was different here, but she refused to allow fear to grip her heart. She had been raised on the streets, lived on them most of her life. This was no different. Search for the familiar; that was how they had taught the new orphans to survive the unknown.

She raised her head and forced herself to look more closely. But try as she might, the differences were too many and far too overshadowing. The houses might have been built of the same grey brick, but the windows were fashioned of colorful glass—red, blue, yellow, green and too many others to name. The folk were human, but their clothes were far too fine, regardless of whether they were gentry strolling by or washerwomen with laundry in hand by the wells. Chickens had strangely colored feathers. Horses had their manes plaited with red and gold strands. The carts rolling past were brightly painted.

With every step, she had to remind herself that she was still in her world, the Realm of Seramight. This was merely the other half of it. This was still Terren, its folk the descendants of her kind. She was glad they had not perished, glad the city lived on.

Suddenly, a building moved beside her and black branches tangled in her hair. She screamed and leapt back in fright, leaving behind a clump of her hair. She stared at the building woven from magic, standing side by side with those built of stone by men. It reminded her starkly of the bridge she had crossed into this world. The walls were a matted web of slick black, moving branches. There were silvery windows you could not see through, and no door she could discern. No one around her paid the monstrous house any mind. Instead, they regarded her with unhidden disdain.

"Bloody Dae magic haters," someone sneered in passing.

Elika walked on quickly, trying to appear unafraid.

In that instant, as if her eyes were suddenly opened, she saw another, even less familiar side to this city. This Terren, unlike her own, was infused with magic. It lurked everywhere. A barrel walked past on legs made of black strands. She jumped out of its way and watched it walk down the stairs into the cellar of a tavern.

Further ahead, the street widened around a thick limbed tree with branches twisted and plaited towards the ground. There was a blue obelisk made of water in the center of a courtyard. Children darted through it and laughed when they came out dry.

Find the familiar, she reminded herself. But the prevalent sense of magic would not allow her to forget that she was far from home. Much farther than the span of the chasm she had crossed to reach this place.

As if on instinct, her feet turned in the direction which would have taken her towards Riftside, and back towards the Hide. She wanted nothing more than to go home. Penny was here somewhere. Elika could find her. The thought was compelling. Walk back to the Hide and see Penny and her pack. Elika shook her head to clear it. Her mind was wandering. The day was fading, and her fingers and toes were numb from the cold. The snow had been melting on her, and her clothes and hair were damp and icy. Panic set its claws into her. She had to find shelter, or else steal a warm blanket before her mind wandered any more.

She looked around frantically. A man caught her eye. Like her, he stood out from the others on the street like a goat amidst the doves. He was clad in a lowly garb made of fabric she recognized as being from her world. It was more than the clothes that marked him as one of her kind. His hands were buried deep in his pockets, and his shoulders were hunched as he glanced at the magic around him with suspicion. He was subdued and edgy, like a thief caught in another man's home. He gave a magic-woven building a wide berth and was still startled when the branches moved.

Excited to find another person from her world, she crossed the road toward him.

He slanted his gaze her way, seeming neither surprised nor interested to see her. Around his neck, he wore a silver band stamped with a mark of three faces and a small hook where a chain might be fastened.

"You're … one of us," she whispered when she caught up to him.

"What do you want, kid?" he said brusquely, glancing about suspiciously.

His abruptness took her aback. "I … I'm looking for someone … a friend. We were separated when we crossed the bridge."

"Leave me alone before they think we're conspiring against them."

"If you could only tell me where to find our kind…"

He sighed with impatience. "One of the last ones to get here, hey? Look. This is how it is. Your friend's likely in one of the many workshops they put us all in when we arrive. At least those of us who cannot buy our own freedom. Do you see any beggars or street urchins here?" He waved his hand at the street.

She had not thought of it. But now she realized that there were no orphans on the street, no sign of gangs, not a single beggar she could speak with, huddled in some corner. Worse still, there were no ruined or abandoned buildings to hide in.

"Not a bad thing either, if you ask me," he continued. "Your kind used to rob me of my last pair of shoes in Dae-Terren."

"My kind?" she echoed, confounded by his hostility.

"Aye, damned street brats, thugs and gangs. Well, they don't tolerate thievery here. So be on your way. If you've half a penny worth of sense, you'll find a kindly master and offer yourself to him before the mages get hold of you. You dress like a boy, but I suspect there's tits beneath that shirt. The mages won't be fooled by your disguise, brat. They have a lust on them somewhat fierce." With that, he crossed the street as if he could not be rid of her fast enough.

Her heart sank. There was no help from her own kind either, it seemed. She noticed more and more Daes, all wearing metal collars around their necks. None of them paid her any mind, or to each other, for that matter.

Out of nowhere, someone grabbed her arm. She looked up in fright into the stern face of a fat pouch in fine silks with a jeweled brooch on his scarf. Years of life on the streets of Terren had sharpened her senses. Here, however, those street senses seemed as lost as she. Never before had anyone snuck up close enough to grab her.

"Who is your master, Dae?" he asked in a soft accent.

"My master...?" she stuttered.

His grip tightened. "It's a crime to be a beggar. Come with me."

She tried to yank her arm back. "I'm not a beggar."

The folk around her watched, some with pity, others with contempt. She imagined how she must look in their eyes, dressed in foreign clothes, scruffy and lost.

"If you've no money, then you're a beggar," the man hissed. "You certainly dress like one. No self-respecting master would send out his servants dressed like that. And where's your master's collar?"

In one smooth motion, Elika snatched out her knife, cut his hand, broke free, and ran. Women jumped aside with a screech. Men berated her, as she ran past. She searched for somewhere to hide but saw only pretty stalls and neat shops. She cursed herself for her carelessness. Somehow, she had blindly stumbled into a wealthy quarter of the city, where she looked like a beggar in truth.

She turned a corner and ran into two guards. One grabbed her in an iron grip, crushing her arm. "Another Othersider without a master," he said with the local accent. He had a ponytail tied with a long piece of a leather strap.

"We'll take him to the magistrate," said the other with a recent cut on his lip. "Must have crossed recently."

With a wash of relief, she realized he spoke with the familiar tongue of her people. She gazed up at him pleadingly. "I stole nothing ... I've done nothing wrong."

Pity touched his eyes. "Not like home, hey, kid?" He smiled kindly. "There are no orphans running the streets here. But don't be afraid. You won't be harmed. They'll just find you a master. Everyone earns their keep. No begging's allowed."

Elika had never had a master. The idea frightened her more than finding herself alone on the streets at night. She imagined being locked in a pitch-dark cellar, beaten and worse.

She wriggled in the other guard's solid grip, then reached for her knife too late. Manacles snapped around her wrists.

"Stop struggling, or we'll have to knock you out, too," said the guard with the ponytail. The threat, though softly spoken, had steely authority behind it. Elika stilled. She was no use to herself unconscious.

As they led her away, she felt every gaze on her. It filled her with shame to be treated like a thief amidst these pristine streets. You are a thief, remember? a deriding voice scoffed inside her head.

At least she had been until there was no one left to steal from. What was she now?

They did not lead her far. The magistrate's office was in a house beneath an arched wall spanning a wide road. Along the road, tall statues of winged animals rose between each doorway. Archers patrolled the wall above the street. Their gazes, however, were not fixed on the street but on the sky and the floating island hovering menacingly over the city, rolling this way and that.

The guard yanked her arm towards the house under the arched wall. Inside, a fat, officious man in red robes was writing in a ledger at his long desk. Thick books of different colors lay in a pile in front of him.

When he looked up at her, it was with bored disinterest. "Another Dae," he drawled, and his jowls wobbled. He put aside his quill, pushed away the ledger he was writing in, took a great big blue tome from the stack of them and opened it. "When will it end, I ask you?" he mumbled to himself and dipped his quill into the inkpot. "Othersider, are you? Recently arrived. Damned mess this is. An invasion is what we thought it. Well, out with your name, girl."

"Girl?" the guard with a cut lip whispered to the other, and they stifled a snorting laugh.

"I'm ... Lika," she said.

The magistrate wrote it dutifully in his ledger. "Parents," he said without raising his face from the page.

"Don't know them. They're dead."

"Age."

"Sixteen ... I'm told."

"Alone or with family here?"

"I'm alone." The words choked her, and the cold reality of that seeped deep into her bones. She was alone in a world where nothing was like it should be. Mite was not waiting for her as he had promised. And she did not know where Penny might be. Everything here was alien and wrong. The people, the way they spoke and dressed, their laws, and the way they regarded her with a mix of disgust and pity, as if she was a wounded wild beast.

"How many more of you are left there?" he asked dully.

One of the guards cleared his throat. "It seems there won't be any more coming. The bridge is gone."

"Gone?" The jowls wobbled. "Where has it gone to?"

The Dae guard shrugged. "Just not there anymore. Only the chasm with no way to cross it."

The magistrate's surprise dissolved into relief. He made another note in his ledger, finished writing, picked up a magnifying glass in a silver frame and peered at her through it. Immediately, he recoiled, lowered the glass to look at her, then raised it again to peer through it. The glass distorted and enlarged his surprised eye. It blinked.

"Hmm," he said and placed the eyeglass on the table. "Strange, but who am I to argue with magic? If it shows me a spider, a spider she is."

Elika's heart stuttered. How could the glass know she was Eli Spider? That had been her street name. What else did the treacherous magic know about her?

"Take her to Mage Aeon-Rah in Yarn Row. Seems magic wants her to weave. He'll know where to place her." The fat magistrate waved them away and turned his attention to the next guard who came in, holding a prisoner in chains.

"Caught this one stealing," the guard announced.

Elika started, for she recognized his prisoner. Blood-Dog. He saw her too and laughed with his head thrown back. "Well, well, look who's here, a little cunny from the past."

Elika ducked her head as she walked past him.

His guard yanked him towards the magistrate. "A Dae, claims to be a freeman, but got no mage's stamp on his skin to prove it."

The magistrate sighed. "All Daes claim to be freemen. Want something for nothing, they do. You have to buy your freedom, you worthless vermin. Same as you buy a horse or a rug."

"Damned magic lovers." Blood-dog spat on the ground. "I was born free, and I'll cut the throat of any man who says otherwise."

Their voices faded as Elika was led outside. The snow was still falling thickly, and she shivered violently. One of the guards whistled and waved a horse-drawn carriage forward from a line of them. As it drew closer, she realized it was not a carriage, but a prison wagon. They pushed her in the back and closed the gate behind her. Slowly, understanding of the magistrate's decree seeped into her cold-numbed mind. She was to be taken to a mage as a prisoner.

The prison wagon lurched and drove onwards. She strained against the numbing cold to remember everything she had ever heard of the vile mages. They had existed long ago, and each tale of them she recalled was more terrible than the last. Men hated and feared them for their cruelty and spite, or so the stories told. Mages in turn hated men. They served the tsaren and magic. She had to escape. But the guards at the back of the wagon watched her closely.

She was a prisoner. The horror of all that meant cut through her frozen mind. She had never before been caught by the guards, but others had. Few returned unmolested, unbeaten or with their fingers intact. The cutting cold was making it hard to think, to plot. She was alone, she reminded herself with an ache in her chest. She had to think sharply to survive. Alone she might be, but not defenseless. Her knife was still tucked in her belt. And she had magic to draw on, as she had done before. She had survived worse than this.

Aye, she could run ... but where?

The wagon rolled through unfamiliar bustling streets. The light was fading fast, and her body was numb. She doubted her fingers could grip the knife even if she could reach it.

The wagon came to a stop outside a house woven of something that looked like a mix of stone and metal, save that it was fluid, like a river. The young guard from her world unlocked the door and helped her down.

Coherent thought fled her mind. "What will the mage do to me?" she asked him in a whisper.

He appeared unconcerned. "'Tis not so bad as you think. He'll just place you with a master so you can earn your keep, weaving. No more stealing and begging for you."

As the cold invaded her body and her stomach tightened with hunger, being placed with a master suddenly did not seem so bad. She would gladly work for a warm bed and a bowl of hot goat stew. Might be it was time she earned honest coin.

The guards approached the strange house without fear and she borrowed her own bravery from them.

Inside, the walls were also fluid and shiny. A human servant told them to wait in the hall whilst the master was notified of their arrival. Elika's gaze roamed over everything in sight. There was nothing here that looked like it was made by human hands—mirrors, vases, urns and even flowers all seemed of a different world. There was also an odd hollowness to everything she saw, as if it was a reflection, or a drawing come to life. Edges seemed to merge with air, and colors shifted as you looked at them. She had a strong urge to touch the urn close by to see if it was real.

A large figure appeared above the stairs, and every thought flew from Elika's mind. None of Bill's stories of mages could have prepared her for their reality. The man, if he could be called that, was dressed in night robes as if he had been pulled from the bed. He came down the stairs, inelegantly, awkwardly, clutching the bannister as if he had never mastered the proper use of his legs.

Mage Aeon-Rah was grim-faced, ugly and foul. A deep sense of repulsion shook her, though she could not grasp the essence of the foulness that hung about him. He was pale, wan and oddly waxen. As he drew closer, she caught a faint stench of death and decay, masked by a thick layer of perfume. Instinctively, she recoiled and took a step back, but the guards blocked her retreat.

The mage looked her up and down with equal disdain. His eyes were bleached of color. With a fumbling movement, he produced an eyeglass, akin to the magistrate's one, and peered at her through it. There was neither surprise, nor interest in his face.

"The spider and the princess." His voice was as vile and strange as he. It sounded as though two men spoke at once, each one echoing what the other said, but not exactly. "The princess and the spider," echoed another voice from deep in his throat, though his lips did not move this time. "How … quaint," he said before that other voice stopped speaking. He lowered the looking glass and probed her next with his gaze. "We can make no sense of this. But aye, she's likely a weaver. Mistress Oblana had another girl run away. Perhaps magic sends this one to replace her. Take this girl to Yarn Row." He waved dismissively in her direction whilst addressing her guards.

The guards bowed as if the king himself addressed them. "As your eminence commands."

Ire rose in her at their deference. When had men begun to bow to magic?

The mage turned away.

"How long am I to serve this woman?" Elika asked.

His back stiffened. Slowly, he turned. "Insolent she-human," he hissed. "She-human," hissed another voice inside him. "You do not address us until we demand it."

"Am I a prisoner?" she persisted. "I committed no crime."

"This is Al-Terren, Dae. You are a bonded servant from the day you come into this world, no matter the manner of your entry. The cost of freedom is fifty sherrings, as set by the laws of the archmage. Do you have wealthy parents or perhaps a freeman lover who might purchase your freedom from us?" When she did not reply, he huffed. "Then you must work until you have the coin to buy it yourself."

Anger and fear made her reckless. "Is it the same true for you, too, Mage?" she asked before she could stop herself.

"Watch your tongue, she-human, before we decide to remove it."

Black tendrils of magic appeared from nowhere to crawl over her face and pry their way into her mouth. She cried out and tried to claw them from her face.

Remove her tongue, an echo added beneath his horrid voice. Rip it out.

Then the strands vanished. Her tongue was still there. She staggered back from the mage in horror.

A hand fell on her shoulder and squeezed. "No more questions," the Dae guard whispered to her. "Forgive her, Master. She's just arrived and hasn't yet learnt our ways."

Elika lowered her gaze, feeling grateful to the guard for saving her from her stupidity.

The mage huffed and turned away. "Then she'd better learn quickly," he threw over his shoulder and began to climb the stairs in the same awkward way, as if his feet could not decide which one should go first or where they should step when they did.

Distracted with watching him, Elika did not notice a servant approach until it was too late. A silver choker snapped shut around her throat. She gripped the metal collar and tried to rip it off. It must have been fastened with magic, for there were no clasps or seals she could feel.

"Too tight," she gasped and tugged.

The guard stopped her. "It's not tight, just breathe. It will not strangle you. You'll be used to it soon enough."

She looked up into his face and her breathing steadied. "How is it you are not wearing one of these? Who bought your freedom?"

"Only freemen can join the city guard, so the captain paid for my freedom. There's coin in each legion's war chest. It's ten years of service to pay it back."

"Do they take girls as guards?" she asked somewhat hopefully.

The guard laughed and ruffled her hair.

In the mirror, she caught sight of an engraving in her collar of a burning tree. The same mark was etched into the door of Mage Aeon-Rah's home.

It was dark by the time she was brought to stand before another house three streets along. It was a shop with lavish fabrics displayed in the windows. Around them, the streets had grown quiet and shops locked their doors. Fresh snow covered the road and paths, cleansing them of signs of men's passage.

The guards took her up a side path. They removed her manacles and led her into the house through the back door. The heat hit her first, and she felt dizzy with the pleasure of it. She was in the kitchen, where a large stove and cooking fire took up most of one wall.

A plump woman with her sleeves rolled above her elbows was working the dough. She scowled at Elika from under her sweaty hair. "What's this then? Another damned Dae? Ain't there any nice girls left in this city save for these magic haters who take their fill of our food then run away?"

"Ask Mage Aeon-Rah, woman, or hold your tongue," answered the guard.

The cook wiped her hands on a cloth. "I'll tell the mistress then. Since lately, she's been casting out every servant who does not weave. Not sure how we'll feed another worthless mouth."

They did not wait long before a prim, stern mistress marched into the kitchen. "An Othersider? I asked for a local girl. Why did you bring me this worthless wretch?"

The cook strolled in behind her and returned to rolling the dough.

"Mage Aeon-Rah sends her. Our job is only to deliver," said the Dae guard with a shrug.

The woman came forward and looked down her long nose into Elika's face. "I am Mistress Oblana. Which workshop have you come from?"

"Arrived recently," replied the guard for her. "You are her first master. Ahem … mistress, that is."

"Well, at least that's something," said Mistress Oblana. "I hate it when they bring bad habits from worthless masters. Meena!" she yelled.

Immediately, a young woman with a cold, unkind face appeared. She wore a plain frock. Three golden plaits fell along her back. Her gaze fell on Elika, and instant dislike lit her eyes.

"Take this girl to the attic room," Mistress Oblana instructed. "Tomorrow morning, she will begin work." She examined Elika's metal collar. "And make sure she is stamped with the mark of my workshop. I do not want her getting lost or thinking she can run away. And I'll be damned if anyone tries to steal another of my girls."

"As you say, mistress," Meena said politely and smiled at Elika in a way that promised some cruelty to come.

The Dae guard nodded to her reassuringly and they left.

Meena led her to the uppermost room, under the low sloping roof. She was a head taller than Elika and carried herself with airs befitting the daughter of a lord.

"Sit there," she pointed at the chair beside the table.

Elika did as she was told, and Meena sat across from her, and with a tip of a thick needle began to engrave. The needle appeared to be made of similar metal to the collar Elika wore. There was a faint blue hue to the silver. Whilst Elika waited, she noticed Meena herself did not wear a metal collar. Instead, she wore two gold bands on her wrists etched with a mark of a yarn carried in a bird's beak. In the mirror, she saw that it was the same mark Meena was now engraving into her collar.

Without warning, the needle pressed deep into her skin. Elika gasped in pain and surprise and grabbed Meena's hand.

The girl's icy eyes were hard and vicious. "Listen to me, Dae. I know your kind. I hate the barbaric sound of your voice. And I wish you'd never come into our city but stayed where you were in your barbaric world."

Elika made not a sound, shocked by her viciousness. The shock quickly stilled to cold anger. She was Eli Spider, no one threatened her. At least no scrap of a whelp like this chit.

But the foolish girl did not know this. "In this house, I'm your mistress," she continued blithely. "And you'll do as I say. One mistake and I'll beat you. And don't think our mistress will do anything but agree. You're here to work, and if you don't earn the money for my mistress, you don't eat."

Elika pushed away Meena's hand. The tip of the needle was bloody. In one quick move, she Elika grabbed the girl's hair and slammed her face into the table. The girl screeched, covered her bloodied nose and ran out, dripping blood through her fingers. That was the way they dealt with mindless bullies in her pack.

Shortly, Mistress Oblana came up, cold and composed. In her hand, she held a cane. "Turn around."

Elika did, unafraid, only shaking with anger. The mistress hit her with the cane, once twice, thrice until Elika groaned and tears filled her eyes.

Then she grabbed Elika's neck and pushed her to her knees in front of an ugly, misshapen statue of black stone. It was decorated with the bones of small animals and dried flowers.

"That is the shrine to magic. You will pray for its favor each night before you go to bed. If magic favors you, you will be a good weaver. If not, you will be sent to the mills." She leant in closer to Elika's face. "Magic hates vicious little rats like you. So watch your manners."

With that, Mistress Oblana left her, closing and locking the door. Once the footsteps had retreated on the stairs, Elika rose to her feet. Her back was throbbing and her shirt stuck to her bleeding wounds. She strode to the window, unlatched it and flung it open. Relief flooded her. The roofs were her escape. They had always been her freedom. Without thought, she climbed out.

Icy air hit her like another sharp cane. The snow continued to fall, the skies were heavy with clouds. The floating island was lit up against the night sky as if swathed in sunshine.

Elika hugged herself and looked around, seeking a path, a place to go, and her heart froze at the city's enormous expanse. In six hundred years, this city, the one they called Al-Terren, had grown far larger than the one she'd come from. In the light of the torches, she could make out the old wall, which was once the boundary of Terren. Now the city extended beyond it, and two more dividing walls had been erected. A great black outer wall with many towers like fangs along it surrounded the outer reaches of the great city.

The cold grew sharp and piercing. Elika looked back into her small attic room. Warmth was coming from it, treacherously enticing. She did not need to run, at least not yet. She climbed inside, closed the window and sat on the bed.

Was it only that morning she had found the courage to cross the bridge? Only that morning she was plunging through the chasm? Just a few vague hours ago that she had been certain only the deadlands awaited her here?

She curled on her bed and wished only for sleep. Might be when she awoke, she would be back home, with her pack and Penny cooking by the fire. Her eyes would not close, however. Before them, the ugly shrine grew more menacing. And when the candle went out, in the dark, the curved stone became a monstrous face watching her sleep.

Eventually, she must have fallen asleep, for deep in the night, dark chanting invaded her dreams. It grew louder until it called forth the giant spider with yellow eyes who hunted her from its shimmering web.

RELEASE DATE
DECEMBER 2023

CPSIA information can be obtained
at www.ICGtesting.com
Printed in the USA
BVHW031723310123
657545BV00010B/166